D1285683

Ungava

"SHE WAS DRAGGED VIOLENTLY FROM
THE ROARING WAVES"—Page 106

Ungava

A Tale of the Eskimos Land

by

R.M. BALLANTYNE

Author of
Post Haste, Fighting the Flames,
Fast In The Ice, etc., etc.

THE VISION FORUM, INC.
SAN ANTONIO, TEXAS

Reprinted from the 1857 Classic by R.M. Ballantyne

FISRT PRINTING

Copyright © 2008 The Vision Forum, Inc.
All Rights Reserved.

"Where there is no vision, the people perish."

www.visionforum.com

ISBN-10 1-934554-23-5
ISBN-13 978-1-934554-23-4

The cloth covers in this series are color-coded to represent the geographic region of each story. The regions and their respective colors are as follows:

NORTH AMERICA—*Forest Green*	SOUTH AMERICA—*Wheat*
SOUTH PACIFIC—*Light Blue*	ARCTIC REGIONS—*Grey*
EUROPE—*Navy Blue*	AFRICA—*Sienna*
ASIA—*Red*	

PRINTED IN THE UNITED STATES OF AMERICA

The "Scotch Thistle," the floral emblem of Scotland, serves as the emblem of the R.M. Ballantyne Series published by Vision Forum.

PREFACE

THE FOLLOWING story is intended to illustrate one of the many phases of the fur-trader's life in those wild regions of North America which surround Hudson's Bay.

Most of its major incidents are facts—fiction being employed chiefly for the purpose of weaving these facts into a readable form.

If this volume should chance to fall into the hands of any of those who acted a part in the first settlement of Ungava, we trust that they will forgive the liberty that has been taken with their persons and adventures, remembering that transpositions, modifications, and transformations are necessary in constructing a tale out of the "raw material."

We take this opportunity of expressing to the Leader of the adventurous band our grateful acknowledgements for his kindness in placing at our disposal the groundwork on which this story has been reared.

R.M. BALLANTYNE

CONTENTS

CHAPTER VII

CHAPTER VIII

CHAPTER IX

CHAPTER X

CHAPTER XI

CHAPTER XII

CHAPTER XIII

CHAPTER XIV

CHAPTER XV

CHAPTER XVI

CHAPTER XVII

Chapter I

"Hallo! where are you!" shouted a voice that rang through the glades of the forest like the blast of a silver trumpet, testifying to lungs of leather and a throat of brass.

The ringing tones died away, and naught was heard save the rustling of the leafy canopy overhead, as the young man, whose shout had thus rudely disturbed the surrounding echoes, leaned on the muzzle of a long rifle, and stood motionless as a statue, his right foot resting on the trunk of a fallen tree, and his head bent slightly to one side, as if listening for a reply. But no reply came. A squirrel ran down the trunk of a neighbouring pine, and paused, with tail and ears erect, and its little black eyes glittering as if with surprise at the temerity of him who so recklessly dared to intrude upon and desecrate with his powerful voice the deep solitudes of the wilderness. They stood so long thus that it seemed as though the little animal and the man had been petrified by the unwonted sound. If so, the spell was quickly broken. The loud report of a fowling-piece was heard at a short distance. The squirrel incontinently disappeared from the spot on which it stood, and almost instantaneously reappeared on the topmost branch of a high tree; while the young man gave a smile of satisfaction, threw the rifle over his shoulder, and, turning round, strode rapidly away in the direction whence the shot proceeded.

A few minutes' walk brought him to the banks of a little brook, by the side of which, on the projecting root of a tree, sat a man, with a dead goose at his feet and a fowling-piece by his side. He was dressed in the garb of a hunter; and, from the number of gray hairs that shone like threads of silver among the black curls on his temples, he was evidently past the meridian of life although, from the upright bearing of his tall, muscular frame, and the quick glance of his fearless black eye, it was equally evident that the vigour of his youth was not yet abated.

"Why, Stanley," exclaimed the young man as he approached, "I've been shouting till my throat is cracked, for at least half an hour. I verily began to think that you had forsaken me altogether."

"In which case, Frank," replied the other, "I should have treated you as you deserve, for your empty game-bag proves you an unworthy comrade in the chase."

"So, so, friend, do not boast," replied the youth with a smile; "if I mistake not, that goose was winging its way to the far north not ten minutes agone. Had I come up half an hour sooner, I suspect we should have met on equal terms; but the fact is that I have not seen hair or feather, save a tree-squirrel, since I left you in the morning."

"Well, to say truth, I was equally unfortunate until I met this luckless goose, and fired the shot that brought him down and brought you up. But I've had enough o' this now, and shall back to the fort again. What say you? Will you go in my canoe or walk?"

The young man was silent for a few seconds; then, without replying to his companion's question, he said, "By-the-bye, is it not to-night that you mean to make another attempt to induce the men to volunteer for the expedition!"

"It is," replied Stanley, with a light frown. "And what if they still persist in refusing to go?"

"I'll try once more to shame them out of their cowardice. But if they won't agree, I'll compel them to go by means of more powerful arguments than words."

"'Tis not cowardice; you do the men injustice," said Frank, shaking his head.

"Well, well, I believe I do, lad; you're right," replied Stanley, while a smile smoothed out the firm lines that had gathered round his lips for a few seconds. "No doubt they care as little for the anticipated dangers of the expedition as any men living, and they hesitate to go simply because they know that the life before them will be a lonely one at such an out-o'-the-way place as

Ungava. But we can't help that, Frank; the interests of the Company must be attended to, and so go they must, willing or not willing. But I'm annoyed at this unexpected difficulty, for there's a mighty difference between men who volunteer to go and men who go merely because they must and can't help it."

The young man slowly rubbed the stock of his rifle with the sleeve of his coat, and looked as if he understood and sympathised with his friend's chagrin.

"If Prince were only here just now," said he, looking up, "there would be no difficulty in the matter. These fellows only want a bold, hearty comrade to step forward and show them the way, and they will follow to the North Pole if need be. They look upon our willingness to go as a mere matter of course, though I don't see why we should be expected to like banishment more than themselves. But if Prince were—"

"Well, well, Prince is not here, so we must do the best we can without him," said Stanley.

As he spoke, the trumpet note of a goose was heard in the distance.

"There he goes—down with you!" exclaimed Frank, darting suddenly behind the stump of the tree, while his companion crouched beside him, and both began to shout at the top of their voices in imitation of the goose. The bird was foolish enough to accept the invitation immediately, although, had it been other than a goose, it would have easily recognised the sound as a wretched counterfeit of the goose language. It flew directly towards them, as geese always do in spring when thus enticed, but passed at such a distance that the elder sportsman was induced to lower his piece.

"Ah! he's too far off. You'd better give him a shot with the rifle, Frank; but you're sure to miss."

"To hit, you mean," cried his companion, flushing with momentary indignation at this disparaging remark. At the same moment he took a rapid aim and fired. For a few yards the goose continued its forward flight as if unhurt; then it wavered once or twice, and fell heavily to the ground.

"Bravo, boy!" cried Stanley. "There, don't look nettled; I only jested with you, knowing your weakness on the score of rifle-shooting. Now, pick up your bird, and throw it into the canoe, for I must away."

Frank finished reloading his piece as his friend spoke, and went to pick up the goose; while the other walked down to the edge of the rivulet, and disengaged a light birch-bark canoe from the long grass and sedges that almost hid it from view.

"Make haste, Frank!" he shouted; "there's the ice coming up with the flood-tide, and bearing down on the creek here."

At a short distance from the spot where the sportsmen stood, the streamlet already alluded to mingled its waters with a broad river, which, a few miles farther down, flows into James's Bay. As every one knows, this bay lies to the south of Hudson's Bay, in North America. Here the river is about two miles wide; and the shores on either side being low, it has all the appearance of an extensive lake. In spring, after the disruption of the ice, its waters are loaded with large floes and fields of ice; and later in the season, after it has become quite free from this wintry encumbrance, numerous detached masses come up with every flood-tide. It was the approach of one of these floes that called forth Stanley's remark.

The young man replied to it by springing towards the canoe, in which his companion was already seated. Throwing the dead bird into it, he stooped, and gave the light bark a powerful shove into the stream, exclaiming, as he did so, "There, strike out, you've no time to lose, and I'll go round by the woods."

There was indeed no time to lose. The huge mass of ice was closing rapidly into the mouth of the creek, and narrowing the only passage through which the canoe could escape into the open water of the river beyond. Stanley might, indeed, drag his canoe up the bank, if so disposed, and reach home by a circuitous walk through the woods; but by doing so he would lose much time, and be under the necessity of carrying his gun, blanket, tin kettle, and the goose, on his back. His broad shoulders were admirably adapted for such a burden, but he preferred the canoe to the woods on the present occasion. Besides, the only risk he ran was that of getting his canoe crushed to pieces. So, plunging his paddle vigorously in the water, he shot through the lessening channel like an arrow, and swept out on the bosom of the broad river just as the ice closed with a crash upon the shore and ground itself to powder on the rocks.

"Well done!" shouted Frank, with a wave of his cap, as he witnessed the success of his friend's exploit.

"All right," replied Stanley, glancing over his shoulder.

In another moment the canoe disappeared behind a group of willows that grew on the point at the river's mouth, and the young man was left alone. For a few minutes he stood contemplating the point behind which his companion had disappeared; then giving a hasty glance at the priming of his rifle, he threw it across his shoulder, and striding rapidly up the bank, was soon lost to view amid the luxuriant undergrowth of the forest.

Chapter II

Moose Fort, the headquarters and depot of the
fur-traders, who prosecute their traffic in almost
all parts of the wild and uninhabited regions of North
America, stands on an island near the mouth of Moose
River. Like all the establishments of the fur-traders, it
is a solitary group of wooden buildings, far removed
beyond the influences—almost beyond the ken—of
the civilised world, and surrounded by the primeval
wilderness, the only tenants of which were, at the time
we write of, a few scattered tribes of Muskigon Indians,
and the wild animals whose flesh furnished them with
food and whose skins constituted their sole wealth.
There was little of luxury at Moose Fort. The walls of
the houses within the stockade, that served more as an

ornament than a defence, were of painted, in some
cases unpainted, planks. The floors, ceilings, chairs,
tables, and, in short, all the articles of furniture in
the place, were made of the same rough material. A
lofty scaffolding of wood rose above the surrounding
buildings, and served as an outlook, whence, at the
proper season, longing eyes were wont to be turned
towards the sea in expectation of "the ship" which
paid the establishment an annual visit from England.
Several large iron field-pieces stood before the front
gate; but they were more for the sake of appearance
than use, and were never fired except for the purpose
of saluting the said ship on the occasions of her arrival
and departure. The first boom of the cannon unlocks
the long-closed portals of connection between Moose
Fort and England; the second salvo shuts them up
again in their frozen domains for another year! A
century and a half ago, the band of "adventurers
trading into Hudson's Bay" felled the first trees and
pitched their tents on the shores of James's Bay, and
successive generations of fur-traders have kept the post
until the present day; yet there is scarcely a symptom
of the presence of man beyond a few miles round the
establishment. Years ago the fort was built, and there
it stands now, with new tenants, it is true, but in its
general aspect unchanged; and there it is likely to
remain, wrapped in its barrier of all but impregnable
solitude, for centuries to come.

Nevertheless, Moose is a comfortable place in
its way, and when contrasted with other trading
establishments is a very palace and temple of luxury.

There are men within its walls who can tell of log-huts and starvation, solitude and desolation, compared with which Moose is a terrestrial paradise. Frank Morton, whom we have introduced in the first Chapter, said, on his arrival at Moose, that it appeared to him to be the very fag-end of creation. He had travelled night and day for six weeks from what he considered the very outskirts of civilisation, through uninhabited forests and almost unknown rivers, in order to get to it; and while the feeling of desolation that overwhelmed him on his first arrival was strong upon him, he sighed deeply, and called it a "horrid dull hole." But Frank was of a gay, hearty, joyous disposition, and had not been there long ere he loved the old fort dearly. Poor fellow, far removed though he was from his fellow-men at Moose, he afterwards learned that he had but obtained an indistinct notion of the signification of the word "solitude."

There were probably about thirty human beings at Moose, when Mr. George Stanley, one of the principal fur-traders of the place, received orders from the governor to make preparations, and select men, for the purpose of proceeding many hundred miles deeper into the northern wilderness, and establishing a station on the distant, almost unknown, shores of Ungava Bay. No one at Moose had ever been there before; no one knew anything about the route, except from the vague report of a few Indians; and the only thing that was definitely known about the locality at all was, that its inhabitants were a few wandering tribes of Eskimos, who were at deadly feud with the Indians, and generally massacred all who came within their reach. What the capabilities of the country were, in regard to timber and provisions, nobody knew, and, fortunately for the success of the expedition, nobody cared! At least those who were to lead the way did not; and this admirable quality of total indifference to prospective dangers is that which, to a great extent, insures success in a forlorn hope.

Of the leaders of this expedition the reader already knows something. George Stanley was nearly six feet high, forty years of age, and endued with a decision of character that, but for his quiet good humour, would have been deemed obstinacy. He was deliberate in all his movements, and exercised a control over his feelings that quite concealed his naturally enthusiastic disposition. Moreover, he was married, and had a daughter of ten years of age. This might be thought a disadvantage in his present circumstances; but the governor of the fur-traders, a most energetic and active ruler, thought otherwise. He recommended that the family should be left at Moose until an establishment had been built, and a winter passed at Ungava. Afterwards they could join him there. As for Frank Morton, he was an inch taller than his friend Stanley, and equally powerful; fair-haired, blue-eyed, hilarious, romantic, twenty-two years of age, and so impulsive that, on hearing of the proposed expedition from one of his comrades, who happened to be present when Stanley was reading the dispatches, he sprang from his chair, which he upset, dashed out at the door, which he banged, and hurried to his friend's quarters in order to be first to volunteer his services as second in command; which offer was rendered unnecessary by Stanley's exclaiming, the moment he entered his room—

"Ha, Frank, my lad, the very man I wanted to see! Here's a letter from headquarters ordering me off on an expedition to Ungava. Now, I want volunteers; will you go!"

It is needless to add that Frank's blue eyes sparkled with animation as he seized his friend's hand and replied, "To the North Pole if you like, or farther if need be!"

It was evening. The sun was gilding the top of the flagstaff with a parting kiss, and the inhabitants of Moose Fort, having finished their daily toil, were making preparations for their evening meal. On the end of the wharf that jutted out into the stream was assembled a picturesque group of men, who, from the earnest manner in which they conversed, and the energy of their gesticulations, were evidently discussing a subject of more than ordinary interest. Most of them were clad in corduroy trousers, gartered below the knee with thongs of deer-skin, and coarse, striped cotton shirts, open at the neck, so as to expose their sunburnt breasts. A few wore caps which, whatever might have been their original form, were now so much soiled and battered out of shape by long and severe service that they were nondescript; but most of these hardy backwoodsmen were content with the covering afforded by their thick, bushy locks.

"No, no," exclaimed a short, thick-set, powerful man, with a somewhat ascetic cast of countenance;

"I've seen more than enough o' these rascally Huskies [Eskimos]. 'Tis well for me that I'm here this blessed day, an' not made into a dan to bob about in Hudson's Straits at the tail of a white whale, like that poor boy Peter who was shot by them varmints."

"What's a dan?" asked a young half-breed who had lately arrived at Moose, and knew little of Eskimo implements.

"What a green-horn you must be, Francois, not to know what a dan is!" replied another, who was inclined to be quizzical. "Why, it's a sort of sea-carriage that the Eskimos tie to the tail of a walrus or sea-horse when they feel inclined for a drive. When they can't get a sea-horse they catch a white whale asleep, and wake him up after fastening the dan to his tail. I suppose they have conjurers or wizards among them, since Massan told us just now that poor Peter was—"

"Bah! gammon," interrupted Francois with a smile, as he turned to the first speaker. "But tell me, Massan, what is a dan?"

"It's a sort o' float or buoy, lad, used by the Huskies, and is made out o' the skin o' the seal. They tie it with a long line to their whale spears to show which way the fish bolts when struck."

"And did they use Peter's skin for such a purpose?" inquired Francois earnestly.

"They did," replied Massan.

"And did you see them do it?"

"Yes, I did."

Francois gazed intently into his comrade's face as he spoke; but Massan was an adept at what is usually called drawing the long bow, and it was with the most imperturbable gravity that he continued—

"Yes, I saw them do it; but I could not render any assistance to the poor child, for I was lying close behind a rock at the time, with an arrow sticking between my shoulders, and a score o' them oily varmints a-shoutin', and yellin', and flourishing their spears in search o' me."

"Tell us how it happened, Massan. Let's hear the story," chorused the men, as they closed round their comrade.

"Well then," began the stout backwoodsman, proceeding leisurely to fill his pipe from an ornamented bag that hung at his belt, "here goes. It was about the year—a—I forget the year, but it don't matter—that we were ordered off on an expedition to the Huskies; 'xactly sich a one as they wants us to go on now, and—but you've heerd o' that business, lads, haven't you?"

"Yes, yes, we've heard all about it; go on."

"Well," continued Massan, "I needn't be wastin' time tellin' you how we failed in that affair, and how the Huskies killed some of our men and burnt our ship to the water's edge. After it was all over, and they thought they had killed us all, I was, as I said, lyin' behind a great rock in a sort o' cave, lookin' at the dirty villains as they danced about on the shore, and took possession of all our goods. Suddenly I seed two o' them carry Peter down to the beach, an' I saw, as they passed me, that he was quite dead. In less time than I can count a hundred they took the skin off him, cut off his head, sewed up the hole, tied his arms and

legs in a knot, blew him full o' wind till he was fit to
bu'st, an' then hung him up to dry in the sun! In fact,
they made a dan of him!"

A loud shout of laughter greeted this startling
conclusion. In truth, we must do Massan the justice to
say, that although he was much in the habit of amusing
his companions by entertaining them with anecdotes
which originated entirely in his own teeming fancy,
he never actually deceived them, but invariably, either
by a sly glance or by the astounding nature of his
communication, gave them to understand that he was
dealing not with fact but fiction.

"But seriously, lads," said Francois, whose
intelligence, added to a grave, manly countenance
and a tall, muscular frame, caused him to be regarded
by his comrades as a sort of leader both in action and
in council, "what do you think of our bourgeois' plan?
For my part, I'm willing enough to go to any reasonable
part o' the country where there are furs and Indians;
but as for this Ungava, from what Massan says, there's
neither Indians, nor furs, nor victuals—nothin' but
rocks, and mountains, and eternal winter; and if we
do get the Huskies about us, they'll very likely serve us
as they did the last expedition to Richmond Gulf."

"Ay, ay," cried one of the others, "you may say that,
Francois. Nothin' but frost and starvation, and nobody
to bury us when we're dead."

"Except the Huskies," broke in another, "who
would save themselves the trouble by converting us
all into dans!"

"Tush, man! stop your clapper," cried Francois,

impatiently; "let us settle this business. You know that Monsieur Stanley said he would expect us to be ready with an answer to-night. What think you, Gaspard? Shall we go, or shall we mutiny?"

The individual addressed was a fine specimen of an animal, but not by any means a good specimen of a man. He was of gigantic proportions, straight and tall as a poplar, and endowed with the strength of a Hercules. His glittering dark eyes and long black hair, together with the hue of his skin, bespoke him of half-breed extraction. But his countenance did not correspond to his fine physical proportions. True, his features were good, but they wore habitually a scowling, sulky expression, even when the man was pleased, and there was more of sarcasm than joviality in the sound when Gaspard condescended to laugh.

"I'll be shot if I go to such a hole for the best bourgeois in the country," said he in reply to Francois' question.

"You'll be dismissed the service if you don't," remarked Massan with a smile.

To this Gaspard vouchsafed no reply save a growl that, to say the best of it, did not sound amiable.

"Well, I think that we're all pretty much of one mind on the point," continued Francois; "and yet I feel half ashamed to refuse after all, especially when I see the good will with which Messieurs Stanley and Morton agree to go."

"I suppose you expect to be a bourgeois too some day," growled Gaspard with a sneer.

"Eh, tu gros chien!" cried Francois, as with flashing eyes and clinched fists he strode up to his ill-tempered comrade.

"Come, come, Francois; don't quarrel for nothing," said Massan, interposing his broad shoulders and pushing him vigorously back.

At that moment an exclamation from one of the men diverted the attention of the others.

"Voila! the canoe."

"Ay, it's Monsieur Stanley's canoe. I saw him and Monsieur Morton start for the swamp this morning."

"I wonder what Dick Prince would have done in this business had he been here," said Francois to Massan in a low tone, as they stood watching the approach of their bourgeois' canoe.

"Can't say. I half think he would have gone."

"There's no chance of him coming back in time, I fear."

"None; unless he prevails on some goose to lend him a pair of wings for a day or two. He won't be back from the hunt for three weeks good."

In a few minutes more the canoe skimmed up to the wharf.

"Here, lads," cried Mr. Stanley, as he leaped ashore and dragged the canoe out of the water; "one of you come and lift this canoe up the bank, and take these geese to the kitchen."

Two of the men instantly hastened to obey, and Stanley, with the gun and paddles under his arm, proceeded towards the gateway of the fort. As he passed the group assembled on the wharf, he turned and said—

"You'll come to the hall in an hour, lads; I shall

expect you to be ready with an answer by that time."

"Ay, ay, sir," replied several of the men.

"But we won't go for all your expectations," said one in an undertone to a comrade.

"I should think not," whispered another.

"I'll be hanged, and burnt, and frozen if I do," said a third.

In the meantime Mr. Stanley walked briskly towards his dwelling, and left the men to grumble over their troubles and continue their debate as to whether they should or should not agree to go on the pending expedition to the distant regions of Ungava.

Chapter III

On reaching his apartment, which was in an angle of the principal edifice in the fort, Mr. Stanley flung down his gun and paddles, and drawing a chair close to his wife, who was working with her needle near a window, took her hand in his and heaved a deep sigh.

"Why, George, that's what you used to say to me when you were at a loss for words in the days of our courtship."

"True, Jessie," he replied, patting her shoulder with a hand that rough service had rendered hard and long exposure had burnt brown. "But the producing cause then was different from what it is now. Then it was love; now it is perplexity."

Stanley's wife was the daughter of English parents, who had settled many years ago in the fur countries. Being quite beyond the reach of any school, they had been obliged to undertake the instruction of their only child, Jessie, as they best could. At first this was an easy matter, but as years flew by, and little Jessie's mind expanded, it was found to be a difficult matter to carry on her education in a country in most parts of which books were not to be had and schoolmasters did not exist. When the difficulty first presented itself, they talked of sending their little one to England to finish her education; but being unable to bring themselves to part with her, they resolved to have a choice selection of books sent out to them. Jessie's mother was a clever, accomplished, and lady-like woman, and decidedly pious, so that the little flower, which was indeed born to blush unseen, grew up to be a gentle, affectionate woman—one who was a lady in all her thoughts and actions, yet had never seen polite society, save that of her father and mother. In process of time Jessie became Mrs. Stanley, and the mother of a little girl whose voice was, at the time her father entered, ringing cheerfully in an adjoining room. Mrs. Stanley's nature was an earnest one, and she no sooner observed that her husband was worried about something, than she instantly dropped the light tone in which she at first addressed him.

"And what perplexes you now, dear George?" she said, laying down her work and looking up in his face with that straightforward, earnest gaze that in days of yore had set the stout backwoodsman's heart on fire, and still kept it in a perennial blaze.

"Nothing very serious," he replied with a smile; "only these fellows have taken it into their stupid heads that Ungava is worse than the land beyond the Styx; and so, after the tough battle that I had with you this morning in order to prevail on you to remain here for a winter without me, I've had to fight another battle with them in order to get them to go on this expedition."

"Have you been victorious?" inquired Mrs. Stanley.

"No, not yet."

"Do you really mean to say they are afraid to go? Has Prince refused? Are Francois, Gaspard, and Massan cowards?" she inquired, her eye kindling with indignation.

"Nay, my wife, not so. These men are not cowards; nevertheless they don't feel inclined to go; and as for Dick Prince, he has been off hunting for a week, and I don't expect him back for three weeks at least, by which time we shall be off."

Mrs. Stanley sighed, as if she felt the utter helplessness of woman in such affairs.

"Why, Jessie, that's what you used to say to me when you were at a loss for words in the days of our courtship," said Stanley, smiling.

"Ah, George, like you I may say that the cause is now perplexity; for what can I do to help you in your present difficulty?"

"Truly not much. But I like to tell you of my troubles, and to make more of them than they deserve, for the sake of drawing forth your sympathy. Bless your heart!" he said, in a sudden burst of enthusiasm, "I would gladly undergo any amount of trouble every day, if by so doing I should secure that earnest, loving, anxious gaze of your sweet blue eyes as a reward!" Stanley imprinted a hearty kiss on his wife's cheek as he made this lover-like speech, and then rose to place his fowling-piece on the pegs from which it usually hung over the fireplace.

At that moment the door opened, and a little girl, with bright eyes and flaxen hair, bounded into the room.

"O mamma, mamma!" she said, holding up a sheet of paper, while a look of intense satisfaction beamed on her animated countenance, "see, I have drawn Chimo's portrait. Is it like, mamma? Do you think it like?"

"Come here, Eda, my darling, come to me," said Stanley, seating himself on a chair and extending his arms. Edith instantly left the portrait of the dog in her mother's possession, and, without waiting for an opinion as to its merits, ran to her father, jumped on his knee, threw her arms round his neck, and kissed him. Edith was by no means a beautiful child, but miserable indeed must have been the taste of him who would have pronounced her plain-looking. Her features were not regular; her nose had a strong tendency to what is called snubbed, and her mouth was large; but to counterbalance these defects she had a pair of large, deep-blue eyes, soft, golden hair, a fair, rosy complexion, and an expression of sweetness at the corners of her mouth that betrayed habitual good-nature. She was quick in all her movements, combined with a peculiar softness and grace of deportment that was exceedingly attractive.

"Would you like to go, my pet," said her father, "to a country far, far away in the north, where there are high mountains and deep valleys, inhabited by beautiful reindeer, and large lakes and rivers filled with fish; where there is very little daylight all the long winter, and where there is scarcely any night all the long, bright summer? Would my Eda like to go there?"

The child possessed that fascinating quality of being intensely interested in all that was said to her. As her father spoke, her eyes gradually expanded and looked straight into his, while her head turned slowly and very slightly to one side. As he concluded, she replied, "Oh! very, very, very much indeed," with a degree of energy that made both her parents laugh.

"Ah, my darling! would that my lazy men were endued with some of your spirit," said Stanley, patting the child's head.

"Is Prince a lazy man, papa?" inquired Edith anxiously.

"No, certainly, Prince is not. Why do you ask?"

"Because I love Prince."

"And do you not love all the men?"

"No," replied Edith, with some hesitation; "at least I don't love them very much, and I hate one."

"Hate one!" echoed Mrs. Stanley. "Come here, my darling."

Eda slipped from her father's knee and went to her mother, feeling and looking as if she had said something wrong.

Mrs. Stanley was not one of those mothers who, whenever they hear of their children having done anything wrong, assume a look of intense, solemnised horror, that would lead an ignorant spectator to suppose that intelligence had just been received of some sudden and appalling catastrophe. She knew that children could not be deceived by such pieces of acting. She expressed on her countenance precisely what she felt—a slight degree of sorrow that her child should cherish an evil passion, which, she knew, existed in her heart in common with all the human race, but which she expected, by God's help and blessing, to subdue effectually at last. Kissing Eda's forehead she said kindly, "Which of them do you hate, darling?"

"Gaspard," replied the child.

"And why do you hate him?"

"Because he struck my dog," said Eda, while her face flushed and her eyes sparkled; "and he is always rude to everybody, and very, very cruel to the dogs."

"That is very wrong of Gaspard; but, dearest Eda, do you not remember what is written in God's Word,—'Love your enemies?' It is wrong to hate anybody."

"I know that, mamma, and I don't wish to hate Gaspard, but I can't help it. I wish if I didn't hate him, but it won't go away."

"Well, my pet," replied Mrs. Stanley, pressing the child to her bosom, "but you must pray for him, and speak kindly to him when you meet him, and that will perhaps put it away. And now let us talk of the far-off country that papa was speaking about. I wonder what he has to tell you about it."

Stanley had been gazing out of the window during the foregoing colloquy, apparently inattentive, though, in reality, deeply interested in what was said. Turning round, he said—

"I was going to tell Eda that you had arranged to follow me to that country next year, and that perhaps you would bring her along with you."

"Nay, George, you mistake. I did not arrange to do so—you only proposed the arrangement; but, to say truth, I don't like it, and I can't make up my mind to let you go without us. I cannot wait till next year."

"Well, well, Jessie, I have exhausted all my powers of persuasion. I leave it entirely to yourself to do as you think best."

At this moment the sound of deep voices was heard in the hall, which was separated from Stanley's quarters by a thin partition of wood. In a few seconds the door opened, and George Barney, the Irish butler and general factotum to the establishment, announced that the "min wos in the hall awaitin'."

Giving Eda a parting kiss, Stanley rose and entered the hall, where Francois, Massan, Gaspard, and several others were grouped in a corner. On their bourgeois entering, they doffed their bonnets and bowed.

"Well, lads," began Stanley, with a smile, "you've thought better of it, I hope, and have come to volunteer for this expedition—" He checked himself and frowned, for he saw by their looks that they had come with quite a different intention. "What have you to say to me?" he continued abruptly.

The men looked uneasily at each other, and then fixed their eyes on Francois, who was evidently expected to be spokesman.

"Come, Francois, speak out," said Stanley; "if you have any objections, out with them; you're free to say what you please here."

As he spoke, and ere Francois could reply, Frank Morton entered the room. "Ah!" he exclaimed, as he deposited his rifle in a corner and flung his cap on the table, "in time, I see, to help at the council!"

"I was just asking Francois to state his objections to going," said Stanley, as his young friend took his place beside him.

"Objections!" repeated Frank; "what objections can bold spirits have to go on a bold adventure? The question should have been, 'Who will be first to volunteer?'"

At this moment the door of Stanley's apartment opened, and his wife appeared leading Eda by the hand.

"Here are two volunteers," she said, with a smile; "pray put us at the head of your list. We will go with you to any part of the world!"

"Bravo!" shouted Frank, catching up Eda, with whom he was a great favourite, and hugging her tightly in his arms.

"Nay, but, wife, this is sheer folly. You know not the dangers that await you—"

"Perhaps not," interrupted Mrs. Stanley; "but you know them, and that is enough for me."

"Indeed, Jessie, I know them not. I can but guess at them.—But, ah! well, 'tis useless to argue further. Be it so; we shall head the list with you and Eda."

"And put my name next," said a deep-toned voice from behind the other men. All turned round in surprise.

"Dick Prince!" they exclaimed; "you here?"

"Ay, lads," said a tall man of about forty, who was not so remarkable for physical development (though in this respect he was by no means deficient) as for a certain decision of character that betrayed itself in every outline of his masculine, intelligent countenance— "ay, lads, I'm here; an' sorry am I that I've jist comed in time to hear that you're sich poor-spirited rascals as to hang back when ye should jump for'ard."

"But how came you so opportunely, Prince?" inquired Stanley.

"I met an Injin, sir, as told me you was goin' off; so I thought you might want me, and comed straight back. And now, sir, I'm ready to go; and so is Francois," he continued, turning to that individual, who seized his hand and exclaimed, "That am I, my boy—to the moon if ye like!"

"And Massan, too," continued Prince.

"All right; book me for Nova Zembla," replied that worthy.

"So, so," cried Mr. Stanley, with a satisfied smile. "I see, lads, that we're all of one mind now. Is it not so? Are we agreed?"

"Agreed! agreed!" they replied with one voice.

"That's well," he continued. "Now then, lads, clear out and get your kits ready. And ho! Barney, give these men a glass of grog. Prince, I shall want to talk with you this evening. Come to me an hour hence. And now," he added, taking Eda by the hand, "come along, my gentle volunteers; let's go to supper."

Chapter IV

EXPLANATORY, BUT NOT DRY!—MURDEROUS DESIGNS
THWARTED BY VIGOROUS TREATMENT—THE CATTLE PAY
FOR IT!—PREPARATIONS FOR A LONG, LONG VOYAGE.

In order to render our story intelligible, it is
necessary here to say a few words explanatory of the
nature and object of the expedition referred to in the
foregoing chapters.

Many years previous to the opening of our tale, it
was deemed expedient, by the rulers of the Hudson's
Bay Fur Company, to effect, if possible, a reconciliation
or treaty of peace between the Muskigon Indians of
James's Bay and the Eskimos of Hudson's Straits. The
Muskigons are by no means a warlike race; on the
contrary, they are naturally timid, and only plucked
up courage to make war on their northern neighbours
in consequence of these poor people being destitute
of firearms, while themselves were supplied with guns

and ammunition by the fur-traders. The Eskimos,
however, are much superior to the Muskigon Indians
physically, and would have held their adversaries in
light esteem had they met on equal terms, or, indeed,
on any terms at all; but the evil was that they never
met. The Indians always took them by surprise, and
from behind the rocks and bushes sent destruction
into their camps with the deadly bullet; while their
helpless foes could only reply with the comparatively
harmless arrow and spear. Thus the war was in fact an
annual raid of murderers. The conceited Muskigons
returned to their wigwams in triumph, with bloody
scalps hanging at their belts; while the Eskimos pushed
farther into their ice-bound fastnesses, and told their
comrades, with lowering brows and heaving bosoms,
of the sudden attack, and of the wives and children
who had been butchered in cold blood, or led captive
to the tents of the cowardly red men.

At such times those untutored inhabitants of the
frozen regions vowed vengeance on the Indians, and
cursed in their hearts the white men who supplied
them with the deadly gun. But the curse was unmerited.
In the councils of the fur-traders the subject of
Eskimo wrongs had been mooted, and plans for the
amelioration of their condition devised. Trading
posts were established on Richmond Gulf and Little
Whale River; but owing to circumstances which it is
unnecessary to detail here, they turned out failures,
and were at length abandoned. Still, those in charge
of the districts around Hudson's Bay and Labrador
continued to use every argument to prevail on the

Indians to cease their murderous assaults on their unoffending neighbours, but without much effect. At length the governor of East Main—a territory lying on the eastern shores of James's Bay—adopted an argument which proved eminently successful, at least for one season.

His fort was visited by a large band of Muskigons from Albany and Moose districts, who brought a quantity of valuable furs, for which they demanded guns and ammunition, making no secret of their intention to proceed on an expedition against their enemies the Eskimos. On hearing of this, the governor went out to them, and, in a voice of extreme indignation, assured them that they should not have an ounce of supplies for such a purpose.

"But we will pay you for what we ask. We are not beggars!" exclaimed the astonished Indians, into whose calculations it had never entered that white traders would refuse good furs merely in order to prevent the death of a few Eskimos.

"See," cried the angry governor, snatching up the nearest bale of furs—"see, that's all I care for you or your payment!" and hurling the pack at its owner's head, he felled him therewith to the ground. "No," he continued, shaking his fist at them, "I'll not give you as much powder or shot as would blow off the tail of a rabbit, if you were to bring me all the skins in Labrador!"

The consequence of this vigorous conduct was that the Indians retired crestfallen—utterly discomfited. But in the camp that night they plotted revenge. In the darkness of the night they slaughtered all the cattle around the establishment, and before daybreak were over the hills and far away in the direction of their hunting-grounds, loaded with fresh beef sufficient for the supply of themselves and their families for the winter! It was a heavy price to pay; but the poor Eskimos remained unmolested that year, while the Indians received a salutary lesson. But the compulsory peace was soon broken, and it became apparent that the only effectual way to check the bloodthirsty propensity of the Indians was to arm their enemies with the gun. The destruction of the first expedition to the Eskimos, and the bad feeling that existed in the minds of the natives of Richmond Gulf consequent thereon, induced the fur-traders to fix on another locality for a new attempt. It was thought that the remote solitudes of Ungava Bay, at the extreme north of Labrador,—where the white man's axe had never yet felled the stunted pines of the north, nor the ring of his rifle disturbed its echoes,—would be the spot best suited for the erection of a wooden fort.

Accordingly, it was appointed that Mr. George Stanley should select a coadjutor, and proceed with a party of picked men to the scene of action as early in the spring as the ice would permit, and there build a fort as he best could, with the best materials he could find; live on whatever the country afforded in the shape of food; establish a trade in oil, whalebone, arctic foxes, etcetera, etcetera, if they were to be got; and bring about a reconciliation between the Eskimos and the Indians of the interior, if that were possible. With the careful minuteness peculiar to documents, Stanley's instructions went on to point out that he was to start from Moose with two half-sized canoes, each capable of carrying ten pieces or packages of 90 pounds weight each, besides the crew and bore through the ice, if the ice would allow him, till he should reach Richmond Gulf; cross this gulf, and ascend, if practicable, some of the rivers which fall into it from the height of land supposed, but not positively known, to exist somewhere in the interior. Passing this height, he was to descend by the rivers and lakes (if such existed) leading to the eastward, until he should fall upon a river reported to exist in these lands, and called by the natives Caniapuscaw, or South River, down which he was to proceed to the scene of his labours, Ungava Bay; on reaching which he was considerately left to the unaided guidance of his own discretion! Reduced to their lowest term and widest signification, the instructions directed our friend to start as early as he could, with whom he chose, and with what he liked; travel as fast as possible over terra incognita to a land of ice— perhaps, also, of desolation and locate himself among bloody savages. It was hoped that there would be found a sufficiency of trees wherewith to build him a shelter against a prolonged winter; in the meantime he might enjoy a bright arctic summer sky for his canopy!

But it was known, or at least supposed, that the Eskimos were fierce and cruel savages, if not cannibals. Their very name implies something of the sort. It signifies eaters of raw flesh, and was bestowed on them by their enemies the Muskigons. They call themselves Innuit-men, or warriors; and although they certainly do eat raw flesh when necessity compels them—which it often does—they asserted that they never did so from choice. However, be this as it may, the remembrance of their misdeeds in the first expeditions was fresh in the minds of the men in the service of the fur-traders, and they evinced a decided unwillingness to venture into such a country and among such a people, an unwillingness which was only at length overcome when Mrs. Stanley and her little daughter heroically volunteered to share the dangers of the expedition in the manner already narrated.

Stanley now made vigorous preparations for his departure. Some of the men had already been enrolled, as we have seen, and there were more than enough of able and active volunteers ready to complete the crews.

"Come hither, lads," he cried, beckoning to two men who were occupied on the bank of the river, near the entrance to Moose Fort, in repairing the side of a canoe.

The men left their work and approached. They were both Eskimos, and good stout, broad-shouldered, thick-set specimens of the race they were. One was called Oolibuck, [This name is spelt as it should be pronounced. The correct spelling is Ouligbuck], the other Augustus; both of which names are now chronicled in the history of arctic adventure as having belonged to the well-tried and faithful interpreters to Franklin, Back, and Richardson, in their expeditions of north-west discovery.

"I'm glad to see you busy at the canoe, boys," said Stanley, as they came up. "Of course you are both willing to revisit your countrymen."

"Yes, sir, we is. Glad to go where you choose send us," answered Oolibuck, whose broad, oily countenance lighted up with good-humour as he spoke.

"It will remind you of your trip with Captain Franklin," continued Stanley, addressing Augustus.

"Me no like to 'member dat," said the Eskimo, with a sorrowful shake of the head. "Me love bourgeois Franklin, but tink me never see him more."

"I don't know that, old fellow," returned Stanley, with a smile. "Franklin is not done with his discoveries yet; there's a talk of sending off another expedition some of these days, I hear, so you may have a chance yet."

Augustus's black eyes sparkled with pleasure as he heard this. He was a man of strong feeling, and during his journeyings with our great arctic hero had become attached to him in consequence of the hearty and unvarying kindness and consideration with which he treated all under his command. But the spirit of enterprise had been long slumbering, and poor Augustus, who was now past the prime of life, feared that he should never see his kind master more.

"Now I want you, lads, to get everything in readiness for an immediate start," continued Stanley, glancing upwards at the sky; "if the weather holds, we shan't be long off paying your friends a visit. Are both canoes repaired?"

"Yes, sir, they is," replied Oolibuck.

"And the baggage, is it laid out? And—"

"Pardon, monsieur," interrupted Massan, walking up, and touching his cap. "I've jest been down at the point, and there's a rig'lar nor' wester a-comin' down.

The ice is sweepin' into the river, an' it'll be choked up by to-morrow, I'm afraid."

Stanley received this piece of intelligence with a slight frown, and looked seaward, where a dark line on the horizon and large fields of ice showed that the man's surmise was likely to prove correct.

"It matters not," said Stanley, hastily; "I've made arrangements to start to-morrow, and start we shall, in spite of ice or wind, if the canoes will float!"

Massan, who had been constituted principal steersman of the expedition, in virtue of his well-tried skill and indomitable energy, felt that the tone in which this was said implied a want of confidence in his willingness to go under any circumstances, so he said gravely—

"Pardon, monsieur; I did not say we could not start."

"True, true, Massan; don't be hurt. I was only grumbling at the weather," answered Stanley, with a laugh.

Just then the first puff of the coming breeze swept up the river, ruffling its hitherto glassy surface.

"There it comes," cried Stanley, as he quitted the spot. "Now, Massan, see to it that the crews are assembled in good time on the beach to-morrow. We start at daybreak."

"Oui, monsieur," replied Massan, as he turned on his heel and walked away. "Parbleu! we shall indeed start to morrow, an it please you, if all the ice and wind in the polar regions was blowed down the coast and crammed into the river's mouth. C'est vrai!"

Chapter V

ICE LOOKS UNPROPITIOUS—THE START—AN IMPORTANT
MEMBER OF THE PARTY NEARLY FORGOTTEN—CHIMO.

Stanley's forebodings and Massan's prognostications
proved partly incorrect on the following morning.
The mouth of the river, and the sea beyond, were
quite full of ice; but it was loose, and intersected in all
directions by lanes of open water. Moreover, there was
no wind.

The gray light of early morning brightened into
dawn, and the first clear ray of the rising sun swept over
a scene more beautiful than ever filled the fancy of the
most imaginative poet of the Temperate Zones. The
sky was perfectly unclouded, and the surface of the sea
was completely covered with masses of ice, whose tops
were pure white like snow, and their sides a delicate
greenish-blue, their dull, frosted appearance forming
a striking contrast to the surrounding water, which

shone, when the sun glanced upon it, like burnished silver. The masses of ice varied endlessly in form and size, some being flat and large like fields, others square and cornered like bastions or towers—here a miniature temple with spires and minarets, there a crystal fortress with embrasures and battlements; and, in the midst of these, thousands of broken fragments, having all the varied outlines of the larger masses, appearing like the smaller houses, cottages, and villas of this floating city of ice.

"Oh how beautiful!" exclaimed little Edith, as her father led her and Mrs. Stanley towards the canoes, which floated lightly in the water, while the men stood in a picturesque group beside them, leaning on their bright red paddles.

"It is indeed, my pet," replied Stanley, a smile almost of sadness playing around his lips.

"Come, George, don't let evil forebodings assail you to-day," said Mrs. Stanley in a low tone. "It does not become the leader of a forlorn hope to cast a shade over the spirits of his men at the very outset." She smiled as she said this, and pressed his arm; but despite herself, there was more of sadness in the smile and in the pressure than she intended to convey.

Stanley's countenance assumed its usual firm but cheerful expression while she spoke. "True, Jessie, I must not damp the men; but when I look at you and our darling Eda, I may be forgiven for betraying a passing glance of anxiety. May the Almighty protect you!"

"Is the country we are going to like this, papa?"

inquired Eda, whose intense admiration of the fairy-like scene rendered her oblivious of all else.

"Yes, dear, more like this than anything else you have ever seen; but the sun does not always shine so brightly as it does just now, and sometimes there are terrible snow-storms. But we will build you a nice house, Eda, with a very large fireplace, so that we won't feel the cold."

The entire population of Moose Fort was assembled on the beach to witness the departure of the expedition. The party consisted of fifteen souls. As we shall follow them to the icy regions of Ungava, it may be worth while to rehearse their names in order as follows—

Mr. and Mrs. Stanley and Edith, Frank Morton, Massan, the guide, Dick Prince principal hunter to the party, La Roche Stanley's servant and cook, Bryan the blacksmith, Francois the carpenter, Oolibuck, Augustus and Moses, Eskimo interpreters, Gaspard, labourer and fisherman, Oostesimow and Ma-istequan Indian guides and hunters.

The craft in which these were about to embark were three canoes, two of which were large and one small. They were made of birch bark, a substance which is tough, light, and buoyant, and therefore admirably adapted for the construction of craft that have not only to battle against strong and sometimes shallow currents, but have frequently to be carried on the shoulders of their crews over rocks and mountains. The largest canoe was sixteen feet long by five feet broad in the middle, narrowing gradually towards the bow and stern to a sharp edge. Its loading consisted of bales, kegs, casks, and bundles of goods and provisions; each bale or cask weighed exactly 90 pounds, and was called a piece. There were fifteen pieces in the canoe, besides the crew of six men, and Mr. Stanley and his family, who occupied the centre, where their bedding, tied up in flat bundles and covered with oiled cloth, formed a comfortable couch. Notwithstanding the size and capacity of this craft, it had been carried down to the beach on the shoulders of Massan and Dick Prince, who now stood at its bow and stern, preventing it with their paddles from rubbing its frail sides against the wharf; for although the bark is tough, and will stand a great deal of tossing in water and plunging among rapids, it cannot sustain the slightest blow from a rock or other hard substance without being cracked, or having the gum which covers the seams scraped off. To those who are unacquainted with travelling in the wild regions of the north it would seem impossible that a long journey could be accomplished in such tender boats; but a little experience proves that, by judicious treatment and careful management, voyages of great length may be safely accomplished in them—that they are well adapted for the necessities of the country, and can be taken with greater ease through a rough, broken, and mountainous region than ordinary wooden boats, even of smaller size, could be.

The second canoe was in all respects similar to the one we have described, excepting that it was a few inches shorter. The third was much smaller—so small that it could not contain more than three men, with their provisions and a few bales, and so light that it could with the greatest ease be carried on the shoulders of one man. It was intended to serve as a sort of pioneer and hunting craft, which should lead the way, dart hither and thither in pursuit of game, and warn the main body of any danger that should threaten them ahead. It was manned by the two Indian guides, Oostesimow and Ma-istequan, and by Frank Morton, who being acknowledged one of the best shots of the party, was by tacit understanding regarded as commissary-general. It might have been said that Frank was the best shot, were it not for the fact that the aim of Dick Prince was perfect, and it is generally admitted that perfection cannot be excelled.

Although differing widely in their dispositions and appearance, the men of the expedition were similar at least in one respect—they were all first-rate, and had been selected as being individually superior to their comrades at Moose Fort. And a noble set of fellows they looked, as they stood beside their respective canoes, leaning on their little, brilliantly coloured paddles, awaiting the embarkation of their leaders. They all wore new suits of clothes, which were sufficiently similar to give the effect of a uniform, yet so far varied in detail as to divest them of monotony, and relieve the eye by agreeable contrast of bright colours. All of them wore light-blue cloth capotes with hoods hanging down behind, all had corduroy trousers gartered below the knee, and all wore moccasins, and had fire-bags stuck in their belts, in which were contained the materials for producing fire, tobacco, and pipes. So far they were alike, but the worsted belts of some were scarlet, of others crimson, and of others striped. Some gartered their trousers with thongs of leather, others used elegant bands of bead-work—the gifts, probably, of sorrowing sweethearts, sisters, or mothers—while the fire-bags, besides being composed some of blue, some of scarlet cloth, were ornamented more or less with flowers and fanciful devices elegantly wrought in the gaily-dyed quills of the porcupine.

On seeing Stanley and his wife and child approaching, Massan gave the order to embark. In a moment every man divested himself of his capote, which he folded up and placed on the seat he was to occupy; then, shaking hands all round for the last time, they stepped lightly and carefully into their places.

"All ready, I see, Massan," said Stanley, as he came up, "and the ice seems pretty open. How say you? shall we make a good day of it?"

Massan smiled dubiously as he presented his thick shoulder as a support to Mrs. Stanley, while she stepped into her place. He remembered the conversation of the previous evening, and determined that, whatever should happen, he at least would not cast the shadow of a doubt on their prospects. But in his own mind he suspected that their progress would be interrupted ere long, as the wind, although very light—almost imperceptible—was coming from the north-west.

"It'll be full flood in less nor half an hour," he replied, "and—(take care, Miss Edith, give me your little hand; there, now, jump light)—and we'll be past the p'int by that time, and git the good o' the ebb till sun-down."

"I fear," said Frank Morton, approaching, "that the

ice is rather thick for us; but it don't much matter, it will only delay us a bit—and at any rate we'll make good way as far as the point."

"True, true," said Stanley; "and it's a great matter to get fairly started. Once off we must go forward. All ready, lads?"

"Ay, ay, sir."

"Now, Frank, into your canoe and show us the way; mind we trust to your guidance to keep us clear of blind alleys among these lanes of water in the ice."

At this moment Edith—who had been for the last few minutes occupied in alternately drying her eyes and kissing her hands to a group of little children who had been her play-fellows during her sojourn at the fort— uttered a loud exclamation.

"Oh! oh! papa, mamma—Chimo!—we've forgot Chimo! Oh me! don't go away yet!"

"So we have!" said her father; "dear me, how stupid to forget our old friend!—Hallo! Frank, Frank, we've forgot the dog," shouted Stanley to his young comrade, who was on the point of starting.

On hearing this, Frank gave a long, shrill whistle. "That'll bring him if he's within ear-shot."

When the well-known sound broke upon Chimo's ear, he was lying coiled up in front of the kitchen fire, being privileged to do so in consequence of his position as Edith's favourite. The cook, having gone out a few minutes previously, had left Chimo to enjoy his slumbers in solitude, so that, when he started suddenly to his feet on hearing Frank's whistle, he found himself a prisoner. But Chimo was a peculiarly strong-minded and strong-bodied dog, and was possessed of an iron will! He was of the Eskimo breed, and bore some resemblance to the Newfoundland, but was rather shorter in the legs, longer in the body, and more powerfully made. Moreover, he was more shaggy, and had a stout, blunt, straightforward appearance, which conveyed to the beholder the idea that he scorned flattery, and would not consent to be petted on any consideration. Indeed this was the case, for he always turned away with quiet contempt from any of the men who attempted to fondle him. He made an exception, however, of little Edith, whom he not only permitted to clap him to any extent, but deliberately invited her to do so by laying his great head in her lap, rubbing himself against her, and wagging his bushy tail, as if to say, "Now, little girl, do what you will with me!" And Eda never refused the animal's dumb-show request. When she was very young and had not much sense—at which time Chimo was young too, but possessed of a great deal of sense—she formed a strong affection for the Eskimo dog, an affection which she displayed by putting her little arms round his neck and hugging him until he felt a tendency to suffocation; she also pulled his ears and tail, and stuffed her fat little hands into his eyes and mouth,—all of which dreadful actions she seemed to think, in her childish ignorance, must be very pleasant to Chimo, and all of which the dog appeared really to enjoy. At all events, whether he liked it or not, he came regularly to have himself thus treated every day. As Eda grew older she left off choking her favourite and poking out his eyes, and contented herself with caressing him. Chimo also evinced a partiality for Mr. Stanley and Frank Morton, and often accompanied the latter on his hunting excursions; but he always comported himself towards them with dignified hauteur, accepting their caresses with a slight wag of acknowledgment, but never courting their favour.

On jumping up, as we have already said, and observing that the door was shut, the dog looked slowly and calmly round the apartment, as if to decide on what was best to be done; for Chimo was a dog of great energy of character, and was never placed in any circumstances in which he did not pursue some decided course of action. On the present occasion there was not a hole, except the key-hole, by which he could hope to make his escape. Yes, by-the-bye, there was a hole in the window, which was made of parchment; but as that was merely the bullet-hole through which the animal that had given his skin for a window had been shot, and was not larger than a shilling, it did not afford much hope. Nevertheless Chimo regarded it with a steady gaze for a minute or two, then he turned to the fire, and having satisfied himself that the chimney was impracticable, being full of flames and smoke, he faced the window once more, and showed his teeth, as if in chagrin.

"Whew-ew! Chimo-o-o!" came Frank's voice, floating faintly from afar. Chimo took aim at the bullet-hole. One vigorous bound—a horrible crash, that nearly caused the returning cook to faint—and the dog was free.

"Ah, here he comes, good dog!" cried Frank, as

the animal came bounding over intervening obstacles towards the canoes. Chimo made straight for the small canoe, in answer to his master's call; but, like many dogs and not a few men, he owned a higher power than that of a master. The voice of his little mistress sounded sweetly in his ear, like the sound of a silver bell. "O Chimo, Chimo! my darling pet! come here—here." It was a soft, tiny voice at the loudest, and was quite drowned amid the talking and laughter of the men, but Chimo heard it. Turning at a sharp angle from his course, he swept past the light canoe, and bounding into that of Mr. Stanley, lay down beside Eda and placed his head in her lap, where it was immediately smothered in the caresses of its young mistress.

Mr. Stanley smiled and patted his little girl on the shoulder, as he said, "That's right, Eda; the love of a faithful dog is worth having and cherishing." Then turning towards the stern of the canoe, where Massan stood erect, with his steering paddle ready for action, he said to that worthy—

"Now, Massan, all ready; give the word."

"Ho, ho, boys; forward!"

The paddles dipped simultaneously in the water with a loud, gurgling sound; the two large canoes shot out into the stream abreast of each other, preceded by the light one, which, urged forward by the powerful arms of Frank and the two Indians, led the way among the floating fields of ice. The people on shore took off their caps and waved a last farewell. Dick Prince, who possessed a deep, loud, sonorous voice, began one of those beautiful and wild yet plaintive songs peculiar to the voyageurs of the wilderness. The men joined, with a full, rich swell, in the chorus, as they darted forward with arrow-like speed—and the voyage began.

Chapter VI

Fortunately the wind veered round to the south-east soon after the departure of the canoes from Moose Fort, and although there was not enough of it to ruffle the surface of the river, it had the effect of checking the influx of ice from James's Bay. The tide, too, began to ebb, so that the progress of the canoes was even more rapid than it appeared to be; and long before the sun set, they were past the point at the mouth of the river, and coasting along the shores of the salt ocean.

Outside of them the sea was covered with hummocks and fields of ice, some of which ever and anon met in the cross currents caused by the river, with a violent shock. Close to the shore, however, the thickness of the ice caused it to strand, leaving a lane of open water, along which the canoes proceeded easily, the depth of water being much more than sufficient for them, as the largest canoe did not draw more than a foot. Sometimes, however, this space was blocked up by smaller fragments, and considerable difficulty was experienced in steering the canoes amongst them. Had the party travelled in boats, they would have easily dashed through many of these checks; but with canoes it is far otherwise. Not only are their bark sides easily broken, but the seams are covered with a kind of pitch which becomes so brittle in ice-cold water that it chips off in large lumps with the slightest touch. For the sea, therefore, boats are best; but when it comes to carrying the craft over waterfalls and up mountain sides, for days and weeks together, canoes are more useful, owing to their lightness.

"Take care, Massan," said Mr. Stanley, on approaching one of these floes. "Don't chip the gum off if you can help it. If we spring a leak, we shan't spend our first night on a pleasant camping-ground, for the shore just hereabouts does not look inviting."

"No fear, sir," replied Massan. "Dick Prince is in the bow, and as long as his mouth's shut I keep my mind easy."

"You appear to have unlimited confidence in Prince," said Stanley, with a smile. "Does he never fail in anything, that you are so sure of him?"

"Fail!" exclaimed the steersman, whose paddle swept constantly in a circle round his head, while he changed it from side to side as the motions of the canoe required—"fail! ay, that does he sometimes. Mortal man must get on the wrong side o' luck now and then. I've seen Dick Prince fail, but I never saw him make a mistake."

"Well, I've no doubt that he deserves your good opinion. Nevertheless, be more than ordinarily careful. If you had a wife and child in the canoe, Massan, you would understand my anxiety better." Stanley smiled as he said this, and the worthy steersman replied in a grave tone,—"I have the wife and child of my bourgeois under my care."

"True, true, Massan," said Stanley, lying back on his couch and conversing with his wife in an undertone.

"'Tis curious," said he, "to observe the confidence that Massan has in Prince; and yet it would be difficult to say wherein consists the superiority of the one over the other."

"Perhaps it is the influence of a strong mind over a weaker," suggested his wife.

"It may be so. Yet Prince is an utterly uneducated man. True, he shoots a hair's-breadth better than Massan; but he is not a better canoe-man, neither is he more courageous, and he is certainly less powerful: nevertheless Massan looks up to him and speaks of him as if he were greatly his superior. The secret of his power must lie in that steady, never-wavering inflexibility of purpose, that characterises our good bowman in everything he does."

"Papa," said Edith, who had been holding a long conversation with Chimo on the wonders of the scene around them—if we may call that a conversation where the one party does all the talking and the other all the listening—"papa, where shall we all sleep to-night?"

The thought seemed to have struck her for the first time, and she looked up eagerly for an answer, while Chimo gave a deep sigh of indifference, and went to sleep, or pretended to do so, where he was.

"In the woods, Eda. How do you think you will like it?"

"Oh, I'm sure I shall like it very much," replied the little one. "I've often wished to live in the woods altogether like the Indians, and do nothing but wander about and pull berries."

"Ah, Jessie," said Stanley, "what an idle little baggage your daughter is! I fear she's a true chip of the old block!"

"Which do you consider the old block," retorted Mrs. Stanley—"you or me?"

"Never mind, wife; we'll leave that an open question.—But tell me, Eda, don't you think that wandering about and pulling berries would be a very useless sort of life?"

"No," replied Edith, gravely. "Mamma often tells me that God wants me to be happy, and I'm quite sure that wandering about all day in the beautiful woods would make me happy."

"But, my darling," said Stanley, smiling at the simplicity of this plausible argument in favour of an idle life, "don't you know that we ought to try to make others happy too, as well as ourselves?"

"Oh yes," replied Eda, with a bright smile, "I know that, papa; and I would try to make everybody happy by going with them and showing them where the finest flowers and berries were to be found; and so we would all be happy together, and that's what God wants, is it not?"

Mr. Stanley glanced towards his wife with an arch smile. "There, Jessie, what think you of that?"

"Nay, husband, what think you?"

"I think," he replied in an undertone, "that your sagacious teaching against idleness, and in favour of diligence and attention to duty, and so forth, has not taken very deep root yet."

"And I think," said Mrs. Stanley, "that however wise you men may be in some things, you are all most incomprehensibly stupid in regard to the development of young minds."

"Take care now, Jessie; you're verging upon metaphysics. But you have only given me your opinion of men as yet; you have still to say what you think of Eda's acknowledged predilection for idleness."

"Well," replied Mrs. Stanley, "I think that my sagacious teaching, as you are pleased to call it, has taken pretty firm root already, and that Eda's speech is one of the first bright, beautiful blossoms, from which we may look for much fruit hereafter; for to make one's self and one's fellow-creatures happy, because such is the will of God, seems to me a simple and comprehensive way of stating the whole duty of man."

Stanley's eyes opened a little at this definition. "Hum! multum in parvo; it may be so," he said; and casting down his eyes, he was soon lost in a profound reverie, while the canoe continued to progress forward by little impulsive bounds, under the rapid stroke of the paddles. Eda rested her fair cheek on the shaggy brow of Chimo, and accompanied him to the land of nod, until the sun began to sink behind the icebergs on the seaward horizon, where a dark line indicated an approaching breeze.

Massan cast an uneasy glance at this from time to time. At length he called to his friend in the bow, "Hello, Prince! will it come stiff; think ye?"

"No," replied Prince, rising and shading his eyes with his hand; "it'll be only a puff; but that's enough to drive the ice down on us, an' shut up the open water."

"It's my 'pinion," said Massan, "that we should hold away for the p'int yonder, an' camp there."

Dick Prince nodded assent, and resumed his paddle.

As he did so the report of a gun came sharply over the water.

"Ha!" exclaimed Stanley, looking out ahead; "what's that?"

"Only Mr. Frank," said Massan; "he's dowsed two birds. I see'd them splash into the water."

"That's right," said Stanley; "we shall have something fresh for the kettle to-night. And, by the way, we'll need all we can kill, for we haven't much provision to depend on, and part of it must be reserved in case of accidents, so that if Frank does not do his duty, we shall have to live on birch bark, Massan."

"That would be rayther tough. I'm afeerd," replied the steersman, laughing. "I've tried the tail o' a deerskin coat afore now, an' it wasn't much to boast of; but I niver tried a birch-bark steak. I doubt it would need a power o' chewin?"

By this time the two large canoes had drawn gradually nearer to the leading one. As they approached, Frank ordered his men to cease paddling.

"Well, Frank, what success?" said Stanley, as they came up.

"There's our supper," cried Frank, tossing a large duck into the canoe; "and there's a bite for the men," he added, sending a huge gray goose into the midst of them. "I saw a herd of reindeer on the other side of the point; but the ice closed up the passage, and prevented me from getting within range. It will stop our further progress for to-night too; so I waited to advise you to camp here."

"There it comes!" cried Dick Prince. "Jump out on the ice, lads, and unload as fast as you can."

As Dick spoke he sprang on to a field of ice which was attached to the shore, and drawing the canoe alongside, began hastily to remove the cargo. His example was instantly followed by the men, who sprang over the gunwales like cats; and in less than five minutes the cargoes were scattered over the ice. Meanwhile, the breeze which Massan had observed continued to freshen, and the seaward ice bore rapidly down on the shore, gradually narrowing and filling up the lanes of water among which the travellers had been hitherto wending their way. Dick Prince's sudden action was caused by his observing a large, solid field, which bore down on them with considerable rapidity. His warning was just in time, for the goods were scarcely landed and the three canoes lifted out of the water, when the ice closed in with a crash that would have ground the frail barks to pieces, and the passage was closed up. So completely was every trace of water obliterated, that it seemed as though there never had been any there before.

Chapter VII

SHOWS HOW THE PARTY MADE THEMSELVES AT
HOME IN THE BUSH—TALK ROUND THE CAMP
FIRE—A FLASH OF TEMPER—TURNING IN.

The spot where they were thus suddenly arrested in their progress was a small bay, formed by a low point which jutted from the mainland, and shut out the prospect in advance. There was little or no wood on the point, except a few stunted willows, which being green and small would not, as La Roche the cook remarked, "make a fire big enough to roast the wing of a mosquito." There was no help for it, however. The spot on which Massan had resolved to encamp for the night was three miles on the other side of the point, and as the way was now solid ice instead of water, there was no possibility of getting there until a change of wind should drive the ice off the shore. Moreover, it was now getting dark, and it behoved them to make their preparations with as much speed as possible. Accordingly, Massan and Prince shouldered one canoe, Francois and Gaspard carried the other, and the light one was placed on the shoulders of Bryan the blacksmith; La Roche took the provision-basket and cooking utensils under his special charge; while the three Eskimo interpreters and the two Indian guides busied themselves in carrying the miscellaneous goods and baggage into camp. As for Chimo, he seated himself quietly on a lump of ice, and appeared to superintend the entire proceedings; while his young mistress and her mother, accompanied by Frank and Stanley, crossed the ice to the shore, to select a place for their encampment.

But it was some time ere a suitable place could be found, as the point happened to be low and swampy, and poor Eda's first experience of a life in the woods was stepping into a hole which took her up to the knees in mud and water. She was not alone, however, in misfortune, for just at the same moment Bryan passed through the bushes with his canoe, and staggered into the same swamp, exclaiming as he did so, in a rich brogue which many years' residence among the French half-breeds of Rupert's Land had failed to soften, "Thunder an' turf! such a blackguard counthry I niver did see. Och, Bryan dear, why did ye iver lave yer native land?"

"Pourquoi, why, mon boy? for ver' goot raison," cried La Roche, in a horrible compound of French and broken English, as he skipped lightly past, with a loud laugh, "for ver' goot raison—dey was tired of you to home, vraiment. You was too grande raskale; dey could not keep you no longer."

"Thrue for ye, La Roche," replied the blacksmith, "thrue for ye, boy; they sartinly could not keep me on nothin', an' as the murphies was all sp'iled wi' the rot, I had to lave or starve."

At last, after a long search, Frank Morton found a spot pretty well adapted for their purpose. It was an elevated plot of gravel, which was covered with a thin carpet of herbage, and surrounded by a belt of willows which proved a sufficient shelter against the wind. A low and rather shaggy willow-tree spread its branches over the spot, and gave to it a good deal of the feeling and appearance of shelter, if not much of the reality. This was of little consequence, however, as the night proved fine and comparatively mild, so that the black vault of heaven, spangled with hosts of brilliant stars, amply compensated for the want of a leafy canopy.

Under the willow-tree, Frank and La Roche busied themselves in spreading a very small white tent for Mr. Stanley and his family. Frank himself, although entitled from his position in the Company's service to the luxury of a tent, scorned to use one, preferring to rough it like the men, and sleep beneath the shelter of the small canoe. Meanwhile, Mr. Stanley proceeded to strike a light with his flint and steel; and Bryan, having deposited his burden near the tent, soon collected a sufficiency of driftwood to make a good fire. Edith and her mother were not idle in the midst of this busy scene. They collected a few bundles of dried twigs to make the fire light more easily, and after the blaze

was casting its broad glare of light over the camp, and
the tent was pitched, they assisted La Roche in laying
the cloth for supper. Of course, in a journey like this,
none but necessary articles were taken, and these were
of the most homely character. The kettle was the tea-
pot, the cups were tin pannikins, and the table-cloth
was a large towel, while the table itself was the ground,
from the damp of which, however, the party in the tent
were protected by an ample oil-cloth.

When all the things were carried up, and the
men assembled, the camp presented the following
appearance: in the centre of the open space, which
nature had arranged in the form of a circle, blazed the
fire; and a right jovial, sputtering, outrageous fire it
was, sending its sparks flying in all directions, like the
artillery of a beleaguered fortress in miniature, and
rolling its flames about in fierce and wayward tongues,
that seemed bent on licking in and swallowing up
the entire party, but more especially La Roche, who
found no little difficulty in paying due attention to his
pots and kettles. Sometimes the flames roared fiercely
upwards, singeing off the foliage of the overhanging
willow as they went, and then, bursting away from
their parent fire, portions of them floated off for a few
seconds on the night air. On the weather side of this
fire stood Mr. Stanley's tent, under the willow-tree, as
before described, its pure white folds showing strongly
against the darkness of the sky beyond. The doorway,
or curtain of the tent, was open, displaying the tea-
equipage within, and the smiling countenances of
Stanley and his wife, Frank and Eda, who, seated on

blankets and shawls around the towel, were preparing to make an assault on the fat duck before mentioned. This duck had been split open and roasted on a piece of stick before the blaze, and now stood with the stumps of its wings and legs extended, as if demanding urgently to be eaten—a demand which Chimo, who crouched near the doorway, could scarce help complying with.

To the right of the tent was placed the small canoe, bottom up, so as to afford a partial protection to the bedding which Oostesimow was engaged in spreading out for Frank and himself and his comrade Ma-Istequan. Facing this, at the other side of the fire, and on the left of the tent, the largest canoe was turned up in a similar manner, and several of the men were engaged in covering the ground beneath it with a layer of leaves and branches, above which they spread their blankets; while others lounged around the fire and smoked their beloved pipes, or watched with impatient eyes the operations of Bryan, who, being accustomed to have familiar dealings with the fire, had been deemed worthy of holding the office of cook to the men, and was inducted accordingly.

It is due to Bryan to say that he fully merited the honour conferred upon him; for never, since the days of Vulcan, was there a man seen who could daringly dabble in the fire as he did. He had a peculiar sleight-of-hand way of seizing hold of and tossing about red-hot coals with his naked hand, that induced one to believe he must be made of leather. Flames seemed to have no effect whatever on his sinewy arms when they licked around them; and as for smoke, he treated it with benign contempt. Not so La Roche: with the mercurial temperament of his class he leaped about the fire, during his culinary operations, in a way that afforded infinite amusement to his comrades, and not unfrequently brought him into violent collision with Bryan, who usually received him on such occasions with a strong Irish growl, mingled with a disparaging or contemptuous remark.

Beyond the circle of light thrown by the fire was the belt of willows which encompassed the camp on all sides except towards the sea, where a narrow gap formed a natural entrance and afforded a glimpse of the ocean with its fields and hummocks of ice floating on its calm bosom and glancing in the faint light of the moon, which was then in its first quarter.

"How comfortable and snug everything is!" said Mrs. Stanley, as she poured out the tea, while her husband carved the duck.

"Yes, isn't it, Eda?" said Frank, patting his favourite on the head, as he held out her plate for a wing. "There, give her a bit of the breast too," he added. "I know she's ravenously hungry, for I saw her looking at Chimo, just before we landed, as if she meant to eat him for supper without waiting to have him cooked."

"O Frank, how can you be so wicked?" said Eda, taking up her knife and fork and attacking the wing with so much energy as almost to justify her friend's assertion.

"Snug, said you, Jessie? yes, that's the very word to express it," said Stanley. "There's no situation that I know of (and I wasn't born yesterday) that is so perfectly snug, and in all respects comfortable, as an encampment in the woods on a fine night in spring or autumn."

"Or winter," added Frank, swallowing a pannikin of tea at a draught, nodding to Chimo, as much as to say, "Do that if you can, old fellow," and handing it to Mrs. Stanley to be replenished. "Don't omit winter—cold, sharp, sunny winter. An encampment in the snow, in fine weather, is as snug as this."

"Rather cold, is it not?" said Mrs. Stanley.

"Cold! not a bit," replied Frank, making a reckless dive with his hand into the biscuit-bag; "if you have enough wood to get up a roaring fire, six feet long by three broad and four deep, with a bank of snow five feet high all around ye, a pine-tree with lots of thick branches spreading overhead to keep off the snow, and two big green blankets to keep out the frost—(another leg of that widgeon, please)—you've no notion how snug it is, I assure you."

"Hum!" ejaculated Stanley, with a dubious smile, "you forgot to add—a youthful, robust frame, with the blood careering through the veins like wildfire, to your catalogue of requisites. No doubt it is pleasant enough in its way; but commend me to spring or autumn for thorough enjoyment, when the air is mild, and the waters flowing, and the woods green and beautiful."

"Why don't you speak of summer, papa?" said Eda, who had been listening intently to this conversation.

"Summer, my pet! because—"

"Allow me to explain," interrupted Frank, laying down his knife and fork, and placing the forefinger of his right hand in his left palm, as if he were about to make a speech. "Because, Eda, because there is such a thing as heat—long-continued, never-ending, sweltering heat. Because there are such reprehensible and unutterably detestable insects as mosquitoes, and sand-flies, and bull-dogs; and there is such a thing as being bitten, and stung, and worried, and sucked into a sort of partial madness; and I have seen such sights as men perpetually slapping their own faces, and scratching the skin off their own cheeks with their own nails, and getting no relief thereby, but rather making things worse; and I have, moreover, seen men's heads swelled until the eyes and noses were lost, and the mouths only visible when opened, and their general aspect like that of a Scotch haggis; and there is a time when all this accumulates on man and beast till the latter takes to the water in desperation, and the former takes to intermittent insanity, and that time is summer. Another cup, please, Mrs. Stanley. 'Pon my conscience, it creates thirst to think of it."

At this stage the conversation of the party in the tent was interrupted by a loud peal of laughter mingled with not a few angry exclamations from the men. La Roche, in one of his frantic leaps to avoid a tongue of flame which shot out from the fire with a vicious velocity towards his eyes, came into violent contact with Bryan while that worthy was in the act of lifting a seething kettle of soup and boiled pork from the fire. Fortunately for the party whose supper was thus placed in jeopardy, Bryan stood his ground; but La Roche, tripping over a log, fell heavily among the pannikins, tin plates, spoons, and knives, which had been just laid out on the ground in front of the canoe.

"Ach! mauvais chien," growled Gaspard, as he picked up and threw away the fragments of his pipe, "you're always cuttin' and jumpin' about like a monkey."

"Oh! pauvre crapaud," cried Francois, laughing; "don't abuse him, Gaspard. He's a useful dog in his way."

"Tare an' ages! you've done it now, ye have. Bad luck to ye! wasn't I for iver tellin' ye that same. Shure, if it wasn't that ye're no bigger or heavier than a wisp o' pea straw, ye'd have druve me and the soup into the fire, ye would. Be the big toe o' St. Patrick, not to mention his riverince the Pope—"

"Come, come, Bryan," cried Massan, "don't speak ill o' the Pope, an' down wi' the kettle."

"The kittle, is it? Sorra a kittle ye'll touch, Massan, till it's cool enough to let us all start fair at wance. Ye've got yer mouth and throat lined wi' brass, I believe, an' would ate the half o't before a soul of us could taste it!"

"Don't insult me, you red-faced racoon," retorted Massan, while he and his comrades circled round the kettle, and began a vigorous attack on the scalding mess; "my throat is not so used to swallowin' fire as your own. I never knowed a man that payed into the grub as you do.—Bah! how hot it is.—I say, Oolibuck, doesn't it remember you o' the dogs o' yer own country, when they gits the stone kettle to clean out?"

Oolibuck's broad visage expanded with a chuckle as he lifted an enormous wooden spoonful of soup to his ample mouth. "Me tink de dogs of de Innuit [Eskimos] make short work of dis kettle if 'e had 'im."

"Do the dogs of the Huskies eat with their masters?"

inquired Francois, as he groped in the kettle with his fork in search of a piece of pork.

"Dey not eat wid der masters, but dey al'ays clean hout de kettle," replied Moses, somewhat indignantly.

"Ha!" exclaimed Massan, pausing for a few minutes to recover breath; "yes, they always let the dogs finish off the feast. Ye must know, comrades, that I've seed them do it myself—anyways I've seed a man that knew a feller who said he had a comrade that wintered once with the Huskies, which is pretty much the same thing. An' he said that sometimes when they kill a big seal, they boil it whole an' have a rig'lar feast. Ye must understand, mes garcons, that the Huskies make thumpin' big kettles out o' a kind o' soft stone they find in them parts, an' some o' them's big enough to boil a whole seal in. Well, when the beast is cooked, they take it out o' the pot, an' while they're tuckin' into it, the dogs come and sit in a ring round the pot to wait till the soup's cool enough to eat. They knows well that it's too hot at first, an' that they must have a deal o' patience; but afore long some o' the young uns can't hold on, so they steps up somewhat desperate like, and pokes their snouts in. Of course they pulls them out pretty sharp with a yell, and sit down to rub their noses for a bit longer. Then the old uns take courage an' make a snap at it now and again, but very tenderly, till it gits cooler at last, an' then at it they go, worryin', an' scufflin', an' barkin', an' gallopin', just like Moses there, till the pot's as clean as the day it wos made."

"Ha! ha! oh, ver' goot, tres bien; ah! mon coeur, just tres splendiferous!" shouted La Roche, whose risibility was always easily tickled.

"It's quite true, though—isn't it, Moses?" said Massan, as he once more applied to the kettle, while some of his comrades cut up the goose that Frank had shot in the afternoon.

"Why, Moses, what a capacity you have for grub!" said Francois. "If your countrymen are anything like you, I don't wonder that they have boiled seals and whales for dinner."

"It'll take a screamin' kittle for a whale," spluttered Bryan, with his mouth full, "an' a power o' dogs to drink the broth."

"You tink you funny, Bryan," retorted Moses, while an oily smile beamed on his fat, good-humoured countenance; "but you not; you most dreadful stupid."

"Thrue for ye, Moses; I was oncommon stupid to let you sit so long beside the kittle," replied the Irishman, as he made a futile effort to scrape another spoonful from the bottom of it. "Och! but ye've licked it as clane as one of yer own dogs could ha' done it."

"Mind your eye!" growled Gaspard, at the same time giving La Roche a violent push, as that volatile worthy, in one of his eccentric movements, nearly upset his can of water.

"Oh! pardon, monsieur," exclaimed La Roche, in pretended sorrow, at the same time making a grotesque bow that caused a general peal of laughter.

"Why, one might as well travel with a sick bear as with you, Gaspard," said Francois half angrily.

"Hold your jaw," replied Gaspard.

"Not at your bidding," retorted Francois, half rising

from his reclining posture, while his colour heightened. Gaspard had also started up, and it seemed as if the little camp were in danger of becoming a scene of strife, when Dick Prince, who was habitually silent and unobtrusive, preferring generally to listen rather than to speak, laid his hand on Gaspard's broad shoulder and pulled him somewhat forcibly to the ground.

"Shame on you, comrades!" he said, in a low, grave voice, that instantly produced a dead silence; "shame on you, to quarrel on our first night in the bush! We've few enough friends in these parts, I think, that we should make enemies o' each other."

"That's well said," cried Massan, in a very decided tone. "It won't do to fall out when there's so few of us." And the stout voyageur thrust his foot against the logs on the fire, causing a rich cloud of sparks to ascend, as if to throw additional light on his remark.

"Pardon me, mes comrades," cried Francois; "I did not intend to quarrel;" and he extended his hand to Gaspard, who took it in silence, and dropping back again to his recumbent posture, resumed his pipe.

This little scene was witnessed by the party in the tent, who were near enough to overhear all that was said by the men, and even to converse with them if they should desire to do so. A shade of anxiety crossed Mr. Stanley's countenance, and some time after, recurring to the subject, he said—

"I don't feel quite easy about that fellow Gaspard. He seems a sulky dog, and is such a Hercules that he might give us a deal of trouble if he were high-spirited."

A slight smile of contempt curled Frank's lip as he

said, "A strong arm without a bold heart is not of more value than that of my Eda here in the hour of danger. But I think better of Gaspard than you seem to do. He's a sulky enough dog, 'tis true; but he is a good, hard worker, and does not grumble; and I sometimes have noticed traces of a better spirit than usually meets the eye. As for his bulk, I think nothing of it; he wants high spirit to make it available. Francois could thrash him any day."

"Perhaps so," replied Stanley; "I hope they won't try their mettle on each other sooner than we expect. Not that I care a whit for any of the men having a round or two now and then and be done with it; but this fellow seems to 'nurse his wrath to keep it warm.' On such an expedition as ours, it behoves us to have a good understanding and a kindly feeling in the camp. One black sheep in the flock may do much damage."

"He's only piebald, not black," said Frank, laughing, as he rose to quit the tent. "But I must leave you. I see that Eda's eyes are refusing to keep open any longer, so good-night to you all, and a sound sleep."

Frank's concluding remarks in reference to him were overheard by Gaspard, who had risen to look at the night, and afterwards kneeled near the tent, in order to be at some distance from his comrades while he said his prayers; for, strange though it may seem, many of the rough and reckless voyageurs of that country, most of whom are Roman Catholics, regularly retire each night to kneel and pray beneath a tree before lying down on their leafy couches, and deem the act quite consistent with the swearing and quarrelling life that too many of them lead. Such is human nature. As Gaspard rose from his knees Frank's words fell upon his ear, and when he drew his blanket over his head that night there was a softer spot in his heart and a wrinkle less on his brow.

When Frank stepped over to the place where his canoe lay, the aspect of the camp was very different from what it had been an hour before. The fire had burned low, and was little more than a mass of glowing embers, from which a fitful flame shot forth now and then, casting a momentary glare on the forms of the men, who, having finished their pipes, were all extended in a row, side by side, under the large canoe. As they possessed only a single green blanket each, they had to make the most of their coverings, by rolling them tightly around their bodies, and doubling the ends down under their feet and over their heads; so that they resembled a row of green bolsters, all their feet being presented towards the fire, and all their heads resting on their folded capotes. A good deal of loud and regular snoring proved that toil and robust health seldom court the drowsy god long in vain. Turning to his own canoe, Frank observed that his Indian friends were extended out under it, with a wide space between them, in which his own bedding was neatly arranged. The grave sons of the forest had lain down to rest long before their white comrades, and they now lay as silent and motionless as the canoe that covered their heads. Being a small canoe, it did not afford protection to their legs and feet; but in fine weather this was of no consequence, and for the morrow they cared not.

Before lying down Frank kneeled to commend himself and his comrades to the protection of God; then stirring up the embers of the fire, he pulled out a small Bible from his breast pocket and sat down on a log to read. Frank was a careless, rollicking, kind-hearted fellow, and how much there was of true religion in these acts none but himself could tell. But the habit of reading the Word, and of prayer, had been instilled into him from infancy by a godly mother, and he carried it with him into the wilderness.

When he drew his blanket over him and laid his head on his capote the stars were still twinkling, and the moon still sailed in a clear sky and gave silver edges to the ice upon the sea. All was calm and solemn and beautiful, and it seemed as if it could never be otherwise in such a tranquil scene. But nature does not always smile. Appearances are often deceitful.

Chapter VIII

BRYAN'S ADVENTURE WITH A POLAR BEAR, ETC.

Ice, ice, ice! everything seemed to have been converted into ice when the day broke on the following morning and awoke the sleepers in the camp. A sharp frost during the night, accompanied by a fall of snow, had, as if by magic, converted spring into winter. Icy particles hung upon and covered, not only the young leaves and buds of the bushes, but the branches also, giving to them a white and extremely airy appearance. Snow lay on the upper sides of the canoes, and weighed heavily on the tent, causing its folds, once seemingly so pure and white, to look dirty by contrast. Snow lay on the protruding legs of the men, and encircled the black spot where rested the ashes of last night's brilliant fire. Ice grated on the pebbles of the shore; ice floated on the sea; icy hummocks and mounds rose above its surface; and icebergs raised their pinnacles on the far-off horizon, and cut sharply into the bright blue sky.

It was cold, but it was not cheerless; for when Eda put out her head at the curtain doorway of the tent, and opened her eyes upon the magic scene, the sun's edge rose above the horizon, as if to greet her, and sent a flood of light far and near through the spacious universe, converting the sea into glass, with islands of frosted silver on its bosom. It was a gorgeous scene, worthy of its great Creator, who in His mysterious working scatters gems of beauty oftentimes in places where there is scarce a single human eye to behold their excellence.

Although the sea was covered with ice, there were, nevertheless, several lanes of open water not far from the shore; so that when Stanley called a council, composed of Frank Morton, Dick Prince, and Massan, it was agreed unanimously that they should attempt to proceed. And it was well that they did so; for they had not advanced many miles, winding their way cautiously among the canals of open water, when they doubled a promontory, beyond which there was little or no ice to be seen, merely a few scattered fragments and fields, that served to enhance the beauty of the scene by the airy lightness of their appearance in contrast with the bright blue of the sea and sky, but did not interrupt the progress of the travellers. The three canoes always maintained their relative positions during the journey as much as possible. That is to say, Frank and the two Indians went first in the small canoe, to lead the way, while the two large canoes kept abreast of each other when the open water was wide enough to permit of their doing so. This, besides being more sociable, enabled the two crews to join in the chorus of those beautiful songs with which they frequently enlivened the voyage.

During all this day, and for many days following, they continued to enjoy fine weather and to make rapid progress. Sometimes the ice was pretty thick, and once or twice they narrowly escaped being nipped by collapsing masses, which caused them to jump out, hastily throw the baggage on the ice, and haul the canoes out of the water. On these occasions the men proved themselves to be sterling fellows, nearly all of them being cool, prompt, and collected in the moment of danger. No doubt there were exceptions. La Roche, when any sudden crisis of danger arose, usually threw himself blindly over the side of the canoe on to the ice with the lightness and agility of a harlequin. He recked not whether he came down on his head or his feet, and more than once nearly broke his neck in consequence of his precipitancy. But La Roche was no coward, and the instant the first burst of excitement was over he rushed to render effective assistance. Bryan, too, although not so mercurial as La Roche, was apt to lose self-command for about five minutes when any sudden danger assailed him, so that he frequently sat still, staring wildly straight before him, while the others were actively unloading the canoes; and once, when the danger was more critical than usual, having sat till the canoe was empty, and paid no attention to a prompt, gruff order to jump ashore, he had been seized by the strong arms of Gaspard and tossed out of the canoe like a puppy dog. On these occasions he invariably endeavoured to make up for his fault by displaying, on recovery, the most outrageous and daring amount of unnecessary recklessness, uttering, at the same time, an amazing number of strange expressions, among which "Tare an' ages!" "Och! murder!" and several others less lucid in signification, predominated. Chimo was always first ashore, and instantly wheeled round to greet Eda, who was also always second, thanks to the strong and prompt arm of Francois, who sat just in front, and by tacit agreement took her under his special charge. As for Mrs. Stanley, the arm that was rightfully her own, and had been her shield in many a scene of danger, proved ever ready and able to succour the "first volunteer" to Ungava.

At times the sea was quite free of ice, and many miles were soon added to the space which separated the little band of adventurers from the rest of the human world. Their encampments varied according to the nature of the coast, being sometimes among pine-trees, or surrounded by dwarf willows; at other times on the bare sand of the sea-shore; and occasionally at the extremity of long-projecting capes and promontories, where they had to pitch their tent and make their beds in the clefts of the solid rock. But wherever they laid them down to rest—on the rock, or on the sand, or within the shade of the forest—it was always found, as Mrs. Stanley remarked of the first night's encampment, that they were extremely comfortable and eminently snug.

They were successful, too, in procuring an ample supply of fresh provisions. There were ducks and geese of various kinds, and innumerable quantities of plover, cormorants, gulls, and eider-ducks, the eggs of which they found in thousands. Many of these birds were good for food, and the eggs of most of them, especially those of the eider-duck, were excellent. Reindeer were also met with; and, among other trophies of his skill as a hunter, Frank one day brought in a black bear, parts of which were eaten with great gusto by the Eskimos and Indians, to the immense disgust of Bryan, who expressed his belief that the "haythens was barely fit to live," and were most justly locked out from society in "thim dissolate polar raygeons." There were many seals, also, in the sea, which put up their ugly, grotesque heads ever and anon, gazed at the canoes with their huge, fishy eyes, as in surprise at the sight of such novel marine monsters, and then sank slowly beneath the wave. These animals were never molested, out of respect to the feelings of the two Indians, who believed them to be gods, and assured Stanley that the destruction of one would infallibly bring down ill-luck and disaster on the heads of the party. Stanley smiled inwardly at this, but gave orders that no seals should be shot— an order which all were very willing to obey, as they did not require the animals either for food or any other purpose. Several white polar bears were seen, but they also were spared, as they require a great deal of shot to kill them, if not hit exactly behind the ear; and besides, neither their bodies nor skins were of any use to the travellers.

Thus all went favourably for a time. But life is a chequered story, and the sun of prosperity does not always shine, as we shall see.

One fine morning, as they were paddling cheerfully along in the neighbourhood of Cape Jones, it struck Mr. Stanley that he might prove the correctness of his sextant and other instruments before entering upon the country which to most of the party was terra incognita. This was the more necessary that he could not depend on the guidance of Oostesimow and Ma-Istequan, they having travelled only once, long ago, through part of the country, while the latter part of it was totally unknown to them. It was one of those beautiful mornings that are peculiar to arctic regions, when the air is inexpressibly still, and all inanimate nature seems hushed in profound repose—a repose which is rather rendered more effective than otherwise by the plaintive cries of wild-fowl or the occasional puffing of a whale. There was a peculiar brilliancy, too, in the atmosphere, caused by the presence of so many fields and hummocks of white ice, looming fantastically through a thin, dry, gauze-like haze, which, while it did not dim the brightness of the solar rays, lent an additional charm to every object by shrouding it in a veil of mystery.

On passing the point the men ceased rowing, and proceeded to solace themselves with a five-minutes' pipe—an indulgence which voyageurs always claim as their due after a long spell at the oars or paddles.

"Put ashore here, Massan," said Stanley, turning to

the guide; "I shall take an observation, if possible, and you can set the men to hunt for eggs. We shall want them, as the larder is rather low just now."

Massan muttered assent, and, shouting to the other canoe to put ashore, ran alongside the rocks.

"You'd better hail the little canoe," said Stanley, as he landed. "I shall want Mr. Morton to assist me."

Massan stepped upon an elevated rock, and, shading his eyes with his hands, looked earnestly ahead where he observed the little canoe almost beyond vision, and just going to double a point of land. Transferring his hands to his mouth, he used them as a trumpet, and gave forth a shout the like of which had never startled the echoes of the place before.

"It's no use, sir," said Massan; "he's past hearin'. I'm afeerd that they're off in the direction o' the White Bear Hills, in hopes o' gittin' a shot."

"Try again, Massan," urged Stanley; "raise your pipe a little higher. Perhaps it will reach them."

Massan shook his head. "Try it, Bryan," he said, turning to the Irishman, who was sitting on a rock leisurely filling his short, black pipe.

"Is it to halloo ye want me?" replied Bryan, rising. "Shure the great gun of Athlone itself could niver hold a candle to ye, Massan, at yellin'; but I'll try, anyhow;" and putting his hands to his mouth he gave forth a roar compared to which Massan's was nothing. There was a sort of crack in the tone of it, however, that was so irresistibly ridiculous that the whole party burst incontinently into a fit of laughter. Loud though it was, it failed to reach the ears of those in the little canoe, which in a few seconds doubled the point and disappeared.

"Ah, bad luck to it!" said Bryan, in disgust; "the pipe's damaged intirely. Small pace to ye, Bob Mahone; for shure it was howlin' and screechin' at your wake like a born scrandighowl that broke it."

"Never mind, lad; what remains of it is not bad," said Stanley, laughing, as he proceeded to open the box containing his scientific instruments.

Meanwhile his wife and Edith wandered along the rocks picking up shells and pebbles; and the men dispersed, some to smoke and chat, others to search for eggs. Bryan and La Roche, who were both aspiring geniuses, and had formed a sort of rough attachment to each other, asked permission to take a walk to the point ahead, where they would wait for the canoes. Having obtained it, they set off at a good round pace, that would have been "throublesome to kape up," as Bryan remarked, "with payse in yer shoes!"

"Why you come for to jine de company?" inquired La Roche, as they jogged along.

"Why? bekase I'd nothin' else to do, as the ould song says. Ye see, Losh," (Bryan had invented a contraction for his friend's name, which he said was "convanient")— "ye see, Losh, there may be more nor wan raison for a gintleman lavin' his native land in order to thravel in furrin parts. It's thrue I had nothin' in the univarse to do, for I could niver git work nohow, an' whin I got it I could niver kape it. I niver could onderstan' why, but so it was. Nivertheless I managed to live well enough in the ould cabin wid the murphies—"

"Vat is murphies?" inquired La Roche.

"Bliss yer innocent face, don't ye know it's praties?"

"'Tis vat?"

"Praties, boy, or pit-taties, if I must be partic'lar."

"Ah! goot, goot, I understan'—pettitoes. Oui, oui, ye call him pomme de terre."

"Hum! well, as I was sayin', I got on pretty well wid the pumdeterres an' the pig, but the pig died wan day—choked hisself on a murphy—that is, a pumbleterre; an' more betoken, it was the last murphy in the house, a powerful big wan that my grandmother had put by for supper. After this ivery thin' wint to smithereens. The rot came, and I thought I should have to list for a sodger. Well, Bob Mahone died o' dhrink and starvation, an' we had a beautiful wake; but there was a rig'lar shindy got up, an' two or three o' the county p'lice misbehaved themselves, so I jist floored them all, wan after the other, an' bolted. Well, I wint straight to Dublin, an' there I met wid an ould friend who was the skipper o' a ship bound for New York. Says he, 'Bryan, will ye go?' Says I, 'Av coorse; 'an 'shure enough I wint, an' got over the say to 'Meriky.' But I could niver settle down, so, wan way or another, I came at last to Montreal and jined the Company; an' afther knockin' about in the Columbia and Mackenzie's River for some years, I was sint to Moose, an' here I am, Losh, yer sarvant to command."

"Goot, ver' goot, mais peculiaire," said La Roche, whose intimacy with this son of Erin had enabled him to comprehend enough of his jargon to grasp the general scope of his discourse.

"Av ye mane that lavin' the ould country was goot,"

said Bryan, stooping to pick up a stone and skim it along the smooth surface of the sea, "p'raps ye're right; but there's wan thing I niver could make my mind aisy about," and the blacksmith's voice became deep and his face grave as he recalled these bygone days.

"Vat were dat?" inquired La Roche.

"Why, ye see, Losh, I was so hard druve by the p'lice that I was forced to lave wid-out sayin' good day to my ould mother, an' they tould me it almost broke her heart; but I've had wan or two screeds from the priest wid her cross at them since, and she's got over it, an' lookin' out for my returnin'—bliss her sowl!—an' I've sint her five pounds ivery year since I left: so ye see, Losh, I've great hope o' seein' her yit, for although she's ould she's oncommon tough, an' having come o' a long-winded stock, I've great hopes o' her."

Poor Bryan! it never entered into his reckless brain to think that, considering the life of almost constant peril he led in the land of his pilgrimage, there was more hope of the longevity of his old mother than of himself. Like many of his countrymen, he was a man of strong, passionate, warm feelings, and remarkably unselfish.

"Is your contry resemblance to dat?" inquired La Roche, pointing, as he spoke, towards the sea, which was covered with fields and mountains of ice as far out as the eye could discern.

"Be the nose o' my great-grandmother (an' that was be no manes a short wan), no!" replied Bryan, with a laugh. "The say that surrounds ould Ireland is niver covered with sich sugar-plums as these. But what have we here?"

As he spoke they reached the point at which they were to await the coming up of the canoes, and the object which called forth Bryan's remark was the little canoe, which lay empty on the beach just beyond the point. From the manner in which it lay it was evident that Frank and his Indians had placed it there; but there was no sign of their presence save one or two footprints on the sand. While La Roche was examining these, his companion walked towards a point of rock that jutted out from the cliffs and intercepted the view beyond. On turning round this, he became suddenly rooted to the spot with horror. And little wonder, for just two yards before him stood an enormous polar bear, whose career was suddenly arrested by Bryan's unexpected appearance. It is difficult to say whether the man or the beast expressed most surprise at the rencounter. They both stood stock still, and opened their eyes to the utmost width. But the poor Irishman was evidently petrified by the apparition. He turned deadly pale, and his hands hung idly by his sides; while the bear, recovering from his surprise, rose on his hind legs and walked up to him—a sure sign that he was quite undaunted, and had made up his mind to give battle. As for La Roche, the instant he cast his eyes on the ferocious-looking quadruped, he uttered a frightful yell, bounded towards a neighbouring tree, and ceased not to ascend until its topmost branches were bending beneath his weight. Meanwhile the bear walked up to Bryan, but not meeting with the anticipated grapple of an enemy, and feeling somewhat uneasy under the cataleptic stare of the poor man's eyes—for he still

stood petrified with horror—it walked slowly round
him, putting its cold nose on his cheek, as if to tempt
him to move. But the five minutes of bewilderment
that always preceded Bryan's recovery from a sudden
fright had not yet expired. He still remained perfectly
motionless, so that the bear, disdaining, apparently,
to attack an unresisting foe, dropped on his forelegs
again. It is difficult to say whether there is any truth
in the well-known opinion that the calm, steady gaze
of a human eye can quell any animal. Doubtless there
are many stories, more or less authentic, corroborative
of the fact; but whether this be true or not, we are
ready to vouch for the truth of this fact—namely, that
under the influence of the blacksmith's gaze, or his
silence it may be, the bear was absolutely discomfited.
It retreated a step or two, and walked slowly away,
looking over its shoulder now and then as it went, as if
it half anticipated an onslaught in the rear.

We have already said that Bryan was no craven,
and that when his faculties were collected he usually
displayed a good deal of reckless valour on occasions
of danger. Accordingly, no sooner did he see his shaggy
adversary in full retreat, than the truant blood returned
to his face with a degree of violence that caused it to
blaze with fiery red, and swelled the large veins of his
neck and forehead almost to bursting. Uttering a truly
Irish halloo, he bounded forward like a tiger, tore the
cap off his head and flung it violently before him, drew
the axe which always hung at his belt, and in another
moment stood face to face with the white monster,
which had instantly accepted the challenge, and rose

IN FRONT OF HIM STOOD A ENORMOUS POLAR BEAR—PAGE 95

on its hind legs to receive him. Raising the axe with both hands, the man aimed a blow at the bear's head; but with a rapid movement of its paw it turned the weapon aside and dashed it into the air. Another such blow, and the reckless blacksmith's career would have been brought to an abrupt conclusion, when the crack of a rifle was heard. Its echo reverberated along the cliffs and floated over the calm water as the polar bear fell dead at Bryan's feet.

"Hurrah!" shouted Frank Morton, as he sprang from the bushes, knife in hand, ready to finish the work which his rifle had so well begun. But it needed not. Frank had hit the exact spot behind the ear which renders a second ball unnecessary—the bear was already quite dead.

Chapter IX

"Ah, Bryan! a friend in need is a friend indeed,'"
said Frank, as he sat on a rock watching the
blacksmith and his two Indians while they performed
the operation of skinning the bear, whose timely
destruction has been related in the last Chapter. "I
must say I never saw a man stand his ground so well,
with a brute like that stealing kisses from his cheek.
Were they sweet, Bryan? Did they remind you of the
fair maid of Derry, hey?"

"Ah! thrue for ye," replied the blacksmith, as he
stepped to a rock for the purpose of whetting his
knife; "yer honour was just in time to save me a power
o' throuble. Bad skran to the baste! It would have
taken three or four rounds at laste to have finished

him nately off, for there's no end o' fat on his ribs that would have kep' the knife from goin' far in."

Frank laughed at this free-and-easy way of looking at it. "So you think you would have killed him, do you, if I had not saved you the trouble?"

"Av coorse I do. Shure a man is better than a baste any day; and besides, had I not a frind at my back ridy to help me?" Bryan cast a comical leer at La Roche as he said this, and the poor Frenchman blushed, for he felt that his conduct in the affair had not been very praiseworthy. It is due to La Roche to say, however, that no sooner had he found himself at the top of the tree, and had a moment to reflect, than he slid rapidly to the bottom again, and ran to the assistance of his friend, not, however, in time to render such assistance available, as he came up just at the moment the bear fell.

In half an hour afterwards the two large canoes came up, and Bryan and his little friend had to undergo a rapid fire of witticism from their surprised and highly-amused comrades. Even Moses was stirred up to say that "Bryan, him do pratty well; he most good 'nuff to make an Eskimo!"

Having embarked the skin of the bear, the canoes once more resumed their usual order and continued on their way. The carcass of the bear being useless for food, was left for the wolves; and the claws, which were nearly as large as a man's finger, were given by Frank to the blacksmith, that he might make them into a necklace, as the Indians do, and keep it in remembrance of his re-encounter.

But the weather was now beginning to change.

Dick Prince, whose black eye was ever roving about observantly, told Massan that a storm was brewing, and that the sooner he put ashore in a convenient spot the better. But Stanley was anxious to get on, having a long journey before him, at the termination of which there would be little enough time to erect a sufficient protection against the winter of the north; so he continued to advance along shore until they came to a point beyond which there was a very deep bay that would take them many hours to coast. By making a traverse, however, in a direct line to the next point, they might cross it in a much shorter time.

"How say you, Prince? Shall we cross?" asked Stanley, as they rested on their paddles and cast furtive glances up at the dark clouds and across the still quiet bay.

Prince shook his head. "I fear we won't have time to cross. The clouds are driving too fast and growin' black."

"Well, then, we had better encamp," said Stanley.— "Is there a proper place, Massan, hereabouts?"

"No, sir," replied the guide. "The stones on the beach are the only pillows within six mile o' us."

"Ho! then, forward, boys, make a bold push for it," cried Stanley; "if it does begin to blow before we're over, we can run back again at all events."

In another moment the canoes swept out to sea, and made for the point far ahead like race-horses. Although the clouds continued to gather, the wind did not rise, and it seemed as though they would get over easily, when a sudden gust came off the shore—a direction whence, from the appearance of the clouds, it had not been expected. Ruffling the surface of the water for a few seconds, it passed away.

"Give way, boys, give way," cried Massan, using his large steering paddle with a degree of energy that sent the canoe plunging forward. "We can't go back, an' if the storm bursts off the shore—"

A loud peal of thunder drowned the remainder of the sentence, and in a few seconds the wind that had been dreaded came whistling violently off the shore and covered the sea with foam. The waves soon began to rise, and ere long the frail barks, which were ill calculated to weather a storm, were careering over them and shipping water at every plunge.

It now became a matter of life and death with them that they should gain the point, for, deeply loaded as they were, it was impossible that they could float long in such a sea. It is true that a wind off the shore does not usually raise what sailors would consider much of a sea; but it must be remembered that, although it was off shore, the bay which they were crossing extended far inland, so that the gale had a wide sweep of water to act upon before it reached them. Besides this, as has already been explained, canoes are not like boats. Their timbers are weak, the bark of which they are made is thin, the gum which makes their seams tight is easily knocked off in cold water, and, in short, they cannot face a sea on which a boat might ride like a sea-gull.

For a considerable time the men strained every nerve to gain the wished-for point of land, but with so little success that it became evident they would never reach it. The men began to show signs of flagging, and cast uneasy glances towards Stanley, as if they had lost all hope of accomplishing their object, and waited for him to suggest what they should do. Poor Mrs. Stanley sat holding on to the gunwale with one hand and clasping Edith round the waist with the other, as she gazed wistfully towards the cape ahead, which was now almost lost to view under the shadow of a dark cloud that rolled towards them like a black pall laden with destruction.

"God help us!" murmured Stanley, in an undertone, as he scanned the seaward horizon, which was covered with leaden clouds and streaks of lurid light, beneath which the foaming sea leaped furiously.

"Call upon Me in the time of trouble, and I will deliver thee," said Mrs. Stanley, who overheard the exclamation.

Stanley either heard her not or his mind was too deeply concentrated on the critical nature of their position to make any reply. As she buried her face in her hands, Edith threw her trembling arms round her mother and hid her face in her bosom. Even Chimo seemed to understand their danger, for he crept closer to the side of his young mistress and whined in a low tone, as if in sympathy. The waves had now increased to such a degree that it required two of the men to bail incessantly in order to prevent their being swamped, and as Stanley cast a hurried glance at the other canoes, which were not far off, he observed that it was as much as they could do to keep afloat. "Could we not run back, Massan?" asked Stanley, in despair.

"Unposs'ble, sir," replied the guide, whose voice was almost drowned by the whistling of the wind. "We're more nor half-way over, an' it would only blow us farther out to sea if we was to try."

While the guide spoke, Stanley was gazing earnestly in the direction of the horizon.

"Round with you, Massan," he exclaimed suddenly; "put the canoe about and paddle straight out to sea.— Hallo!" he shouted to the other canoes, "follow us out to sea—straight out."

The men looked aghast at this extraordinary order. "Look alive, lads," continued their leader; "I see an island away there to leeward. Perhaps it's only a rock, but any way it's our only chance."

The canoes' heads were turned round, and in another moment they were driving swiftly before the wind in the direction of the open sea.

"Right, right," murmured Dick Prince, as they made towards this new source of hope; "mayhap it's only a bit o' ice, but even that's better than nothin'."

"If 'tis only ice," cried La Roche, "ye have ver' pauvre chance at all."

"Shure, an' if we are to go ashore, at all," said Bryan, whose spirits had suddenly risen with this gleam of hope from fifty degrees below to fifty above zero—"if we are to go ashore at all, at all, it's better to land on the ice than on the wather."

With such a breeze urging them on, the three canoes soon approached what appeared to be a low sand-bank, on which the sea was dashing in white foam. But from the tossing of the waves between them and the beach, it was difficult to form a conjecture as to its size. Indeed, at times they could scarcely see it at all, owing to the darkness of the day and the heavy rain which began to fall just as they approached; and more than once Stanley's heart sank when he lost sight of the bank, and he began to think that he had made a mistake, and that they were actually flying out to the deep sea, in which case all hope would be gone for ever. But God's mercy was extended to them in this hour of peril. The island appeared to grow larger as they neared it, and at last they were within a stone's-throw of the shore. But a new danger assailed them here. The largest canoe, which neared the island first, had begun to leak, and took in water so fast that the utmost efforts of those who bailed could not keep it under, and from the quantity that was now shipped they made very little way. To add to the horror of the scene, the sky became very dark, and another crash of thunder pealed forth accompanied by a blinding flash of lightning.

"Paddle, boys, paddle for your lives!" cried Stanley, throwing off his coat, and seizing a tin dish, with which he began to throw out the water.

The canoe rose on a huge wave which broke all round it. This nearly filled it with water, and carried it towards the shore with such velocity that it seemed as if they should be dashed in pieces; but they fell back into the trough of the sea, and lay motionless like a heavy log, and in a sinking condition.

"Now, lads, look out for the next wave, and give way with a will," cried Massan. The worthy steersman acted rather too energetically on his own advice, for he dipped his paddle with such force that it snapped in two.

"Be ready to jump out," cried Dick Prince, standing up in the bow in order to give more power to his strokes.

As he spoke, Stanley turned to his wife, and said, "Jessie, hold on by my collar; I'll take Eda in my arms." At that instant the canoe gave a lurch, and before Stanley could grasp his child, they were all struggling in the sea! At this awful moment, instead of endeavouring to do as her husband directed, Mrs. Stanley instinctively threw her arms around Edith, and while the waves were boiling over her, she clasped the child tightly to her bosom with her left arm, while with her right she endeavoured to raise herself to the surface. Twice she succeeded, and twice she sank, when a box of merchandise providentially struck her arm. Seizing this, she raised herself above the water, and poor Edith gasped convulsively once or twice for air. Then the box was wrenched from her grasp by a wave, and with a wild shriek she sank again. Just then a strong arm was thrown around her, her feet touched the ground, and in a few seconds she was dragged violently from the roaring waves and fell exhausted on the beach.

"Thanks be to God, we are saved!" murmured Mrs. Stanley, as her husband assisted her to rise and led her beyond the reach of the waves, while Edith still clung with a deadly grasp to her mother's neck.

"Ay, Jessie, thank God indeed! But for His mercy we should have all been lost. I was floundering about beside the canoe when your scream showed me where you were, and enabled me to save you. But rest here, in the lee of this bale. I cannot stay by you. Frank is in danger still."

Without waiting for a reply, he sprang from her side and hurried down to the beach. Here everything was in the utmost confusion. The two large canoes had been saved and dragged out of the reach of the waves, and the men were struggling in the boiling surf to rescue the baggage and provisions, on which latter their very lives depended. As Stanley reached the scene of action, he observed several of the men watching the small canoe which contained Frank and his two Indians. It had been left some distance behind by the others, and was now approaching with arrow speed on the summit of a large wave. Suddenly the top of the billow curled over, and in another moment the canoe was turned bottom up! Like a cork it danced on the wave's white crest, then falling beneath the thundering mass of water, it was crushed to pieces and cast empty upon the beach. But Frank and his men swam like otters, and the party on shore watched them with anxious looks as they breasted manfully over the billows. At last a towering wave came rolling majestically forward. It caught the three swimmers in its rough embrace, and carrying them along on its crest, launched them on the beach, where it left them struggling with the retreating water. Those who have bathed in rough weather on an exposed coast know well how difficult it is to regain a firm footing on loose sand while a heavy wave is sweeping backward into its parent ocean. Frank and the two Indians experienced this; and they might have struggled there till their strength had been exhausted, were it not for Stanley, Prince, and Massan, who rushed simultaneously into the water and rescued them.

As the whole party had now, by the goodness of God, reached the land in safety, they turned their undivided energies towards the bales and boxes which were rolling about in the surf. Many of these had been already collected, and were carried to the spot where Mrs. Stanley and Edith lay under the shelter of a bale. As the things were successively brought up they were piled around the mother and child, who soon found themselves pretty well sheltered from the wind, though not from the rain, which still fell in torrents. Soon after Frank came to them, and said that all the things were saved, and that it was time to think of getting up some sort of shelter for the night. This was very much needed, for poor Edith was beginning to shiver from the wet and cold.

"Now then, Francois, Massan," shouted Frank, "lend a hand here to build a house for Eda. We'll be all as snug as need be in a few minutes."

Despite the cold and her recent terror, the poor child could not help smiling at the idea of building a house in a few minutes, and it was with no little curiosity that she watched the operations of the men. Meanwhile Mr. Stanley brought some wine in a pannikin, and made Edith and his wife drink a little. This revived them greatly, and as the rain had now almost ceased they rose and endeavoured to wring the water out of their garments. In less than half an hour the men piled the bales and boxes in front of the largest canoe, which was turned bottom up, and secured firmly in that position by an embankment of sand. Over the top of all, three oil-cloths were spread and lashed down, thus forming a complete shelter, large enough to contain the whole party. At one end of this curious house Mr. Stanley made a separate apartment for his wife and child, by placing two large bales and a box as a partition; and within this little space Edith soon became very busy in arranging things, and "putting the house to rights," as she said, as long as the daylight lasted, for after it went away they had neither candles nor fire, as the former had been soaked and broken, and as for the latter no wood could be found on the island. The men's clothes were, of course, quite wet, so they cut open a bale of blankets, which had not been so much soaked as the other goods, having been among the first things that were washed ashore.

At the time they were wrecked the dashing spray and the heavy rain, together with the darkness of the day, had prevented the shipwrecked voyageurs from ascertaining the nature of the island on which they had been cast; and as the night closed in while they were yet engaged in the erection of their temporary shelter, they had to lie down to rest in ignorance on this point. After such a day of unusual fatigue and excitement, they all felt more inclined for rest than food; so, instead of taking supper, they all lay down huddled together under the canoe, and slept soundly, while the angry winds whistled round them, and the great sea roared and lashed itself into foam on the beach, as if disappointed that the little band of adventurers had escaped and were now beyond the reach of its impotent fury.

Chapter X

Of all the changes that constantly vary the face of nature, the calm that succeeds a storm is one of the most beautiful, and the most agreeable, perhaps, to the feelings of man. Few conditions of nature convey to the mind more thoroughly the idea of complete repose—of deep rest after mortal strife, of sleep after exhausting toil; and those who have passed through the violence of the storm and done battle with its dangers are, by the physical rest which they enjoy after it is over, the more fitted to appreciate and sympathise with the repose which reigns around them.

When the sun rose, on the morning after the storm, it shone upon a scene so calm and beautiful, so utterly unconnected with anything like the sin of a fallen world, and so typical, in its deep tranquillity, of the mind of Him who created it, that it seemed almost possible for a moment to fancy that the promised land was gained at last, and that all the dark clouds, the storms and dangers, the weary journeyings and the troubles of the wilderness, were past and gone for ever. So glorious was the scene that when Edith, rising from her rude couch and stepping over the prostrate forms of her still slumbering companions, issued from the shelter of the canoe and cast her eyes abroad upon the glassy sea, she could not restrain her feelings, and uttered a thrilling shout of joy that floated over the waters and reverberated among the glittering crags of the surrounding icebergs.

The island on which the travellers had been cast was a mere knoll of sand, not more than a few hundred yards in circumference, that scarcely raised its rounded summit above the level of the water, and at full tide was reduced to a mere speck, utterly destitute of vegetation. The sea around it was now smooth and clear as glass, though undulated by a long, regular swell, which rolled, at slow, solemn intervals, in majestic waves towards the sand-bank, where they hovered for a moment in curved walls of dark-green water, then, lipping over, at their crests, fell in a roar of foam that hissed a deep sigh on the pebbles of the beach, and left the silence greater than before. Masses of ice floated here and there on the surface of the deep, the edges and fantastic points of which were tipped with light. Not far from the northern extremity of the sand-bank a large iceberg had grounded, from the sides of which several pinnacles had been hurled by the shock and now lay stranded on the beach.

The shout with which Edith had welcomed the morning roused the whole party, and in a few minutes they were all assembled outside of their little hut, some admiring the scene, others—of a less enthusiastic and more practical turn—examining the circumstances of their position, and considering the best course that should be pursued in their difficulty.

Mr. Stanley, Dick Prince, and Massan, as was their wont, held a council upon the existing state of things, and after much gazing round at the sea and up at the sky, and considerable grunting of his deep voice and rubbing of his capacious chin, on the part of the latter, he turned to Dick Prince, as if appealing to his superior sagacity, and said—

"Well, ye see, my 'pinion's jist this: yonder's the mainland there" (pointing to the eastward, where, about ten miles distant, the rocks and trees were seen distorted and faintly looming through a tremulous haze), "an' there's our canoes there" (jerking his thumb over his shoulder in the direction of the large canoes, whose torn sides and damaged ribs, as they lay exposed on the sand, bore sad testimony to the violence of the previous night's storm), "and there's the little canoe yonder," (glancing towards the craft in question, which lay on the beach a hopelessly-destroyed mass of splinters and shreds of bark that projected and bristled in all directions, as in uncontrollable amazement at the suddenness and entirety of its own destruction). "Now, that bein' the case, an' the baggage all wet, an' the day parfitly beautiful, an' the sun about hot enough to bile the sea, we can't do better nor stay where we are, an' mend the canoes, dry the goods, an' start fair to-morrow mornin'."

Stanley looked at Prince, as if expecting a remark from him; but the grave countenance of the silent bowman indicated that he was absorbed in contemplation.

"'Tis quite evident, Massan," said Stanley, "that we must repair the canoes; but a few hours could do that, and I don't like the idea of staying another night on a strip of sand like this, which, I verily believe, another stiff nor'-wester would blow away altogether. But what say you, Prince? Do you advise our remaining?"

"Yes," replied Dick, "I do. Ye see there's no fear of another storm soon. 'Tis a good chance for dryin' the goods, so I vote for stoppin'."

"Well, then, we shall stay," replied Stanley. "To say truth, I agreed with you at first, Massan, but it's always advisable to look at both sides of a question—"

"Yes, and in the multitude of counsellors there is wisdom,'" said Frank Morton, coming up at the moment, and tapping his friend on the shoulder. "If you will include me in your confabulation, you shall have the benefit of deep experience and far-sighted sagacity."

"Come, then, Master Frank," replied Stanley, "what does your sagacity advise on the point of our staying on this sandbank? Shall we spend another night on it in order to dry the goods, or shall we up and away to terra firma as soon as the canoes are seaworthy?"

"Stay, of course," said Frank. "As to the sand-bank,

'tis firm enough, to my mind, after resisting the shock of the wave that dashed me ashore last night. Then we have everything we need—shelter and food, and even fuel." As Frank mentioned the last word, he glanced round with a rueful countenance and pointed to the bark and timbers of his broken canoe.

"True, Frank, we have wherewith to boil the kettle, and as the water-cask was full when we started yesterday morning, there will be enough at least for one or two days."

"By the way, that reminds me that Eda and your wife are particularly desirous of having breakfast," said Frank. "In fact they sent me specially to lay their melancholy case before you; and I have great fears that Eda will lay violent hands on the raw pork if her morning meal is delayed much longer. As for Chimo, he is rushing about the island in a state of ravenous despair; so pray let us be going."

"Be it so, Frank," said Stanley, taking his friend's arm, and sauntering towards the canoe, while Massan and Prince went to inform their comrades of the determination of their leader.

In an hour after the above discourse breakfast was over, and the men, under Stanley's inspection, arranged and examined the baggage, which, considering that it had been rolled about by the surf for a considerable time, was not so much soaked as might have been expected. The two kegs of gunpowder were first inspected, being the most valuable part of the cargo, as on them depended much of their future livelihood. They were found to be quite dry, except a small portion of powder at the seams of the staves, which, having caked with the moisture, had saved the rest from damage. Some of the bales, however, containing knives and other hardware, were very wet, and had to be opened out and their contents wiped and spread out to dry. Blankets, too, and other woollen garments that had suffered, were also spread out on the sand, so that in a short time the little island was quite covered with a strange assortment of miscellaneous articles, that gave to it the appearance of a crowded store. The entire wealth of the fur-traders was now exposed to view, and it may perhaps be interesting to enumerate the different articles, in order to give some idea of the outfit deemed necessary on such an expedition.

And, first, there were two kegs of gunpowder, as before mentioned, containing each thirty pounds, with four bags of ball and three of shot of various sizes—in all, about 250 pounds of lead. Six nets of four and a half inch mesh. A large quantity of twine for making nets—most of the men being able to construct these useful articles. A small bag of gun-flints. Sixty pounds of roll tobacco. Twelve large axes. Six augers. Seven dozen scalping-knives. Six pounds of variously-coloured beads. Two dozen fire-steels, and a pretty large assortment of awls, needles, thread, nails, and such like small articles, which, though extremely useful, were too numerous and comparatively insignificant to mention in detail. Besides these, there was a small bale containing gaudy ornaments and attractive articles, which were intended as propitiatory presents to the Eskimos when they should be met with.

Then there were two runlets of salt pork, containing about ninety pounds each, and in the centre of each runlet were two hams. A barrel of flour and a barrel of oatmeal constituted all their provision, if we except a small cask of hard biscuit, and a little tea and sugar, which were the private property of Stanley and Frank Morton. There was also a large deerskin tent, capable of holding from twenty to thirty men, which was intended to be used while they were engaged in building their winter residence at Ungava. As to arms, each man had one of the long single-barrelled fowling-pieces that are supplied by the Fur Company to the natives, and are styled Indian guns. Stanley had a double-barrelled flint fowling-piece; and Frank had a rifle, besides a single gun of a description somewhat finer than that supplied to the Indians. Of course each man carried a scalping-knife and an axe in his belt, not for the purpose of self-defence, but for carving their food and cutting their fuel.

It may be well to remark here that the goods and provisions which we have detailed above were merely intended as a supply for their immediate necessities, and to enable them to commence active operations at once on arriving at their destination, while the heavy stores and goods necessary for the year's trade were to be forwarded in a small sloop from the depot direct through Hudson's Straits to Ungava Bay.

When the work of unpacking and exposing the things to dry in the sun was accomplished, it was long past noon, and high time for dinner; so a fire was lighted by Bryan, who cut up another portion of

Frank's canoe for the purpose. A rasher of pork and a flour cake were disposed of by each of the party in a surprisingly short time, and then the men bestirred themselves in mending the canoes. This was a more troublesome job than they expected, but being accustomed not only to mend but to make canoes, they worked with a degree of skill and diligence that speedily put all to rights. In Massan's canoe there was a hole large enough, as Bryan remarked, to stick his head through, though it was a "big wan, an' no mistake." Taking up a roll of bark, which was carried with them for the purpose, Massan cut from it a square patch, which he sewed over the hole, using an awl for a needle and the fibrous roots of the pine tree, called wattape, for thread. After it was firmly sewed on, the seams were covered with melted gum, and the broken spot was as tight and strong as ever. There were next found several long slits, one of them fully three feet, which were more easily managed, as they merely required to be sewed and covered with gum. Several broken ribs, however, were not so easily repaired. Had there been any wood on the island, Massan's quick knife would have soon fashioned new ribs; as it was, he had to make the best job he could, by splicing the old ones with several pieces abstracted from Frank's little canoe.

It was sunset before all was put in complete order, the goods repacked, and placed in readiness for a start at daybreak on the following morning. After all was done, the remains of the small canoe were converted into a bonfire, round which the tired and hungry travellers assembled to smoke and chat, while supper was being prepared by the indefatigable Bryan and his friend La Roche. As the day faded away the stars came out, one by one, until they glittered in millions in the sky, while the glare of the fire became every moment more and more intense as the darkness deepened. It was a strange, wild scene,—especially when viewed from the extremity of the little sand-bank, which was so low as to be almost indiscernible in the dark night, and seemed scarce a sufficient foundation for the little busy group of human beings who stood radiant in the red light of their camp-fire, like a blazing gem cast upon the surface of the great, cold sea.

Chapter XI

START AFRESH—SUPERSTITIOUS NOTIONS—THE
WHIRLPOOL—THE INTERIOR— FISHING IN THE
OLD WAY ON NEW GROUND, AND WHAT CAME
OF IT—A COLD BATH— THE RESCUE—SAVED—
DEEPER AND DEEPER INTO THE WILDERNESS.

As if to make amends for its late outrageous conduct, the weather, after the night of the great storm, continued unbrokenly serene for many days, enabling our travellers to make rapid progress towards their destination: It would be both tiresome and unnecessary to follow them step by step throughout their journey, as the part of it which we have already described was, in many respects, typical of the whole voyage along the east coast of Hudson's Bay. Sometimes, indeed, a few incidents of an unusual character did occur. Once they were very nearly being crushed between masses of ice; twice the larger canoe struck on a hummock, and had to be landed and repaired; and frequently mishaps of a slighter nature befell them. Their beds, too, varied occasionally. At one time they laid them down to rest on the sand of the sea-shore; at another, on the soft turf and springy moss of the woods. Sometimes they were compelled to content themselves with a couch of pebbles, few of which were smaller than a man's fist; and, not unfrequently, they had to make the best they could of a flat rock, whose unyielding surface seemed to put the idea of anything like rest to flight, causing the thin men of the party to growl and the fat ones to chuckle. Bryan was one of the well-favoured, being round and fleshy; while his poor little friend La Roche possessed a framework of bones that were so sparingly covered with softer substance, as to render it a matter of wonder how he and the stones could compromise the matter at all, and called forth from his friend frequent impertinent allusions to "thridpapers, bags o' bones, idges o' knives, half fathoms o' pump water," and such like curious substances. But whatever the bed, it invariably turned out that the whole party slept soundly from the time they lay down till the time of rising, which was usually at the break of day.

Owing to the little Indian canoe having been wrecked on the sand-bank, Frank and his men had to embark in the smaller of the large canoes; a change which was in some respects a disadvantage to the party, as Frank could not now so readily dash away in pursuit of game. However, this did not much matter, as, in a few days afterwards, they arrived at the mouth of the river by which they intended to penetrate into the interior of the country. The name of the river is Deer River, and it flows into Richmond Gulf, which is situated on the east shore of Hudson's Bay, in latitude 56 degrees North. Richmond Gulf is twenty miles long, and about the same in breadth; but the entrance to it is so narrow that the tide pours into it like a torrent until it is full. The pent-up waters then rush out on one side of this narrow inlet while they are running in at the other, causing a whirlpool which would engulf a large boat and greatly endanger even a small vessel. Of course it was out of the question to attempt the passage of such a vortex in canoes, except at half flood or half ebb tide, at which periods the waters became quiet. On arriving at the mouth of the gulf, the travellers found the tide out and the entrance to it curling and rolling in massive volumes, as if all the evil water-spirits of the north were holding their orgies there. Oostesimow and Ma-Istequan, being by nature and education intensely superstitious, told Stanley—after they had landed to await the flow of the tide—that it was absolutely necessary to perform certain ceremonies in order to propitiate the deities of the place, otherwise they could not expect to pass such an awful whirlpool in safety. Their leader smiled, and told them to do as they thought fit, adding, however, that he would not join them, as he did not believe in any deities whatever, except the one true God, who did not require to be propitiated in any way, and could not be moved by any other means than by prayer in the name of Jesus Christ. The red men seemed surprised a little at this, but, with their proverbial stoicism, refrained from any further or more decided expression of feeling.

Nevertheless, the Indians sufficiently showed their

faith in their own doctrines by immediately setting about a series of curious and elaborate ceremonies, which it was impossible to comprehend, and decidedly unprofitable to describe. They appeared, however, to attach much importance to their propitiatory offerings, the chief among which seemed to be a few inches of tobacco, with which it was fondly hoped the deities of the gulf would condescend to smoke the pipe of peace while their red children ventured to trespass a little on their domain; and hard indeed must have been the hearts of the said spirits had they refused so valuable an offering, for tobacco is the life and marrow, the quintessence of terrestrial felicity, the very joy and comfort of a voyageur, and the poor Indians had but little of it to spare.

While this was going on, Bryan stood with his back to the fire, a remarkably short and peculiarly black pipe in his mouth, and his head inclined sagaciously to one side, as if he designed, by dint of a combination of intense mental abstraction, partial closing of his eyes, severe knitting of his brows, and slow but exceedingly voluminous emission of smoke, to come to a conclusion in regard to the unfathomable subject of Indian superstition. La Roche, steeped in unphilosophic indifference on such matters, and keenly alive to the gross cravings of hunger, busied himself in concocting a kettle of soup; while the rest of the party rambled about the beach or among the bushes in search of eggs. In this latter search Frank and Edith were very successful, and returned with pockets laden with excellent eggs of the eider-duck, which were immediately put into the kettle, and tended not a little to increase the excellence of the soup and the impatience of the men.

Meanwhile the tide rose, the power of the current was gradually checked, and towards noon they passed the dangerous narrows in safety. From the view that was now obtained of the interior, it became evident that the worst of their journey yet lay before them. On arriving at the mouth of Deer River, the mountains were seen to rise abruptly and precipitously, while far away inland their faint blue peaks rose into the sky. Indeed from this point the really hard work of the voyage may be said to have commenced; for scarcely had they proceeded a few miles up the river, when their further progress, at least by water, was effectually interrupted by a rapid which came leaping madly down its rocky bed, as if the streams rejoiced to escape from the chasms and mountain gorges, and find rest at last on the ample bosom of the great deep.

"What think ye of that, boy?" said Stanley to Frank Morton, as they leaped from their respective canoes, and stood gazing at the rugged glen from which the rapid issued, and the wild appearance of the hills beyond. "It seems to me that report spoke truly when it said that the way to Clearwater Lake was rugged. Here is no despicable portage to begin with; and yonder cliffs, that look so soft and blue in the far distance, will prove to be dark and hard enough when we get at them, I warrant."

"When we get at them!" echoed Mrs. Stanley, as she approached, leading Edith by the hand. "Get at them,

George! Had any one asked me if it were possible to pass over these mountains with our canoes and cargoes, I should have answered, 'Decidedly not!'"

"And yet you were so foolish and reckless as to be the first to volunteer for this decidedly impossible expedition!" replied Stanley.

"There you are inconsistent," said Mrs. Stanley, smiling. "If reckless, I cannot be foolish, according to your own showing; for I have heard you give it as your opinion that recklessness is one of the most essential elements in the leaders of a forlorn hope. But really the thing does seem to my ignorant mind impossible. What think you, Eda?"

Mrs. Stanley bent down and looked into the face of her child, but she received no reply. The expanded eyes, indeed, spoke volumes; and the parted lips, on which played a fitful, exulting smile, the heightened colour, and thick-coming breath, told eloquently of her anticipated delight in these new regions, which seemed so utterly different from the shores of the bay: but her tongue was mute.

And well might Mrs. Stanley think the passage over these mountains impossible; for, except to men accustomed to canoe travelling in the American lakes and rivers, such an attempt would have appeared as hopeless as the passage of a ship through the ice-locked polar seas in winter.

Not so thought the men. Already several of the most active of them were scrambling up the cliffs with heavy loads on their backs; and, while Stanley and his wife were yet conversing, two of them approached rapidly, bearing the large canoe on their shoulders. The exclamation that issued from the foremost of these proved him to be Bryan.

"Now, bad luck to ye, Gaspard! can't ye go stidy? It's mysilf that'll be down on me blissid nose av ye go staggerin' about in that fashion. Sure it's Losh, the spalpeen, that would carry the canoe better than you."

Gaspard made no reply. Bryan staggered on, growling as he went, and in another minute they were hid from view among the bushes.

"What do you see, Frank?" inquired Stanley; "you stare as earnestly as Bryan did at the white bear last week. What is't, man? Speak!"

"A fish," replied Frank. "I saw him rise in the pool, and I'm certain he's a very large one."

"Very likely, Frank; there ought to be a fish of some sort there. I've been told—hist! there he's again. As I live, a salmon, a salmon, Frank! Now for your rod, my boy."

But Frank heard him not, for he was gone. In a few minutes he returned with a fishing-rod, which he was busily engaged in putting up as he hurried towards the rocks beside the pool.

Now, Frank Morton was a fisher. We do not mean to say that he was a fisher by profession; nor do we merely affirm that he was rather fond of the gentle art of angling, or generally inclined to take a cast when he happened to be near a good stream. By no means. Frank was more than that implies. He was a steady, thorough-going disciple of Izaak Walton; one who, in the days of his boyhood, used to flee to the water-side at all seasons, in all weathers, and despite all obstacles.

Not only was it his wont to fish when he could, or how he could, but too often was he beguiled to fish at times and in ways that were decidedly improper; sometimes devoting those hours which were set apart expressly for the acquirement of Greek and Latin, to wandering by mountain stream or tarn, rod in hand, up to the knees in water, among the braes and woodlands of his own native country. And Frank's enthusiasm did not depend entirely on his success. It was a standing joke among his school-fellows that Frank would walk six miles any day for the chance of a nibble from the ghost of a minnow. Indeed he was often taunted by his ruder comrades with being such a keen fisher that he was quite content if he only hooked a drowned cat during a day's excursion. But Frank was good-natured; he smiled at their jests, and held on the even tenor of his way, whipping the streams more pertinaciously than his master whipped him for playing truant; content alike to bear ignominy and chastisement, so long as he was rewarded by a nibble, and overjoyed beyond expression when he could return home with the tail of a two-pounder hanging over the edge of his basket. Far be it from us to hold up to ridicule the weakness of a friend, but we cannot help adding that Master Frank made the most of his tails. His truthful and manly nature, indeed, would not stoop to actual deception, but he had been known on more than one occasion to offer to carry a friend's waterproof fishing-boots in his basket, when his doing so rendered it impossible to prevent the tails of his trout from protruding arrogantly, as if to insinuate that there were shoals within. Another of Frank's weaknesses was, upon the hooking of every fish, to assert, with overweening confidence and considerable excitement, that it was a tremendously big one. Experience had, during all his piscatorial career, contradicted him ninety-nine times out of every hundred; but Frank's firm belief in his last minnow being a big trout—at least until it lay gasping on the bank at his feet—was as unshaken after long years of mistaken calculation as when first he sallied forth to the babbling brook with a willow branch, a fathom of twine, and a crooked pin!

Such untiring devotion, of course, could not fail to make Frank particularly knowing in all the details and minutiae of his much-loved sport. He knew every hole and corner of the rivers and burns within fifteen miles of his father's house. He became mysteriously wise in regard to the weather; knew precisely the best fly for any given day, and, in the event of being unhappily destitute of the proper kind, could dress one to perfection in ten minutes. As he grew older and taller, and the muscles on his large and well-made limbs began to develop, Frank slung a more capacious basket on his back, shouldered a heavier rod, and, with a pair of thick shoes and a home-spun shooting suit, stretched away over the Highland hills towards the romantic shores of the west coast of Scotland. Here he first experienced the wild excitement of salmon-fishing; and here the Waltonian chains, that had been twining and thickening around him from infancy, received two or three additional coils, and were finally riveted for ever. During his sojourn in America, he had happened to dwell in places where the fishing, though good, was not of a very exciting nature; and he had not seen a salmon since the day he left home, so that it is not matter for wonder that his stride was rapid and his eye bright while he hurried towards the pool, as before mentioned.

He who has never left the beaten tracks of men, or trod the unknown wilderness, can have but a faint conception of the feelings of a true angler as he stands by the brink of a dark pool which has hitherto reflected only the antlers of the wild deer—whose dimpling eddies and flecks of foam have been disturbed by no fisher since the world began, except the polar bear. Besides the pleasurable emotions of strong hope, there is the additional charm of uncertainty as to what will rise, and of certainty that if there be anything piscatine beneath these fascinating ripples it undoubtedly will rise—and bite too! Then there is the peculiar satisfaction of catching now and then a drop of spray from, and hearing the thunder of, a cataract, whose free, surging bound is not yet shackled by the tourist's sentimental description; and the novelty of beholding one's image reflected in a liquid mirror whose geographical position is not yet stereotyped on the charts of man. Alas for these maps and charts! Despite the wishes of scientific geographers and the ignorance of unscientific explorers, we think them far too complete already; and we can conceive few things more dreadful or crushing to the enterprising and romantic spirits of the world than the arrival of that time (if it ever shall arrive) when it shall be said that terra incognita exists no longer—when every one of those fairy-like isles of the southern seas, and all the hidden wonders of the polar regions, shall be put down, in cold blood, on black and white, exposed profanely on the schoolroom walls, and drummed into the thick heads of wretched little boys who don't want to learn, by the unsympathising hands of dominies who, it may be, care but little whether they do or not!

But to return. While Frank stood on the rocks, attaching to the line a salmon-fly which he had selected with much consideration from his book, he raised his eyes once or twice to take a rapid glance at his position and the capabilities of the place. About fifty yards further up the river the stream curled round the base of a large rock, and gushed into a pool which was encircled on all sides by an overhanging wall, except where the waters issued forth in a burst of foam. Their force, however, was materially broken by another curve, round which they had to sweep ere they reached this exit, so that when they rushed into the larger pool below they calmed down at once, and on reaching the point where Frank stood, assumed that oily, gurgling surface, dimpled all over with laughing eddies, that suggests irresistibly the idea of fish not only being there, as a matter of course, but being there expressly and solely for the purpose of being caught! A little further down, the river took a slight bend, and immediately after, recurring to its straight course, it dashed down, for a distance of fifty yards, in a tumultuous rapid, which swept into sudden placidity a few hundred yards below. Having taken all this in at a glance, Frank dropped the fly into the water and raised his rod to make a cast. In this act he almost broke the rod, to his amazement; for, instead of whipping the fly lightly out of the water, he dragged a trout of a pound weight violently up on the bank.

"Bravo!" cried Stanley, laughing heartily at his friend's stare of mingled wonder and amazement,— "bravo, Frank! I'm no fisher myself, but I've always understood that fish required a little play before being landed. However, you have convinced me of my ignorance. I see that the proper way is to toss them over your head! A salmon must be rather troublesome to toss, but no doubt, with your strong arms, you'll manage it easily, hey?"

"Why, what an appetite they must have!" replied Frank, answering his friend's badinage with a smile. "If the little fellows begin thus, what will not the big ones do?"

As he spoke, he disengaged the fish and threw it down, and made the next cast so rapidly, that if another trout was waiting to play him a similar trick, it must have been grievously disappointed. The line swept lightly through the air, and the fly fell gently on the stream, where it had not quivered more than two seconds when the water gurgled around it. The next moment Frank's rod bent like a hoop, and the line flew through the rings with whirring rapidity, filling these lonely solitudes for the first time with the pleasant "music of the reel." Almost before Frank had time to take a step in a downward direction, fifty yards were run out, the waters were suddenly cleft, and a salmon sprang like a bar of burnished silver twice its own height into the air. With a sounding splash it returned to its native element; but scarcely had its fins touched the water, when it darted towards the bank. Being brought up suddenly here, it turned at a tangent, and flashed across the pool again, causing the reel to spin with renewed velocity. Here the fish paused for a second, as if to collect its thoughts, and then coming, apparently, to a summary determination as to what it meant to do, it began steadily to ascend the stream, not, indeed, so rapidly as it had descended, but sufficiently so to give Frank some trouble, by means of rapidly winding up, to keep the line tight. Having bored doggedly towards the head of the rapid, the fish stopped and began to shake its head passionately, as if indignant at being foiled in its energetic attempts to escape. After a little time, it lay sulkily down at the bottom of the pool, where it defied its persecutor to move it an inch.

"What's to be done now?" asked Stanley, who stood ready to gaff the fish when brought near to the bank.

"We must rouse him up," said Frank, as he slowly wound up the line. "Just take up a stone and throw it at him."

Stanley looked surprised, for he imagined that such a proceeding would frighten the fish and cause it to snap the line; but seeing that Frank was in earnest, he did as he was directed. No sooner had the stone sunk than the startled fish once more dashed across the river; then taking a downward course, it sped like an arrow to the brink of the rough water below. To have allowed the salmon to go down the rapid would have been to lose it, so Frank arrested the spinning of his reel and held on. For a second or two the rod bent almost in a circle, and the line became fearfully rigid.

"You'll break it, Frank," cried Stanley, in some anxiety.

"It can't be helped," said Frank, compressing his lips; "he must not go down there. The tackle is new; I think it will hold him."

Fortunately the tackle proved to be very good. The fish was arrested, and after one or two short runs, which showed that its vigour was abated, it was drawn carefully towards the rocks. As it drew near it rolled over on its side once or twice—an evident sign of being much exhausted

"Now, Stanley, be careful," said Frank, as his friend stepped cautiously towards the fish and extended the gaff. "I've seen many a fine salmon escape owing to careless gaffing. Don't be in a hurry. Be sure of your distance before you strike, and do it quickly. Now, then—there—give it him! Hurrah!" he shouted, as Stanley passed the iron hook neatly into the side of the fish, and lifted it high and dry on the rocks.

The cheer to which Frank gave vent, on this successful termination to the struggle, was re-echoed heartily by several of the men, who, on passing the spot with their loads, had paused and become deeply interested spectators of the sport.

"Powerful big fish, sir," said Bryan, throwing down his pack and taking up the salmon by the gills. "Twinty pounds at laste, av it's an ounce."

"Scarcely that, Bryan," said Stanley; "but it's not

much less, I believe."

"Ah! oui, 'tis ver' pritty. Ver' superb for supper," remarked La Roche.

The little Frenchman was right in saying that it was pretty. Unlike the ordinary salmon, it was marked with spots like a trout, its head was small and its shoulders plump, while its silvery purity was exceedingly dazzling and beautiful.

"'Tis a Hearne-salmon," said Massan, approaching the group. "I've seed lots o' them on the coast to the south'ard o' this, an' I've no doubt we'll find plenty o' them at Ungava."

While the men were discussing the merits of the fish, Frank had hooked another, which, although quite as large, gave him much less trouble to land; and before the men had finished carrying the canoes and goods over the portage, he had taken three fish out of the same pool. Wishing, however, to try for a larger one nearer the sea, he proceeded to take a cast below the rapid.

Meanwhile, La Roche, whose activity had enabled him to carry over his portion of the cargo long before his comrades, came to the pool which Frank had just left, and seating himself on a large stone, drew forth his tobacco-pouch. With a comical leer at the water which had so recently been deprived of its denizens, he proceeded leisurely to fill a pipe.

It is impossible to foresee, and difficult to account for, the actions of an impulsive human being. La Roche sat down to smoke his pipe, but instead of smoking it, he started to his feet and whirled it into the river.

This apparently insane action was followed by several others, which, as they were successively performed, gradually unfolded the drift of his intentions. Drawing the knife which hung at his girdle, he went into the bushes, whence he quickly returned, dragging after him a large branch. From this he stripped the leaves and twigs. Fumbling in his pocket for some time, he drew forth a piece of stout cord, about four yards long, with a cod-hook attached to the end of it. This line had been constructed some weeks before when the canoes were wind-bound at a part of the coast where La Roche, desirous of replenishing the kettle, had made an unsuccessful attempt at sea-fishing. Fastening this line to the end of his extemporised rod, La Roche proceeded to dress his hook. This he accomplished by means of the feather of a duck which Frank shot the day before, and a tag from his scarlet worsted belt; and, when finished, it had more the appearance of some hideous reptile than a gay fly. However, La Roche surveyed it for a moment or two with an expression of deep satisfaction, and then, hurrying to the brink of the water, made a violent heave.

"Oh! cent milles tonnerres!" he exclaimed angrily, as the enormous hook caught in the leg of his trousers. The large and clumsy barb was deeply imbedded, so there was no help for it but to use the knife. The second throw was more successful, and the hook alighted in the water with a splash that ought to have sent all the fish in the pool away in consternation. Instead of this, however, no sooner did the reptile trail upon the stream than a trout dashed at it in such violent haste that it nearly missed it altogether. As it was, it hooked itself very slightly, and the excitable Frenchman settled the matter by giving the line a violent tug, in his anxiety to land the fish, that pulled the hook entirely out of its mouth.

"Ah! c'est dommage, ver' great; mais try it encore, my boy," exclaimed the mortified angler. The next throw, although well accomplished, produced nothing; but at the third attempt, ere the reptile had settled on the water for a second, it was engulfed by a salmon fully six pounds weight, and La Roche's rod was almost drawn out of his grasp.

"Hilloa, Losh! what have ye got there?" exclaimed Bryan, as, with several of the men, he approached to where the Frenchman and the salmon strove in uncertain conflict.

"By the mortial, he's hucked a whale! Out with it, boy, afore it pulls ye in!" said the Irishman, running to the rescue.

Just then the salmon gave a pull of more than ordinary vigour, at the same moment La Roche slipped his foot, and, ere Bryan could lay hold of him, fell headlong into the water and disappeared. Bryan's hands hung helplessly down, his jaw dropped, and his eyes opened wide, as he gazed in mute wonderment at the spot where his friend's toes had vanished. Suddenly he wrenched off his cap and flung it down, and proceeded to tear off his coat, preparatory to leaping into the river to the rescue, when his arms were pinioned to his sides by the powerful grip of Massan.

"Come, Bryan," said he, "you know very well that

you can't swim; you'd only make things worse."

"Och! murder! He can't swim neither. Let me go, ye black villain. Thunder an' turf! will ye see the poor lad drownded forenint yer two eyes?" cried the poor Irishman, as he made violent but unavailing struggles to get free. But Massan knew that to allow him to escape would only add to the number requiring to be saved, and as he himself could not swim, he saw at once that the only service he could render under the circumstances would be to hold the Irishman down. Clasping him, therefore, as in a vice, he raised his head and gave a shout for help that rolled in deep echoes among the overhanging cliffs. Another shout was uttered at the same instant. Edith, who happened to come up just as La Roche's head emerged from the water gasping for breath, uttered a wild shriek that made more than one heart among the absentees leap as they flew to the rescue.

Meanwhile La Roche rose and sank several times in the surges of the pool. His face on these occasions exhibited a mingled expression of terror and mischievous wildness; for although he could not swim a stroke, the very buoyancy of his mercurial temperament seemed partially to support him, and a feeling of desperate determination induced him to retain a death-like gripe of the rod, at the end of which the salmon still struggled. But his strength was fast going, and he sank for the fourth time with a bubbling cry, when a step was heard crashing through the adjacent bushes, and Dick Prince sprang down the slope like a deer. He did not pause when the scene burst upon his view, but a smile of satisfaction played upon his usually grave face when he saw Edith safe on the banks of the stream. Another spring and an agile bound sent him headlong into the pool about a yard from the spot where La Roche had last sunk. Scarcely had he disappeared when the dog Chimo bounded towards the scene of action, and, with what intent no one could tell, leaped also into the water. By this time Frank, Stanley, and nearly all the party had assembled on the bank of the river, ready to render assistance. In a few seconds they had the satisfaction of seeing Dick Prince rise, holding poor La Roche by the collar of his capote with his left hand, while he swam vigorously towards the shore with his right. But during the various struggles which had taken place they had been gradually sucked into the stream that flowed towards the lower rapid, and it now became apparent to Prince that his only chance of safety was in catching hold of the point of rock that formed the first obstruction to the rush of water. Abandoning all effort, therefore, to gain the bank beside him, he swam with the current, but edged towards the shore as he floated down.

"Hallo! La Roche!" he exclaimed loudly. "Do you hear? Do you understand me?"

"Ah! oui, vraiment. I not dead yit."

"Then let go that rod and seize my collar, and mind, sink deep in the water. Show only enough o' your face to breathe with, or I'll drown ye."

The Frenchman obeyed to the extent of seizing Dick's collar and sinking deep in the water, so as not to overburden his friend; but nothing could induce him to quit the rod to which he had clung so long and so resolutely. Prince's arms being now free, one or two powerful strokes placed him beyond the influence of the strong current, and as he passed the rocks before mentioned, he seized an overhanging branch of a small shrub, by which he endeavoured to drag himself ashore. This, however, he found to be impossible, partly owing to the steepness of the shelving rock, and partly to the fact that Chimo, in his ill-directed attempts to share in the dangers of his friends, had seized La Roche by the skirts of the coat in order to prevent himself from going down the stream. Those on shore, on seeing Prince make for the rock, ran towards the spot; but having to make a slight detour round the bend of the river, they did not reach it until he seized the branch, and when Frank, who was the first, sprang down, the slope to the rescue, he found them streaming out and waving to and fro in the current, like some monstrous reptile—Dick holding on to the branch with both hands, La Roche holding on to Dick, Chimo holding on by his teeth to La Roche, and the unfortunate salmon holding on to the line which its half-drowned captor scorned to let go.

A few seconds sufficed to drag them dripping from the stream; and the energetic little Frenchman no sooner found his feet on solid ground than he hauled out his fish and landed it triumphantly with his own hand.

"'Tis a pretty fish, La Roche," said Frank, laughing, as he busied himself in taking down his rod, while several of the men assisted Dick Prince to wring the water out of his clothes, and others crowded round

La Roche to congratulate him on his escape—"'tis a pretty fish, but it cost you some trouble to catch it."

"Throuble, indeed!" echoed Bryan, as he sat on a rock smoking his pipe; "troth it's more nor him came to throuble by that same fish: it guve me the throuble o' bein' more nor half choked by Massan."

"Half choked, Bryan! what mean you?" asked Frank.

"Mane? I just mane what I say; an' the raison why's best known to himself."

A loud peal of laughter greeted Massan's graphic explanation of the forcible manner in which he had prevented the Irishman from throwing himself into the river.

The party now turned earnestly to the more serious duties of the journey. Already too much time had been lost in this "playing themselves with fish," as Stanley expressed it, and it behoved them to embark as speedily as possible. About a mile above the pool which had nearly proved fatal to La Roche was the head of a series of insurmountable rapids, which extended all the way down to the waterfall. Beyond this was a pretty long reach of calm water, up which they proceeded easily; but as they advanced the current became so strong that no headway could be made with the paddles, and it was found necessary to send a party of the men ashore with a long line, by means of which the canoes were slowly dragged against the current. At length they came to shallow water, which necessitated another portage; and as it was about sunset when they reached it, Stanley ordered the tent to be pitched for the night, and the fire lighted, under the shadow of a stupendous mountain, the rocky sides of which were sprinkled with dwarf pine trees, and partially covered with brush and herbage. Here Edith and her mother discovered multitudes of berries, the most numerous being cloud and crow berries; both of which were found to be good, especially the former, and a fragrant dish of these graced the towel that evening at supper.

Thus, day by day, our adventurous travellers penetrated deeper and deeper into the heart of the wilderness, which became more savage and mountainous as they left the coast. Stanley drew forth his quadrant and compass, wherewith he guided the party towards their future home. At night, after the labour of the day was over, he and Frank would spread their charts in the blaze of the camp fire, and study the positions of the land so far as it was laid down; while Edith sat beside her mother, helping her to repair the torn and way-worn habiliments of her husband and Frank, or listening with breathless interest to the men, as they recounted their experiences of life in the different regions through which they had travelled. Many of these tales were more or less coloured by the fancy of the narrators, but most of them were founded on fact, and proved an unfailing source of deep interest to the little child. Frank's fishing-rod was frequently in requisition, and often supplied the party with more than enough of excellent fish; and at every new bend and turn of the innumerable lakes and rivers through which they passed, reindeer were seen bounding on the mountain-sides, or trotting down the ravines to quench their thirst and cool their sides in the waters;

so that food was abundant, and their slender stock of provisions had not to be trenched upon, while the berries that grew luxuriantly everywhere proved a grateful addition to their store. Thus, day by day, they slowly retreated farther and farther from the world of mankind— living in safety under the protection of the Almighty, and receiving the daily supply of all their necessities from His fatherly and bountiful hand; thus, day by day, they rose with the sun, and lay down at night to rest upon the mountain's side or by the river's bank; and thus, day by day, they penetrated deeper and deeper into the heart of the unknown wilderness.

Chapter XII

A NEW SCENE—THE ESKIMO—DEER-
SLAYING—ENEMIES IN THE BUSH.

Turn we now to another, a more distant, and a
wilder scene. Near the bleak shores of Hudson's
Straits there flows a river which forms an outlet to the
superfluous waters of the almost unknown territory
lying between the uninhabited parts of Labrador
and that tract of desert land which borders Hudson's
Bay on the east, and is known to the fur-traders by
the appellation of East Main. This river is called the
Caniapuscaw, and discharges itself into Ungava Bay.

The scene to which we would turn the reader's
attention is upwards of twenty miles from the mouth of
this river, at a particular bend, where the stream spreads
itself out into a sheet of water almost worthy of being called
a lake, and just below which two bold cliffs shut out the
seaward view, and cause an abrupt narrowing of the river.

The scene is peculiar, and surpassingly grand. On each side of the stream majestic mountains raise their bald and rugged peaks almost into the clouds. Little herbage grows on the more exposed places, and nothing, save here and there a stunted and weather-worn pine, breaks the sharp outline of the cliffs. But in the gorges and dark ravines—for there are no valleys—clumps of small-sized spruce—fir and larch trees throw a softness over some of the details of a spot whose general aspect is one of sterility. The mountains rise in a succession of irregular steps or terraces, whose faces are so precipitous that they cannot be ascended. To accomplish the feat of scaling the mountain-tops it would be necessary to clamber up a ravine until the first terrace should be gained, then, walking along that, ascend the next ravine, and so on. At the upper end of the lake (as we shall hereafter call this wide part of the river) lies a low island, fringed with a scanty growth of willows; and not far from this, on the eastern bank of the river, lies a small patch of level sand. This spot is somewhat peculiar, inasmuch as it is backed by a low platform of rock, whose surface is smooth as a table. At the foot of this rock bubbles a little spring, which, meandering through a tangled spot of stunted shrubbery ere it mingles with the sand, gives unusual green-ness and vitality to the surrounding herbage. On the edge of this rocky platform sat the figure of a man.

It was evening. The declining sun shot its last few rays over the brow of the opposite mountains, and bathed him in mellow light, as he sat apparently contemplating the scene before him. The man's costume bespoke him a native of the savage region in the midst of which he seemed the only human being. But although an Eskimo, he exhibited several physical peculiarities not commonly supposed to belong to that people. To an altitude of six feet three he added a breadth of shoulder and expansion of chest seldom equalled among men of more highly-favoured climes; and his real bulk being very greatly increased by his costume, he appeared to be a very giant—no unfitting tenant of such giant scenery. The said costume consisted of an extremely loose coat or shirt of deerskin, having the hair outside, and a capacious hood, which usually hung down behind, but covered his head at this time, in order to protect it from a sharp north-west breeze that whirled among the gullies of the mountains, and surging down their sides, darkened the surface of the water. A pair of long sealskin boots encased his limbs from foot to thigh; and a little wallet or bag of sealskin, with the hair outside, hung from his shoulders. Simple although this costume was, it had a bulky rotundity of appearance that harmonised well with the giant's frank, good-humoured countenance, which was manly, firm, and massive, besides being rosy, oily, and fat. In the latter peculiarity he partook of the well-known characteristic of his tribe; but the effeminacy in appearance that is produced by a round, fat face was done away in the case of our giant by a remarkably black though as yet downy moustache and beard, of a length suitable to twenty-three winters. His hair was long, straight, and black, besides being uncommonly glossy—an effect attributable to the prevalence of whale-oil in these regions. On the forehead the locks were cut short, so as to afford free scope to his black eyes and sturdy-looking nose. By his side lay a long hunting spear, and a double-bladed paddle, fully fifteen feet long; which latter belonged to a kayak, or Eskimo canoe, that lay on the sand close to the water's edge. Sitting there, motionless as the rocks around him, the giant looked like a colossal statue of an Eskimo. He was no figure of stone, however, but a veritable human being, as was proved by his starting suddenly from his reverie and hastening towards the spring before mentioned, at which he stooped and drank rapidly, like one who had to make up for lost time.

After a few hurried gulps, the man strode towards his canoe; but as he went his restless eye became fixed on the branching antlers of a deer, that were tossed in the air on the summit of a neighbouring cliff. Like one who is suddenly paralysed, the Eskimo stood transfixed in the attitude in which he had been arrested. He did not even seem to breathe, as the antlers moved to and fro, clearly defined against the blue sky. At length they disappeared, and the animal to which they belonged slowly descended a ravine towards the river. Then, as if set free from a spell, the man glided into his kayak, and swept rapidly but noiselessly behind a projecting point of rock, where he waited patiently till the deer took to the water. He had not long to wait, however, for in a few minutes afterwards the deer, followed by several companions, walked out upon the patch of sand, snuffed the air once or twice, and entered the stream with the intention of crossing.

But there was an enemy near whom they little

dreamed of—not an enemy who would dash excitedly into the midst of them, or awaken the thunders of the place with his noisy gun, but a foe who could patiently bide his time, and take cool and quiet advantage of it when it came. When the deer had proceeded about a hundred yards into the river, the Eskimo dipped his paddle twice, and the narrow, sharp-pointed canoe, which, at a short distance, seemed little more than a floating plank, darted through the water and ranged alongside of the startled animals. The fattest of the herd was separated from its fellows and driven towards the shore from which it had started, while the others struggled across the river. Once or twice the separated deer endeavoured to turn to rejoin its comrades—an attempt which was frustrated by the Eskimo, who could paddle infinitely faster over the water in his skin canoe than the deer could swim. As they neared the shore, the giant cast on it one or two glances, and having made up his mind as to the most convenient spot for landing, he urged the point of his canoe between the antlers of the deer, and steered it in this manner to the sand-bank. The deer, thus directed, had no resource but to land where its persecutor chose; but no sooner did its foot touch ground, than it sprang convulsively forward in the vain hope to escape. The same instant its captor's canoe shot beside it. Grasping the long lance before mentioned in his hand, he placed its glittering point on the deer's side, tickled it slowly to ascertain that it was between two ribs, and, with a quick thrust, stabbed it to the heart. A convulsive shudder, as the deer's head sank in the stream, proved that, though cold-blooded in appearance, the action was more effective and less cruel than many other more approved methods of killing game.

Our Eskimo thought neither of the method of slaying his deer nor of man's opinion regarding it. His sole object was to procure supper, having tasted nothing since early morning; and the manner in which he ate showed at once the strength of his appetite and his total indifference to cookery, for he ate it raw. There was a certain appearance of haste in all his actions which, however, seemed unaccountable, considering the peaceful nature of the vast solitudes around him. Scarcely had he cut off and devoured a portion of the deer than he hastened again to his canoe, and darted like an arrow from the shore. This is no exaggerated simile. The long, thin, sharp Eskimo kayak is highly suggestive of an arrow in its form, and much more so in its extraordinary speed. It consists of an extremely light framework of wood covered with sealskin parchment, which is stretched upon it all over as tight as a drum. The top of the canoe being covered as well as the bottom, it is thus, as it were, decked; and a small hole in the middle of this deck admits its occupant. The kayak can only hold one person. The paddle, as already said, is a long pole with a blade at each end. It is dipped alternately on each side, and is used not only to propel the kayak, but to prevent it from upsetting. Indeed, so liable is it to upset that nothing but the wonderful adroitness of its occupant prevents it from doing so with every swing of his body.

Quick, however, though the kayak sped over the

rippling wave, it could not have escaped the messenger of death that seemed about to be dispatched after it by a dark-skinned, red-painted Indian, who, at the moment the vessel left the shore, leapt from behind a rocky point, and, levelling a long gun, took a steady aim at the unconscious Eskimo. A little puff of powder answered to the click of the lock, as the gun missed fire. With an exclamation of anger the savage seized his powder-horn to reprime, when a rude grasp was laid on his shoulder, and another Indian, who, from the eagle feather in his hair, and his general bearing, appeared to be a chief, exclaimed—

"Fool! you have the impatience of a woman, and you have not yet shown that you have the heart of a man. Would the scalp of yon Eater-of-raw-flesh pay us for coming so far from our hunting-grounds? If your gun had spoken among these mountains, we would have found the empty wigwams of his people, instead of fringing our belts with their scalps."

With a frown of anger the chief turned on his heel and retraced his steps into the ravine from which he had emerged, followed by his abashed and silent companion.

Meanwhile the Eskimo, ignorant of the fate from which he had just escaped, continued to ply his paddle with right good will. The little craft, obedient to the powerful impulse, combined as it was with the current of the ebb-tide, flew rather than floated toward the narrows, through which it passed, and opened up a view of the ice-encumbered waters of Ungava Bay. Directing his course along the western shores of the river, the Eskimo speedily reached the coast at a point where several low, rough-built summer huts clustered near the shore. Here he ran his kayak into a little creek, and, having lifted it beyond tide mark, betook himself to his dwelling.

Chapter XIII

SAVAGE LOVE—A WIFE PURCHASED—THE ATTACK—
THE FLIGHT—THE ESCAPE—THE WOUNDED MAN.

Scarcely had the stout Eskimo proceeded a few steps along the shore, when he was met by a young girl who laid her hand on his arm. Taking her gently by the shoulders, he drew her towards him and kissed her on both cheeks—an action which caused her to blush deeply as, with a half smile half frown on her face, she pushed him away.

Love is the same all the world over, whether it glows beneath the broad-cloth and spotless linen of a civilised gentleman, or under the deerskin coat of a savage. And its expression, we suspect, is somewhat similar everywhere. The coy repulse of pretended displeasure came as naturally from our plump little arctic heroine as it could have done from the most civilised flirt, and was treated with well-simulated contrition by our arctic giant, as they walked slowly towards the huts. But the Eskimo had other matters than love in his head just then, and the girl's face assumed a grave and somewhat anxious look as he continued to whisper in her ear.

At the little hamlet they separated, and the maiden went to her grandfather's abode; while her lover, lifting the skin-curtain door of a rudely-constructed hut, entered his own humble dwelling. The room was empty, and its owner did not seem as if he meant to cheer it with his presence long. In one corner lay a pile of miscellaneous articles, which he removed, and, taking the tusk of a walrus which lay near his hand, began to dig with it in the sand. In a few seconds it struck a hard substance, and the Eskimo, putting his hand into the hole, drew forth a glittering axe, upon which he gazed with supreme satisfaction.

Now be it known to you, reader, that among the Eskimos of the frozen north iron is regarded with about as much delight as gold is by ourselves. And the reason is simple enough. These poor people live entirely upon the produce of the chase. Polar bears, seals, walruses, and whales are their staff of life. To procure these animals, spears are necessary; to skin and cut them up, knives are needful. But bone and stone make sorry knives and spears; so that, when a bit of iron, no matter how poor its quality or small its size, can be obtained, it is looked on as the most valuable of possessions; and the ingenuity displayed by Eskimos in fashioning the rudest piece of metal into the most useful of implements is truly astonishing, proving, in the most satisfactory way, that necessity is indeed the mother of invention. The precious metal is obtained in two ways: by the discovery of a wreck, which is extremely rare; and by barter with those tribes which sometimes visit the Moravian settlements of Labrador. But neither source is very productive. Even a nail is treasured as a blessing, while an axe is a fortune! When our giant, therefore, drew forth the shining implement, and gazed with delight at its keen edge, he experienced as great satisfaction as a miser does when gloating over his banker's book!

Having satisfied himself that the axe was free from all approximation to rust, he stuck it into a belt of raw hide, which he put on for the express purpose of sustaining it, as Eskimos do not generally wear belts. He then sallied forth, and walked with the air of a man who wears the grand cross of the Legion of Honour. As he went to the hut in which lived the oldest man of the tribe, the shade of anxiety, which had clouded his brow more than once during the day, again rested on his face. On entering, he observed the old Eskimo listening with anxious countenance to the young girl whom we have already introduced to the reader.

Now this girl—Aneetka by name—was by no means an angel in Eskimo habiliments. Among civilised folk probably she would not have been deemed even pretty. Nevertheless, in the eyes of her lover she was most decidedly beautiful, and round, and fat, and rosy, and young, awkward, and comfortable! And the giant loved her—never so strongly, perhaps, as when he saw her striving to allay the fears of her old grandfather. But this same grandfather was obstinate. He wanted her to become the wife of an Eskimo who lived far to the westward, and who once had dealings with the fur-traders, and from whom he expected to derive considerable advantages and gifts of bits of hoop-iron and nails. But shewanted to become the giant's wife; so there the matter stood.

"The spirits o' the wind and sea protect us, and may the god o' the mist cover us!" said the old man, as the young Eskimo sat down on a dead seal beside him. "Is it true that you saw the men of fire?"

This was, of course, said in the language of the Eskimos, and we render it as literally as possible.

"Yes, it is true," replied the young man. "I saw them at the rapid water in Caniapuscaw, and I took kayak to bring the news."

Various exclamations of mingled surprise and anger escaped from the compressed lips of several stalwart natives, who had crowded into the tent on hearing of the arrival of their comrade.

"Yes," continued the young man, "we must go away this night. They had fire-tubes, and there were thirty men. We have only ten."

Again a murmur ran through the listeners, but no one spoke for a few seconds.

"Did they see you?" asked the old man anxiously.

"No. I came on them suddenly, when I was chasing deer, and almost ran into their camp; but I saw, and fell in the grass. I thought the chief raised his head quickly when I fell; but he looked down again, and I crawled away."

In this the young Eskimo was mistaken. He knew

little of the craft and the quickness of the Red Indian, and easily fell into the snare of his savage enemy, who, having been momentarily startled by the sudden sound of the Eskimo approach, had endeavoured to throw him off his guard, by pretending that although he heard the sound he thought nothing of it. But no sooner had the Eskimo retired than he was closely followed and watched by the whole party. They could have easily shot him, but refrained from doing so, that he might unwittingly be their guide to the habitations of his people. The rapid flight of his kayak distanced his pursuers at first, but they made up for this during an hour or two in the night, when the tired Eskimo allowed himself a short season of repose to recruit his energies for the following day's journey. During this period the Indians shot far ahead of him, and when he arrived at the coast next day they were not much in the rear.

"And now, old man," said our young Eskimo, "it is time that I should have my wife. If the Allat comes here to-night, as I know they will, I want to have a right to defend her, and carry her away when we flee. Are you willing?"

The young giant said this with a degree of roughness and decision that at any other time would have made the obstinate old grandfather refuse point blank; but as there was every probability of having to flee for his life ere the break of another day, and as his old heart trembled within him at the thought of the dreaded guns of the Indians, he merely shook his head and pondered a little.

"What will you give me?" he said, looking up.

The young man answered by drawing the axe from his belt and laying it on the ground before him. The old man's eyes glistened with pleasure as he surveyed the costly gift.

"Good; that will do. Take her and go."

A second bidding was not needed. The young man arose hastily, took his blushing bride by the hand, and led her from the tent of her grandfather towards his own. Here she set to work instantly to assist her husband in hurriedly packing up their goods and chattels; and, immediately afterwards, the little village became a perfect Babel of confusion, as the alarmed inhabitants, on learning the threatened danger, prepared for instant flight. In less than an hour the most of them were ready. The men launched their kayaks, while the women, having loaded their oomiaks with their goods, tossed their dogs and children on the top of them.

The oomiak, or women's boat, is quite a different affair from the kayak, in which the men travel singly. It is usually made large and capacious, in order to hold the entire household of the Eskimo. Like the kayak it is made of skin, but has no covering above, and is propelled by means of short single-bladed paddles, which are worked by the women, upon whom devolves the entire care and management of the oomiak. It is a clumsy affair to look at, but, like the boats of savages generally, it is uncommonly useful and a good sea-boat.

While the Eskimos were busied in completing their arrangements, one of the dogs rushed towards the bushes that lined the shore just behind the village, and barked vociferously. Instantly it was joined by the whole pack, and the Eskimos, who, ever since they had heard of the proximity of their Indian foes, were in a state of the utmost trepidation, made a general rush towards their canoes. Before they reached them, however, a volley of musketry was fired from the bushes, and three of their number—a man and two women—filled the air with their death-shriek, as they fell dead upon the beach; while the Indians sprang from their concealment, and, brandishing their knives and tomahawks, rushed with a fearful yell upon the terror-stricken Eskimos.

Shrill and terrible though the Indian war-cry is proverbially known to be, it was excelled in appalling wildness by the shriek which arose from the Eskimos, as they hurried tumultuously into their canoes and put off to sea. These poor creatures were naturally brave—much more so, indeed, than their assailants; but the murderous effects of the terrible gun caused the sternest brow among them to blanch and the stoutest heart to quail. The arrow and the spear, however rapid, could be avoided, if observed in time; but this dreaded implement of destruction was so mysterious to them, and its death-dealing bullet so quick, and the smoke, the fire, and the loud report so awful, that they shuddered even when they thought of it. No wonder, then, that they uttered a despairing cry when it actually sounded in their ears.

When the dogs first gave tongue, our tall Eskimo was alone in his hut, having just sent his wife down with a bundle to the oomiak. When the volley rang in his ears, he rushed towards the beach, supposing that she was there before him. This was not the case, however. Aneetka had gone towards her grandfather's hut, and when the Indians fired she rushed in to assist him to fly. But the old man was already gone. Turning instantly, she sprang nimbly towards the shore. At that moment a single shot was fired, and she saw her husband stumble forward and fall headlong to the earth, where he lay motionless. Her first impulse was to run towards the body and throw herself upon it; but this intention was effectually checked by a strong, dark-skinned arm which encircled her waist, and, despite her cries and struggles, bore her away into the bushes. Her captor was the Indian whose gun once before on that day had been levelled at her lover's head.

When the young Eskimo fell, as already related, he was so close to the water that he stumbled into it, and, fortunately, not a yard distant from an oomiak which the women were frantically thrusting into the sea. They had no time to lift so heavy a weight on board, but, as the light craft darted from the shore, an old woman, who had often received kind attentions from the good-natured youth, leant over the stern and seized him by the hair. In this manner he was dragged through the water until they were out of gun-shot, when he was lifted inside and laid beside the dogs and children.

Meanwhile the Indians had rushed into the water up to their middle, in the hope of catching the last of the little fleet, but without success. Mad with disappointed rage, they waded back to the shore, and, standing in a line along the edge of the waves, reloaded their guns with the utmost rapidity. The poor Eskimos knew well what would follow, and strained every nerve to increase their distance. Once more the guns belched forth their leaden shower, which went skipping over the water towards the flotilla. Only one kayak was hit by the discharge. It was that of the old grandfather already mentioned. The ball ripped up the side of the canoe, which filled and upset, and the poor old man would certainly have been drowned but for the opportune coming up of the oomiak containing his wounded grandson. The old woman who had already saved the life of the young giant of the tribe, again put forth her skinny hand and grasped the patriarch, who was soon hauled on board in safety. A few minutes more placed the whole party out of danger.

In the meantime, the Indians, furious with disappointment, scalped the three dead bodies and tossed them into the sea; after which they went into the huts in order to collect all the valuables that might have been left behind. Very little, however, was to be found, as the entire property of an Eskimo is not worth much to a red man. The most useful thing they laid hands on was the axe which the old grandfather had left behind in his hurried flight. Having taken all they could carry, the savages destroyed the rest; and then, setting fire to the village, they returned to the bush. Here a fire was made, and a council of war held.

When the Indian who had captured the Eskimo girl led her forward towards the fire, there was a general yell of indignation. Tomahawks were grasped, and more than one knife was unsheathed. But the chief commanded silence.

"What does White Heart mean to do with the Eater-of-raw-flesh?" he inquired, turning to the young man.

"He will take her to the hunting-grounds of the Crees."

"That cannot be," said the chief. "The girl must die, and White Heart must kill her."

The young man made no reply.

"If," continued the chief sarcastically, "White Heart is afraid to see blood on his knife, another warrior will show him how to do it!"

As he spoke, a dark-visaged savage drew his scalping-knife, and, with one stride, stood beside the trembling girl, who, during the consultation of the savages, had stood silently beside her captor listening intently to the words which she did not comprehend.

Seizing her by the shoulder, the savage plunged his knife at her bosom; but, ere the keen point reached it, the arm was caught by the young Indian, and the scowling savage was hurled violently back. With dilated eye and expanded nostril, the young man, not deigning to bestow a glance upon his fallen comrade, turned to his chief and said—

"Did not I take her? The girl is mine. I will carry her to my tent and make her my wife."

"Be it so," replied the chief abruptly. Then turning to his followers, he gave orders to start immediately.

In a few minutes all was ready. The chief led the way into the bush. The Eskimo girl and her captor followed; and the whole band, silently and in single file, commenced to retrace their steps to the far distant hunting-grounds of the Cree Indians.

Chapter XIV

THE PURSUIT—SEAL-SPEARING—THE GIANT'S DESPAIR.

When the young Eskimo began to recover from the lethargic state into which his wound had thrown him, he found himself lying at the bottom of the women's oomiak with his old grandfather by his side, and a noisy crew of children and dogs around him. Raising himself on his elbow, he brushed the clotted blood and hair from his temples, and endeavoured to recall his scattered faculties. Seeing this, the old crone who had saved his life laid down her paddle and handed him a sealskin cup of water, which he seized and drank with avidity. Fortunately the wound on his forehead, although it had stunned him severely at first, was trifling, and in a few minutes after partaking of the cool water, he recovered sufficiently to sit up and look around him.

Gradually his faculties returned, and he started up

with a troubled look.

"Where are the Allat? Where is my wife?" he exclaimed vehemently, as his eye fell on the prostrate form of his still insensible grandfather.

"Gone," answered several of the women.

"Gone!" repeated the youth, gazing wildly among the faces around him in search of that of his wife. "Gone! Tell me, is she in one of the other oomiaks?"

The women trembled as they answered, "No."

"Have the Allat got her?"

There was no reply to this question, but he did not need one. Springing like a tiger to the stern of the oomiak, he seized the steering paddle, and turning the head of the boat towards the shore, paddled with all his energy. Nearly two hours had elapsed since they had commenced their flight, and as all danger of pursuit was over the moment the Indians turned their backs on the sea, the Eskimos had gradually edged in-shore again, so that a few minutes sufficed to run the prow of the oomiak on the shingle of the beach. Without saying a word, the young man sprang over the side, drew a hunting-spear from the bottom of the boat, and hurried back in the direction of the deserted village at the top of his speed. The women knew that nothing could stop him, and feeling that he was quite able to take care of himself, they quietly put to sea again, and continued their voyage.

The limbs of the young Eskimo, as we have already said, were gigantic and powerful, enabling him to traverse the country at a pace which few of his fellows could keep up with; and although a stern-chase is proverbially a long one, and the distance between two parties travelling in opposite directions is amazingly increased in a short space of time, there is no doubt that he would have overtaken his Indian foes ere many hours had passed, but for the wound in his head, which, although not dangerous, compelled him more than once to halt and sit down, in order to prevent himself from falling into a swoon. Hunger had also something to do with this state of weakness, as he had eaten nothing for many hours. In his hasty departure from the boat, however, he had neglected to take any provisions with him, so that he had little hope of obtaining refreshment before arriving at the village, where some scraps might perhaps be picked up.

Slowly, and with a reeling brain, he staggered on; but here no relief awaited him, for every scrap of food had been either taken away or destroyed by the Indians, and it was with a heavy sigh and a feeling akin to despair that he sat down beside the blackened ruins of his late home.

But Eskimos, more than other men, are accustomed to reverses of fortune, and the sigh with which he regarded the ruins of his hut had no reference whatever to the absence of food. He knew that about this time the mouth of the river would be full of ice, carried up by the flood-tide, and that seals would, in all probability, be found on it; so he started up, and hastening along the beach soon gained the floes, which he examined carefully. A glance or two sufficed to show him that he was right in his conjecture. On a sheet of ice not more than a couple of hundred yards from shore were two

seals fast asleep. These he prepared to stalk. Between
the floe and the shore ran a stream of water twenty
yards broad. Over this he ferried himself on a lump
of loose ice; and, on reaching the floe, he went down
on his hands and knees, holding the spear in his right
hand as he advanced cautiously towards his victim.

The Eskimo seal-spear is a curious weapon, and
exhibits in a high degree the extraordinary ingenuity
of the race. The handle is sometimes made of the horn
of the narwal, but more frequently of wood. It has a
movable head or barb, to which a long line of walrus hide
or sealskin is attached. This barb is made of ivory tipped
with iron, and is attached to the handle in such a way
that it becomes detached from it the instant the animal is
struck, and remains firmly imbedded in the wound with
the line fastened to it, while the handle floats away on
the water or falls on the ice, as the case may be.

When the Eskimo had approached to within a
hundred yards, he lay down at full length and slowly
worked himself forward. Meanwhile the seals raised
their heads, but seeing, as they imagined, a companion
coming towards them, they did not make for their
holes, which were a few yards distant from them. Having
drawn near enough to render the animals suspicious,
the young giant now sprang up, rushed forward, and
got between one seal and its hole just as its more active
companion dived into the water. In another moment
the deadly lance transfixed its side and killed it. This
was a fortunate supply to the Eskimo, whose powers of
endurance were fast failing. He immediately sat down
on his victim, and cutting a large steak from its side,

speedily made a meal that far exceeded the powers of any alderman whatsoever! It required but a short time to accomplish, however, and a shorter time to transfer several choice chunks to his wallet; with which replenished store he resumed his journey.

Although the man's vigour was restored for a time, so that he travelled with great speed, it did not last long, owing to the wound in his head, which produced frequent attacks of giddiness, and at last compelled him, much against his will, to halt for a couple of hours' repose. Glancing round, in order to select a suitable camping ground, he soon observed such a spot in the form of a broad, overhanging ledge of rock, beneath which there was a patch of scrubby underwood. Here he lay down with the seal blubber for a pillow, and was quickly buried in deep, untroubled slumber. In little more than two hours he awoke with a start, and, after a second application to the contents of the wallet, resumed his solitary march. The short rest seemed to have quite restored his wonted vigour, for he now stalked up the banks of the river at a rate which seemed only to accelerate as he advanced. As has been already said, these banks were both rugged and precipitous. In some places the rocks jutted out into the water, forming promontories over which it was difficult to climb; and frequently these capes terminated in abrupt precipices, necessitating a detour in order to advance. In other places the coast was indented with sandy bays, which more than doubled the distance the traveller would have had to accomplish had he possessed a kayak. Unfortunately

in his hasty departure he neglected to take one with
him; but he did his best to atone for this oversight by
making almost superhuman exertions. He strode over
the sands like an ostrich of the desert, and clambered
up the cliffs and over the rocks—looking, in his hairy
garments, like a shaggy polar bear. The thought of his
young and pretty bride a captive in the hands of his
bitterest foes, and doomed to a life of slavery, almost
maddened him, and caused his dark eye to flash and
his broad bosom to heave with pent-up emotion, while
it spurred him on to put forth exertions that were far
beyond the powers of any member of his tribe, and
could not, under less exciting circumstances, have
been performed even by himself. As to what were his
intentions should he overtake the Indians, he knew
not. The agitation of his spirits, combined with the
influence of his wound, induced him to act from
impulse; and the wild tumult of his feelings prevented
him from calculating the consequences or perceiving
the hopelessness of an attack made by one man, armed
only with knife and spear, against a body of Indians
who possessed the deadly gun.

Alas! for the sorrows of the poor human race. In
all lands they are much the same, whether civilised
or savage—virtue and vice alternately triumphing.
Bravery, candour, heroism, in fierce contest with
treachery, cowardice, and malevolence, form the
salient points of the record among all nations, and
in all ages. No puissant knight of old ever buckled
on his panoply of mail, seized his sword and lance,
mounted his charger, and sallied forth singlehanded

to deliver his mistress from enchanted castle, in the face of appalling perils, with hotter haste or a more thorough contempt of danger than did our Eskimo giant pursue the Indians who had captured his bride; but, like many a daring spirit of romance, the giant failed, and that through no fault of his.

On arriving at the rocky platform beside the spring where we first introduced him to the reader, the Eskimo sat down, and, casting his spear on the ground, gazed around him with a look of despair. It was not a slight matter that caused this feeling to arise. Notwithstanding his utmost exertions, he had been unable to overtake the Indians up to this point, and beyond this point it was useless to follow them. The mountains here were divided into several distinct gorges, each of which led into the interior of the country; and it was impossible to ascertain which of these had been taken by the Indians, as the bare, rocky land retained no mark of their light, moccasined feet. Had the pursuer been an Indian, the well-known sagacity of the race in following a trail, however slight, might have enabled him to trace the route of the party; but the Eskimos are unpractised in this stealthy, dog-like quality. Their habits and the requirements of their condition render it almost unnecessary; so that, in difficult circumstances, their sagacity in this respect is not equal to the emergency. Add to this the partial confusion created in the young giant's brain by his wound, and it will not appear strange that despair at length seized him, when, after a severe journey, he arrived at a spot where, as it were, half a dozen cross-roads met, and he had not the most distant idea which he had to follow. It is true the valley of the river seemed the most probable route; but after pursuing this for a whole day without coming upon a vestige of the party, he gave up the pursuit, and, returning to the spring beside the rock, passed the night there with a heavy heart. When the sun rose on the following morning he quitted his lair, and, taking a long draught at the bubbling spring, prepared to depart. Before setting out, he cast a melancholy glance around the amphitheatre of gloomy hills; shook his spear, in the bitterness of his heart, towards the dark recesses which had swallowed up the light of his eyes, perchance for ever; then, turning slowly towards the north, with drooping head, and with the listless tread of a heart-broken man, he retraced his steps to the sea-coast, and, rejoining his comrades, was soon far away from the banks of the Caniapuscaw River.

Chapter XV

END OF THE VOYAGE—PLANS AND
PROSPECTS—EXPLORING PARTIES SENT OUT.

Three weeks alter the departure of the Eskimos
from the neighbourhood of Ungava Bay, the
echoes of these solitudes were awakened by the merry
song of the Canadian voyageurs, as the two canoes of
Stanley and his comrades swept down the stream and
approached the spring at the foot of the flat rock.

As the large canoe ran its bow lightly on the sand, the
first man who leaped ashore was La Roche. He seemed
even more sprightly and active than formerly, but was
a good deal darker in complexion, and much travel-
stained. Indeed, the whole party bore marks of having
roughed it pretty severely for some time past among
the mountains. Edith's face was decidedly darker than
when she left Moose, and her short frock considerably
shorter in consequence of tear and wear.

"Bad luck to ye, Losh! Out o' the way, an' let yer betters land before ye," exclaimed Bryan, as he jumped into the water, and dragged the canoe towards the beach.

The only marks that rough travelling had put on Bryan were one or two additional wrinkles in his battered white hat; as for his face, it was already so thoroughly bronzed by long exposure, that a week or two more or less made no difference in its hue.

"Jump into my arms, Miss Edith," said Francois, as he stood in the water beside the canoe.

"Steady, boy; mind the gum," cried Massan, as Oolibuck strained the canoe roughly in shouldering a package.

"Look out ashore, there," cried Dick Prince, throwing the tent poles on the beach as he spoke.

Regardless of the warning, Gaspard did not "look out," and received a rap on the leg from one of the poles, whereat he growled savagely, and threw down a sack, which rested on his shoulder, so violently that it nearly knocked over Ma-istequan, who was passing at the time with the camp-kettle in his hand.

"What an ould buffalo it is!" exclaimed Bryan, pushing Gaspard rudely aside with his left shoulder, and hitching off La Roche's cap with his right, as he sprang back to the canoe for another load. "Pardonay mwa, Losh, may garson," he exclaimed, with a broad grin. "Now thin, boys, out wid the fixin's. Faix it's mysilf is plazed to git ashore anyhow, for there's nothin' gone into my intarior since brickfust this mornin'."

At this moment the bow of the other canoe grated on the sand, and Frank Morton leaped ashore.

"Capital place to camp, Frank," said Stanley, who had just finished pitching the tent on the scrimp herbage that forced its way through the sand. "There's a splendid spring of pure water below yonder rock. I've just left my wife and Eda busy with the tea-cups, and La Roche preventing them from getting things ready, by way of helping them."

"It does indeed seem a good place," replied Frank, "and might do for temporary headquarters, perhaps, while we make excursions to the coast to fix on a spot for our new home."

Stanley gazed contemplatively around him as his friend spoke. "Hand me the telescope, Frank; it strikes me we are nearer the sea than you think. The water here is brackish, and yonder opening in the mountains might reveal something beyond, if magnified by the glass."

After a lengthened survey of the surrounding hills, Frank and Stanley came to the conclusion that they could make nothing of it, at least that night; and as it was becoming gradually dark, they resolved to postpone all further consideration of the subject till the next day.

Meanwhile, the men busied themselves in preparing supper, and Chimo unexpectedly lent them some assistance by bringing into camp a ptarmigan which he had just killed. True, Chimo had, in his innocence, designed this little delicacy of the season for his own special table; but no sooner was he seen with the bird between his teeth, than it was snatched from him and transferred to the pot forthwith.

The following day was an era in the existence of the

travellers. For the first time since commencing their arduous voyage, the cargoes were left behind, and the canoes paddled away, light and buoyant, on a trip of investigation. Stanley had rightly judged that they were now near the sea, and the great breadth of the river led him to believe that there might be water sufficient to float the vessel in which the goods for the station were to be forwarded. If this should turn out as he expected, there could not be a better spot for establishing a fort than that on which they had encamped, as it was situated just below the last rapids of the river; had a fine spring of fresh water in its vicinity; and was protected from the cold blasts of winter, to some extent at least, by the surrounding mountains.

"Now, Frank," added Mr. Stanley, after stating his opinion on this point, "what I mean to do is this: I shall take the large canoe, with Dick Prince, Francois, Gaspard, La Roche, and Augustus—the last to interpret should we fall in with Eskimos, whom I am surprised not to have found hereabouts. With these I will proceed to the sea, examine the coast, observe whether there be any place suitable for building on, and, if all goes well, be back to supper before sunset. You will take the other canoe, with Bryan, Massan, Oolibuck, and Ma-istequan, and proceed down the opposite side of the river a short way. Examine the shores there, and above the island; see whether there be any place better than where we stand for a permanent residence; and at night we shall compare notes. My wife and Eda shall remain in camp under the care of Oostesimow and Moses."

"And pray who is to defend your poor wife and

innocent child in the event of an attack by a band of savage natives?" inquired Mrs. Stanley, as she joined her husband and Frank.

"No fear of the wife and child," replied Stanley, patting his better half on the shoulder. "If Indians should find out the camp, Oostesimow can palaver with them; and should Eskimos pay you a visit, Moses will do the polite. Besides, had you not interrupted, I was going to have given special instructions to Frank regarding you. So, Master Frank, be pleased to take Eda off your shoulder, and give ear to my instructions. While you are examining the other side of the water, you will keep as much as possible within eye-shot, and always within ear-shot, of the camp. In a still day like this a gun-shot can be heard five or six miles off; and should you see any sign of the natives having been here recently, return instantly to the camp."

Frank promised implicit obedience to these instructions, and the whole party then set to work to pile the goods on a ledge in the steep cliffs behind the spring, so that a fortress was soon formed, which, with two such stout and courageous men as Moses and Oostesimow, armed with two guns each, a brace of pistols, two cutlasses, and an ample supply of ammunition, could have stood a prolonged siege from much more practised enemies than Indians or Eskimos. After having completed these defensive arrangements, and provided occupation for those who remained in camp, by laying on them the duty of having the goods examined, in order to see that nothing had been damaged by wet or rough usage, the two canoes pushed from the shore, and bounded lightly away, while the men sang merrily at their easy labour; for now that the canoes were light, they might have been propelled by two men. Frank directed his course obliquely up the river, towards the island already alluded to, and Stanley proceeded with the current towards the narrows beyond which he expected to catch sight of the sea.

After passing above the island, which was found to be low and thinly covered with vegetation and a few scrubby bushes, Frank and his men pushed over to the other side and proceeded carefully to examine the coast. It was found to be much the same as that which they had just left. A narrow belt of sandy and shingly beach extended along the margin of the river, or, as it might be more appropriately termed, the lake, at least in as far as appearance went. This strip or belt was indented here and there with numerous bays and inlets, and in many places was intersected by rocky capes which jutted out from the mountains. These mountains were bare and precipitous, rising abruptly, like those on the other side, from the edge of the sand, and ascending in a succession of terraces, whose faces were so steep that it was almost impossible to scale them. They could be ascended in succession, however, by means of the ravines and numerous gullies which rose in rugged and zigzag lines from the beach to the mountain tops. In the very first of these gullies in which the exploring party landed, they found the remains of an Eskimo summer encampment. These consisted of a few stunted trees, which appeared to have been built in the form of rude huts; but they were thrown about in some confusion, and altogether bore evidence of having remained in a state of ruin for many years. Another discovery of a more satisfactory kind was made—namely, the tracks of deer, which were so fresh as to induce Frank to take his rifle and mount the ravine in search of the animals, accompanied by Massan, whose natural temperament was exceedingly prone to enjoy the excitement of the chase. So much, indeed, was this the case, that the worthy guide had more than once been on the point of making up his mind to elope to the backwood settlements of the States, purchase a rifle and ammunition there, don a deerskin hunting-shirt, and "make tracks," as he styled it, for the prairies, there to dwell and hunt until his eye refused to draw the sight and his finger to pull the trigger of a Kentucky rifle. But Massan's sociable disposition came in the way of this plan, and the thought of leading a solitary life always induced him to forego it.

"It's my 'pinion, sir," remarked the guide, as he followed Frank up the ravine, the sheltered parts of which were covered with a few clumps of stunted pines—"it's my 'pinion that we'll have to cut our logs a long bit up the river, for there's nothin' fit to raise a fort with hereabouts."

"True, Massan," replied Frank, glancing from side to side, hunter fashion, as he walked swiftly over the broken ground; "there's not a tree that I can see big enough to build a backwoods shanty with."

"Well, master, 'twill do for firewood, if it's fit for

nothin' else, and that's a blessin' that's not always to be comed by everywhere. Let's be thankful for small matters. I see sticks growin' up them gullies that'll do for stakes for the nets, an' axe handles, an' paddles, an' spear shafts, an'-"

The honest guide's enumeration of the various articles into which the small timber of the place might be converted was brought to a sudden pause by Frank, who laid his hand on his shoulder, and while he pointed with the butt of his rifle up the ravine, whispered, "Don't you see anything else up yonder besides trees, Massan?"

The guide looked in the direction indicated, and by an expressive grunt showed that his eye had fallen on the object referred to by his companion. It was a deer which stood on an overhanging ledge of rock, high up the cliffs—so high that it might easily have been mistaken for a much smaller animal by less practised sportsmen. Below the shelf on which it stood was a yawning abyss, which rendered any attempt to get near the animal utterly hopeless.

"What a pity," said Frank, as he crouched behind a projecting rock, "that it's out of shot! It would take us an hour at least to get behind it, and there's little chance, I fear, of its waiting for us."

"No chance whatever," replied Massan decidedly. "But he's big enough to cover from where we stand."

"To cover! Ay, truly, I could point straight at his heart easy enough— indeed I would think it but slight boasting to say I could cover his eye from this spot—but the bullet would refuse to go,

Massan; it's far beyond shot."

"Try, sir, try," exclaimed the guide quickly, for as they spoke the deer moved. "I've been huntin' on the Rocky Mountains afore now, an' I know that distance cheats you in sich places. It's not so far as you think—"

He had scarcely finished speaking when Frank's rifle poured forth its contents. The loud echoes of the crags reverberated as the smoke floated away to leeward. The next instant the deer sprang with one wild bound high into the air—over the cliff—and descending with lightning speed through the dark space, was dashed almost in pieces on the rocks below.

Massan gave a low chuckle of satisfaction as he walked up to the mangled animal, and pointing to a small round hole just over its heart, he said, "The old spot, Mr. Frank; ye always hit them there."

Having paid Frank this compliment, Massan bled the animal, which was in prime condition, with at least two inches of fat on its flanks, and having placed it on his shoulders, returned with his companion to the canoe.

While Frank was thus engaged, Stanley had descended towards the shores of Ungava Bay, which he found to be about twenty-five miles distant from the encampment beside the spring. He made a rapid survey of the coast as they descended, and sounded the river at intervals. When he reached its mouth he had made two important discoveries. The one was, that there did not seem to be a spot along the whole line of coast so well fitted in all respects for an establishment as the place whereon their tents were already pitched. The other was, that the river, from its mouth up to that point, was deep enough to float a vessel of at least three or four hundred tons burden. This was very satisfactory, and he was about to return to the camp when he came upon the deserted Eskimo village which, a few weeks before, had been the scene of a murderous attack and a hasty flight. On a careful examination of the place, the marks of a hasty departure were so apparent that Stanley and his men made a pretty near guess at the true state of affairs; and the former rightly conjectured that, having made a precipitate flight in consequence of some unexpected attack, there was little probability of their returning soon to the same locality. This was unfortunate, but in the hope that he might be mistaken in these conjectures, and that the natives might yet return before winter, he set up a pole on a conspicuous place, and tied to the top of it a bag containing two dozen knives, one dozen fire-steels, some awls and needles, several pounds of beads, and a variety of such trinkets as were most likely to prove acceptable to a savage people.

While Bryan was engaged in piling a heap of stones at the foot of this pole to prevent its being blown down by the wind, the rest of the party re-embarked, and prepared to return home; for although the camp beside the spring was scarcely one day old, the fact that it was likely to become the future residence of the little party had already invested it with a species of homelike attraction. Man is a strange animal, and whatever untravelled philosophers may say to the contrary, he speedily makes himself "at home" anywhere!

"Hallo, Bryan!" shouted Stanley from the canoe,

"look sharp; we're waiting for you!"

"Ay, ay, yer honour," replied the Irishman, lifting a huge mass of rock; "jist wan more, an' it'll be stiff an' stidy as the north pole himself." Then in an undertone he added, "'Look sharp,' is it ye say? It's blunt ye are to spake that way to yer betters. Musha! but it's mysilf wouldn't give a tinpinny for all that bag houlds, twinty times doubled; an' yit thim haythens, thim pork-faced Huskimos, 'll dance round this here pole wi' delight till they're fit to dhrop. Och! but salvages is a quare lot; an', Bryan, yer a cliver boy to come this far all the way to see thim."

With this self-complimentary conclusion, Bryan resumed his place at the paddle, and the party returned to the camp.

Here they found things in a most satisfactory state. Frank and his party had returned, and the deer, now cut up into joints and steaks, was impaled on a number of stakes of wood, and stuck up to roast round a large and cheering fire. The savoury steam from these, with the refreshing odour of the tea-kettle, produced a delectable sensation in the nostrils of the hungry explorers. Stanley's tent was erected with its back towards the mountains and its open door towards the fire, which lighted up its snug interior, and revealed Mrs. Stanley and Edith immersed in culinary operations, and Chimo watching them with a look of deep, grave sagacity—his ears very erect, and his head a good deal inclined to one side, as if that position favoured the peculiar train of his cogitations. La Roche was performing feats of agility round the fire, that led one to believe he must be at least half a salamander. At a respectful distance from Stanley's tent, but within the influence of the fire, the men were employed in pitching, for the first time, the large skin tent which was to be their residence until they should build a house for themselves; and on a log, within dangerous proximity to the mercurial La Roche, sat Frank Morton, busily employed in entering in his journal the various events of the day.

There was much talk and loud laughter round the fire that night, for the different parties had much to tell and much to hear regarding the discoveries that had been made, and discussions as to the prospects of the expedition were earnest and long. It was generally admitted that first appearances were, upon the whole, favourable, although it could not be denied that the place looked dreadfully barren and rugged. Under the happy influence of this impression, and the happier influence of the savoury steaks on which they had supped, the entire party lay down to rest, and slept so profoundly that there was neither sound nor motion to indicate the presence of human beings in the vast solitudes of Ungava, save the fitful flame of the fire as it rose and fell, casting a lurid light on the base of the rugged mountains, and a sharp reflection on the dark waters.

Chapter XVI

RESOURCES OF THE COUNTRY BEGIN
TO DEVELOP—BRYAN DISTINGUISHES
HIMSELF— FISHING EXTRAORDINARY.

There is a calm but deep-seated and powerful pleasure which fills the heart, and seems to permeate the entire being, when one awakens to the conviction that a day of arduous toil is about to begin—toil of an uncertain kind, perhaps connected with danger and adventure, in an unexplored region of the earth. Ignorance always paints coming events in glowing colours; and the mere fact that our adventurers knew not the nature of the country in which their tent was pitched—knew not whether the natives would receive them as friends or repel them as foes—knew not whether the nature and capabilities of the country were such as would be likely to convert the spot on which they lay into a comfortable home or a premature grave; the mere fact of being utterly ignorant on these points was, in itself, sufficient to fill the poorest spirit of the band (had there been a poor spirit among them) with a glow of pleasurable excitement, and a firm resolve t0o tax their powers of doing and suffering to the uttermost.

When the sun rose on the following morning the whole party was astir, the fire lighted, and an early breakfast in course of preparation. Much had to be done, and it behoved them to set about it with energy and at once, for the short autumn of these arctic regions was drawing on apace, and a winter of great length and of the utmost severity lay before them.

There was also one consideration which caused some anxiety to Stanley and Frank, although it weighed little on the reckless spirits of the men, and this was the possibility of the non-arrival of the ship with their winter supply of provisions and goods for trade. Without such a supply a winter on the shores of Ungava Bay would involve all the hardships and extreme perils that too often fall to the lot of arctic discoverers; and he who has perused the fascinating journals of those gallant men, knows that these hardships and perils are neither few nor light. The leaders of the expedition were not, indeed, men to anticipate evils, or to feel unduly anxious about possible dangers; but they would have been more or less than human had they been able to look at Mrs. Stanley and little Edith without a feeling of anxiety on their account. This thought, however, did not influence them in their actions; or, if it did, it only spurred them on to more prompt and vigorous exertions in the carrying out of their undertaking.

After breakfast Stanley assembled his men, and gave each special directions what to do. One of the most important points to ascertain was whether there were many fish in the river. On this hung much of the future comfort and well-being, perhaps even the existence, of the party. Gaspard was, therefore, ordered to get out his nets and set them opposite the encampment. Oolibuck, being officially an interpreter of the Eskimo language, and, when not employed in his calling, regarded as a sort of male maid-of-all-work, was ordered to assist Gaspard. The next matter of primary importance was to ascertain what animals inhabited the region, and whether they were numerous. Dick Prince, being the recognised hunter of the party, was directed to take his gun and a large supply of ammunition, and sally forth over the mountains in search of game; and as Massan was a special friend of his, a good shot, and, moreover, a sagacious fellow, he was ordered to accompany him. They were also directed to observe particularly the state of the woods and the quality of the timber growing therein; but as this last required special attention, the style and size of the future fort being dependent on it, Francois, the carpenter, was appointed to make a journey of observation up the Caniapuscaw River, in company with Augustus the Eskimo and Ma-istequan the Indian—it being thought probable that if natives were to be met with at all, they would be on the banks of the river rather than in the mountains. It was further arranged that Frank Morton should ascend the mountains in company with Bryan, and ascertain if there were any lakes, and whether or not they contained fish. As for Mr. Stanley, he resolved to remain by the camp. On entering his tent after dispatching the several parties, he said to his wife—

"I'm going to stay by you to-day, Jessie. All the men, except Moses, Oostesimow, Gaspard, and La Roche, are sent off to hunt and fish in the mountains, and I have kept these four to paddle about this neighbourhood, in order to take soundings and examine the coast more carefully; because, you see, it would be an unfortunate thing if we began our establishment in a place not well suited for it."

Mrs. Stanley and Edith were, of course, quite pleased with this arrangement, and while the males of the party were absent, the former employed herself in dressing the skin of the deer that had been shot the day before. She accomplished this after the Indian fashion, by scraping and rubbing it with the animal's brains. Afterwards she smoked it over a fire of green wood, and in this way produced a soft, pliant substance similar to chamois leather, but coarser and stouter. As for Edith, she rambled at will among the bushes of the nearest ravine, under the faithful guardianship of Chimo, and hurried back to the camp almost every hour, laden with cloudberries, cranberries, blaeberries, and crowberries, which grew in profusion everywhere.

Opposite to the camp the water was found to be eight fathoms deep. This was of great importance, as affording facility for unloading the ship abreast of the establishment. Higher up the river the ground was more favourable for building, both on account of its being more sheltered and better wooded with timber fit for the construction of houses; but the water was too shallow to float the ship, and the island before mentioned, which was named Cross Island, proved an effectual barrier to the upward progress of any craft larger than a boat. But as Stanley surveyed the spot on which the tent was pitched, and observed the sheltering background of mountains, with their succession of terraces; the creek or ravine to the right, with its growth of willows and stunted pines; the level parcel of greensward, with the little fountain under the rock; and the fine sandy bay in which Gaspard and Oolibuck were busily engaged in setting a couple of nets,—when he surveyed all this, he felt that, although not the best locality in the neighbourhood, it was, nevertheless, a very good one, and well suited in many respects for the future establishment.

"Please, sir, the net him set," shouted Oolibuck from the shore to his master, who floated in the bay at the distance of a hundred yards, busily engaged with the sounding-line. On receiving this piece of information, Stanley ran the canoe on the beach, and said to his follower—

"Oolibuck, I have been thinking much about that river which we saw yesterday, off the mouth of this one; and I cannot help fearing that the ship will run into it, instead of into this, for the land is very deceptive."

"Me t'ink dat is true," answered the Eskimo, with a look of grave perplexity. "If de ship go into dat riv'r he t'ink we no arrive, and so he go 'way, and we all starve!"

"Nay, Oolibuck, I trust that such would not be the sad result of the ship failing to find us; but in order to prevent this, if possible, I intend to send you down to the coast, with a few days' provisions, to keep a look-out for the ship, and light a fire if you see her, so that she may be guided to the right place. So get a blanket and your gun as fast as you can, and be off. I can only afford you four days' provisions, Oolibuck, so you will have to prove yourself a good hunter, else you'll starve. Will four days' provisions do?"

Oolibuck's eyes disappeared. We do not mean to say that they flew away, or were annihilated. But Oolibuck was fat—so fat that, when he laughed, his eyes reduced themselves into two little lines surrounded by wrinkles; a result which was caused by a physical incapacity to open the mouth and eyes at the same time. As a general rule, when Oolibuck's mouth was open his eyes were shut, and when his eyes were open his mouth was shut. Being a good-humoured fellow, and of a risible nature, the alternations were frequent. It was the idea of Stanley doubting the sufficiency of four days' provisions that closed the eyes of the Eskimo on the present occasion.

"Two days' grub more dan 'nuff," said Oolibuck. "Give me plenty powder and shot, and me no starve—no fear."

"Very well," rejoined Stanley, laughing, "take as much ammunition as you require, but be careful of it; if the ship fails us we shall need it all. And don't be too eager after the deer, Oolibuck; keep a sharp look-out seaward, be on the hill-tops as much as you can, and keep your eyes open."

Oolibuck replied by closing the said eyes with a

smile, as he hurried towards the tent to prepare for his expedition. In the meantime Stanley directed Oostesimow and La Roche to set about building a small canoe out of the birch bark which they had carried with them for the purpose, the large canoes being too cumbrous for the purpose of overhauling the nets.

The nets had been set by Gaspard in the usual way—that is, with stones attached to the lower lines to act as sinkers, and floats attached to the upper lines to keep them spread; and it was with no little impatience that the party in the camp awaited the issue. Indeed they scarcely permitted an hour to pass without an inspection being ordered; but to their chagrin, instead of finding fish, they found the nets rolled up by the conflicting currents of the river and the tide into the form of two ropes.

"This will never do," cried Stanley, as they brought the nets ashore. "We must set stake-nets immediately. It is nearly low tide now, so if we work hard they may be ready to set up before the tide has risen much."

In pursuance of this plan, Stanley and his men went to the ravine, of which mention has been already made, and proceeded to cut stakes for the nets; while Oolibuck, having explained to Mrs. Stanley and Edith that he was "going to look hout for de ship," shouldered his wallet and gun, and ascending the ravine, speedily gained the first terrace of the mountains, along which he hastened in the direction of the sea-coast.

While the party in the camp were thus engaged, Frank Morton and Bryan instituted a thorough investigation of the country that lay directly in the rear of the camp, in the course of which investigation they made sundry interesting discoveries.

After ascending the ravine in which we left Stanley and his men cutting stakes for the nets, Frank and Bryan reached the first terrace, and proceeded along it in the opposite direction from that pursued by Oolibuck. A walk of a quarter of a mile, or less, brought them to another ravine, into which they turned, and the first thing that greeted them as they pushed their way through the stunted willows that thickly covered this gorge in the mountains was a covey of ptarmigan. These birds are similar in form and size to ordinary grouse, perhaps a little smaller. In winter they are pure white—so white that it is difficult to detect them amid the snow; but in summer their coats become brown, though there are a few of the pure white feathers left which never change their colour. Being unaccustomed to the sight of man, they stood gazing at Frank and Bryan in mute surprise, until the latter hastily threw forward his gun, when they wisely took to flight. But Frank arrested his follower's arm.

"Don't waste your powder and shot, Bryan, on such small game. There may be something more worthy of a shot among the mountains; and if you once raise the echoes among these wild cliffs, I fear the game will not wait to inquire the cause thereof."

"Maybe not, sir," replied Bryan, as he fell back a pace, and permitted Frank to lead the way; "but there's an ould proverb that says, 'A bird in the hand's worth two in the buss,' an' I've great belaif in that same."

"Very true, Bryan, there is much wisdom in old

proverbs; but there are exceptions to every rule, and this is a case in point, as you will admit if you cast your eyes over yonder valley, and observe the edge of the mountain-top that cuts so clear a line against the sky."

Frank pointed, as he spoke, to the shoulder or spur of one of the mountains which rose at a considerable distance in the interior, and from which they were separated by a dark glen or gorge; for none of the ravines in this part of the country merited the name of valley, save that through which flowed the Caniapuscaw River. The ravine up which they had been toiling for some time led into this darksome glen, and it was on rounding a bold precipice, which had hitherto concealed it from view, that Frank's quick eye caught sight of the object to which he directed the attention of his companion.

"'Tis a crow," said Bryan, after a gaze of five minutes, during which he had gone through a variety of strange contortions—screwing up his features, shading his eyes with his hand, standing on tip-toe, although there was nothing to look over, and stooping low, with a hand on each knee, though there was nothing to look under, in the vain hope to increase by these means his power of vision.

Frank regarded him with a quiet smile, as he said, "Look again, Bryan. Saw you ever a crow with antlers?"

"Anthlers!" exclaimed the Irishman, once more wrinkling up his expressive face, and peering under his palm; "anthlers, say you? Sorra a thing duv I see 'xcept a black spot on the sky. If ye see anthlers on it, ye're nothin' more nor less than a walkin' spy-glass."

"Nevertheless I see them, Bryan; and they grace the head of a noble buck. Now, you see, it is well you did not fire at the ptarmigan. Away with you, lad, down into that ravine, and clamber up the mountain through yonder gap with the fallen rock in the middle of it—d'ye see?— and wait there, lest the deer should turn back. In the meantime I'll run round by the way we came, and descend to the water's edge, to receive him when he arrives there. Now don't lose yourself, and take care not to fire at smaller game."

As Frank concluded these orders, which he issued in a quick low voice, he threw his gun into the hollow of his left arm and strode rapidly away, leaving his companion gazing after him with an expression of blank stupidity on his face. Gradually his cheeks and brow were overspread with a thousand wrinkles and a smile took possession of his lips.

"'Don't lose yersilf!' Faix, Master Frank, ye're free an' aisy. Arrah now, Bryan dear, don't lose yersilf; you that's crossed the salt saes, an' followed the Red Injins to the prairie, and hunted in the Rocky Mountains, and found yer way to Ungava—not to mintion havin' comed oraginally from ould Ireland—which ov itsilf secures ye agin mistakes of every kind whatsumdiver. Lose yersilf! Musha, but ye had better git some wan to look after ye, Bryan boy. Take care now; go softly and kape yer eyes open, for fear ye lose yersilf!"

As Bryan mumbled forth this bantering soliloquy, he lifted up a large bag which contained a couple of fishing-lines and a few hooks, and throwing it across the stock of his gun, and both across his shoulder, he took his way down the rugged but well-beaten deer-path which led to the ravine or glen. The idea of losing himself seemed to have taken such a hold of Bryan's mind, and afforded him so much amusement and such scope for the continued flow of bantering soliloquy to which he was in truth much addicted, that he failed to note the fact that he was walking along the edge of a steep declivity, at the foot of which lay a small, dark sheet of water, which was connected by a short river or strait with a larger lake, whose wavelets rippled at the base of the mountain beyond. The scene was magnificently wild and lonely, and would have riveted the attention and excited the admiration of any one less absent than Bryan. High, rugged, and to all appearance inaccessible mountains surrounded the vale on all sides; and although there were several outlets from it, these were so concealed by the peculiar formation of the wild mountains that they could not be seen until they were actually entered.

Had Bryan's eyes been more active, he would have seen that the fringe of bushes by the side of the deer-track, along which he walked, concealed a declivity so steep that it almost merited the name of a precipice. But Bryan was lost in philosophic contemplation, and the first thing that awakened him to the fact was the slipping of a stone, which caused him to trip and fall headlong over the bank! The Irishman grasped convulsively at the bushes to arrest his fall, but the impetus with which he had commenced the descent tore them from his grasp, and after one or two unpleasant bounds and a good deal of crashing through shrubs that tore his garments sadly, he found himself stretched at full length on the margin of the river that connected the two lakes. So nearly had he been hurled into this strait by the violence of his descent that his head was hanging over the bank ere he stopped! Being partially stunned by the fall, Bryan lay for a few seconds motionless. As his shaken faculties returned, however, he became aware of the fact that a fish of fully two feet long lay at the bottom of the pool over which his head hung. Starting up, and totally forgetting his bruises, he turned to look for the bag containing the fishing-lines, and observing it lying on the ground not far distant, still wrapped round the gun, he ran to pick it up.

"Oh! wow! poor thing!" he exclaimed, on lifting up his gun, which, though fortunately not broken, was sadly bent, "ye're fit for nothin' but shootin' round the corner now! It's well for you, Bryan, ye spalpeen, that your backbone is not in the same fix."

While he thus muttered to himself, Bryan drew from the bag a stout cod-line, to which he fastened a hook of deadly dimensions, and dressed it into the form of a fly, much in the same manner as was formerly done by La Roche. This line and fly he fastened to the end of a short stout pole which he cut from a neighbouring tree, and approaching cautiously to the bank of the strait—for there was too little motion in it to entitle it to be called a stream—he cast the fly with a violent splash into the water. The violence was unintentional— at least the exclamations of reproach that followed the cast would lead us to suppose so. The fish here were as tame as those caught in Deer River. In a few seconds the fly was swallowed, and Bryan, applying main force to the pole, tossed a beautiful trout of about two pounds weight over his head.

"Och! ye purty crature," exclaimed the delighted Irishman, rubbing his hands with glee as he gazed at the fish after having unhooked it. "Shure ye'll make a beautiful fagure in the kittle this night. An' musha! there's wan o' yer relations to kape ye company," he added, as, exerting an enormous degree of unnecessary force, he drew another trout violently from the water. The second trout was larger than the first, and Bryan soon became so excited in the sport that he totally forgot Frank's orders, and the deer, and everything else in the world, for the time being. Having caught six or seven trout, varying from two to four pounds in weight, he changed his position a little, and made a cast over a deep pool nearer to the large lake. As heretofore, the fly was engulfed the instant it fell on the water; but Bryan did not, as heretofore, haul the fish violently out of its native element. It is true he attempted to do so, but the attempt proved utterly futile; moreover, the fish darted with such velocity and strength towards the lake, that the angler, albeit entirely ignorant of his art, experienced an inward conviction that the thick cord would snap altogether if not eased of the enormous strain. He therefore followed the fish at the top of his speed, uttering incomprehensible sounds of mingled rage and amazement as he went, and tripping over rocks and bushes in his headlong career. After a smart run of half a minute the fish stopped, turned, and darted back so rapidly that Bryan tripped in turning and fell into the water! The place was shallow, but having fallen on his back, he was thoroughly drenched from head to foot. He did not lose the grasp of his rod, however. Spluttering, and gasping, and dripping, he followed the fish in its wild career until it turned again at a tangent, and darted towards the bank on which he stood. There was a shelving bed of pebbles, where the water shoaled very gradually. Bryan saw this. Availing himself of the fish's impetus, and putting all his force to the rod, he dragged it into two inches of water, when the line broke. Instantly the fish struggled towards deep water; but it was so large, and the place to which it had been dragged so shallow, that it afforded the excited angler time to rush forward and throw himself bodily on the top of it!

The battle that now ensued was of an energetic and deadly character on the part of both man and fish. Those who have not grasped a live salmon in their arms have no conception of the strength of a fish; and perhaps it may be said with equal truth that those who have never wielded a forehammer have but a faint conception of the strength of a blacksmith's knuckles. Bryan had thrown his whole weight on the fish, and grasped it, as with a vice, in both hands; but at every struggle of its powerful frame he felt how uncertain was the hold he had of its slippery body. Once it almost escaped, and dashed the spray over its adversary's face with its tail, as it wriggled out of his grasp; but with a desperate plunge Bryan seized it by the head and succeeded in thrusting his thumb under its gill and choking it, while himself was well-nigh choked at the same moment by unintentionally swallowing a gulp of the muddy compound which they had stirred up in their struggles. Slowly and with caution Bryan rose on one knee, while he crushed the fish against the bottom with both hands; then making a last exertion, he hurled it up the bank, where it fell beyond all hope of return to its native element.

The fish thus captured was a beautiful trout of about twenty pounds weight. The lake trout of North America are, some of them, of enormous size, being not unfrequently taken of sixty pounds weight, so that as a specimen of those inhabiting these lakes this was by no means a large one. Nevertheless it was a splendid fish, and certainly the largest that had ever been captured by the worthy son of Vulcan.

The thick coat of liquid mud with which his face was covered could not entirely conceal the smile of intense satisfaction with which he regarded his prize, as he sat down on the bank before it.

"Kape quiet now, honey!" he exclaimed, as the trout made a last fluttering attempt to escape; "kape quiet. Have patience, darlint. It's o' no manner o' use to hurry natur'. Just lie still, an' it'll be soon over."

With this consolatory remark, Bryan patted the fish on the head, and proceeded to wring the water from his upper garments, after which he repaired his broken tackle, and resumed his sport with an eagerness and zest that cold and water and mud could not diminish in the smallest degree.

Chapter XVII

SUCCESSES AND ENCOURAGEMENT—
BRYAN LOST AND FOUND.

It was evening before the tide began to fall and uncover the stake-nets, which were eagerly and earnestly watched by those who had remained in the camp. Mrs. Stanley and Edith were seated on an empty box by the margin of the sandy bay; Mr. Stanley sat on a nail-keg beside them; La Roche and the Indian were still working at the small canoe a few yards from the tent; and Gaspard, with folded arms, and an unusual smile of good humour playing on his countenance, stood close behind Stanley.

None of the hunting and exploring parties had returned, although the sun had long since disappeared behind the mountains, and the mellow light of evening was deepening over the bay.

"There's a tail, sir," said Gaspard, as he hurried

towards the net.

"So it is!" cried Stanley, leaping up. "Come along, Eda, and take the first fish."

Edith needed no second invitation, but bounded towards the edge of the water, which was now gradually leaving the nets. Gaspard had already disengaged a white fish from the mesh, and wading to the beach, gave it to the little girl, who ran with it joyously to her mother. Meanwhile, another and another fish was left by the tide, and Stanley soon after brought up a splendid salmon of about twenty-five pounds weight, and laid it at Edith's feet.

"Oh, how very beautiful!" cried the child, as she gazed in delight at the silvery scales of the fish.

"My mind is much relieved by this, Jessie," said Stanley, reseating himself on the keg, while Oostesimow and La Roche carried the fish ashore as Gaspard freed them from the nets. "I now see that there are plenty of fish in the river, and if the hunters bring in a good report to-night, our anxiety on the score of food will be quite removed."

Although none of the party had ever set a net on stakes before, they had frequently heard of this manner of fishing, and their first attempt proved eminently successful. At low tide stakes had been driven into the sand, extending from the edge of the water towards high-water mark. On these the nets had been spread, and thus the misfortune which had attended the setting of the nets with floats and sinkers was avoided. The quantity of fish taken gave promise of an ample supply for the future. There were two Hearne-salmon (that is, spotted like trout), and one large common salmon, besides thirty white-fish, averaging between two to six pounds weight each, all of which were in excellent condition. The white-fish is of the salmon species, but white in the flesh, and being less rich than the salmon, is much preferred by those who have to use it constantly as an article of food.

"This is a most fortunate supply," remarked Stanley, "and will prevent the necessity of putting the men on short allowance."

"Short allowance!" exclaimed his wife; "I thought we had more than enough of food to last us till the arrival of the ship."

"Ay, so we have. But until now I did not feel at liberty to use it; for if through any accident the ship does not come, and if there had chanced to be no fish in the river, the only course open to us would be to retrace our steps, and as that would be a long and slow process, we would require to economise our food. In fact, I had resolved to begin operations by putting the men on short allowance; but this haul of fish shows me that we shall have more than enough.

"But who comes here?" he added, on observing the figure of a man approaching the camp. "He seems to carry a burden on his back, as far as I can make out in the uncertain light."

"Did any of the men go out alone?" inquired Mrs. Stanley.

"No; but I suppose that this one must have separated from his comrade. Hallo! who goes there?"

The man tossed the bundle from his shoulders, and

hastening forward revealed the flushed countenance of Frank Morton.

"What! Frank! why, man, you seem to have had a hard day of it, if I may judge by your looks."

"Not so hard but that a good supper will put its effects to flight," replied Frank, as he rested his gun against a rock and seated himself on the keg from which Stanley had risen. "The fact is, I have slain a noble buck, and being desirous that the men should have as much of it as possible, I loaded myself rather heavily. The ground, too, is horribly bad; but pray send Gaspard for the bundle. I should have been here sooner but for the time required to dissect the animal."

"Where is Bryan, Frank?" inquired Mrs. Stanley. "You went away together."

"Bryan! I know not. He and I parted in the mountains some hours ago; and as he failed to keep his appointment with me, I concluded that he must have become foot-sore and returned to camp."

"He has not returned," said Stanley; "but I have no fear for the honest blacksmith. He's too old a nor'wester to lose himself, and he's too tough to kill. But come, Frank, let us to our tent. I see that La Roche has already prepared our salmon for the kettle, and so—"

"Salmon!" interrupted Frank.

"Ay, lad, salmon! a twenty-five pounder too! But come, change your foot-gear, and then we shall have our supper, in the course of which we shall exchange news."

As they proceeded towards the camp the voices of some of the men were heard in the distance; it was now too dark to see them. In a few minutes Francois, followed by Augustus and Ma-istequan, strode into the circle of light around the fire, and laying aside their guns proceeded to light their pipes, while they replied to the questions of Frank and Stanley.

"You do not come empty-handed," remarked the latter, as Francois and his comrades threw down several fat ducks and a few grouse, which, after the fashion of hunters, they had carried pendent by the necks from their belts.

"We only shot a few, monsieur," replied Francois, "to put in the kettle for supper. We might have loaded a canoe had we chosen."

"That is well," said Stanley; "but the kettle is full already, and supper prepared. See, Frank has shot a deer, so that we shall fare well to-night. Ah, Prince! come along. What! more game?" he added, as Dick and Massan entered the halo of light, and threw down the choice morsels of a fat deer which they had killed among the mountains.

"Ah! oui, monsieur," said Massan, chuckling as he laid aside his axe and gun; "we might ha' killed three o' them if we had been so minded; but we couldn't ha' brought them into camp, an', as Dick said, 'tis a pity to kill deer to feed the wolves with."

"Right!" exclaimed Frank; "but did any of you see Bryan? He gave me the slip in the mountains, and, I fear, has lost himself."

To this the men replied in the negative, and some of them smiled at the idea of the blacksmith being lost.

"No fear, vraiment! He no lost," cried La Roche with a laugh, as he lifted the huge kettle from the fire and placed it in the midst of the men, having previously abstracted the best portions for the special benefit of his master. "No fear of Bryan, certainment; he like one bad shilling—he come up toujours. Ah! mauvais chien, him give me all de trouble ov get supper ready mylone."

"I trust it may be so," said Stanley. "We are all here except him and Oolibuck, whom I have sent to the coast for a few days to watch for the ship. But let us have supper, La Roche, and spread ours nearer the fire to-night—it is rather cold; besides, I want to hear the reports of the men."

In compliance with this order, the lively Frenchman spread the supper for his master's family close beside that of the men, and in a few minutes more a most vigorous attack was made on the viands, during the first part of which the hungry travellers maintained unbroken silence. But as the cravings of nature began to be satisfied, their tongues found time to remark on the excellence of the fare. The salmon was superb. Even Edith, who seldom talked about what she ate, pronounced it very good. The white-fish were better than any of the party had ever eaten in their lives, although most of them had travelled over the length and breadth of the North American wilderness. The ducks were perfect. Even the ptarmigan were declared passable; and the venison, with an inch of fat on the haunches—words were not found sufficiently expressive to describe it. Those who are philosophically inclined may suspect that some of this super-excellence lay in the keen appetites of the men. Well, perhaps it did.

While the travellers were in the midst of this, and ere yet their tongues were fairly loosened, a loud unearthly shout rang with appalling reverberations among the surrounding cliffs, causing the entire party to start up and rush for their arms. Again the cry was heard.

"Ah! bad skran to ye, Losh!—Hould on, Moses, ye fat villain. Lave me wan mouthful, jist wan, to kape me from givin' up the ghost intirely."

A shout of laughter greeted the advent of Bryan's voice, but it was nothing to the peals that burst forth on the appearance of that individual in propria persona. To say that he was totally dishevelled would convey but half the truth. Besides being covered and clotted with mud, he was saturated with water from head to foot, his clothes rent in a most distressing manner, and his features quite undistinguishable.

"Why, Bryan, what ails you? Where have you been?" inquired Stanley, in a tone of sympathy.

"Bin, is it? Sorra wan o' me knows where I've bin. It's mysilf is glad to be sartin I'm here, anyhow."

"I'm glad you're certain of it," said Frank, "for if it were not for the sound of your voice, I should doubt it."

"Ah monsieur," said La Roche, "make your mind easy on dat. No von but Bryan ever regard de kettle dat way."

"Taizy voo, ye petit varmint," said Bryan, approaching the said kettle, and smiling rapturously through the mud that encrusted his face on beholding its contents. Without waiting to change his garments the hungry blacksmith began supper, having first, however, directed attention to the bag which he had brought in. From this bag La Roche now extracted about a dozen trout, some of which were of great size— especially one, whose bulk exceeded that of the large salmon.

"There's plinty more where thim comed from," said Bryan, through a mouthful of venison; "but I'll tell ye ov it afther supper."

"Ah, true! don't let us interrupt him just now," said Stanley. "In the meantime, Francois, since you seem to be about done, tell us what you have seen, and let us hear what you have to say of the country."

Francois having lighted his pipe, cleared his throat and began—

"Well, monsieur, after we had paddled a short bit beyond the point below the last rapid in Caniapuscaw River, we shoved the canoe ashore, and landed Prince and Massan, who set off to look for game, leavin' Augustus, Ma-istequan, and me to paddle up the river as well as we could. But we soon found that three men in a big canoe could not make much way agin the strong current of the river, so we put ashore again and took to our legs.

"After making a long tramp up the banks o' the river, we fell in with some good-sized pines; but although they are big for this part of the country, they are not big enough for building. Then we pushed into the gullies, which are sheltered from the cold winds off the bay, and here we found the trees a good deal bigger. There are pines and larch in abundance, and some of the larch are even bigger than we require."

"Are they far inland?" inquired Stanley.

"No, monsieur, they are only a few hundred yards from the banks of the river, and growin' on the edge of a small creek, which I noticed is deep enough to float them down."

"Good, very good," said Stanley, filling his pipe with a fresh charge of tobacco; "that is most fortunate, for it will save time, and take fewer men to bring them here. Go on, Francois."

"Bien, monsieur. Then I felled one or two o' the trees, to see what like they are; and I found that they are very tough and good. The pines are firmer and tougher than any I ever saw in the Indian country, owing, I suppose, to their stunted growth. While I was thus employed, Augustus shot the grouse we brought home, and we saw a great many coveys of them. In fact, we might have shot many more; but as we did not know how far we should have to walk, we thought it best not to burden ourselves too much. We also saw a great many ducks, and shot a few, as you see."

"Did you see goose?" inquired La Roche, whose mind had a natural tendency to culinary matters.

"No," replied Francois, "I saw no geese; but I did not go out of my way to look for them. I was more taken up with the timber than replenishing the kettle."

"Ah! that ver' great pity. Oui, grand dommage. De kittle toujours de most importance t'ing on de voyage. If you forget him, you goot for not'ing. Mais, Francois, did you look into the deep clear pool at de foot of de rapid?"

Francois emitted a cloud of smoke with a negative in the middle of it.

"An!" said La Roche with a sigh, "I thought not; mais it was pity. You see one goose for certain, if you have look straight down into dat pool."

"Bien," continued Francois, turning to Stanley. "I then went into one or two more gullies, and saw some more sticks fit for building; but after all it is only in the gullies they grow, and there are not very many. The trees on the banks of the river are chiefly pines, and only fit for firewood."

"And an important item is firewood, as we shall find ere long," remarked Stanley. "Your account of the timber is very satisfactory, Francois. Did you see traces of Indians or Eskimos?"

"No; I saw none."

"Perhaps you did, Prince," continued Stanley, turning to that worthy, who was stretched, along with Massan, at full length before the blaze, and had been listening attentively to the conversation while he solaced himself with his pipe.

"Yes, sir, we seed the marks they left behind them," answered Prince, while he glanced towards Massan, as if to invite him to give the desired information.

"Ay, we saw their marks, no doubt," said the guide, knocking the ashes out of his pipe, and raising himself from his reclining posture to that of a tailor, the more conveniently to recharge that beloved implement. "Ay, we saw their marks, and they was by no means pleasant to look on. After we had landed above the p'int, as Francois told ye, Dick Prince and me went up one o' the gullies, an' then gettin' on one o' them flat places that run along the face of all the mountains hereabouts, we pushed straight up the river. We had not gone far when, on turnin' a p'int, we both clapped eyes at the same moment on the most ill-lookin' blackguard of a wolf I ever saw. Up went both our guns at once, and I believe we were very near puttin' a bullet in each of his eyes, when we noticed that these same eyes were not bookin' at us, but starin', most awful earnest like, up a gully in the mountains; so we looked up, an', sure enough, there we saw a deer on the mountain-top, tossin' its head and snuffin' round to see that the coast was clear before it came down to the water. We noticed that a regular beaten deer-track passed down this gully, and master wolf, who knowed the walk very well, was on the lookout for his dinner; so we waited quiet till the deer came down, an' Dick put a bullet in its heart, an' I put one into the wolf's head, so they both tumbled down the cliffs together. The shot made another deer, that we had not seen, start off into the river; but before it got a few yards from the shore, Dick loaded again and put a bullet into its head too, an' it was washed ashore at the p'int below us.

"Havin' fixed them off comfortably, we cut up the deer, and put all we could carry on our shoulders, for we knowed that if we left them we'd find nothin' but the bones when we came back. About an hour after this we came upon a deserted camp of Indians. It was so fresh that we think they must have passed but a few weeks ago. The whole camp was strewed with bones of deer, as if the red varmints had been havin' a feast. An' sure enough, a little farther on we came upon the dead carcasses of ninety-three deer! The rascals had taken nothin' but the tongues an' tit-bits, leavin' the rest for the wolves."

"Ay, they're a reckless, improvident set," remarked Stanley. "I've been told that the Eskimos are quite different in this respect. They never kill what they don't require; but the redskins slaughter the deer by dozens for the sake of their tongues."

"We also found the broken head of an Eskimo seal-spear, and this little bit of sealskin." Massan handed these as he spoke to Stanley.

"I fear," said Frank, "this looks as if they had made an attack on the Eskimos very recently."

"I fear it much," said Stanley, examining the little shred of sealskin, which had beautifully glossy hair on one side, and on the other, which was dressed, there were sundry curious marks, one of which bore a rude resemblance to an Indian wigwam, with an arrow pointing towards it.

"I found the bit o' sealskin hanging on a bush a little apart from the place where they camped, an' from what I've seen o' the ways o' redskins, it's my 'pinion that it was put there for some purpose or other."

"Very likely. Take care of it, Jessie," said Stanley, throwing it to his wife; "it may be explained some day.—Well, Massan, did you see any other animals?"

"Yes, sir, lots o' them. We saw deer on the hill-tops, and might ha' shot more o' them if we could have brought them into camp. An' we saw porcupines in all the pine bluffs. An' we saw fish in the lakes among the mountains. There are lots o' them lakes—small things some o' them—in all the gullies, and fish in most o' them; but we had neither lines nor hooks, so we catched none."

"Faix, if ye catched none, yer betters catched plinty," said Bryan, who, having concluded supper and changed his garments, was now luxuriating in a smoke. The blacksmith pointed as he spoke to the bag of splendid trout which lay at a short distance from the fire. "'Tis mysilf's the boy to catch them. I would have brought ye two times as much, if it wasn't that I lost my hook and line. I think it must have bin a fresh-water whale, the last wan, bad luck to it! for it pulled me into the wather three times, an' wint off at last with two fathom o' cod-line trailin' behind it."

"So then, Bryan," said Frank, "it must have been the yells with which you accompanied your fishing that frightened the deer I was after and caused me to lose him. However, as I got another soon afterwards which must have been frightened towards me by the same halloos, I forgive you."

Frank now gave the party an account of what he had seen, but as his experience merely corroborated that of Dick Prince and Massan, we will not trouble the reader with the details. The evidence of the various exploring parties, when summed up, was undoubtedly most satisfactory, and while it relieved the mind of the leaders of the band, it raised and cheered the spirits of the men. Timber, although not plentiful or very large, was to be had close to the spot where they proposed to erect their fort; game of all kinds swarmed in the mountains in abundance; and the lakes and rivers were well stocked with excellent fish: so that, upon the whole, they considered that they had made an auspicious commencement to their sojourn in the land of the Eskimos.

Chapter XVIII

The band of fur-traders now set earnestly about
the erection of their winter dwelling. The season
was so far advanced that the men could no longer be
spared from the work to hunt or fish in the mountains,
so that they lived chiefly on the produce of the stake-
nets in front of the camp, and a small allowance of the
provisions with which they had started from Moose
Fort. Occasionally Frank sallied forth and returned
with the best parts of a deer on his shoulders; but
these excursions were rare, as both he and Stanley
worked with the men in the erection of the fort. No
one was idle for a moment, from the time of rising—
shortly after daybreak—to the time of going to rest
at night. Even little Edith found full occupation in
assisting her mother in the performance of a host of

little household duties, too numerous to recapitulate. The dog Chimo was the only exception to the general rule. He hunted the greater part of the forenoon, for his own special benefit, and slept when not thus occupied, or received with philosophical satisfaction the caresses of his young mistress.

The future fort was begun on the centre of the level patch of green-sward at the foot of the flat rock by the spring, where the party had originally encamped. A square was traced on the ground to indicate the stockade; and within this, Stanley marked off an oblong patch, close to the back stockade, for the principal dwelling-house, facing the river. Two other spaces were on either side of this—one for a store, the other for a dwelling for the men. When finished, the fort would thus have the form of three sides of a square surrounded by a stockade. In the centre of this, and the first thing that was erected, was a flag-staff, on which the H.B.C.—Hudson's Bay Company—flag was hoisted, and saluted with three cheers as its crimson folds fluttered out in the breeze for the first time. The plan on which the houses were constructed was that on which all the dwellings of the fur-traders are built—namely, a framework of timber, the interstices of which are filled up with logs sliding into grooves cut in the main posts and beams. This manner of building is so simple that a house can be erected without any other instruments than an axe, an auger, and a large chisel; and the speed with which it is put up would surprise those whose notions of house-building are limited to stone edifices.

The axes of the wood-cutters resounded among the gullies and ravines of Ungava, and awakened the numerous echoes of the mountains. The encampment no longer presented a green spot, watered by a tiny rill, but was strewn with logs in all stages of formation, and chips innumerable. The frameworks of the dwelling-houses began to rise from the earth, presenting, in their unfinished condition, a bristling, uncomfortable appearance, suggesting thoughts in the beholder's mind highly disparaging to art, and deeply sympathetic with outraged nature. The tents still stood, and the campfire burned, but the superior proportions of the rising fort threw these entirely into the shade. A rude wharf of unbarked logs ran from the beach into the river. It had been begun and finished in a couple of days, for the convenience of Gaspard while visiting his nets, as he sometimes did before the water left them. Everything, in short, bore evidence of the most bustling activity and persevering energy; and in a few weeks from the time of their first landing, the dwelling-houses were sufficiently weather-tight to be habitable, and the other portions of the establishment in an advanced condition.

The openings between the logs of the houses were caulked with a mixture of mud and moss, and left in that condition in the meantime, until the pit-saw could be set to work to produce boards for the better protection of the walls without and within. The window and door frames were also made, and covered temporarily with parchment, until the arrival of the

ship should enable them to fill the former with glass
and the latter with broad panels.

The effect of the parchment-covered door, however,
was found to be somewhat troublesome. Being large,
and tightly covered, it sounded, when shut violently,
with a noise so strongly resembling the report of
a distant cannon that, during the first day after its
erection, the men more than once rushed down to
the beach in the expectation of seeing the long and
ardently wished-for ship, which was now so much
beyond the time appointed for her arrival that Stanley
began to entertain serious apprehensions for her
safety. This ship was to have sailed from York Fort, the
principal depot of the fur-traders in Hudson's Bay, with
supplies and goods for trade with the Eskimos during
the year. She was expected at Ungava in August, and it
was now September. The frost was beginning, even at
this early period, to remind the expedition of the long
winter that was at hand, and in the course of a very few
weeks Hudson's Straits would be impassable; so that
the anxiety of the traders was natural.

Just before the partitions of the chief dwelling-house
were completed, Stanley went to the tent in which his
wife and child were busily employed in sewing.

"Can you spare Edith for a short time, wife?" said
he, as his partner looked up to welcome him.

"Yes, for a short time; but she is becoming so useful
to me that I cannot afford to spare her long."

"I'm afraid," said Stanley, as he took his child by the
hand and led her away, "that I must begin to put in my
claim to the services of this little baggage, who seems

to be so useful. What say you, Eda; will you allow me to train you to shoot, and fish, and walk on snow-shoes, and so make a trader of you?"

"I would like very much, papa, to learn to walk on snowshoes, but I think the gun would hurt me—it seems to kick so. Don't you think I am too little to shoot a gun off?"

Stanley laughed at the serious way in which the child received the proposal.

"Well, then, we won't teach you to shoot yet, Eda; but, as you say, the snow-shoe walking is worth learning, for if you cannot walk on the long shoes when the snow falls, I fear you'll not be able to leave the fort at all."

"Yes, and Francois has promised to make me a pair," said Edith gaily, "and to teach me how to use them; and mamma says I am old enough to learn now. Is it not kind of Francois? He is always very good to me."

"Indeed it is very kind of him, my pet; but all the men seem to be very good to you—are they not?"

"Oh yes, all of them! Even Gaspard is kind now. He never whips Chimo, and he patted me on the head the other day when I met him alone in the ravine—the berry ravine, you know, where I go to gather berries. I wonder if there are berries in all the other ravines? But I don't care much, for there are thousands and thousands of all kinds in my own ravine, and—where are you going, papa?"

This abrupt question was caused by her father turning into the square of the new fort, in which the most of the men were at work.

"I'm going to show you our house, Eda, and to ask

you to fix on the corner you like best for your own room. The partitions are going to be put up, so we must fix at once."

As he spoke they passed through the open doorway of the new dwelling, which was a long, low building; and, placing his little daughter in the centre of the principal hall, Stanley directed her to look round and choose a corner for herself.

For a few minutes Edith stood with an expression of perplexity on her bright face; then she began to examine the views from each of the corner windows. This could only be done by peeping through the bullet-hole in the parchment skins that in the meantime did duty for glass. The two windows at the back corners looked out upon the rocky platform, behind which the mountains rose like a wall, so they were rejected; but Edith lingered at one of them, for from it she saw the spring at the foot of the rock, with its soft bed of green moss and surrounding willow-bushes. From the front corner on the left hand Cross Island and the valley of the river beyond were visible; but from the window on the right the view embraced the whole sweep of the wide river and the narrow outlet to the bay, which, with its frowning precipices on either side, and its bold flanking mountains, seemed a magnificent portal to the Arctic Sea.

"I think this is the nicest corner," said Edith, turning with a smile to her father.

"Then this shall be yours," said Stanley.

"But," exclaimed Edith, as a sudden thought occurred to her, "perhaps Frank would like this corner.

I would not like to have it if Frank wants it."

"Frank doesn't want it, and Frank shan't have it. There now, run to your mother, you little baggage; she can't get on without you. Off you go, quick!"

With a merry laugh Edith bounded through the doorway, and disappeared like a sunbeam from the room.

On the 25th of September, Stanley was standing on the beach, opposite the fort, watching with a smile of satisfaction the fair, happy face of his daughter, as she amused herself and Chimo by throwing a stick into the water, which the latter dutifully brought out and laid at her feet as often as it was thrown in. Frank was also watching them.

"What shall we call the fort, Frank?" said his companion. "We have a Fort Good Hope, and a Fort Resolution, and a Fort Enterprise already. It seems as if all the vigorous and hearty words in the English language were used up in naming the forts of the Hudson's Bay Company. What shall we call it?"

"Chimo! Chimo! Chimo!" shouted Edith to the dog, as the animal bounded along the beach.

Both gentlemen seemed to be struck with the same idea simultaneously.

"There's an answer to your question," said Frank; "call the fort 'Chimo.'"

"The very thing!" replied Stanley; "I wonder it did not occur to me before. Nothing could be more appropriate. I salute thee, Fort Chimo," and Stanley lifted his cap to the establishment.

In order that the peculiar appropriateness of the name may appear to the reader, it may be as well to explain that Chimo (the i and o of which are sounded long) is an Eskimo word of salutation, and is used by the natives when they meet with strangers. It signifies, "Are you friendly?" by those who speak first, and seems to imply, "We are friendly," when returned as an answer. So well known is the word to the fur-traders who traffic with the natives of Hudson's Straits that they frequently apply it to them as a name, and speak of the Eskimos as Chimos. It was, therefore, a peculiarly appropriate name for a fort which was established on the confines of these icy regions, for the double purpose of entering into friendly traffic with the Eskimos, and of bringing about friendly relations between them and their old enemies, the Muskigon Indians of East Main.

After playing for some time beside the low wharf, Edith and her dog left the beach together, and rambled towards a distant eminence, whence could be obtained a commanding bird's-eye view of the new fort. She had not sat many minutes here when her eye was arrested by the appearance of an unusual object in the distance. Frank, who was yet engaged in conversation with Stanley on the beach, also noticed it. Laying his hand on the arm of his companion, he pointed towards the narrows, where a small, white, triangular object was visible against the dark cliff. As they gazed, a second object of similar form came into view; then a fore and top sail made their appearance; and, in another second, a schooner floated slowly through the opening! Ere the spectators of this silent apparition could give utterance to their joy, a puff

IN ANOTHER SECOND A SCHOONER FLOATED
THROUGH THE OPENING—Page 222

of white smoke sprang from the vessel's bow, and a cannon-shot burst upon the mountains. Leaping on from cliff to crag, it awakened a crash of magnificent echoes, which, after prolonged repetitions, died away in low mutterings like distant thunder. It was followed by a loud cheer from the schooner's deck, and the H.B.C. flag was run up to the main, while the Union Jack floated at the peak.

"Now, Frank, give the word," cried Stanley, taking off his cap, while the men ran down to the beach en masse.

"Hip, hip, hurrah!"

"Hurrah!" echoed the men, and a cheer arose among the cliffs that moved to the very centre the hearts of those who heard and gave it.

Again and again the stirring shout arose from the fort, and was replied to from the schooner. It was no matter of form, or cheer of ceremony. There was a deep richness and a prolonged energy in the tone, which proved that the feelings and lungs of the men were roused to the uttermost in its delivery. It told of long gathering anxieties swept entirely away, and of deep joy at seeing friendly faces in a sterile land, where lurking foes might be more likely to appear.

At all times the entrance of a ship into port is a noble sight, and one which touches the heart and evokes the enthusiasm of almost every human being; but when the ship arriving is almost essential to the existence of those who watch her snowy sails swelling out as they urge her to the land—when her keel is the first that has ever ploughed the waters of their distant bay—and when her departure will lock them up in solitude for a long, long year—such feelings are roused to their utmost pitch of intensity.

Cheer upon cheer rose and fell, and rose again, among the mountains of Ungava. Even Edith's tiny voice helped to swell the enthusiastic shout; and more than one cheer was choked by the rising tide of emotion that forced the tears down more than one bronzed cheek, despite the iron wills that bade them not to flow.

Chapter XIX

BUSTLE AND BUSINESS—A GREAT FEAST, IN
WHICH BRYAN AND LA ROCHE ARE PRIME
MOVERS—NEW IDEAS IN THE ART OF COOKING.

The scene at Fort Chimo was more bustling and active than ever during the week that followed the arrival of the schooner. The captain told Stanley, as they sat sipping a glass of Madeira in the hall of the new fort, that he had been delayed by ice in the straits so long, that the men were afraid of being set fast for the winter, and were almost in a state of mutiny, when they fortunately discovered the mouth of the river. As had been anticipated by Stanley, the ship entered False River by mistake, unseen by Oolibuck, notwithstanding the vigilance of his lookout. Fortunately he observed it as it came out of the river, just at the critical period when the seamen began to threaten to take the law into their own hands if the search were continued any longer. Oolibuck no sooner beheld the object of his hopes than he rushed to the top of a hill, where he made a fire and sent up a column of smoke that had the immediate effect of turning the vessel's head towards him. Soon afterwards a boat was sent ashore, and took the Eskimo on board, who explained, in his broken English, that he had been watching for them for many days, and would be happy to pilot the vessel up to the fort.

"You may be sure," continued the captain, "that I was too happy to give the ship in charge to the fellow, who seemed to understand thoroughly what he was about. He is already quite a favourite with the men, who call him Oily-buss, much to his own amusement; and he has excited their admiration and respect by his shooting, having twice on the way up shot a goose on the wing."

"Not an unusual exhibition of skill among fur-traders," said Stanley; "but I suppose your men are not much used to the gun. And now, captain, when must you start?"

"The moment the cargo is landed, sir," replied the captain, who was distinguished by that thorough self-sufficiency and prompt energy of character which seem peculiar to sea-captains in general. "We may have trouble in getting out of the straits, and, after getting to Quebec, I am bound to carry a cargo of timber to England."

"I will do my best to help you, captain. Your coming has relieved my mind from a load of anxiety, and one good turn deserves another, so I'll make my fellows work night and day till your ship is discharged."

Stanley was true to his word. Not only did the men work almost without intermission, but he and Frank Morton scarce allowed themselves an hour's repose during the time that the work was going on. Night and day "yo heave ho" of the Jack Tars rang over the water; and the party on shore ran to and fro, from the beach to the store, with bales, kegs, barrels, and boxes on their shoulders. There were blankets and guns, and axes and knives, powder and shot, and beads and awls, and nets and twine. There were kettles of every sort and size; cloth of every hue; capotes of all dimensions, and minute etceteras without end: so that, had it been possible to prevail on the spirits of the ice to carry to the Eskimos intelligence of the riches contained in the store at Chimo, an overwhelming flood of visitors would speedily have descended on that establishment. But no such messengers could be found—although Bryan asserted positively that more than "wan o' them" had been seen by him since his arrival; so the traders had nothing for it but to summon patience to their aid and bide their time.

When the work of discharging was completed, and while Stanley and the captain were standing on the beach watching the removal of the last boat-load to the store, the former said to the latter: "Now, captain, I have a favour to request, which is that you and your two mates will dine with me to-morrow. Your men will be the better of a day's rest after such a long spell of hard work. You could not well get away till the evening of to-morrow at any rate, on account of the tide, and it will be safer and more pleasant to start early on the day after."

"I shall be most happy," replied the captain heartily.

"That's right," said Stanley. "Dinner will be ready by four o'clock precisely; and give my compliments to your crew, and say that my men will expect them all to dinner at the same hour."

Ten minutes after this, Stanley entered his private apartment in the fort, which, under the tasteful management of his wife, was beginning to look elegant and comfortable.

"Wife," said he, "I will order La Roche to send you a box of raisins and an unlimited supply of flour, butter, etcetera, wherewith you will be so kind as to make, or cause to be made—on pain of my utmost displeasure in the event of failure—a plum-pudding large enough to fill the largest sized washing-tub, and another of about quarter that size; both to be ready boiled by four to-morrow afternoon."

"Sir, your commands shall be obeyed. I suppose you intend to regale the sailors before they leave. Is it not so?"

"You have guessed rightly for once; and take care that you don't let Eda drown herself in the compost before it is tied up. I must hasten to prepare the men."

Two minutes later and Stanley stood in the midst of his men, who, having finished their day's work, were now busy with supper in their new house, into which they had but recently moved.

"Lads," said Stanley, "you have stuck to your work so hard of late that I think it a pity to allow you to fall into lazy habits again. I expect you all to be up by break of day to-morrow."

"Och! musha!" sighed Bryan, as he laid down his

knife and fork with a look of consternation.

"I have invited the ship's crew," continued Stanley, "to dine with you before they leave us. As the larder is low just now, you'll all have to take to the hills for a fresh supply. Make your arrangements as you please, but see that there is no lack of venison and fish. I'll guarantee the pudding and grog."

So saying, he turned and left the house, followed by a tremendous cheer.

"Oh! parbleu! vat shall I do?" said La Roche, with a look of affected despair. "I am most dead for vant of sleep already. C'est impossible to cook pour everybody demain. I vill be sure to fall 'sleep over de fire, prehaps fall into him."

"Och, Losh, Losh, when will ye larn to think nothin' o' yoursilf? Ye'll only have to cook for the bourgeois; but think o' me! All the min, an' the ship's crew to boot!"

The blacksmith concluded by knocking La Roche's pipe out of his mouth, in the excess of his glee at the prospective feast; after which he begged his pardon solemnly in bad French, and ducked his head to avoid the tin can that was hurled at it by the indignant Frenchman.

At the first streak of dawn the following morning, and long before the sun looked down into the ravines of Ungava, Massan and Dick Prince were seen to issue with noiseless steps from the fort, with their guns on their shoulders, and betake themselves to the mountains. Half an hour later Bryan staggered out of the house, with a bag on his shoulder, scarcely half awake, rubbing his eyes and muttering to himself in a low tone, as he plunged rather than walked into the ravine which led to the first terrace on the mountain.

When the sun rose over the mountain-tops and looked down upon the calm surface of the river, there was not a man remaining in the fort, with the exception of Stanley and Frank, and their active servant La Roche.

A deep calm rested on the whole scene. The sailors of the vessel, having risen to dispatch breakfast, retired to their hammocks again and went to sleep; Stanley, Frank, and their household, were busy within doors; Chimo snored in the sunshine at the front of the fort; and the schooner floated on a sheet of water so placid, that every spar and delicate rope was clearly reflected. Nothing was heard save the soft ripple on the shore, the distant murmur of mountain streams, and, once or twice through the day, the faint reverberation of a fowling-piece.

But as the day advanced, evidences of the approaching feast began to be apparent. Early in the forenoon Massan and Prince returned with heavy loads of venison on their shoulders, and an hour later Bryan staggered into the fort bending under the weight of a well-filled bag of fish. He had been at his favourite fishing quarters in the dark valley, and was dripping wet from head to foot, having fallen, as usual, into the water. Bryan had a happy facility in falling into the water that was quite unaccountable— and rather enviable in warm weather. As the cooking operations were conducted on an extensive scale, a fire was kindled in the open air in the rear of the men's house; round which fire, in the course of the forenoon, Bryan and La Roche performed feats of agility so extravagant, and apparently so superhuman, that they seemed to involve an element of wickedness from their very intensity. Of course no large dinner ever passed through the ordeal of being cooked without some accidents or misfortunes, more or less. Even in civilised life, where the most intricate appliances are brought to bear on the operation by artistes thoroughly acquainted with their profession, infallibility is not found. It would be unjust, therefore, to expect that two backwoodsmen should be perfectly successful, especially when it is remembered that their branch of the noble science was what might be technically termed plain cookery, the present being their first attempt in the higher branches.

Their first difficulty arose from the larger of the two plum-puddings, which La Roche had compounded under the directions of Mrs. Stanley and the superintendence of Edith.

"I say, Losh," cried Bryan to his companion, whose head was at the moment hid from view in a cloud of steam that ascended from a large pot over which he bent, apparently muttering incantations.

"Vell, fat you want?"

"Faix, and it's just fat that I don't want," said Bryan, pointing, as he spoke, to the large pudding, which, being much too large for the kettle, was standing on the rim thereof like the white ball of foam that caps a tankard of double X. "It's more nor twice too fat already. The kittle won't hould it, no how."

"Oh, stuff him down, dat is de way," suggested La Roche.

"Stuff it down, avic, an' what's to come o' the wather?" said Bryan.

"Ah! true, dat is perplexible, vraiment."

At this moment the large pot boiled over and a cloud of scalding steam engulfed the sympathetic Frenchman, causing him to yell with mingled pain and rage as he bounded backwards.

"Musha! but ye'll come to an early death, Losh, if ye don't be more careful o' yer dried-up body."

"Taisez vous, donc," muttered his companion, half angrily.

"Taisin' ye? avic, sorra wan o' me's taisin' ye. But since ye can't help me out o' me throubles, I'll try to help mysilf."

In pursuance of this noble resolve, Bryan went to the store and fetched from thence another large tin kettle. He then undid the covering of the unwieldy pudding, which he cut into two equal parts, and having squeezed them into two balls, tied them up in the cloth, which he divided for the purpose, and put them into the separate kettles, with the air of a man who had overcome a great difficulty by dint of unfathomable wisdom. It was found, however, that the smaller pudding, intended for Stanley's table, was also too large for its kettle; but the energetic blacksmith, whose genius was now thoroughly aroused, overcame this difficulty by cutting off several pounds of it, and transferring the pudding thus reduced to the kettle, saying in an undertone as he did so, "There's more nor enough for the six o' ye yit, av yer only raisonable in yer appetites."

But the superfluity of the pudding thus caused became now a new source of trouble to Bryan.

"What's to be done wid it, Losh? I don't like to give it to the dogs, an' it's too small intirely to make a dumplin' of."

"You better heat him raw," suggested La Roche.

"Faix, an' I've half a mind to; but it would spile my dinner. Hallo! look out for the vainison, Losh."

"Ah, oui; oh! misere!" cried La Roche, springing over the fire, and giving a turn to the splendid haunch of venison which depended from a wooden tripod in front of the blaze, and, having been neglected for a few minutes, was beginning to singe.

"What have ye in the pot there?" inquired Bryan.

"Von goose, two duck, trois plovre, et von leetle bird—I not know de name of—put him in pour experiment."

"Very good, Losh; out wid the goose and we'll cram the bit o' dumplin' into him for stuffin'."

"Ah! superb, excellent," cried La Roche, laughing, as he lifted out the goose, into which Bryan thrust the mass of superfluous pudding; after which the hole was tied up and the bird re-consigned to the pot.

Everything connected with this dinner was strikingly suggestive of the circumstances under which it was given. The superabundance of venison and wild-fowl; the cooking done in the open air; the absence of women, and the performance of work usually allotted to them by bronzed and stalwart voyageurs; the wild scenery in the midst of which it took place; and the mixture of Irish, English, French, Indian, Eskimo, and compound tones, that fell upon the ear as the busy work went on,—all tended to fill the mind with a feeling of wild romance, and to suggest powerfully the idea of being, if we may so express it, far, far away! As the proceedings advanced towards completion, this feeling was rather increased than removed.

Tables and chairs were a luxury that still remained to be introduced at Fort Chimo, when the men found leisure from more urgent duties to construct them. Therefore the dining-table in Stanley's hall was composed of three large packing-cases turned bottom up. There was no cloth wherewith to cover its rough boards; but this was a matter of little importance to the company which assembled round it, punctually at the hour of four. In place of chairs there were good substantial nail-kegs, rather low, it is true, and uncommonly hard, but not to be despised under the circumstances. Owing to the unusual demand for dishes, the pewter plates and spoons and tin drinking-cups—for they had little crockery—were of every form and size that the store contained; and the floor on which it all stood was the beaten ground, for the intended plank flooring was still growing in the mountain glens.

But if the equipage was homely and rude, the fare was choice and abundant; and an odour that might have gladdened the heart of an epicure greeted the nostrils of the captain and his two mates when they entered the hall, dressed in blue surtouts with bright brass buttons, white duck trousers, and richly flowered vests [waistcoats]. There was a splendid salmon, of twenty pounds weight, at one end of the board; and beside it, on the same dish, a lake-trout of equal size and beauty. At the other end smoked a haunch of venison, covered with at least an inch of fat; and beside it a bowl of excellent cranberry jam, the handiwork of the hostess. A boiled goose and pease-pudding completed the catalogue. Afterwards, these gave place to the pudding which had caused Bryan so much perplexity, and several dishes of raisins and figs. Last, but not least, there was a bottle of brandy and two of port wine; which, along with the raisins and figs, formed part of the limited supply of luxuries furnished by the Hudson's Bay Company to Stanley, in common with all the gentlemen in the service, in order to enable them, now and then, on great occasions, to recall, through the medium of a feast, the remembrance of civilised life.

The display in the men's house was precisely similar to that in the hall. But the table was larger and the viands more abundant. The raisins and figs, too, were wanting; and instead of wine or brandy, there was a small supply of rum. It was necessarily small, being the gift of Stanley out of his own diminutive store, which could not, even if desired, be replenished until the return of the ship next autumn.

On the arrival of the guests a strange contrast was presented. The sailors, in white ducks, blue jackets with brass buttons, striped shirts, pumps, and straw hats, landed at the appointed hour, and in hearty good-humour swaggered towards the men's house, where they were politely received by the quiet, manly-looking voyageurs, who, in honour of the occasion, had put on their best capotes, their brightest belts, their gayest garters, and most highly-ornamented moccasins. The French Canadians and half-breeds bowed, shook hands, and addressed the tars as messieurs. The sailors laughed, slapped their entertainers on the shoulders, and called them messmates. The Indians stood, grave and silent, but with looks of good-humour, in the background; while the Eskimos raised their fat cheeks, totally shut up their eyes, and grinned perpetually, not to say horribly, from ear to ear. But the babel that followed is beyond the powers of description, therefore we won't attempt it.

Here, however, the characteristic peculiarity of our scene ceases. The actual demolition of food is pretty much the same among all nations that are not absolutely savage; and, however much contrast might have been observed in the strange mixture of human beings assembled under the hospitable roof of Fort Chimo, there was none whatever in the manner in which they demolished their viands. As the evening advanced, a message was sent to Monsieur Stanley for the loan of his violin.

"Ay," said he, as the instrument was delivered to Bryan, who happened to be the messenger and also the performer—"ay, I thought it would come to that ere long. Don't be too hard on the strings, lad. 'Twill be a rough ball where there are no women."

"Thrue, yer honour," replied the blacksmith, as he received the instrument, "there's a great want of faymales in thim parts; but the sailors have consinted to ripresint the purty craytures on the present occasion, which is but right, for, ye see, the most o' thim's shorter nor us, an' their wide breeches are more like the pitticoats than our leggin's."

Many were the stories that were told and retold, believed, disbelieved, and doubted, on that memorable night; and loud were the songs and long and strong the dancing that followed. But it was all achieved under the influence of pure animal spirits, for the rum supplied afforded but a thimbleful to each. The consequence was that there were no headaches the following morning, and the men were up by break of day as fresh and light as larks. A feeling of sadness, however, gradually crept over the band as the dawn advanced and the schooner prepared for her departure.

By six o'clock the flood-tide turned, and a few minutes later all the sailors were aboard, hoisting the sails and anchor, while the men stood silently on the beach where they had just parted from their guests.

"Good-bye once more, Mr. Stanley; good-bye, Mr. Morton," said the captain, as he stepped into his boat. "I wish you a pleasant winter and a good trade."

"Thank you, thank you, captain," replied Stanley; "and don't forget us out here, in this lonely place, when you drink the health of absent friends at Christmas time."

In a few minutes the anchor was up, and the schooner, bending round with a fair wind and tide, made for the narrows.

"Give them a cheer, lads," said Frank.

Obedient to the command, the men doffed their caps and raised their voices; but there was little vigour in the cheer. It was replied to from the schooner's deck. Just as the flying-jib passed the point a gun was fired, which once more awakened the loud echoes of the place. When the smoke cleared away, the schooner was gone.

Thus was severed the last link that bound the civilised world to the inhabitants of Fort Chimo.

Chapter XX

WINTER APPROACHES—ESKIMOS ARRIVE—EFFECT OF
A WORD—A SUCKING BABY— PROSPECTS OF TRADE.

For many days after the ship's departure the work of completing the fort went forward with the utmost rapidity, and not until the houses and stores were rendered weather-tight and warm did Stanley consider it advisable to send out hunting and fishing parties into the mountains. Now, however, the frosts continued a great part of the day as well as during the night, so it was high time to kill deer and fish, in order to freeze, and so preserve them for winter's consumption.

Up to this time no further traces of Eskimos had been discovered, and Stanley began to express his fears to Frank that they had left the neighbourhood altogether, in consequence of the repeated attacks made upon them by Indians. Soon after this, however, the fur-traders were surprised by a sudden visit from a party of these denizens of the north.

It happened on the afternoon of a beautiful day towards the close of autumn, that charming but brief season which, in consequence of its unbroken serenity, has been styled the Indian summer. The men had all been dispatched into the mountains in various directions, some to fish, others to shoot; and none were left at the fort except its commandant with his wife and child, and Oolibuck the Eskimo. Stanley was seated on a stone at the margin of the bay, admiring the vivid alterations of light and shade, as the sun dipped behind the mountains of the opposite shore, when his eye was attracted towards one or two objects on the water near the narrows. Presently they advanced, and were followed by several others. In a few minutes he perceived that they were Eskimo canoes.

Jumping hastily up, Stanley ran to the fort, and bidding his wife and child keep out of sight, put two pair of pistols in his pockets and returned to the beach, where he found Oolibuck gazing at the approaching flotilla with intense eagerness.

"Well, Oolibuck, here come your countrymen at last," said Stanley. "Do they look friendly, think you?"

"Me no can tell; they most too quiet," replied the interpreter.

Eskimos in general are extremely noisy and full of animated gesticulation on meeting with strangers, especially when they meet on decidedly friendly terms. The silence, therefore, maintained by the natives as they advanced was looked upon as a bad sign. The fleet consisted of nine kayaks, and three large oomiaks full of women and children; and a curious appearance they presented at a distance, for the low kayaks of the men being almost invisible, it seemed as if their occupants were actually seated on the water. The oomiaks being much higher, were clearly visible. On coming to within a quarter of a mile of the fort, the men halted to allow the women to come up; then forming in a crescent in front of the oomiaks, the whole flotilla advanced slowly towards the beach. When within a hundred yards or so, Stanley said, "Now, Oolibuck, give them a hail."

"Chimo! Chimo! Chimo-o-o!" shouted the interpreter.

The word acted like a talisman.

"Chimo!" yelled the Eskimos in reply, and the kayaks shot like arrows upon the sand, while the women followed as fast as they could. In another minute a loud chattering and a brisk shaking of hands was taking place on shore.

The natives were dressed in the sealskin garments with which arctic travellers have made us all more or less acquainted. They were stout burly fellows, with fat, oily, and bearded faces.

"Now tell them, Oolibuck, the reason of our coming here," said Stanley.

Oolibuck instantly began, by explaining to them that they had come for the purpose of bringing about peace and friendship between them and the Indians; on hearing which the Eskimos danced and shouted for nearly a minute with joy. But when the interpreter went on to say that they intended to remain altogether among them, for the purpose of trading, their delight knew no bounds; they danced and jumped, and whooped and yelled, tossed up their arms and legs, and lay down on the sand and rolled in ecstasy. In the midst of all this, Mrs. Stanley rushed out of the house, followed by Edith, in great terror at the unearthly sounds that had reached her ears; but on seeing her husband and Oolibuck laughing in the midst of the grotesque group, her fears vanished, and she stood an amused spectator of the scene.

Meanwhile, Stanley went down and stepped into the midst of one of the oomiaks, with a few beads and trinkets in his hands; and while Oolibuck entertained the men on shore, he presented gifts to the women, who received them with the most childish demonstrations of joy. There was something irresistibly comic in the childlike simplicity of these poor natives. Instead of the stiff reserve and haughty demeanour of their Indian neighbours, they danced and sang, and leaped and roared, embraced each other and wept, with the most reckless indifference to appearances, and seemed upon all occasions to give instant vent to the feelings that happened to be uppermost in their minds. As Stanley continued to distribute his gifts, the women crowded out of the other oomiaks into the one in which he stood, until they nearly sank it; some of them extending their arms for beads, others giving a jolt to the hoods on their backs, which had the effect of bringing to light fat, greasy-faced little babies, who were pointed to as being peculiarly worthy of attention.

At length Stanley broke from them and leaped ashore, where he was soon followed by the entire band. But here new objects—namely, Mrs. Stanley and Edith—attracted their wondering attention. Approaching towards the former, they began timidly to examine her dress, which was indeed very different from theirs, and calculated to awaken curiosity and surprise. The Eskimo women were dressed very much like the men—namely, in long shirts of sealskin or deerskin with the hair on, short breeches of the same material, and long sealskin boots. The hoods of the women were larger than those of the men, and their boots much more capacious; and while the latter had a short stump of a tail or peak hanging from the hinder part of their shirts, the women wore their tails so long that they trailed along the ground as they walked. In some cases these tails were four and six inches broad, with a round flap at the end, and fringed with ermine. It was, therefore, with no little surprise that they found Mrs. Stanley entirely destitute of a tail, and observed that she wore her upper garment so long that it reached the ground. Becoming gradually more familiar, on seeing that the strange woman permitted them to handle her pretty freely, one of them gently lifted up her gown to see whether or not she wore boots; but receiving a somewhat prompt repulse, she began to caress her, and assured her that she did not mean to give offence.

By this time Frank and some of the men had joined the group on the shore, and as it was getting late Stanley commanded silence.

"Tell them I have somewhat to say to them, Oolibuck."

The interpreter's remark instantly produced

a dead silence.

"Now ask them if they are glad to hear that we are going to stay to trade with them."

A vociferous jabbering followed the question, which, by Oolibuck's interpretation, meant that their joy was utterly inexpressible.

"Have they been long on the coast?"

"No; they had just arrived, and were on their way up the river to obtain wood for building their kayaks."

"Did they see the bundle of presents we left for them at the coast?"

"Yes, they had seen it; but not knowing whom it was intended for, they had not touched it."

On being told that the presents were intended for them, the poor creatures put on a look of intense chagrin, which, however, passed away when it was suggested to them that they might take the gifts on their return to the coast.

"And now," said Stanley, in conclusion, "'tis getting late. Go down to the point below the fort and encamp there for the night. We thank you for your visit, and will return it in the morning. Good-night."

On this being translated, the Eskimos gave a general yell of assent and immediately retired, bounding and shouting and leaping as they went, looking, in their gleesome rotundity, like the infant progeny of a race of giants.

"I like the look of these men very much," said Stanley, as he walked up to the house with Frank. "Their genuine trustfulness is a fine trait in their character."

"No doubt of it," replied Frank. "There is much truth

in the proverb, 'Evil dreaders are evil doers.' Those who fear no evil intend none. Had they been Indians, now, we should have had more trouble with them."

"I doubt it not, Frank. You would have been pleased to witness the prompt alacrity with which the poor creatures answered to our cry of Chimo, and ran their kayaks fearlessly ashore, although, for all they knew to the contrary, the rocks might have concealed a hundred enemies."

"And yet," said Frank, with an air of perplexity, "the Eskimo character seems to me a difficult problem to solve. When we read the works of arctic voyagers, we find that one man's experience of the Eskimos proves them to be inveterate thieves and liars, while another speaks of them as an honest, truthful people—and that, too, being said of the same tribe. Nay, further, I have read of a tribe being all that is good and amiable at one time, and all that is bad and vile at another. Now the conduct of these good-natured fellows, in reference to the bundle of trinkets we left at the mouth of the river, indicates a degree of honesty that is almost too sensitive; for the merest exertion of common-sense would show that a bundle hung up in an exposed place to public view must be for the public good."

"Nevertheless they seem both honest and friendly," returned Stanley, "and I trust that our experience of them may never change. To-morrow I shall give them some good advice in regard to procuring furs, and show them the wealth of our trading store."

When the morrow came the visit of the Eskimos

was returned by the entire force of Fort Chimo, and the childish delight with which they were received was most amusing. The childishness, however, was only applicable to these natives when expressing their strong feelings. In other respects, particularly in their physical actions, they were most manly; and the thick black beards and moustaches that clothed the chins of most of the men seemed very much the reverse of infantine. The children were so exactly like to their parents in costume that they seemed miniature representations of them. In fact, were a child viewed through a magnifying glass it would become a man, and were a man viewed through a diminishing glass he would become a child—always, of course, excepting the beard.

Bryan became a special favourite with the natives when it was discovered that he was a worker in iron, and the presents with which he was overwhelmed were of a most extraordinary, and, in some cases, perplexing nature. One man, who seemed determined to get into his good graces, offered him a choice morsel of broiled seal. "No, thankee, lad," said Bryan; "I've had my brickfust."

Supposing that the broiling had something to do with the blacksmith's objection, the Eskimo hastily cut off a slice of the raw blubber and tendered it to him.

"D'ye think I'm a haythen?" said Bryan, turning away in disgust.

"Ah, try it, Bryan," cried La Roche, turning from an Eskimo baby, in the contemplation of which he had been absorbed—"try it; 'tis ver' goot, I 'sure you. Ver' goot for your complaint, Bryan. But come, here, vitement.—Just regardez dat hinfant. Come here, queek!"

Thus urged, Bryan broke away from his host (who had just split open the shinbone of a deer, and offered him the raw marrow, but without success), and, going towards La Roche, regarded the baby in question. It was a remarkably fine child, seemingly about ten months old, with a round, rosy, oily face, coal-black hair, and large, round, coal-black eyes, with which it returned the stare of the two men with interest. But that which amused the visitors most was a lump of fat or blubber, with a skewer thrust through it, which its mother had given to the child to suck, and which it was endeavouring to thrust down its throat with both hands.

"Come here, Oolibuck; pourquoi is de stick?"

"Ho, ho, ho!" laughed Oolibuck. "Dat is for keep de chile quiet; and de stick is for no let him choke; him no can swallow de stick."

"Musha! but it would stick av he did swallow it," said Bryan, turning away with a laugh.

In the course of the day Stanley and Frank conducted the natives to the fort, and having given them all an excellent dinner and a few gifts of needles, scissors, and knives, led them to the store, where the goods for trade were ranged temptingly on shelves round the walls. A counter encompassed a space around the entrance-door, within which the natives stood and gazed on wealth which, to their unsophisticated minds, seemed a dream of enchantment.

Having given them time to imbibe a conception of the room and its treasures, Stanley addressed them through the interpreter; but as reference to this worthy individual is somewhat hampering, we will discard him forthwith—retaining his style and language, however, for the benefit of his fellow-countrymen.

"Now, you see what useful things I have got here for you; but I cannot give them to you for nothing. They cost us much, and give us much trouble to bring them here. But I will give them for skins and furs and oil, and the tusks of the walrus; and when you go to your friends on the sea-coast, you can tell them to bring skins with them when they come."

"Ye vill do vat you vish. Ye most happy you come. Ye vill hunt very mush, and make your house empty of all dese t'ings if ye can."

"That's well. And now I am in need of boots for my men, and you have a good many, I see; so, if you can spare some of these, we will begin to trade at once."

On hearing this, the natives dispatched several of their number down to the camp, who soon returned laden with boots. These boots are most useful articles. They are neatly made of sealskin, the feet or soles being of walrus hide, and perfectly waterproof. They are invaluable to those who have to walk much in ice-cold water or among moist snow, as is the case in those regions during spring and autumn. In winter the frost completely does away with all moisture, so that the Indian moccasin is better at that season than the Eskimo boot

For these boots, and a few articles of native clothing, Stanley paid the natives at the rates of the regular tariff throughout the country; and this rate was so much beyond the poor Eskimo estimate of the relative value of boots and goods, that they would gladly have given all the boots and coats they possessed for what they received as the value of one pair.

Overjoyed at their good fortune, and laden with treasure, they returned to their camp to feast, and to sing the praises of the Kublunat, as they termed the fur-traders.

Chapter XXI

SILENT CONVERSATION—RAW FOOD—FEMALE
TAILS—A TERRIBLE BATTLE TERMINATED
BY THE INTERPOSITION OF A GIANT.

Of all the people at Fort Chimo no one was more interested in the Eskimos than little Edith. She not only went fearlessly among them, and bestowed upon them every trinket she possessed, but, in her childlike desire for the companionship and sympathy of human beings of her own age and sex, she took forcible possession of two little girls who happened to be cleaner, and, therefore, prettier than the others, and led them away to her own ravine, where she introduced them to her favourite berries and to her dog Chimo. At first the dog did not seem to relish the intrusion of these new favourites, but seeing that they did not induce his mistress to caress him less than before, he considerately tolerated them. Besides, the

Eskimos had brought their dogs along with them; and Chimo, being of an amicable disposition, had entered into social fellowship with his own kind. We have said that Chimo was sagacious, and it is quite possible he may have felt the propriety of granting to Edith that liberty which he undoubtedly claimed for himself.

But Edith's intercourse with her little Eskimo protegees was necessarily confined to looks—the language of the eye making up for the absence of that of the tongue. There were many things, however, in which language was not required as a medium of communication between the children. When the berries were good, the brightening eyes and smacking lips spoke a language common to all the human race. So, also, when the berries were sour or bitter, the expression of their faces was peculiarly emphatic. The joyous shout, too, as they discovered a new scene that pleased their eyes, while they roved hand in hand through the ravines, or the shrinking glance of fear as they found themselves unexpectedly on the edge of a precipice, was sufficiently intelligible to the trio. The little friends presented a striking and grotesque contrast. It would have been difficult to say whether the little Eskimos were boys or girls. If anything, the costume seemed more to indicate the former than the latter. Like their mothers, they wore loose deerskin shirts with the hair on the outside, which gave them a round, soft, burly appearance—an appearance which was increased by their little boots, which were outrageously wide, and quite as long as their legs. The frocks or shirts had hoods and tails, which latter, according to fashion, were so long that they trailed on the ground. The inconvenience of the tail is so great that the women, while travelling on a journey, get rid of it by drawing it between their legs, and, lifting up the end, fastening it in front to a button sewed to their frock for the purpose. In travelling, therefore, Eskimo women seem to be destitute of this appendage; but, on arriving at camp, they undo the fastening, and walk about with flowing tails behind them!

Edith's costume consisted of a short frock made of dark blue cloth, and a head-dress peculiar to the Indian women among the Crees. It was preferred by the little wearer to all other styles of bonnet, on account of the ease with which it could be thrown off and on. She also wore ornamented leggings and moccasins. Altogether, with her graceful figure, flaxen curls, and picturesque costume, she presented a strong contrast to the fat, dark, hairy little creatures who followed her by brook and bush and precipice the livelong day.

One morning, about two weeks after the arrival of the Eskimos, Edith went down to the camp after breakfast, and found her two companions engaged in concluding their morning meal. The elder, whose name was Arnalooa, was peering with earnest scrutiny into the depths of a marrowbone, from which she had already extracted a large proportion of the raw material. The younger, Okatook, seized a lump of raw seal's flesh, as Edith entered their hut, and, cutting therefrom a savoury morsel, put it into her mouth as she rose to welcome her visitor.

"Oh! how can you?" said Edith, with a look of disgust

at this ravenous conduct on the part of her friend. But Edith had said, "Oh! how can you?" and "Oh! shocking!" and "Oh! why don't you give up eating it raw?" and "Oh! why won't you have it cooked?" nearly every day for the last two weeks, without producing any other effect than a gleeful laugh from the little Eskimos; for, although they did not comprehend her words, they clearly understood her looks of disapproval. But although they would not give up the habit of eating raw flesh, which they had been accustomed to from their infancy, they were prevailed on so far to break through the habits of their people as to wash their hands and faces before going out to play. This they did because Edith positively refused to go with them unless they did so.

Lifting up the end of her tail and wiping her mouth therewith, Arnalooa smiled at Edith's look of reproach, and ran laughing towards the shore, where she and Okatook washed their hands, after which they followed Edith and Chimo to their favourite ravine. Although she knew that they did not understand a word of what she said, Edith invariably kept up a running fire of small talk, in reference chiefly to the objects of nature by which they were surrounded. To this the little hairy creatures listened intently with smiling faces, and sometimes they laughed prodigiously, as though they understood what was said, so that their companion felt as if she were really conversing with them, although she was sadly perplexed at the utter impossibility of obtaining an intelligible reply to a question when she chanced to put one.

"Oh, what a lovely glen!" cried Edith, her eyes

beaming with delight, as, on turning the point of a projecting crag, she and her companions found themselves in a spot which they had not before seen during their rambles. It was a wild, savage gorge, full of fallen rocks, hemmed in with high cliffs, fringed here and there with willows and mosses, among which were a few brilliant wild-flowers. The lights and shadows of the spot were thrown into powerful contrast by a gleam of sunshine which flashed down among the rugged masses, lighting up peaks and sharp edges in some spots, while in others they were thrown into the profoundest gloom.

"Oh! is it not a delightful place?" cried Edith, as she bounded up the rugged path, followed by Chimo, while the two Eskimo girls buttoned up their tails, and followed her as fast as their more cumbrous habiliments would permit.

For a quarter of an hour the party toiled up the steep ascent, pausing now and then to pluck a flower, or to look back on the wild path by which they had come, until they reached a ridge of rock, beyond which lay a small lake or pool. So dark and still did it lie within the shadow of the overhanging cliffs that it resembled a pool of ink. Here the adventurous explorers sat down to recover breath, and to gaze in childish delight, not unmixed with awe, at the wild scene around them.

The peculiar wildness of the spot seemed to exercise an unusual influence over the dog; for, instead of lying down, as it was wont to do, at the feet of its young mistress, it moved about uneasily, and once or twice uttered a low growl.

"Come here, Chimo," said Edith, when these

symptoms of restlessness had attracted her attention; "what is the matter with you, my dear dog? Surely you are not frightened at the appearance of this wild place! Speak, dog; see, Arnalooa is laughing at you."

Edith might have said with more propriety that Arnalooa was laughing at herself, for the little Eskimo was much amused at the serious manner in which her Kublunat friend spoke to her dog. But Chimo refused to be comforted. He raised his snout, snuffed the air once or twice, and then, descending the gorge a short distance, put his nose close to the ground and trotted away.

"That is very odd of Chimo," said Edith, looking into Arnalooa's face with an expression of perplexity.

As she spoke Okatook pointed, with an eager glance, up the ravine. Turning her eyes hastily in the direction indicated, Edith beheld a deer bounding towards them. It was closely followed by a savage wolf. The deer seemed to be in the last stage of exhaustion. Its flanks were wet with moisture, its eyes starting from their sockets, and its breath issued forth in deep sobs, as it bounded onwards, seemingly more by the force of its impetus than by any voluntary exertion. More intent on the danger behind than on that which lay before it, the deer made straight for the pass in which the three girls stood, and scarcely had they time to spring to the sides of the cliff, when it swept by like an arrow. Instantly after, and ere it had taken two bounds past them, the wolf sprang forward; caught it by the throat, and dragged it to the ground, where in a few seconds it worried the noble animal to death. It is probable that the chase now terminated had begun at early dawn that day, for deer being fleeter than wolves they prolong the chase until overcome by the superior strength and dogged perseverance of their ravenous enemies. Over mountain and hill they had bounded along together, through glen and gorge, across river and lake, bursting headlong through bush and brake, or under the shadow of frowning cliffs, and toiling, at a foot pace and with panting sides, up the steep hills, in the fierce blaze of the sun, the one impelled by hunger, the other by fear, until at length the scene closed in the wild pass, almost at the feet of the three children.

But retribution was in store for the savage destroyer. Ere yet the life's blood had teased to flow from the throat of the dying deer, and while the wolf's fangs were still dripping with its gore, a fierce bark, followed by a terrific growl, rang among the cliffs, and Chimo, with his ears laid back and his formidable row of teeth exposed, rushed up the gorge and seized the wolf by the neck! Thus assailed, the wolf returned the bite with interest, and immediately a fight of the most energetic character ensued.

The wolf was much larger and more powerful than Chimo, but was greatly exhausted by its long chase, while the dog was fresh and vigorous. Once or twice Chimo tossed his huge adversary by main strength, but as often he was overturned and dreadfully shaken, while the long fangs of the wolf met in his neck, and mingled the blood of the deer, which bespattered his black muzzle, with the life's blood that began to flow copiously from Chimo's veins. At this moment a shout was heard farther up the ravine. The three girls turned hastily, and saw, on a point of rock which projected from the mountain side and overhung the dark pool, the figure of a man, of such immense proportions that they instinctively shrank back with terror. The position in which he stood made him appear larger than he really was. The scattered gleams and slant rays of sunshine that played around the spot invested him as with a supernatural halo, while a bright glow of light on the cliff behind detached him prominently from the surrounding shadows. He poised a spear in his right hand, and, while Edith gazed at him in terror, the weapon flew whistling through the air and was buried in the side of the wolf. But so close did the spear pass, that Edith involuntarily stepped back as she heard it whiz. In doing so she lost her balance and fell over the cliff. Fortunately, Arnalooa caught her by the dress and partially broke her fall, but the descent was sufficiently steep and rugged to render the child insensible.

When Edith recovered consciousness, her first emotion was that of terror, on beholding a large, dark-bearded face bending over her; but a second glance showed her that the eyes of the stranger gazed upon her with a look of tenderness, and that Arnalooa and Okatook were kneeling beside her with an expression of anxiety. Had anything further been wanting to allay her fears, the sight of Chimo would have done it. It is true the sturdy dog panted heavily, and occasionally licked his wounds, as he sat on his haunches at her feet; but he was wonderfully calm and collected after his recent mortal conflict, and regarded his young mistress from time to time with an air of patronising assurance.

As Edith opened her eyes, the stranger muttered some unintelligible words, and, rising hastily, went to a neighbouring spring, at which he filled a rude cup with water. In doing this, he revealed the huge proportions of the gigantic Eskimo whom we introduced to our reader in a former chapter. He was dressed in the same manner as when we first saw him, but his face was somewhat altered, and his black eyebrows were marked by that peculiar curve which is expressive of deep melancholy. Returning quickly from the spring, he kneeled beside the little girl, and, raising her head on his broad hand, held the goblet to her lips.

"Thank you," said Edith faintly, as she swallowed a few drops; "I think I had better go home. Is Chimo safe? Chimo!" She started up as the recollection of the fight with the wolf flashed upon her; but the fall had stunned her rather severely, and scarcely had she risen to her feet when she staggered and fell back into the arms of the Eskimo.

Seeing that she was quite unable to walk, he raised her in his powerful arm as if she had been a young lamb. Catching the dead wolf by the neck as he passed, and springing from rock to rock with catlike agility, he bore his burden down the ravine, and strode towards the fort under the guidance of Okatook and Arnalooa.

Chapter XXII

MAXIMUS—DEER SPEARING—A SURPRISINGLY
BAD SHOT—CHARACTER OF THE NATIVES.

"Hallo! What have we here?" exclaimed Stanley, starting from his seat in amazement, as the giant entered the hall of Fort Chimo—his left hand grasping a blood-stained wolf by the throat, and Edith resting in his right arm.

At first the startled father imagined his child must have been wounded, if not killed, by the savage animal; but his mind was immediately relieved on this point by Edith herself, who was no sooner laid on her bed than she recovered sufficiently to narrate the circumstances attending her fall.

"Well, Maximus," said Stanley, returning to the hall and applying to the bulky savage the term that seemed most appropriate to him, "shake hands with me, my good fellow. You've saved Chimo's life, it seems; and

that's a good turn I'll not forget. But a—. I see you
don't understand a word I say. Hallo! Moses, Moses!
you deaf rascal, come here!" he shouted, as that worthy
passed the window.

"Yis, mossue," said Moses, entering the hall. "Oh,
me, what a walrus am dis! Me do b'lieve him most high
as a tree an' more broader nor iveryt'ing!"

"Hold thy tongue, Moses, and ask the fellow where
he came from; but tell him first that I'm obliged to
him for saving Chimo from that villainous wolf."

While Moses interpreted, Arnalooa and Okatook,
being privileged members of the tribe, crossed over to
Edith's room.

"Well, what says he?" inquired Stanley, at the end of a
long address which the giant had delivered to Moses.

"Him say he heered we have come to trade, from
Eskeemo to west'ard, and so him come for to see us."

"A most excellent reason," said Stanley. "Has he
brought any furs?"

"Yis; him brought one two fox, and two t'ree deer.
No have much furs in dis country, him say."

"Sorry to hear that. Perhaps his opinion may change
when he sees the inside of our store. But I would like him
to stay about the fort as a hunter, Moses; he seems a first-
rate man. Ask him if he will consent to stay for a time."

"P'raps he fuss-rate, p'raps not," muttered Moses in
a disparaging tone, as he turned to put the question.

"Him say yis."

"Very good; then take him to your house, Moses, and
give him some food and a pipe, and teach him English as
fast as you can, and see that it is grammatical. D'ye hear?"

"Yis, mossue, me quite sure for to teach him dat."

As Moses turned to quit the hall, Stanley called him back. "Ask Maximus, by-the-bye, if he knows anything of a party of Eskimos who seem to have been attacked, not long ago, by Indians in this neighbourhood."

No sooner was this question put than the face of Maximus, which had worn a placid, smiling expression during the foregoing conversation, totally changed. His brows lowered, and his lips were tightly compressed, as he regarded Stanley for a few moments ere he ventured to reply. Then, in a deep, earnest tone, he related the attack, the slaughter of his people, their subsequent escape, and the loss of his bride. Even Moses was agitated as he went on, and showed his teeth like an enraged mastiff when the Eskimo came to speak of his irreparable loss.

"Stay one moment," said Stanley, when Maximus concluded. "I have something to show you;" and hastening into his room, he quickly returned with the little piece of sealskin that had been found at the deserted Indian camp. "Do you know anything of this, Maximus? Do you understand these marks?"

The Eskimo uttered a cry of surprise when his eye fell on the piece of skin, and he seemed much agitated while he put several quick, earnest questions to Moses, who replied as earnestly and quickly; then turning rapidly on his heel, he sprang through the doorway, and was soon lost to view in the stunted woods of the ravine above the fort.

"That fellow seems in a hurry," exclaimed Frank Morton, entering the room just as the savage made his exit. "Who is he, and wherefore in so great haste?"

"As to who he is," answered Stanley, "I'll tell you that after Moses has explained the cause of his sudden flight."

"He say that him's wife make dat skin, and de arrow on him skin show dat de Injuns take her to deir tents."

"But did you not tell him that we found the skin long ago, and that the Indians must be far, far away by this time—nobody knows where?" demanded Frank.

"Yis, me tell him. But he go for to see de spot. T'ink him find more t'ings, p'raps."

"Oh, messieurs, voila!" shouted La Roche, pointing towards the river, as he rushed, breathless with haste, into the hall; "les Eskimos, dem kill all de deer dans le kontry. Oui, voila! dans les kayak. Two dozen at vonce—vraiment!" Without waiting a reply, the excited Frenchman turned round and rushed out of the house, followed by Stanley and Frank, who seized their guns, which always hung ready loaded on the walls of the apartment.

On reaching the water's edge, the scene that met their eye was indeed sufficient to account for the excitement of La Roche. A herd of perhaps fifty or sixty deer, on their way to the coast, and ignorant of the foes who had so recently invaded their solitudes, had descended the ravine opposite the fort, with the intention of crossing the river. The Eskimos had perceived this, and keeping themselves and their kayaks concealed until most of the animals were in the water, and the leaders of the herd more than two-thirds over, they then gave chase, and getting between the deer and the opposite shore, cut off their retreat, and drove them towards their encampment.

Here the slaughter commenced, and Stanley and Frank arrived at the scene of action while they were in the midst of the wholesale destruction. In all directions the kayaks, with their solitary occupants, were darting about hither and thither like arrows in the midst of the affrighted animals; none of which, however, were speared until they were driven quite close to the shore. In their terror, the deer endeavoured to escape by swimming in different directions; but the long double-bladed paddles of the Eskimos sent the light kayaks after them like lightning, and a sharp prick on their flanks turned them in the right direction. There were so many deer, however, that a few succeeded in gaining the land; but here the guns of the traders awaited them. In the midst of this wild scene, Frank's attention was arrested by the cool proceedings of an Eskimo, whose name was Chacooto. He had several times exhibited a degree of shrewdness beyond his fellows during his residence near the fort, and was evidently a man of importance in the tribe. Chacooto had collected together a band of the herd, amounting to fifteen, and, by dint of cool decision and quick movements, had driven them to within a few yards of the shore, exactly opposite the spot whereon his tent stood. One young buck, of about two years old, darted away from the rest more than once, but, with a sweep of the paddle and a prick of the lance, Chacooto turned it back again, while a quiet sarcastic smile played on his countenance. Having driven the herd close enough in for his purpose, the Eskimo ended the career of the refractory buck with a single thrust of his lance, and then proceeded coolly to stab them all one after another.

"Och, the spalpeen!" said a voice at Frank's ear. "'Tis himsilf knows how to do it, an' no mistake. Musha! His lance goes out and in like a thailor's needle; an' he niver strikes more nor wance, the haythen!"

"He certainly does know how to do it, Bryan," replied Frank; "and it's a comfort to know that every thrust kills in a moment. I like to see as little of the appearance of cruelty as possible in work of this kind."

"Arrah! there's wan that'll chate 'im, anyhow," cried Bryan, throwing forward his gun in nervous haste, as one of the deer gained the land, despite Chacooto's rapidity, and bounded towards the hills.

Frank smiled at the eager haste of his companion, who was one of the poor shots of the party, and, consequently, always in a hurry. "Now, Bryan, there's a chance. Take your time. Just behind the shoulder; a little low, for that gun kicks horribly."

"Murder and blazes, she won't go off!" cried the exasperated Irishman, as, after a wavering effort to take aim, he essayed unsuccessfully to pull the trigger.

"Half-cock, man! Cock it!" said Frank quickly.

"So 'tis, be the mortial! Och, Bryan, yer too cliver, ye are!" he exclaimed, rectifying his error with a force that nearly tore off the dog-head. At that instant there was a sharp crack, and the deer, bounding into the air, fell dead on the sand at the edge of the willows.

"Forgive me, Bryan," said Massan, chuckling and

reloading his piece as he walked up to his comrade. "I would not ha' taken't out o' yer teeth, lad, if ye had been ready; but one bound more would ha' put the beast beyond the reach o' a bullet."

"Faix, Massan, ye desarve to be hanged for murther. Shure I was waitin' till the poor crayture got into the bushes, to give it a chance o' its life, before I fired. That's the way that gintlemen from the ould country does when we're out sportin'. We always put up the birds first, and fire afterwards; but you salvages murther a poor brute on the sand, whin it's only two fathoms from ye. Shame on ye, Massan."

"See, Massan," cried Frank, pointing to another deer, which, having escaped its pursuers, had gained the heights above. "That fellow is beyond us both, I fear. Be ready when it comes into view beyond the cliff there."

But Massan did not move; and when Frank threw forward his gun, he felt his arm arrested.

"Pardon me, monsieur," said Massan respectfully; "there's a sure bullet about to start for that deer."

As he spoke, he pointed to Dick Prince, who, ignorant of the fact that the deer had been seen by Frank, was watching its reappearance from behind a neighbouring rock, at some distance from where they stood. In a second it came into view—the bullet sped—and the deer bounded lightly into the bushes, evidently unhurt!

It is difficult to say whether Dick Prince or his comrades exhibited most amazement in their looks at this result. That the crack shot of the party—the man who could hit a button in the centre at a hundred yards, and cut the head off a partridge at a hundred and fifty—should miss a deer at ninety yards, was utterly incomprehensible.

"Is it yer own gun ye've got?" inquired Bryan, as the discomfited marksman walked up.

"No; it's yours," replied Prince.

A smile, which resolved itself into a myriad of wrinkles, flitted over the blacksmith's face as he said—

"Ah, Prince! ye'll requare long practice to come to the parfect use o' that wipon. I've always fired three yards, at laste, to the left, iver since we fell over the hill togither. If it's a very long shot, it requares four to take the baste in the flank, or four an' a half if ye want to hit the shoulder, besides an allowance o' two feet above its head, to make up for the twist I gave it the other day in the forge, in tryin' to put it right!"

This explanation was satisfactory to all parties, especially so to Prince, who felt that his credit was saved; and if Prince had a weakness at all, it was upon this point.

The deer were now all killed, with the exception of those of the band that had been last in entering the river. These, with a few stragglers, had returned to the shore from which they started. The remainder of the evening was devoted to skinning and cutting up the carcasses—an operation requiring considerable time, skill, and labour.

While the people at the fort were thus employed, Maximus (who adopted at once the name given to him by Stanley) returned from his fruitless journey to the Indian camp, and assisted the men at their work. He made no allusion whatever to his visit to the deserted Indian camp; but, from the settled expression of deep sadness that clouded his countenance, it was inferred that what he had seen there had not tended to raise his hopes.

The supply of deer obtained at this time was very seasonable, for the frost had now begun to set in so steadily that the meat could be hung up to freeze, and thus be kept fresh for winter's consumption. Some of it, however, was dried and stored away in bales; while a small quantity was pounded after being dried, made into pemmican, and reserved for future journeys.

As for the Eskimos, they gave themselves up, during the first night, to feasting and rejoicing. During the short time that they had been at the fort, they had converted the promontory on which they were encamped into a scene of the utmost confusion and filth. A regard for truth constrains us to say, that although these poor creatures turned out to be honest, and simple, and kind-hearted, they did not by any means turn out to be cleanly; quite the reverse.

They had erected four summer tents on the beach, which were composed of skins sewed together, and supported on poles in such a way as to afford ample room for the accommodation of their families. The entrance to each tent was through a passage, which was also made of skins, hung over a line fastened to a pole at the distance of twelve or fifteen feet from the tent. Each side of this entrance was lined with piles of provisions—seals, fish, ducks, and venison, in various stages of decay, which rendered the passage into the interior a trying operation. True, it was intended that the frost should prevent this decay; but, unfortunately, the frost did not always do its duty. The manner in which they cut up their deer and prepared them for future use was curious. After cutting the animals into two, without skinning them, they pinned up the front half with the heart and liver in the cavity. The other half they treated in a similar way, minus the heart and liver, and then put them out to freeze until required. When frozen, they were frequently used in their tents as seats, until the gradual diminution of the larder demanded that they should be appropriated to their proper use.

The tribe of Eskimos who resided near Fort Chimo at this time were possessed of an enormous stone kettle, in which they boiled an entire deer at one time; and while the good people luxuriated on the flesh of the animal in their tents, the dogs assembled round the boiler to await the cooling of the soup—thus verifying the assertion formerly made by Massan on that head.

The dogs resembled those of the Newfoundland breed in some respects, but were scarcely so large or good-looking, and had erect instead of pendent ears. There were about a dozen of them; and it was wonderful to observe the patience with which they sat in a circle round the kettle, gazing earnestly at the soup, licking their chaps the while, in anticipation of the feast.

The successful hunt was regarded as worthy of being specially celebrated by the distribution of a glass of grog to the men, and also to the Eskimos; for at the time we write of, the Hudson's Bay Company had not yet instituted the wise and humane regulation which has since become a standing order throughout all parts of the country, except where there is opposition— namely, that ardent spirits shall not be given to the natives. However, Stanley's natural disposition led him to be very circumspect in giving spirits to the men and natives, and the supply now issued was very small.

In the men it produced a desire for the violin, and created a tendency to sing and tell stories. In the Eskimos it produced at first dislike, and afterwards wild excitement, which, in the case of Chacooto, ended in a desire to fight. But his comrades, assisted by his wives, overpowered him, tied him in a sack made of sealskin, and left him to roar and kick till he fell asleep!

The honesty of these natives was exhibited very strikingly in all their dealings with the fur-traders. Although iron tools of every description were scattered about the fort, while the men were engaged in erecting the several buildings, not one was missed; and even the useless nails and scraps of metal that were thrown away, when they were found by chance by the Eskimos, were always brought to the house, and the question asked, "Were they of any use?" before being appropriated. They were great beggars, however; which was not surprising, considering the value of the articles possessed by the traders, and their own limited means of purchasing them. Their chief wealth at this time lay in boots and deerskins, which the women were constantly employed in preparing; but Stanley urged them to go into the interior and hunt, as, although deerskins and boots were useful, furs were infinitely more valuable. But the Eskimos had much too lively a dread of the Indians to venture away from the coast, and seemed inclined to hang about the place in comparative idleness much longer than was desirable.

Chapter XXIII

A day or two after the successful deer-hunt above related, several bands of Eskimos arrived at Fort Chimo, and encamped beside their comrades. This unusual influx of visitors soon exhausted the venison that had been procured; but hunting parties were constantly on the alert, and as game of all kinds was plentiful, they lived in the midst of abundance. To all of these Stanley made small presents of beads and tobacco, and recommended them strongly to go and hunt for furs. But they seemed to like their quarters, and refused to move. The new arrivals, along with those who had first come, formed a band of about three hundred, and were found, almost without exception, to be a quiet, inoffensive, and honest people.

As a proof of this latter quality, we may mention a circumstance that occurred a few days after the arrival of the last band. Being desirous of taking some additional soundings, Stanley launched his boat by the help of the Eskimos, for his own men were all absent hunting and fishing. The boat referred to had been sent to the fort in the ship, and was a most useful and acceptable gift from the Governor of the Fur Company to the gentleman in charge of Ungava. Stanley hoisted his sails, and prepared to run down the river; but ere he had advanced a hundred yards, he was startled by a burst of loud cries from the shore, and, looking back, he observed the whole band of natives pouring like a torrent into the fort! His heart leaped within him as he thought of his unprotected wife and child. Turning the boat towards the shore, he ran it on the beach, and, leaving it with all the sails standing, he rushed into the square of the fort, forcing his way through the crush of natives, whose vociferous talking rendered what they said, for a time, unintelligible. At length Moses forced his way through the crowd, followed by one of the natives, who led a large dog by a line fastened round its neck.

"What's the matter, Moses? What's wrong?" cried Stanley.

"Oh, not'ing at all," replied Moses, casting a look of pity at his countrymen. "Dem are great gooses. Die man here wid de dog, him say dat de child'n was play in de square of dis fort, an' one o' dem trow stone and broke a window. It was de son ob dis man what do it, an' him say he most awful sorry—an' all de people sorry, so dey bring de dog to pay for de broken window."

"I'm glad it's nothing worse," cried Stanley, much relieved. "Tell them I'm happy to find they are sorry, and I hope they will keep the children out of the square in future; but I don't want the dog. It was an accident, and not worth making such a noise about."

The Eskimos, however, would not agree to look upon this accident as a light matter. They said truly, that glass was not to be got so easily as the ice-blocks with which they formed windows to their own winter houses, so they insisted on the dog being accepted; and at length Stanley gave in, but took care that the native who gave it should not be a loser in consequence of his honesty. Moreover, Stanley begged of them to send up several of their best dogs, saying that he would purchase them, as he was in want of a team for hauling the winter firewood.

Next day, while Stanley was engaged in the trading store with a party of Eskimos, he was surprised by hearing a volley of musketry fired at the back of the fort. Snatching up a loaded gun as he ran hastily out, he found that the shots had been fired by a band of Indians as a salute to the fort on their arrival.

This was the first time that Indians had made their appearance since the arrival of the fur-traders; and their advent at the present time was most fortunate, as it afforded Stanley an opportunity of commencing his negotiations as peacemaker in the presence of a considerable band of both parties. The Indians, fifteen in number, were all clothed, with the exception of their chief, in deerskin hunting shirts, ornamented moccasins of the same material, and cloth leggings. They wore no head-dress, but their long, straight, black hair was decorated with feathers and small metallic ornaments, among which were several silver thimbles. Their powder-horns and shot-pouches were gaily ornamented with bead and quill work; and they were all armed with long guns, on which they leaned as they stood silently, in a picturesque group, on the flat, rocky platform above the spring, which has been more than once alluded to.

This platform overlooked the fort, and was a favourite promenade of the traders. At present it formed a sort of neutral ground, on which the Indians took their stand. The red men were overawed by the very superior number of the Eskimos, and felt that they were safe only so long as they stood on the flat rock, which was the only path leading to the ravine, through which, if need be, they could easily escape into the mountains.

The chief of the Indians, unlike his fellows, was dressed in a costume of the most grotesque and brilliant character, and, certainly, one which, however much it might raise the admiration of his savage companions, did not add to his dignity in the eyes of the traders. He wore a long, bright scarlet coat, richly embroidered with gold lace, with large cuffs, and gilt buttons; a pair of blue cloth trousers, and a vest of the same material; a broad worsted sash, and a hat in the form of the ordinary beaver or silk hat of Europe. The material, however, was very coarse; but this was made up for by the silver, and gilt cords, and tassels with which it was profusely decorated. He evidently felt his own importance, and stood with a calm, dignified gaze, waiting to be addressed.

Hailing Ma-istequan, who leaned on the axe with which he had been cutting firewood when the volley of the Indians arrested him, Stanley bade him invite them to enter the fort.

"We cannot come down," replied the chief, after Ma-istequan had given the invitation. "The Eskimos are in numbers like the stars; we are few. If the pale-faces are our friends, let them come up here and take us by the hand and bring us down."

"Very reasonable," said Stanley to Frank, who stood beside him; "we must take care that the Eskimos do not take advantage of their numbers to avenge their ancient wrongs."

Then, turning to the natives, who had now crowded in large numbers into the fort, Stanley addressed them in a serious tone; told them that the time had now come when he hoped to reconcile the Innuit and the Allat [Eskimo name for Indians] together; and that he expected they would show their gratitude for his many kindnesses to them by treating the Indians, who were his friends, with hospitality. The Eskimos promised obedience, after which Stanley ascended to the promenade, and taking the Indian chief by the hand, led him towards the fort, followed by the whole band in single file.

It is not necessary to detail the speeches that followed on both sides on this occasion, and the eloquence that was expended that evening in the cause of peace. Suffice it to say that the Indians and Eskimos shook hands and exchanged gifts in the presence of the assembled garrison of Fort Chimo. But although the traders had reason to congratulate themselves on having so far succeeded in the establishment of peace, they could not conceal from themselves the fact that while, on the one hand, the Eskimos appeared to be perfectly sincere and cordial in their professions, on the other hand the Indians evinced a good deal of taciturnity at first, and even after their reserve was overcome, seemed to act as men do who are constrained to the performance of a distasteful action.

In general character, the Indians of Labrador do not contrast well with the Eskimos—at least this may with truth be said of those who afterwards became attached to the district of Ungava. The Indian is reserved and taciturn, while the Eskimo is candid, frank, and communicative. Of course there are exceptions on both sides.

On the evening of the same day, Stanley had much difficulty in overcoming the reserve of the Indians, so as to procure information regarding the interior; and it was not until their hearts were opened by the influence of tobacco, that they condescended to give the required information. This was to the effect that there were not many fur-bearing animals in the immediate vicinity of Ungava, but that there were a good many in the wooded country lying to the southward and eastward. Here, however, the Indians do not care to hunt, preferring rather to keep to the heights of land, and near the coast, where the deer are numerous. In fact, Stanley afterwards found that the facility with which the Indians procured deer in this part of the country was a serious drawback to the fur trade, as they contented themselves with trapping just enough of otters, foxes, etcetera, to enable them to procure a supply of ammunition with which to hunt the deer.

The Indians had brought a few beaver and other furs to trade, and, after receiving a good meal and a few presents, they took up their quarters on a plot of ground close to the fort. Here they lived a short time in perfect friendship with the Eskimos, visiting them, and hunting in company; but more than once they exhibited their natural disposition by stealing the goods of their neighbours. On one occasion, two Eskimo children were missed from the camp, and in the course of the day they returned to their parents clothed in Indian costume! This was a very polite piece of attention on the part of the Indians, but the effect of it was much marred, the same day, by the abstraction of a knife from an Eskimo tent. Stanley insisted on the article being restored, and severely reprimanded the offender. But, although the general harmony of the camp was sometimes broken by such events, the friendship between the two parties seemed to be gradually increasing, and Stanley saw with satisfaction that the Allat and the Innuit bade fair to become fast friends for the future.

But an event occurred at this time which put an end to their intercourse, and very much altered the aspect of affairs. For some time past the men at the fort had been subject to rather severe attacks of cold, or a species of influenza. This they unfortunately communicated to the Eskimos, who seemed to be peculiarly susceptible of the disease. Being very fat and full-blooded, it had the most dreadful effect on the poor creatures, and at a certain stage almost choked them. At last one night it was reported that ten of their number had died from absolute suffocation. All of these had been strong and robust, and they died after two days' illness.

One of those who were attacked was Edith's little friend, Arnalooa, and just before the ten Eskimos died, Edith had gone down to the camp with a present of beads to console her. She found her much better, and, after talking to her for some time, she took her leave, promising to pay her another visit next day. True to her promise, Edith sallied forth after breakfast with a little native basket on her arm. About half an hour afterwards, while Stanley was sitting in the hall with his wife and Frank, they were startled by the sudden appearance of Edith, out of breath from the speed with which she had run home, and her face overspread with a deadly paleness.

"What is the matter, my darling?" cried her mother, starting up in alarm.

"Oh! the Eskimos are lying dead on the sand," gasped Edith, as she laid her head on her mother's breast, "and the rest are all gone."

Without waiting to hear more, Frank and Stanley took down their guns and hastened to the camp. Here a scene of the most horrible kind presented itself. The whole camp exhibited evidences of a hasty flight, and eight of the people who had died during the night were lying exposed on the rocks, with their white faces and ghastly eyeballs turned towards the sky. The other two had been buried on the rocks under a heap of stones, which did not conceal them entirely from view.

"No wonder poor Edith was alarmed," said Stanley sadly, as he leaned on his fowling-piece and surveyed the scene of desolation and death.

"I have been told," remarked Frank, "that the Eskimos have a superstitious dread of this river. Oolibuck mentioned to me this morning that he has had a good deal of conversation with the natives about this disease, and they told him that it invariably attacks them when they enter this river, and carries them off by dozens; so that they never come into it except when they require wood, and always stay as short a time as possible."

"Ah! That's bad," said Stanley; "I fear that it will go much against the success of the establishment. But we must hope better things; and, truly, with this exception, all has gone well hitherto. Said they anything more, Frank?"

"Yes; they hinted, it seems, their intention of flying away from this fatal spot, and taking up their abode for the winter at the mouth of False River, where they can obtain a livelihood by seal-fishing; but Oolibuck thought they did not mean to put the threat in execution, and did not imagine that they were in such alarm that they would go off without burying their dead."

"We must do that for them, Frank," said Stanley, turning to retrace his steps to the fort; "send down as many of the men as you can spare to-day, and get it done at once."

"By the way," said Frank, as they walked along the beach, "it seems that many years ago the Moravian missionaries came to the mouth of this river, and talked of setting up a trading-fort here; but, from some cause unknown, they gave up their design and went away. Maximus has been telling me all he knows about the matter; but his reports are vague, and the event must have occurred, if it occurred at all, when he was a child."

"Very possibly, Frank. You know the Moravians have settlements along the coasts of Labrador, to the eastward of this. They may have made an attempt long ago to push as far as this. I have always had a high opinion of the energy and perseverance of these missionaries, but I cannot get over the incongruity of their strange way of mingling trade with religion. It seems to me an unnatural sort of thing for missionaries to be fur-traders. I do not mean by this to object to their system, however; I daresay it works well, but I've had no means of judging."

"It is strange," replied Frank; "yet it seems a good plan. The missionaries trade there in order that they may live and preach. 'Twould be a good thing for the Indian country if the same principles and practice actuated the traders; with this difference, that instead of missionaries becoming fur-traders, the fur-traders would become missionaries. It does seem a species of infatuation," continued Frank, energetically, as he warmed with the subject, "that men, calling themselves

Christians, should live for years and years among the poor Indians of America and never once name to them the great and saving name of Christ. Of course I do not wonder at those who make little or no profession of Christianity; but there are men in the fur-trade who seem to be deeply impressed with the truths of God's Word—who are alive to the fact that there is no name under heaven given among men whereby we can be saved except the name of Christ—who know and feel that the Indians around them are living without God, and therefore without hope in the world—who feel that Christ is all in all, and that the Christian religion, however perfect and beautiful as a code of morals, is utterly worthless as to salvation unless there be in the heart the special love of Jesus Christ;—men who admit and profess to believe all this, yet never speak of Christ to the natives—never mention the name that can alone save them from eternal destruction."

"Be not hasty, Frank," replied Stanley. "I agree with you, that it is strange indeed we do not see and hear more of this missionary spirit among the traders, and I, for one, take your words as a deserved rebuke to myself; but if there are, as you say, many among us who are deeply impressed with the truths of God's Word, how know you that we never mention our Saviour's name to the Indians? Although fur-traders do not mount the pulpit, they may, in private, make mention of that name, and do an amount of good that will only be fully known when the trader, the trapper, and the Indian shall stand side by side before the judgment-seat of Christ. Observe, I do not say that this is actually the case; I only suggest that it is possible—may I not add, probable?"

"It may be so," returned Frank, "it may be so, and God forgive me if I have judged the men of the fur-trade unjustly; but I certainly know one who has made somewhat of a profession of Christianity in his day, and yet has done next to nothing, and that one is Frank Morton."

"I'll not gainsay that, Frank," said Stanley, with a quiet smile; "and I think we are not likely to err much when we apply censure to ourselves. It is curious that you and I should have been thinking of the very same subject. A few days ago, while my wife and I were conversing together about the Eskimos, we agreed to devote a good deal of our leisure time next winter to reading and explaining the Bible to our Eskimo interpreters, in the hope that they may afterwards be the means of much good among their poor countrymen."

Whether or not the good resolutions made at this time were ever put in practice we cannot say. Let us hope that they were.

Not long after the sudden flight of the Eskimos, the Indians struck their tents and took their departure for the interior, with the intention, as they said, of hunting for furs, but more probably, as Ma-istequan suggested, to hunt the deer. During all the time of their residence at the fort, Maximus had kept out of their way as much as possible. He seldom met them without a frown of hatred, for he regarded them as the representatives of a race which had robbed him of his bride; and there were times when the giant's spirit chafed so fearfully at the sight of the red men, that nothing but the remembrance of his promise to Stanley, to offer them no injury, prevented him from stirring up his tribe to overwhelm and destroy them. It was, therefore, with a feeling of relief that Maximus beheld them march single file over the rocky platform, and disappear in the ravine that led into the mountains.

The traders of Ungava were once more left in solitude, and from this time forward, until the winter set in, they devoted all their energies to laying up a stock of provisions sufficient to last till spring.

Dick Prince and Massan were sent after the deer in company. Augustus and Bryan were dispatched to a small lake to establish a fishery; in which they were very successful, and soon caught a large supply of excellent white-fish, trout, and carp, which they gutted and hung up by their tails to dry and freeze. Frank and Moses went to another small lake, about ten miles down the river, and built a hut of willows, in which they dwelt while engaged at the fishery. As there was still much to be done in the way of completing the fort, and making furniture, Stanley retained La Roche, Oolibuck, and the two Indians to assist him in this, as well as in the performance of the miscellaneous minor duties about the station, such as cutting up firewood, covering the roofs of the stores with tarpaulin, shooting such birds and animals as came near the fort, constructing rude chairs and tables, cooking, etcetera, etcetera; while Francois and Gaspard were sent up the river to fell trees, for the purposes both of building and firewood. Edith and her mother found ample occupation—the latter in the use of her needle and the cares of the household; the former in learning her lessons, visiting her berry-ravine, dressing her doll (for she had a doll, as a matter of course), and in holding long and frequent converse with Chimo.

Thus they spent their time; too busily occupied to take much note of its rapid flight, and scarce noticing the lengthening nights and shortening days, until needles of ice began with slow and silent progress to shoot across and solidify the waters of the bay.

Chapter XXIV

EFFECT OF SNOW ON THE FEELINGS, NOT TO MENTION
THE LANDSCAPE—A WONDERFUL DOME OF ICE.

There are times and seasons, in this peculiar world of ours, when the heart of man rejoices. The rejoicing to which we refer is not of the ordinary kind. It is peculiar; and, whether its duration be long or short, its effect powerful or slight, it is quite distinct and emphatic. We do not intend to enter into a detail of the occasions that call forth this feeling of exultation. Far be it from us to venture into such perilous depths of philosophy. Our sole reason for making these preliminary observations is, that we may, with proper emphasis, introduce the statement, that one of these occasions of rejoicing is, when man arises from his couch, on a brilliant, sunny, sparkling morning, gazes forth from his window, and beholds the landscape— which yesterday was green, and red, and brown, and blue—clad in a soft mantle of whitest snow!

What! you don't agree with us? You shudder at the preposterous idea of such a sight being fitted to rejoice the heart of man in any degree whatever? Well, well; do not sneer at our weakness. If we cannot sympathise with each other on this subject, perchance there are other things in which we can. But whatever be our opinion in regard to this, the point that we have to deal with at present is, the opinion of Edith Stanley, who, on rising hastily one morning, and looking forth from her little window, evinced the rejoicing of her heart most emphatically, by her loud exclamation of delight and the sparkling of her bright blue eyes.

Independently of the cheerful lightness and the virgin purity of the mantle, which in itself tended to awaken emotions of gladness in Edith's heart, there was something in its sudden appearance that carried her back violently and vividly to bygone days. The winter garb had no associations, yet, with Ungava; but it had with Moose Fort, and the dear companions she used to play with there. It recalled the time when she and her little friends sallied forth, each with her small wooden sledge drawn after her by a line, to slide thereon down the banks of the frozen river with headlong speed, and upset at the bottom amid shouts of laughter. It recalled the time when she made the first attempt to walk in snow-shoes, upon which occasion she tripped and fell into the snow, as a matter of course, and was advised to wait till she was older. It recalled the memory of her father's team of dogs, and the delightful drives she used to have over the frozen river; which drives often resulted in an upset, perhaps several, and always resulted in fun. It recalled the house in the old fort that used to be her home; the row of houses belonging to the men, to which she often went, and was always welcomed as a great favourite; the water-hole on the river from which the old Canadian drew his daily supply; and the snow-house in the yard which she built in company with Frank Morton, and which stood the whole winter through, but gave way at last before the blazing sun of spring, and fell—as ill luck would have it—when she and Chimo were sitting there, so that she and the dog together had a hard struggle ere they got free. All these, and many more thick-coming memories of other days, were aroused by the vision of snow that met Edith's gaze that morning, and caused her heart with peculiar fervour to rejoice.

Winter had now descended with iron grasp upon Ungava. For some weeks the frost had been so intense that every lake and pool was frozen many inches thick, and the salt bay itself was fringed with a thick and ever-accumulating mass of ice. The snow which now fell was but the ceremonial coronation of a king whose reign had commenced in reality long before.

But the sunshine did not last long. The rolling fogs and vapours of the open and ice-laden sea beyond ascended over the wild mountains, obscured the bright sky, and revealed the winter of the north in all its stern, cold reality. Every cliff and crag and jagged peak had its crown of snow, and every corrie, glen, and gorge its drifted shroud. In places where the precipices were perpendicular, the grey rocks of the mountains formed dark blotches in the picture; but, dark although they were, they did not equal in blackness the river, on which floated hundreds of masses of ice and several ponderous icebergs, which had been carried up from the sea by the flood-tide. Over this inky expanse the frost-smoke hung like a leaden pall—an evil spirit, as it were, which never left the spot till protracted and intense frost closed the waters of the river altogether, and banished it farther out to sea. But this entire closing of the river very seldom happened, and never lasted long.

Fort Chimo itself, at least as much of it as remained unburied, was a mere speck on the edge of the white plain at the mountain's foot, scarce distinguishable, at a short distance, from the straggling black pines and willow bushes that seemed thrust out into the waste from the ravines above and below the fort. But on a nearer approach, the fort assumed an air of greater importance; the influences, too, of the cold, cheerless scene we have described, were broken and dissipated by the sights of comfort and sounds of cheerfulness within. The shout of the water-drawer, as he roused the dogs and went forth with his empty cask, hauled on a little sledge, to draw from the bubbling spring behind the fort; the sounds of the hammer, the chisel, and the axe, in the carpenter's shop; the merry clank of Bryan's hammer, and the bright flame that gleamed from the window of the forge,—all bore evidence of the fact, that however powerful the influence of winter might be without, it had little power within the wooden walls of Fort Chimo, and could not check the life, or heart, or industry of man.

The only other human being visible in the open air, besides the water-drawer, was La Roche, who, with a fur cap covering his head and ears, and leathern mittens on his hands, hewed and hacked the billets with which he purposed to replenish the fire for cooking the midday meal.

Pausing in his labour, and dusting off the hoarfrost that covered his eyebrows and whiskers, he looked at the edge of his hatchet for a few seconds with an expression of contempt. Then, throwing the implement on his shoulder, he crossed the yard and entered the blacksmith's shop.

"Bryan," said he, seating himself on the edge of the forge and filling his pipe, while Vulcan's votary scattered a shower of gems from a white-hot bar of iron at every blow of his hammer—"Bryan, you no fit for not'ing. Dat axe is blont encore. Oui, c'est vrai. Now dat is tres mal. How you not can temper him edge better?"

"Timper it better, is it?" answered Bryan, putting the iron bar in the fire, and regarding his companion earnestly while he blew the bellows. "Faix, 'tis mysilf I'd need to timper better, in order to put up wi' the likes o' you, ye wretched crature. How can ye expict it to kape its idge when ye lave it for iver lyin' among yer pots and kittles?"

"Dat is not it," replied La Roche, applying a glowing coal to his pipe. "'Tis de mauvais steel. But I not com for to fight wid you. Your tongue trop long pour dat.

I com for ax you to give me turn ov de grindstone, s'il vous plait."

"Ye don't desarve it, Losh; but wait till I've finished this job and I'll lind ye a hand."

"Be-the-bye," resumed Bryan, when the metal was cooled, "has Francois finished that sled for Miss Edith?"

"Oui," replied La Roche, seating himself at the grindstone. "(Ah! pas si vite, a leet more slow, Bryan.) Oui, him make it all ready; only want de ring-bolts."

"Thin it won't want thim long. Ye can take thim over to the shop when ye go across. There they are on the binch."

Bryan continued to turn the handle of the stone for some time in silence.

"D'ye know, Losh," he resumed, "whin Mister Frank is goin' to the fishery?"

"He go demain, I b'lieve, and Mademoiselle Edith go too."

"None o' the min goin'?" inquired the blacksmith.

"Non. Monsieur Frank just go for to try if dere be any fish to be cotch by de hook; and I t'ink he go more for to give Edith one drive dan dat."

"Very likely, Losh. The poor purty little crature. She's very fond o' sledgin' and walkin' in snow-shoes. 'Tis well for her, bekase there's a want o' companions for her here intirely."

"Ah! mercy, dat is superb, magnifique!" said the Frenchman, feeling the edge of the axe with his thumb. "It sharp 'nuff to shave de hair off your ugly face, Bryan."

"Thin be off wid ye, an' don't kape me longer from

my work. An' shut the door quick behind ye; there's cowld enough in the place already."

So saying, Bryan resumed his hammer, and La Roche, following the snow-track across the yard, recommenced his labour of chopping firewood.

Next day, Frank and Edith made preparations for the excursion alluded to in the foregoing conversation.

The object for which this excursion was undertaken was twofold—first, to ascertain if there were any fish in a large lake about ten miles distant from the fort; and, secondly, to give little Edith a drive for the good of her health. Not that her health was bad, but several weeks of bad weather had confined her much to the house, and her mother thought the change would be beneficial and agreeable; and tenderly did that mother's heart yearn over her little child, for she felt that, although she was all to Edith that a mother could be, nature had implanted in her daughter's mind a longing desire for the companionship of little ones of her own age, which could not be satisfied by any substitute—not even that of a tender mother, who sought, by all the means in her power, to become a child again for Edith's sake.

Immediately after breakfast that day Frank took Edith by the hand, and led her round by the back of the fort, towards the kennel where the dogs were kept, intending to release Chimo, who was to have the honour of hauling the sledge of his young mistress. In passing the spring, Edith paused, as she had often done before during the winter, to gaze with wonder on the transformation that had taken place in the appearance of the once green and fertile spot. Not only was it covered with deep snow, but over the spring there was formed a singular dome of ice. This dome was a subject of continual astonishment to every one at Ungava. It had commenced to rise soon after the first hard frosts had sealed up the little fountain from the open air. As time passed by, the covering became thick ice, and was bulged gradually up above the surrounding waste, until it reached an elevation of not much less than twelve or thirteen feet. Inside of this the spring bubbled up as of yore.

"What think you, Edith?" said Frank, as a sudden thought occurred to him; "shall I cut a doorway into that crystal house, and see if the spirit of the spring dwells there?"

Edith clapped her hands with delight at the idea, and urged her companion to begin at once. Then, checking him as he was about to commence the work with his hatchet, she said earnestly—

"Do spirits really dwell in the springs, Frank?"

"Why, Eda, we must send to England for a lot of fairy tales to teach you what I mean. I do but jest when I speak of spirits living there. But I daresay there are no spirits in this spring."

"Faix, an' it would be a rale misfortune if there was, sir," remarked Bryan, who came up at this moment, and touched his cap; "for it would be only sperits and wather, which wouldn't kape in this cowld climate. I've finished the ring-bolts for the sled, sir, an' came to see when ye would have them fixed."

"Put them in your pocket, Bryan, for a few minutes,

and lend a hand here to cut a hole through this dome."

As Frank spoke, he drew a small axe from his belt, and began to lay about him so vigorously that the icy splinters flew in all directions like a shower of broken crystal. Bryan seconded his efforts, and in less than half an hour a block of solid ice, about four feet high and two broad, was cut out and detached from the side of the dome.

"That'll do, Bryan," said Frank, when their work was nearly completed; "I'll finish it myself now. Go to the carpenter's house, and Francois will show you what to do with the sled."

As Bryan walked away, Frank dealt the mass of ice a blow that split it into several pieces, which he quickly removed, revealing to the astonished and eager gaze of his young companion a cavern of a most beautiful light blue colour. Taking Edith by the hand, he led her into this icy cave. Its walls were quite luminous and delicately blue, except in places where the green moss and earth around the spring had been torn from the ground and lifted up along with the dome. Icicles hung in various places from the roof, and the floor was hard and dry, except in the centre, where the spring bubbled up through it, and cut a channel across towards one side of the icy wall, where it disappeared under the snow.

"Oh, what a beautiful palace!" cried Edith, with delight, after she had gazed around her for a few minutes in silent wonder and admiration. "I shall come and live here, Frank. Oh! do come, and let us get chairs and a small table, and make it our sitting-room. We can come every day when the sun shines and read!"

"A good idea, Eda; but I fear we would need a stove to keep us warm. It strikes me it will make a capital ice-house in spring to keep our fresh meat in. It will last long after the snow is melted."

"Then we shall make a palace of it in winter and a meat-store in spring," cried Edith, laughing, as she walked round this newly-discovered house, examining its blue walls and peeping into the cold black spring. Meanwhile Frank examined it with a view to the utilitarian purpose, and, after both of them had gone round it several times, they continued on their way towards the dog-kennel.

The sledge which Francois had constructed for Edith was made after the model of those used by the Eskimos. There were two stout runners, or skates, made of wood, for sliding over the snow. These were slightly turned up, or rather rounded up, in front, and attached to each other by means of cross bars and thin planks of wood; all of which were fastened, not by nails (for iron-work snaps like glass in such a cold climate as that of Ungava), but by thongs of undressed sealskin, which, although they held the fabric very loosely together in appearance, were, nevertheless, remarkably strong, and served their purpose very well. Two short upright bars behind served as a back to lean against. But the most curious part of the machine was the substance with which the runners were shod, in order to preserve them. This was a preparation of mud and water, which was plastered smoothly on in a soft condition, and then allowed to freeze. This it did in a few minutes after being exposed to the open air, and thus became a smooth, hard sheathing, which was much more durable and less liable to break than iron, or indeed any other sheathing that could be devised. This substance is, of course, easily repaired, and is always used by the Eskimos in winter.

Eskimo sledges being heavy, and meant for carrying a number of people, require large teams of dogs. But Edith's sledge—or sled, as the men called it—was little. Moreover, Edith herself was little and light, therefore Chimo was deemed sufficiently powerful to draw it. So thoroughly correct were they in this supposition, that when Edith was seated in her sledge for a trial trip, and Chimo harnessed, he ran away with her and gave Frank a chase of half a mile over the river ere he condescended to stop in his wild career.

But the intended excursion was suddenly interrupted and postponed, by an event which we shall relate in the next Chapter.

Chapter XXV

BURIED ALIVE—BUT NOT KILLED—THE
GIANT IN THE SNOW-STORM.

The event which prevented the excursion referred to in the last Chapter was neither more nor less than a snowstorm. "Was that all?" say you, reader? Nay, that was not all. Independently of the fact that it was a snowstorm the like of which you have never seen, unless you have travelled in northern climes, it was a snowstorm that produced results. Of these, more hereafter.

The storm began with a sigh—a mysterious sigh, that swept over the mountains of Ungava with a soft, mournful wail, and died slowly away in the distant glen of the Caniapuscaw, as if the spirit of the north wind grieved to think of the withering desolation it was about to launch upon the land.

The gathering clouds that preceded and accompanied this sigh induced Frank Morton to countermand his orders for the intended journey. In order to console Edith for the disappointment, he went with her into the hall, and, drawing a low stool towards the blazing stove, placed a draught-board upon it. Then he placed another and a lower stool beside the first, on which he seated Edith. Spreading a deerskin robe upon the ground, he stretched himself thereon at full length, and began to arrange the men.

The hall, which was formerly such a comfortless apartment, was now invested with that degree of comfort which always gathers, more or less, round a place that is continually occupied. The ceiling was composed of a carpet of deerskin stretched tightly upon the beams. The walls were hung all round with the thick heavy coats and robes of leather and fur belonging to the inmates, and without which they never ventured abroad. The iron stove in the centre of the apartment, with its pipe to conduct away the smoke, and its radiant fire of logs, emitted a cheerful glow in its immediate vicinity; which glow, however, was not intense enough to melt the thick ice, or rather hoar-frost, an inch deep, with which the two windows were encrusted, to the almost total exclusion of the view and the serious diminution of the light. The door was padded all round its edges with fur, which tended to check the bitter wind that often blew against it, and tempered the slight draught that did force its way through. Altogether the hall at Fort Chimo was curious and comfortable—rather shaggy in its general appearance, but sound and trustworthy at bottom.

A small rough table, the work of Frank Morton,

stood close to the stove; and beside it was seated Mrs. Stanley, with a soft yellow deerskin before her, which she was carefully transforming into a hunting coat for her husband. On another and a larger table was spread the tea equipage. Those who would understand this aright must for tea read supper. Among fur-traders the two are combined. Candles—dips made at the fort— had been brought some time ago by La Roche, who entered the hall by a back door which communicated with a passage leading to the kitchen behind.

"What can have become of Papa, I wonder?" Mrs. Stanley designated her husband by this epithet, in consequence of her desire to keep up the fiction of her being Edith's little sister or playfellow.

Frank looked up from the board. "I know not," said he. "I left him giving some orders to the men. We have been getting things made snug about the fort, for we expect a pretty stiff breeze to-night.—Take care, Eda; your crown's in danger."

"Oh! so it is," cried Edith, snatching back her piece, and looking with intense earnestness at the board.

Frank might have observed, had he not been too deeply engaged with his game, that the expected stiff breeze had already come, and was whistling round the fort with considerable vigour.

"You'll beat me, Eda, if you play so boldly," said Frank, with a smile. "There, give me another crown."

"And me too," said Edith, pushing up her piece. As she spoke, the door burst open, and Stanley sprang into the room.

"Whew! what a night!" he cried, shutting the door

with a forcible bang, in order to keep out the snow-drift that sought to enter along with him.

Two moves would have made Frank the conqueror, but the gust of wind upset the board, and scattered the men upon the floor.

Stanley looked like a man of white marble, but the removal of his cap, coat, and leggings produced a speedy and entire metamorphosis.

"Ho! La Roche!"

"Oui, monsieur."

"Here, take my coat and shake the snow off it, and let's have supper as speedily as may be. The draughts without, Frank, are a little too powerful for the draughts within, I fear. What, wife, making another coat? One would think you had vowed to show your affection for me by the number of coats you made. How many have you perpetrated since we were married?"

"Never mind; go and put on one now, and come to supper while it is hot."

"I'm glad it is hot," cried Stanley from his bedroom. "One needs unusual heat within to make up for the cold without. The thermometer is thirty below."

While the party in the hall were enjoying their evening meal, the men were similarly employed beside the stove in their own habitation. There was not much difference in the two apartments, save that the confusion in that of the men was much greater, in consequence of the miscellaneous mass of capotes, caps, belts, discarded moccasins, axes, guns, and seal-spears, with which they saw fit to garnish the walls. The fumes of tobacco were also more dense, and the conversation more uproarious.

"'Tis a howlin' night," observed Massan, as a gust of more than usual violence shook the door on its hinges.

"Me t'ink de snow-drift am as t'ick in de sky as on de ground," said Oolibuck, drawing a live coal from the fire and lighting his pipe therewith.

"Hould on, boys!" cried Bryan, seizing his chair with both hands, half in jest and half in earnest, as another blast shook the building to its foundation.

The two Indians sat like statues of bronze, smoking their calumets in silence, while Gaspard and Prince rose and went to the window. But the frozen moisture on the panes effectually prevented their seeing out.

It was indeed an awful night—such a night as had not, until now, visited the precincts of Fort Chimo. Viewed from the rocky platform on the hill, the raging of the storm was absolutely sublime. The wind came sometimes in short, angry gusts, sometimes in prolonged roars, through the narrows, sweeping up clouds of snow so dense that it seemed as though the entire mass had been uplifted from the earth, hurling it upwards and downwards and in circling eddies, past the ravines, and round the fort, and launching it with a fierce yell into the valley of the Caniapuscaw. The sky was not altogether covered with clouds, and the broken masses, as they rolled along, permitted a stray moonbeam to dart down upon the turmoil beneath, and render darkness visible. Sometimes the wind lulled for a second or two, as if to breathe; then it burst forth again, splitting through the mountain gorges with a shriek of intensity; the columns of snow sprang in thousands from every hollow, cliff and glen, mingled in wild confusion, swayed, now hither, now thither, in mad uncertainty, and then, caught by the steady gale, pelted on, like the charging troops of ice-land, and swept across the frozen plain.

Could human beings face so wild a storm as this? Ay, they could—at least they could dare to try!

There was one traveller out upon the hills on that tremendous night. The giant was in the midst of it; but weak as the bulrush were the mighty limbs of Maximus before the rushing gale. Several days previous to this the Eskimo had been sent down to his brethren at False River, to procure some seal-meat for the dogs, and to ascertain the condition of the natives and their success in fishing. On arriving, he found that they had been so far successful, that starvation (their too frequent guest) had not yet visited their dwellings of snow. But Maximus found the old woman who had formerly saved his life very ill, and apparently about to die. Having learned from experience the efficacy of Stanley's medicines, he resolved to procure some for the old woman, whom he had tenderly watched over and hunted for ever since the eventful day of the attack. His dogs were exhausted, and could not return. But the bold Eskimo was in the prime of life, and animated by the fire of vigorous youth. The storm was beginning to mutter in the distance. What then? Had he not faced the blasts of the frozen regions many a time before?— Without saying a word, he threw a junk of seal-flesh into his wallet, and, striding back upon his track at the mountain's base, he disappeared in the driving snow.

Before reaching the fort, however, the full fury of the storm had burst upon him. It cast him headlong into the snow; but he rose and staggered on. Again it burst forth, and again he fell before it like a stately pine. Rising to his knees, Maximus draw the hood of his hairy garment close round his head and face, and tried to peer through the driving snow; but he could not see until a slight lull came; then he observed a hummock of ice at a short distance, and, rising, made towards it. The lulls were short-lived, however. The storm threw him down again; instantly he was drifted over with snow; another blast came, lifted the drift into the air, and left the Eskimo exposed to all its fury. But Maximus was not conquered. He rose again, panting, it is true, but sturdy as ever, and ready to take advantage of the next lull. It came soon; and he saw a rock, or, it might be, the base of a cliff close at hand. With a quick run he reached it; and, going down on his knees, began with his gloved hands to scrape a hollow in the snow. Having made a hole big enough to contain his body, he lay down in it, and, pulling the superincumbent snow down upon him, was almost buried in the ruin. Scarcely had he drawn the hood of his coat well over his face, when another burst of the storm dashed a column of curling drift upon the rock, and the place where he lay was covered up; not a wrinkle in the drift remained to mark the spot where he was buried!

All that night the storm roared among mountains with bitter fury; but next day the wind was subdued, and the sun shone brightly on the grey rocks and on the white wreaths of snow. It shone in all the lustre of an unclouded winter sky. Not only did the sun smile upon the scene, but two mock suns or parhelia, almost as bright as himself, shone on either side of him. Yet no ray of light illuminated the dwellings of the fur-traders. All was darkness there, until Stanley rose from his couch and lighted a candle, for the purpose of examining his watch.

"Hallo! Frank, Frank!" he cried, entering the hall, while he hastily threw on his garments; "turn out, man; there's something wrong here. 'Tis past noon, and dark as midnight. Bring your watch; perhaps I'm wrong."

Frank yawned vociferously, and sprang from his bed. In two seconds more he made his appearance in his trousers and shirt.

"Past twelve, no doubt of—yea-o-ow! That accounts for my waking three times and going off again; but—"

"Hey! what have we here?" cried Stanley, as he opened the front door, and disclosed to view a solid wall of snow.

"Snowed up; dear me! eh! that's odd," said Frank, beginning to comprehend the state of matters.

Snowed up they were, undoubtedly; so thoroughly snowed up that there was not a ray of daylight within their dwelling. Had Frank been above the snow, instead of below it, he would have seen that the whole fort was so completely buried that nothing was visible above the surface except the chimneys and the flagstaff. After the first few moments of surprise had passed, it occurred to Stanley that they might ascend to the regions above by the chimney, which was wide enough, he thought, to admit a man; but on looking up, he found that it also was full of drifted snow. This, however, could have been easily removed; but there was a bar of iron stretching across, and built into the clay walls, which rendered escape by that passage impossible.

"There's nothing for it, Frank, but to dig ourselves out, so the sooner we begin the better."

By this time they were joined by Edith and her mother, who, although much surprised, were not at all alarmed; for rough travelling in a wild land had taught them to regard nothing as being dangerous until it was proved to be so. Besides, Stanley had assured them that they had nothing to fear, as the only evil he anticipated would be the trouble they were sure to have in getting rid of the superabundant snow. While they were talking, the back door was opened violently, and La Roche, in a state of dishabille, burst into the room.

"O messieurs, c'est fini! Oui, le world him shut up tout togedder. Oh, misere! Fat shall ye to do?"

"Hold your tongue, La Roche," said Frank, "and bring the kitchen shovel."

The cook instantly turned to obey, and as he rushed towards the kitchen his voice was heard exclaiming in the passage—

"Ah, c'est terrible! Mais I ver' moshe fear de shovel be out in de neige. Ah, non; here it is. C'est bien."

Returning in haste to the hall, he handed a much dilapidated iron shovel to Frank, who threw off his coat and set to work with vigour. The tables and chairs, and all the furniture, were removed into the inner

apartments, in order to afford room for the snow which
Frank dug from the open doorway and shovelled into
the centre of the room. As only one at a time could work
in the narrow doorway, the three men wrought with the
shovel by turns; and while one was digging the tunnel,
the other two piled the debris in a compact mound
beside the stove. As no fire had yet been kindled, the
snow, of course, did not melt, but remained crisp and
dry upon the floor. Meanwhile Edith looked on with
deep interest, and occasionally assisted in piling the
snow; while her mother, seeing that her presence was
unnecessary, retired to her own room.

"There," cried Frank, pausing and surveying an
immense cavern which he had dug into the drift,
"that's a good spell. Take a turn now, La Roche, and
dig upwards; we should see daylight soon."

"Ah, vraiment, it be time, for it am von o'clock,"
replied La Roche, as he plied the shovel.

The tunnel was cut in such a way as that, while it ran
outwards, it also sloped upwards; and, from the angle
at which it lay, Stanley calculated that thirty feet or
thereabouts would bring them to the surface. In this
he was correct, for when La Roche had worked for half
an hour, the snow above became slightly luminous. But
the labour of conveying it from the end of the tunnel
into the hall became, of course, greater as the work
advanced. At length the light penetrated so clearly that
La Roche was induced to thrust his shovel upwards, in
the expectation of penetrating the mass. The effect of
this action was striking and unexpected. Instantly the
roof fell in, and a flood of sunshine poured into the

tunnel, revealing the luckless Frenchman struggling amid the ruins.

"Oh, pull me hout!" he spluttered, as Frank and Stanley stood laughing heartily at his misfortune. One of his legs happened to protrude from the mass as he made this earnest request; so Frank seized it, and dragged the poor man by main force from his uncomfortable position. Immediately afterwards they all three scrambled through the aperture, and stood in open day.

The sight that met their eyes was a curious though not a satisfactory one. All that remained visible of Fort Chimo were, as we have said, the chimneys and the flagstaff. In regard to the general aspect of the neighbourhood, however, there was little alteration; for the change of position in the drifts among the mountain gorges, and the addition to their bulk, made no striking alteration in the rugged landscape. In some places the gale had cleared the sides of the mountains and left their cliffs exposed to view; in other spots the gorges and ravines were choked up, and the pine tops nearly covered; and the open water in the lake was more encumbered than usual with icebergs.

"Now, La Roche," said Stanley, after they had surveyed the desolate scene for a few minutes in silence, "go fetch the shovel and we'll dig out the men. I daresay, poor fellows, they're beginning to wonder at the length of the night by this time."

La Roche prepared to descend into the tunnel, when their attention was arrested by a strange sound beneath the snow. In a few minutes the crust began to crack at a spot not more than two yards from where they stood; then there was a sudden rupture, accompanied by a growl, and followed by the appearance of the dishevelled head and arms of a man.

"Musha, boys, but I'm out!" Bryan coughed the snow from around his mouth, and winked it from his eyes, as he spoke. The first sight that met his bewildered gaze was three pair of expanded eyeballs and three double rows of grinning teeth, a few feet from his face. Uttering a cry of terror, he fell back into the hole, the snow closed over him, and he was gone!

It need scarcely be added that Frank and Stanley commenced to dig into this hole with as much vigour as their frequent explosions of laughter would allow. In a few minutes it was re-opened, and the men issued one by one from durance vile.

"Och, sirs, ye gave me a mortial start!" exclaimed Bryan, as he rose to view the second time. "I thought for sartin ye were all polar bears. Faix we've had a job o't down there. I'll be bound to say there's twinty ton o' snow—bad luck to it—in the middle o' the floor."

"There's work for us here that'll last two weeks, I guess," said Massan, as he and several of the others stooped down and gazed into the tunnel leading to the hall, at the end of which Edith's laughing face met their view.

"When did you awake, and begin to suspect that something was wrong?" inquired Stanley of Dick Prince.

"Awake!" cried Bryan, answering the question; "we awoke at laste a dozen times. I suppose it must have bin the time for brikfust; for, ye see, although we could ha' slept on long enough; our intariors couldn't, be no manes, forgit their needcessities."

"We shall have to work a bit yet ere these necessities are attended to, I fear," said Stanley. "Go, Francois, and one or two of you, and open up the dog-kennel. The rest of you get all the shovels you can lay hands on, and clear out the houses as fast as you can."

"Clear out de chimbleys fust, mes garcons," cried La Roche, looking up from the tunnel. "Den ve vill git dejeuner ready toute suite."

"That will we, lad," said Bryan, shouldering a spade and proceeding towards the chimney of the hall; while the rest of the party, breaking up into several groups, set to work, with spades, shovels, and such implements as were suitable, to cut passages through the square of the fort towards the doors of the several buildings. As Massan had said, it proved to be no light work. The north-west gale had launched the snow upon the exposed buildings of Fort Chimo until the drift was fifteen or sixteen feet deep, so that the mere cutting of passages was a matter of considerable time and severe labour.

Meanwhile, Maximus awoke, and sought to raise himself from his lair at the foot of the rock. But his first effort failed. The drift above him was too heavy. Abandoning, therefore, the idea of freeing himself by main force, he turned round on his side and began to scrape away the snow that was directly above his head. The masses that accumulated in the course of this process he forced down past his chest; and, as his motions tended to compress and crush the drift around him in all directions, he soon made room enough to work with ease. In ten minutes he approached so near to the surface as to be able, with a powerful effort, to burst it upwards, and step out of his strange dormitory into the sunshine.

This method of spending the night has been resorted to more than once by arctic travellers who had lost their way; and it is sad to think that many who have perished might have saved their lives had they known that burrowing could be practised with safety. The Eskimos frequently spend the night in this manner, but they prefer building a snow-house to burrowing, if circumstances will permit.

Cutting a slice of seal-meat, and eating as he went, Maximus resumed his journey, and soon afterwards arrived at the fort, where he found the men busied in excavating their buried dwellings.

Here he stated the case of the old woman, and received such medicines as Stanley, in his amateur medical wisdom, saw fit to bestow. With these he started immediately to retrace his steps, having been directed to proceed, after administering them, to the lake where Frank meant to try the fishing under the ice. A family of Eskimos had been established on another lake not so far distant from the fort; and having been taught by the fur-traders how to set nets under the ice, they succeeded in procuring more than enough for their subsistence. It was hoped, therefore, that the larger lake would afford a good supply; and, the weather having become decidedly fine, Frank prepared to set out on the following day.

Chapter XXVI

AN EXCURSION—IGLOO BUILDING, AND FISHING
UNDER THE ICE—A SNOW-TABLE AND A GOOD
FEAST—EDITH SPENDS THE NIGHT UNDER A SNOW-
ROOF FOR THE FIRST BUT NOT THE LAST TIME.

"Now then, Edith," cried Frank, looking in at
the door of the hall, "your carriage waits, and
Chimo is very restive."

"Coming, coming," exclaimed a treble voice within;
"I'm getting new lines put to my snow-shoes, and will
be ready in two minutes."

Two minutes, translated into female language,
means ten, sometimes twenty. Frank knew this, and
proceeded to re-adjust the sash that secured his
leathern capote, as he walked towards the little sledge
in front of the fort. He then tied down the ear-pieces
of his fur cap more carefully, for it was very cold,
though clear and sunny. The frost had set fast the lake

opposite the fort, and, by thus removing the frost-cloud that overhung the open water farther out to sea, relieved the fort from the mists in which it was usually enveloped. By this time fifteen out of the "two" minutes having elapsed, he re-examined the lock of his gun, and adjusted the warm deerskin robe on Edith's little sledge, patted Chimo on the head, looked up at the clouds, and began to whistle.

"Now, Frank, here I am," cried Edith, running towards him with her snow-shoes in her hand, followed by her father and mother.

"Quiet, Chimo—down, sir!" said Frank, restraining the dog as it sought to bound towards its mistress. Being harnessed to the sledge, this was a very improper proceeding and was rebuked accordingly; so Chimo was fain to crouch on the snow and look back at Edith as Frank placed her in the sledge, and arranged the deerskin robes round her.

Edith wore a long fur cloak and cloth leggings. Her feet were protected from the cold by two pair of blanket socks, besides very thick moccasins of deerskin. The usual head-dress of civilised females in these regions is a round fur cap; but Edith had a peculiar affection for the Cree Indian headdress, and, upon the present occasion, wore one which was lined with fur and accommodated with ear-pieces, to defy the winter cold. The child's general appearance was somewhat rotund. Painters would probably have said there was a little too much breadth, perhaps, in the picture. Her pointed cap, however, with the little bow of ribbon on the top, gave her a piquant air, and did away with the heavy appearance of her costume to some extent; in fact, Edith looked like a fat little witch. But if she looked fat before being wrapped up in the sledge furs, she looked infinitely fatter when thus placed, and nothing of her visible except her two twinkling eyes. So grotesque was she that the whole party burst into a loud laugh as they surveyed her. The laugh made Chimo start off at full gallop, which caused Frank to grasp the line of the sledge that trailed behind, and hurry over the snow at a most undignified pace.

"Take care of her," cried Mr. Stanley.

"Ay, ay," shouted Frank—"Softly, Chimo—softly, you rascal!"

In ten minutes the travellers were round the point and fairly out of sight; but the shouts of Frank, and an occasional howl from Chimo, floated back on the breeze as Stanley and his wife returned leisurely to the hall.

The road, or rather the ground, over which Frank Morton drove Edith that day was exceedingly rough and rugged—so rough that we will not try the endurance of the reader by dragging him over it. We will merely indicate its general features. First of all, they drove about three miles along the level snow at the foot of the mountains. So far the road was good; and Chimo went along merrily to the music of the little thimble-like brass bells with which his harness was garnished. Then they came to a ravine, and Edith had to get out, put on her snow-shoes, and clamber up, holding by Frank's hand; while Chimo followed, dragging the sledge as he best could. Having gained one of the terraces, Edith slipped her feet out of the snow-shoe lines, jumped into the sledge, and was swept along to the next ravine, where she got out again, resumed her snow-shoes, and ascended as before. Thus they went up the ravines and along the terraces until the summit of the first mountain range was reached. Having rested here a few minutes, Edith once more got into the sledge, and Chimo set off. But as there was now a long piece of level ground over which for some miles they could travel in the direction of the coast, Frank took the sled-line in his hand, and held the dog at a quick walking pace. Afterwards they turned a little farther inland, and came into a more broken country, where they had sometimes to mount and sometimes to descend the hills. There were many gorges and narrow fissures in the ground here, some of which were covered over and so concealed with snow that the travellers ran some risk of falling into them. Indeed, at one place, so narrow was their escape that Chimo fell through the crust of snow, and disappeared into a fissure which descended a hundred feet sheer down; and the sledge would certainly have followed had not Frank held it back by the line; and Chimo was not hauled up again without great difficulty. After this, Frank went in front with a pole, and sounded the snow in dangerous-looking places as he went along.

Towards the afternoon they arrived at the lake where they intended to encamp, and, to their great delight, found Maximus there already. He had only arrived a few minutes before them, and was just going to commence the erection of a snow-house.

"Glad to see you, Maximus," cried Frank, as he

drove up. "How's the old woman, eh?"

"She small better," replied Maximus, assisting Edith to alight. "Dis goot for fish."

Maximus was a remarkably intelligent man, and, although his residence at the fort had been of short duration as yet, he had picked up a few words of English.

"A good lake, I have no doubt," replied Frank, looking round. "But we need not search for camping ground. There seems to be very little wood, so you may as well build our hut on the ice. We shall need all our time, as the sun has not long to run."

The lake, on the edge of which they stood, was about a mile in circumference, and lay in a sort of natural basin formed by savage-looking hills, in which the ravines were little more than narrow fissures, entirely devoid of trees. Snow encompassed and buried everything, so that nothing was to be seen except, here and there, crags and cliffs of gray rock, which were too precipitous for the snow to rest on.

"Now, Eda, I will take a look among these rocks for a ptarmigan for supper; so you can amuse yourself watching Maximus build our house till I return."

"Very well, Frank," said Edith; "but don't be long. Come back before dark; Chimo and I will weary for you."

In a few minutes Frank disappeared among the rocks upon the shore; and Maximus, taking Edith by the hand, and dragging her sledge after him, led her a couple of hundred yards out on to the ice, or, more properly speaking, the hard beaten snow with which the ice was covered. Chimo had been turned loose, and, being rather tired after his journey, had coiled himself up on a mound of snow and fallen fast asleep.

"Dis place for house," said Maximus, pausing near a smooth, level part of the lake. "You stop look to me," he added, turning to the little girl, who gazed up in his large face with an expression half of wonder and half of fun. "When you cold, run; when you hot, sit in sled and look at me."

In compliance with this request, Edith sat down in her sledge, and from this comfortable point of view watched the Eskimo while he built a snow-hut before her.

First of all, he drew out a long iron knife, which had been constructed specially for him by Bryan, who looked upon the giant with special favour. With the point of this he drew a circle of about seven feet in diameter; and so well accustomed was he to this operation that his circle, we believe, could not have been mended even by a pair of compasses. Two feet to one side of this circle he drew a smaller one, of about four feet in diameter. Next, he cut out of the snow a number of hard blocks, which were so tough that they could not be broken without a severe blow, but were as easily cut as you might have sliced a soft cheese with a sharp knife. These blocks he arranged round the large circle, and built them above each other, fashioning them, as he proceeded, in such a manner that they gradually rose into the form of a dome. The chinks between them he filled compactly with soft snow, and the last block, introduced into the top of the structure, was formed exactly on the principle of the key-stone of an arch. When the large dome was finished, he commenced the smaller; and in the course of two hours both the houses—or, as the Eskimos call them, igloos—were completed.

Long before this, however, Frank had returned, from an unsuccessful hunt, to assist him; and Edith had wondered and wearied, grown cold and taken to running with Chimo, and grown warm and returned to her sledge, several times. Two holes were left in the igloos to serve as doors; and, after they were finished, the Eskimo cut a square hole in the top of each, not far from the key-stones, and above the entrances. Into these he fitted slabs of clear ice, which formed windows as beautiful and useful as if they had been made of glass. There were two doorways in the large igloo, one of which faced the doorway of the smaller. Between these he built an arched passage, so that the two were thus connected, and the small hut formed a sort of inner chamber to the larger.

"Now, dem done," said Maximus, surveying his work with a satisfied smile.

"And very well done they are," said Frank. "See here, Eda, our snow-fort is finished. The big one is to be the grand hall and banqueting-room, and yonder little hut is your private boudoir."

"Mine!" exclaimed Edith, running away from Chimo, with whom she had been playing, and approaching the new houses that had been so speedily put up. "Oh, how nice! what fun! only think!—a snow bedroom! But won't it be cold, Frank? And is the bed to be of snow too?"

The black moustache of the giant curled with a smile at the energy with which this was said.

"We will make the bedsteads of snow, Eda," replied Frank, "but I think we shall manage to find blankets of a warmer material. Now, Maximus, get the things put inside, and the lamp lighted, for we're all tired and very hungry."

The lamp to which Frank referred was one which Maximus had brought, along with a few other articles, from the Eskimo camp. It was made of soft stone, somewhat in the form of a half moon, about eight inches long and three broad, and hollowed out in the inside. Eskimos burn seal-fat in it, and in winter have no other means of warming their houses or cooking their food. But for both purposes it is quite sufficient. The heat created by these lamps, combined with the natural warmth of the inhabitants, is frequently so great in the igloos of the Eskimos that they are fain to throw off a great portion of their upper garments, and sit in a state of partial nudity; yet the snow-walls do not melt, owing to the counteracting influence of the intense cold without.

Maximus had brought some seal-fat, or blubber, along with him. A portion of this he now put into the lamp, and, placing the latter on a snow-shelf prepared expressly for it, he set it on fire. The flame, although not very steady, was bright enough to illuminate the large igloo, and to throw a strong gleam into the smaller one. Over this lamp Frank placed a small tin kettle, filled with snow, which was speedily converted into water; and while this was being boiled, he assisted Edith in spreading out the bedding. As we have already said, the floor of this snow-house was of the same material as the walls. But one-half of it was raised about a foot above the other half, according to Eskimo rules of architecture. This elevated half was intended for the bed, which consisted of a large deer-skin robe, spread entirely over it, with the soft hair upwards. Another large robe was placed above this for a blanket, and a smaller one either for a pillow or an additional covering if required; but both of these were tossed down in a heap at the present time, to form a luxuriant seat for Frank and Edith. As their legs hung over the edge of the elevated couch, they were thus seated, as it were, on an ottoman. A mat of interlaced willows covered the floor, and on this sat Maximus, towering in his hairy garments like a huge bear, while his black shadow was cast on the pure white wall behind him. In the midst stood a small table, extemporised by Frank out of a block of snow, and covered with the ample skirt of his leathern topcoat, which the increasing temperature of the air inside the igloo rendered too warm.

Beside Edith, on the most comfortable portion of the ottoman, sat Chimo, with an air of majestic solemnity, looking, as privileged dogs always do look under like circumstances, as if the chief seat belonged to him as a matter not of favour but of right. On the table was spread a solid lump of excellent pemmican—excellent, because made by the fair hands of Mrs. Stanley. It stood vis-a-vis to a tin plate whereon lay three large steaming cuts of boiled fresh salmon—fresh, because, although caught some months before, it had been frozen solid ever since. There was a large tin kettle of hot tea in the centre of the board—if under the circumstances we may use the term—and three tin cups out of which to drink it; besides a plate containing broken pieces of ship-biscuit and a small quantity of sugar wrapped up in a morsel of paper. Also a little salt in a tin box.

All these things, and tempting delicacies, had up till now been contained within the compass of a small, compact, insignificant-looking parcel, which during the journey had occupied a retiring position in the hinder part of Edith's sledge—so true is it that the really greatand the useful court concealment until duty calls them forth and reveals their worth and their importance to an admiring world. The admiring world on the present occasion, however, consisted only of Frank, Edith, Maximus, and Chimo; unless, indeed, we may include the moon, who at that moment poured her bright beams through the ice-window of the hut and flooded the centre of the snow-table with light.

"Aren't we snug, Eda?" cried Frank, as he filled her tin with tea. "What a charming house! and so cheap, too! There's sugar beside you. Take care you don't use salt by mistake.—Maximus, hold out your pannikin. That's the true beverage to warm your heart, if you take it hot enough."

"Tankee, sur," said the giant, extending his cup with one hand, while with the other he forced into his capacious mouth as much pemmican as it could hold.

"Frank," said Edith, "we must build an igloo at the fort when we return."

"So we will, now that I know how to do it. Hand me the salt, please, and poke Chimo's nose away from the salmon. Yes, and we'll invite papa and mamma to come and take supper at our house. Maximus, is this the exact way your friends build their winter houses?"

"Yis, sur," answered the Eskimo, looking up from the cut of salmon which he lifted with his fingers in preference to a fork or knife. "Dey always buil' um so. But not dis t'ing," he added, touching the snow-table.

"No, I suppose not," said Frank. "I flatter myself that that is a recent improvement."

"We do great many igloo sometime," continued Maximus, "vid two, t'ree, four—plenty pass'ges goin' into von a-doder."

"What does he mean by that?" inquired Edith, laughing.

"I suppose he means that they connect a number of their igloos together by means of passages. And do they keep them as clean and snug as this, Maximus?"

The Eskimo replied by a loud chuckle, and a full display of his magnificent teeth, which Frank understood to signify a decided negative.

When supper was ended Chimo was permitted to devour the scraps, while Frank assisted Edith to arrange her little dormitory. It was much the same in its arrangements as the larger apartment, and was really as comfortable and warm as one could desire. Returning to the large apartment, Frank spread out the couch on which he and Maximus were to repose; and then, sitting down beside the stone lamp, he drew forth his Bible, as was his wont, and began to read.

Soon after lying down Edith heard the deep voices of her companions engaged in earnest conversation; but these sounds gradually died away, and she fell asleep, to dream of her berry-ravine at Fort Chimo. As the night wore on, the deep breathing of the men told that they, too, had sought and found repose. The lamp burned slowly down and went out, and, when the moon threw her parting rays over the scene, there was nothing to tell of the presence of human beings in that cold, wild spot, save two little white mounds on the frozen lake below.

Chapter XXVII

FRANK MORTON GETS INTO DIFFICULTIES.

Chimo's loud bark and the angry snarl of a large wolf, as it darted away to seek the shelter of the kills, were the sounds that awoke our travellers in the grey dawn of the following morning.

Frank started up, seized his gun, and darted through the doorway of the igloo; in doing which he dashed the door of snow to atoms. He had only the satisfaction, however, of seeing the wolf's tail flourish in the air, as the animal bounded over a snow-drift and disappeared in a ravine.

"Ha! how cold it is!" he exclaimed, re-entering the igloo hastily; far having issued forth without his coat or cap, the two minutes during which he stood exposed to the open air cooled him down nearly to the freezing point. "Hallo, Maximus! jump up; light the lamp while I fill the kettle. Heyday! it solidifies the very marrow in one's bones. Ho, Edith! up with you, lazy thing; there has been a wolf to bid you good-morrow."

While Frank rattled on thus he belted his leathern coat round him, put on his fur cap, and prepared breakfast; while Edith rose and resumed the cap and cloak which she had put off on lying down to rest.

"Maximus," said Frank, after the first duties of the day were concluded, "we must now go and set the hooks; but as cutting holes in the ice will occupy you some time, I'll take a short walk along the margin of the lake with my gun. Be careful of Edith till I return."

So saying, Frank went off, taking Chimo along with him; while Maximus seized the axe and ice-chisel, and began the laborious process of digging through to the water. The ice on the lake was five feet thick, but by dint of great perseverance the Eskimo succeeded in making several holes through it ere Frank returned. Each hole was large enough to contain the body of a man, but a little wider above than below. In these holes were set stout cod-lines, with hooks of about half an inch or more in diameter. They were made of white metal, and clumsy enough to look at; but fish in the lakes of Ungava are not particular. These hooks were baited with lumps of seal-fat, and ere half an hour elapsed the success of the anglers was very decided and satisfactory.

Frank hauled up a white-fish of about six pounds weight at the first dip, and scarcely had he thrown it on the ice when Maximus gave a galvanic start, hauled up his line a few yards with laughable eagerness, then stopped suddenly, under the impression, apparently, that it was a false alarm; but another tug set him again in motion, and in three seconds he pulled a fine lake-trout of about ten pounds weight out of the hole. Edith, also, who had a line under her care, began to show symptoms of expectation.

"Capital!" cried Frank, beating his hands violently against his shoulders; for handling wet line, with the thermometer at twenty below zero is decidedly cold work—"capital! we must set up a regular fishery here, I think; the fish are swarming. There's another,—eh? no—he's off—"

"Oh! oh!! oh!!!" shrieked Edith in mingled fear and excitement, as, at each successive "oh!" she received a jerk that well-nigh pulled her into the ice-hole.

"Hold hard!" cried Frank; "now then, haul away." Edith pulled, and so did the fish; but as it was not more than five pounds weight or so, she overcame it after a severe struggle, and landed a white-fish on the ice.

The next shout that Edith gave was of so very decided and thrilling a character that Frank and Maximus darted to her side in alarm, and the latter caught the line as it was torn violently from her grasp. For a few minutes the Eskimo had to allow the line to run out, being unable to hold the fish—at least without the risk of breaking his tackle; but in a few seconds the motion of the line became less rapid, and Maximus held on, while his huge body was jerked violently, notwithstanding his weight and strength. Soon the line relaxed a little, and Maximus ran away from the hole as fast as he could, drawing the line after him. When the fish reached the hole it offered decided resistance to such treatment; and being influenced, apparently, by the well-known proverb, "Time about's fair play," it darted away in its turn, causing the Eskimo to give it line again very rapidly.

"He must be an enormously big fellow," said Frank, as he and Edith stood close to the hole watching the struggle with intense interest.

The Eskimo gave a broad grin.

"Yis, he most very biggest—hie!"

The cause of this exclamation of surprise was the slacking of the line so suddenly that Maximus was induced to believe the fish had escaped.

"Him go be-off. Ho yis!"

But he was wrong. Another violent tug convinced him that the fish was still captive—though an unwilling one—and the struggle was renewed. In about a quarter of an hour Maximus dragged this refractory fish slowly into the hole, and its snout appeared above water.

"Oh! what a fish!" exclaimed Edith.

"Put in de spear," cried the Eskimo.

Frank caught up a native spear which Maximus had provided, and just as the fish was about to recommence the struggle for its life, he transfixed it through the gills, and pinned it to the side of the ice-hole. The battle was over; a few seconds sufficed to drag the fish from its native element and lay it at full length on the ice.

And few anglers have ever had the pleasure of beholding such a prize. It was a trout of fully sixty pounds weight, and although such fish are seldom if ever found in other parts of the world, they are by no means uncommon in the lakes of North America.

Having secured this noble fish, Maximus cut it open and cleaned it, after which it was left to freeze. The other fish were then similarly treated; and while the Eskimo was thus engaged, Frank and Edith continued their sport. But daylight in these far northern regions is very short-lived in winter, and they were soon compelled unwillingly to leave off.

"Now, Maximus," said Frank, as they rolled up their lines, "I don't intend to keep you longer with us. Edith and I can manage the fishing very well, so you may return to your friends at False River, and take the seal-flesh for the dogs up to the fort. Get the loan of some of their dogs and a sled to haul it; and come round this way in passing, so as to pick up any fish we may have ready for you. The moon will be up in a little, so be off as fast as you can."

In obedience to these orders, Maximus packed up a small quantity of provisions, and bidding good-bye to his two friends, set off to make the best of his way to the coast.

That night Frank and his little charge sat down to sup together in the igloo at the head of their snow-table, and Chimo acted the part of croupier in the room of the Eskimo. And a pleasant evening they spent, chatting, and laughing, and telling stories, by the light of the stone lamp, the mellow flame of which shed a warm influence over the sparkling dome of snow. Before retiring to rest, Frank said that they must be up with the first light, for he meant to have a hard day's fishing; but man little knows what a day may bring forth. Neither Frank nor Edith dreamed that night of the events that were to happen on the morrow.

On awaking in the morning they were again roused by the voice of the wolf which had visited them the day before. In order to catch this wolf, Maximus had, just before starting, constructed a trap peculiar to the Eskimos. It was simply a hole dug down through the ice at the edge of the lake, not far from the igloo. This hole was just wide enough to admit the body of a wolf, and the depth sufficient to render it absolutely impossible for the animal to thrust his snout to the bottom, however long his neck might be. At the bottom a tempting piece of blubber, in very highcondition, was placed. The result of this ingenious arrangement was most successful, and, we may add, inevitable. Attracted by the smell of the meat, our friend the wolf came trotting down to the lake just about daybreak, and sneaked suspiciously up to the trap. He peeped in and licked his lips with satisfaction at the charming breakfast below. One would have thought, as he showed his formidable white teeth, that he was laughing with delight. Then, spreading out his fore legs so as to place his breast on the ice, he thrust his head down into the hole and snapped at the coveted blubber. But he had mistaken the depth, and blaming himself, no doubt, for his stupidity, he slid a little further forward, and pushed his head deeper down. What! not at it yet? Oh! this is preposterous! Under this impression he rose, shook himself, and advancing his shoulders as far as prudence would allow, again thrust down his head and stretched his neck until the very sinews cracked. Then it was, but not till then, that the conviction was forced on him that that precious morsel was totally and absolutely beyond his reach altogether. Drawing himself back he sat down on his haunches and uttered a snarling bark of dissatisfaction. But the odour that ascended from that hole was too much for the powers of wolfish nature to resist. Showing his teeth with an expression of mingled disappointment and ferocity, he plunged his head into the hole once more. Deeper and deeper still it went, but the blubber was yet three inches from his eager nose. Another shove—no! dislocation alone could accomplish the object. His shoulders slid very imperceptibly into the hole. His nose was within an inch of the prize, and he could actually touch it with his tongue. Away with cowardly prudence! what recked he of the consequences? Up went his hind legs, down went his head, and the tempting bait was gained at last!

Alas for wolfish misfortunes! His fore legs were jammed immovably against his ribs. A touch of his hind foot on the ice would remedy this mishap, but he was too far in for that. Vigorously he struggled, but in vain. The blood rushed to his head, and the keen frost quickly put an end to his pains. In a few minutes he was dead, and in half an hour he was frozen, solid as a block of wood, with his hind legs and tail pointing to the sky.

It was at the consummation of this event that another wolf, likewise attracted by the blubber, trotted down the wild ravine and uttered a howl of delighted surprise as it rushed forward to devour its dead companion—for such is the custom among wolves.

And this was the howl that called Frank forth in time to balk its purpose.

Frank happened to be completely dressed at the time, and as he saw the wolf bound away up the mountain gorge, he seized his gun and snow-shoes, and hastily slung on his powder-horn and shot-belt.

"Edith," he cried, as he was about to start, "I must give chase to that wolf. I won't be gone long. Light the lamp and prepare breakfast, dear—at least as much of it as you can; I'll be back to complete it.— Hallo, Chimo! here, Chimo!" he shouted, whistling to the dog, which bounded forth from the door of the hut and followed his master up the ravine.

Edith was so well accustomed to solitary wanderings among the rugged glens in the neighbourhood of Fort Chimo that she felt no alarm on finding herself left alone in this wild spot. She knew that Frank was not far off, and expected him back in a few minutes. She knew, also, that wild animals are not usually so daring as to show themselves in open ground after the break of day, particularly after the shouts of human beings have scared them to their dens; so, instead of giving a thought to any possible dangers that might threaten her, she applied herself cheerfully and busily to the preparation of their morning meal. First she lighted the lamp, which instantly removed the gloom of the interior of the igloo, whose little ice-window as yet admitted only the faint light of the grey dawn. Then she melted a little snow, and cleaned out the kettle, in which she placed two cuts of fresh trout; and having advanced thus far in her work, thought it time to throw on her hood and peep out to see if Frank was coming. But there was no sign of Frank, so she re-entered the igloo and began to set things to rights. She folded up the deerskins on which she had reposed, and piled them at the head of the willow matting that formed her somewhat rough and unyielding mattress, after which she arranged the ottoman, and laid out the breakfast things on the snow-table. Having accomplished all this to her entire satisfaction, Edith now discovered that the cuts of salmon were sufficiently well boiled, and began to hope that Frank would be quick, lest the breakfast should be spoiled. Under the influence of this feeling she threw on her hood a second time, and going out upon the lake, surveyed the shore with a scrutinising gaze. The sun was now so far above the natural horizon that the daylight was pretty clear, but the high mountains prevented any of his direct rays from penetrating the gloom of the valley of the lake. Still there was light enough to enable the solitary child to distinguish the objects on shore; but Frank's tall form was not visible anywhere.

Heaving a slight sigh, Edith returned to the hut, soliloquising thus as she went—"Dear me! it is very strange that Frank should stay away so long. I fear that the trout will be quite spoiled. Perhaps it would be very good cold. No doubt of it. We shall have it cold, and then I can get the tea ready."

In pursuance of this plan, the anxious little housekeeper removed the trout from the kettle, which she cleaned out and refilled with snow. When this was melted and boiled, she put in the tea. In due time this also was ready, and she sallied forth once more, with a feeling approaching to anxiety, to look for Frank. Still her companion did not make his appearance, and for the first time a feeling of dread touched her heart. She strove to avert it, however, by considering that Frank might have been obliged to follow the wolf farther than he expected or intended. Then a thrill of fear passed through her breast as the thought occurred, "What if the wolf has attacked and killed him?" As time wore on, and no sound of voice or gun or bark of dog broke the dreary stillness of that gloomy place, a feeling of intense horror took possession of the child's mind, and she pictured to herself all kinds of possible evils that might have befallen her companion; while at the same time she could not but feel how awful was her unprotected and helpless condition. One thought, however, comforted her, and this was that Maximus would certainly come to the hut on his return to the fort. This relieved her mind in regard to herself; but the very relief on that point enabled her all the more to realise the dangers to which Frank might be exposed without any one to render him assistance.

The morning passed away, the sun rose above the hills, and the short-lived day drew towards its close; still Frank did not return, and the poor child who watched so anxiously for him, after many short and timid wanderings towards the margin of the lake, returned to the igloo with a heart fluttering from mingled anxiety and terror. Throwing herself on the deerskin couch, she burst into a flood of tears. As she lay there, sobbing bitterly, she was startled by a noise outside the hut, and ere she could spring from her recumbent position, Chimo darted through the open doorway, with a cry between a whine and a bark, and laid his head on Edith's lap.

"Oh! what is it, my dog? Dear Chimo, where is Frank?" cried the child passionately, while she embraced her favourite with feelings of mingled delight and apprehension. "Is he coming, Chimo?" she said, addressing the dumb animal, as if she believed he understood her. Then, rising hastily, she darted out once more, to cast a longing, expectant gaze towards the place where she had seen her companion disappear in the morning. But she was again doomed to disappointment. Meanwhile Chimo's conduct struck her as being very strange. Instead of receiving with his usual quiet satisfaction the caresses she heaped upon him, he kept up a continual whine, and ran about hither and thither without any apparent object in view. Once or twice he darted off with a long melancholy howl towards the hills; then stopping short suddenly, stood still and looked round towards his young mistress. At first Edith thought that the dog must have lost his master, and had come back to the hut expecting to find him there. Then she called him to her and examined his mouth, expecting and dreading to find blood upon it. But there were no signs of his having been engaged in fighting with wolves; so Edith felt sure that Frank must be safe from them at least, as she knew that Chimo was too brave to have left his master to perish alone. The dog submitted with much impatience to this examination, and at last broke away from Edith and ran yelping towards the hills again, stopping as before, and looking back.

The resolute manner with which Chimo did this, and the frequency of its recurrence, at length induced Edith to believe that the animal wished her to follow him. Instantly it occurred that he might conduct her to Frank; so without bestowing a thought on the danger of her forsaking the igloo, she ran in for her snow-shoes, and putting on her hood and thick mittens, followed the dog to the margin of the lake. Chimo's impatience seemed to subside immediately, and he trotted rapidly towards the ravine into which Frank had entered in pursuit of the wolf that morning. The dog paused ever and anon as they proceeded, in order to give the child time to come up with him; and so eager was Edith in her adventure, and so hopeful was she that it would terminate in her finding Frank, that she pressed forward at a rate which would have been utterly impossible under less exciting circumstances.

At the foot of the ravine she found the remains of the wolf which had been caught in the snow-trap that morning. Frank had merely pulled it out and cast it on the snow in passing, and the torn fragments and scattered bones of the animal showed that its comrades had breakfasted off its carcass after Frank had passed. Here Edith paused to put on her snow-shoes, for the snow in the ravine was soft, being less exposed to the hardening action of the wind; and the dog sat down to wait patiently until she was ready.

"Now, Chimo, go forward, my good dog. I will follow you without fear," she said, when the lines were properly fastened to her feet.

Chimo waited no second command, but threaded his way rapidly up the ravine among the stunted willow bushes. In doing so he had frequent occasion to wait for his young mistress, whose strength was rapidly failing under the unwonted exertion she forced herself to make. At times she had to pause for breath, and as she cast her eyes upwards and around at the dreary desolation of the rugged precipices which everywhere met her view, she could with difficulty refrain from shedding tears. But Edith's heart was warm and brave. The thought of Frank being in some mysterious, unknown danger, infused new energy into her soul and strengthened her slight frame. Having now recovered somewhat from the nervous haste which urged her to travel at a rate much beyond her capacity, she advanced into the ravines of the mountains with more of that steady, regular tramp which practice in the use of her snow-shoes had taught her to assume; so that, being of a robust constitution naturally, she became stronger and more able for her undertaking as she advanced.

For nearly two hours Chimo led Edith into the midst of the mountains. The scenery became, if possible, more savage as they proceeded, and at length grew so rugged and full of precipices and dark gorges, or rather splits in the hills, that Edith had much difficulty in avoiding the danger of falling over many of the latter, which were partially concealed by, and in some places entirely covered over with, a crust of snow. Fortunately, as daylight waned, a brilliant galaxy of stars shone forth, enabling her to pick her steps.

Hitherto they had followed Frank's snow-shoe track undeviatingly, but near the top of a cliff Chimo suddenly diverged to the left, and led his mistress by a steep and tortuous natural path to the bottom. Here he ran quickly forward, uttering a low whine or whimper, and disappeared round the corner of the precipice. Hastening after the dog with a beating heart, Edith speedily gained the projection of the cliff, on turning which she was startled and terrified by hearing a loud snarling bark mingled with a fierce growl. In another moment she beheld Chimo bounding towards a gaunt savage-looking wolf, which stood close beside the body of a man extended at full length upon the snow.

At first the wolf did not seem inclined to retreat, but the shriek which Edith uttered on suddenly beholding the scene before her induced him to turn tail and fly. In another moment the terrified child sank exhausted on the snow beside the insensible form of Frank Morton.

THE WOLF DID NOT SEEM INCLINED TO RETREAT —PAGE 340

Chapter XXVIII

EDITH BECOMES A HEROINE INDEED.

The shock which Edith received on beholding the bloodstained countenance of her companion completely paralysed her at first, but only for a few minutes.

The feeling of certainty that Frank would perish if assistance were not rendered tended to restore her scattered faculties, and nerve her heart for the duties now required of her; and she rose with a feeling of determination to save her companion or die beside him. Poor child! she little knew the extent of her own feebleness at that moment; but she breathed an inward prayer to Him who can, and often does, achieve the mightiest results by the feeblest means.

Raising Frank's head from the snow, she placed it in her lap, and with her handkerchief removed the blood from his forehead. In doing this she observed, to her inexpressible relief, that he breathed freely, and seemed rather to be in a state of stupor than insensibility. The place where he lay was a dark rent or split in the mountain, the precipices of which rose on either side to a height of between thirty and forty feet. The top of this chasm was entirely covered over with a crust of snow, through which there was a large gap immediately above the spot where Frank lay, revealing at once the cause of his present sad condition. He had evidently been crossing the ravine by means of the deceptive platform of snow, unaware of the danger of his position, and had been suddenly precipitated to the bottom. In descending, his head had struck the side of the cliff, which cut it severely; but the softness of the snow into which he fell saved him from further injury, except the stunning effect of the fall. How long he had lain in this state Edith had no means of knowing, but it must have been a considerable time, as Chimo could not have left him until after his fall. Fortunately the wolf had not touched him, and the wound in his head did not appear to be very deep. Observing that parts of his face were slightly frostbitten, Edith commenced to rub them vigorously, at the same time calling upon him in the most earnest tones to speak to her. The effect of this roused him a little. In a few minutes he opened his eyes, and gazed languidly into the child's face.

"Where am I, Eda?" he said faintly, while a gentle smile played about his lips.

"You are in the mountains, Frank. Dear Frank! Do open your eyes again. I'm so glad to hear your voice!

Are you better now?"

The sound of his voice attracted Chimo, who had long ago abandoned the pursuit of the wolf, and was seated beside his master. Rising, he placed his cold nose on Frank's cheek. The action seemed to rouse him to the recollection of recent events. Starting up on his knees, with an angry shout, Frank seized the gun that lay beside him and raised it as if to strike the dog; but he instantly let the weapon fall, and exclaiming, "Ah, Chimo, is it you, good dog?" He fell back again into the arms of his companion.

Edith wept bitterly for a few minutes, while she tried in vain to awaken her companion from his state of lethargy. At length she dried her tears hastily, and, rising, placed Frank's head on her warm cloak, which she wrapped round his face and shoulders. Then she felt his hands, which, though covered with thick leather mittens, were very cold. Making Chimo couch at his feet, so as to imbue them with some of his own warmth, she proceeded to rub his hands, and to squeeze and, as it were, shampoo his body all over, as vigorously as her strength enabled her. In a few minutes the effect of this was apparent. Frank raised himself on his elbow and gazed wildly round him.

"Surely I must have fallen. Where am I, Edith?" Gradually his faculties returned. "Edith, Edith!" he exclaimed, in a low, anxious voice, "I must get back to the igloo. I shall freeze here. Fasten the lines of my snowshoes, dear, and I will rise."

Edith did as she was desired, and immediately Frank made a violent effort and stood upright; but he swayed to and fro like a drunken man.

"Let me lean on your shoulder, dear Eda," he said in a faint voice. "My head is terribly confused. Lead me; I cannot see well."

The child placed his hand on her shoulder, and they went forward a few paces together—Edith bending beneath the heavy weight of her companion.

"Do I lean heavily?" said Frank, drawing his hand across his forehead. "Poor child!"

As he spoke he removed his hand from her shoulder; but the instant he did so, he staggered and fell with a deep groan.

"O Frank! Dear Frank! why did you do that?" said Edith, anxiously. "You do not hurt me. I don't mind it. Do try to rise again."

Frank tried, and succeeded in walking in a sort of half-sleeping, half-waking condition for about a mile—stumbling as he went, and often unwittingly crushing his little guide to the ground. After this he fell once more, and could not again recover his upright position. Poor Edith now began to lose heart. The utter hopelessness of getting the wounded man to advance more than a few yards at a time, and her own gradually increasing weakness, induced the tears once more to start to her eyes. She observed, too, that Frank was sinking into that state of lethargy which is so dangerous in cold climates, and she had much difficulty in preventing him from falling into that sleep which, if indulged in, is indeed the sleep of death. By persevering, however, she succeeded in rousing him so far as to creep a short distance, now and then, on his hands and knees—sometimes to stagger a few paces forward; and at length, long after the cold moon had arisen on the scene, they reached the margin of the lake.

Here Frank became utterly powerless, and no exertion on the part of his companion could avail to rouse him. In this dilemma, Edith once more wrapped him in her warm cloak, and causing Chimo to lie at his feet, hastened over the ice towards the igloo. On arriving she lighted the lamp and heated the tea which she had made in the morning. This took at least a quarter of an hour to do, and during the interval she endeavoured to allay her impatience by packing up a few mouthfuls of pemmican and biscuit. Then she spread the deerskins out on the couch; and when this was done, the tea was thoroughly heated. The snow on the river being quite hard, she needed not to encumber herself with snow-shoes; but she fastened the traces of her own little sledge over her shoulders, and, with the kettle in her hand, ran as fast as her feet could carry her to the place where she had left Frank and Chimo, and found them lying exactly as they lay when she left them.

"Frank! Frank! here is some hot tea for you. Do try to take some."

But Frank did not move, so she had recourse to rubbing him again, and had soon the satisfaction of seeing him open his eyes. The instant he did so, she repeated her earnest entreaties that he would take some tea. In a few minutes he revived sufficiently to sit up and sip a little of the warm beverage. The effect was almost magical. The blood began to course more rapidly through his benumbed limbs, and in five minutes more he was able to sit up and talk to his companion.

"Now, Frank," said Edith, with an amount of decision that in other circumstances would have seemed quite laughable, "try to get on to my sled, and I'll help you. The igloo is near at hand now."

Frank obeyed almost mechanically, and creeping upon the sled with difficulty, he fell instantly into a profound sleep. Edith's chief anxiety was past now. Harnessing Chimo to the sled as well as she could, she ran on before, and a very few minutes brought them to the snow-hut. Here the work of rousing Frank had again to be accomplished; but the vigour which the warm tea had infused into his frame rendered it less difficult than heretofore, and soon afterwards Edith had the satisfaction of seeing her companion extended on his deerskin couch, under the sheltering roof of the igloo. Replenishing the lamp and closing the doorway with a slab of snow, she sat down to watch by his side. Chimo coiled himself quietly up at his feet; while Frank, under the influence of the grateful warmth, fell again into a deep slumber. As the night wore on, Edith's eyes became heavy, and she too, resting her head on the deerskins, slept till the lamp on the snow-shelf expired and left the hut and its inmates in total darkness.

Contrary to Edith's expectations, Frank was very little better when he awoke next day; but he was able to talk to her in a faint voice, and to relate how he had fallen over the cliff, and how afterwards he had to exert his failing powers in order to defend himself from a wolf.

In all these conversations his mind seemed to wander a little, and it was evident that he had not recovered from the effects of the blow received on his head in the fall. For two days the child tended him with the affectionate tenderness of a sister, but as he seemed to grow worse instead of better, she became very uneasy, and pondered much in her mind what she should do. At last she formed a strange resolution. Supposing that Maximus must still be at the Eskimo village at the mouth of False River, and concluding hastily that this village could not be very far away, she determined to set out in search of it, believing that, if she found it, the Eskimo would convey her back to the igloo on the lake, and take Frank up to Fort Chimo, where he could be properly tended and receive medicine.

Freaks and fancies are peculiar to children, but the carrying of their freaks and fancies into effect is peculiar only to those who are precocious and daring in character. Such was Edith, and no sooner had she conceived the idea of attempting to find the Eskimo camp than she proceeded to put it in execution. Frank was in so depressed a condition that she thought it better not to disturb or annoy him by arousing him so as to get him to comprehend what she was about to do; so she was obliged to commune with herself, sometimes even in an audible tone, in default of any better counsellor. It is due to her to say that, in remembrance of her mother's advice, she sought the guidance of her heavenly Father.

Long and earnest was the thought bestowed by this little child on the subject ere she ventured to leave her companion alone in the snow-hut. Frank was able to sit up and to assist himself to the articles of food and drink which his little nurse placed within his reach, so that she had no fear of his being in want of anything during the day—or two at most—that she expected to be absent; for in her childlike simplicity she concluded that if Maximus could travel thither in a few hours, she could not take much longer, especially with such a good servant as Chimo to lead the way. Besides this, she had observed the way in which the Eskimo had set out, and Frank had often pointed out to her the direction in which the camp lay. She knew also that there was no danger from wild animals, but determined, nevertheless, to build up the door of the igloo very firmly, lest they should venture to draw near. She also put Frank's loaded gun in the spot where he was wont to place it, so as to be ready to his hand.

Having made all her arrangements, Edith glided noiselessly from the hut, harnessed her dog, closed the door of the snow-hut, and jumping into the furs of her sledge, was soon far away from the mountain lake. At first the dog followed what she thought must be the track that Maximus had taken, and her spirits rose when, after an hour's drive, she emerged upon a boundless plain, which she imagined must be the shores of the frozen sea where the Eskimos lived. Encouraging Chimo with her voice, she flew over the level surface of the hard frozen snow, and looked round eagerly in all directions for the expected signs of natives.

But no such signs appeared, and she began to fear that the distance was greater than she had anticipated.

Towards the afternoon it began to snow heavily. There was no wind, and the snow fell in large flakes, alighting softly and without any sound. This prevented her seeing any great distance, and, what was worse, rendered the ground heavy for travelling.

At length she came to a ridge of rocks, and supposing that she might see to a greater distance from its summit, she got out of the sledge and clambered up, for the ground was too rough for the sledge to pass. Here the view was dreary enough—nothing but plains and hummocks of ice and snow met her view, except in one direction, where she saw, or fancied that she saw, a clump of willows and what appeared to be a hut in the midst of them. Running down the rugged declivity, she crossed the plain and reached the spot; but although the willows were there, she found no hut. Overcome with fatigue, fear, and disappointment, she sat down on a wreath of snow and wept. But she felt that her situation was much too serious to permit of her wasting time in vain regrets, so she started up and endeavoured to retrace her steps. This, however, was now a matter of difficulty. The snow fell so thickly that her footsteps were almost obliterated, and she could not see ten yards before her. After wandering about for a few minutes in uncertainty, she called aloud to Chimo, hoping to hear his bark in reply. But all was silent.

Chimo was not, indeed, unfaithful. He heard the cry and responded to it in the usual way, by bounding in the direction whence it came. His progress, however, was suddenly arrested by the sledge, which caught upon and was jammed amongst the rocks. Fiercely did

Chimo strain and bound, but the harness was tough and the sledge immovable. Meanwhile the wind arose, and although it blew gently, it was sufficient to prevent Edith overhearing the whining cries of her dog. For a time the child lost all self-command, and rushed about she knew not whither, in the anxious desire to find her sledge; then she stopped, and restrained the pantings of her breath, while with both hands pressed tightly over her heart, as if she would fain stop the rapid throbbing there, she listened long and intently. But no sound fell upon her ear except the sighing of the cold breeze as it swept by, and no sight met her anxious gaze save the thickly falling snow-flakes.

Sinking on her knees, Edith buried her face in her hands and gave full vent to the pent-up emotions of her soul, as the conviction was at length forced upon her mind that she was a lost wanderer in the midst of that cold and dreary waste of snow.

Chapter XXIX

A DARK CLOUD OF SORROW ENVELOPS FORT CHIMO.

Three days after the events narrated in the last Chapter the fort of the fur-traders became a place of weeping; for on the morning of that day Maximus arrived with the prostrate form of Frank Morton, whom he had discovered alone in the igloo on the lake, and with the dreadful news that little Edith Stanley was nowhere to be found!

It may be more easily imagined than described the state of mind into which the parents of the child were thrown; but after the first burst of emotion was past, Stanley felt that a thorough and immediate search was the only hope that remained to him of finding his little one alive. Still, when he considered the intensity of the cold to which she must have been exposed, and the length of time which had already elapsed since she was missed, his heart sank, and he could scarcely frame

words of comfort to his prostrated partner. Maximus
had examined the immediate neighbourhood of the
lake, in the hope of finding the tracks of the lost one;
but a heavy fall of snow had totally obliterated these,
and he wisely judged that it would be better to convey
the sick man to the fort as quickly as possible and give
the alarm, so that parties might be sent out to scour
the country in all directions.

Frank was immediately put to bed on his arrival,
and everything done in order to restore him. In this
attempt they succeeded so far as to obtain all the
information he could give concerning his fall; but
he remembered nothing further than that Edith had
been the means of bringing him to the snow-hut,
where he lay in a deep, torpid slumber, until the voice
and hand of Maximus awakened him. When Frank
was told that Edith was lost, he sprang from his bed
as if he had received an electric shock. The confusion
of his faculties seemed swept away, and he began to
put on his garments with as much vigour as if he were
well and strong; but ere he belted on his leather coat
his cheek grew pale, his hand trembled, and he fell
in a swoon upon the bed. This convinced him of the
impossibility of doing anything in the search, and he
was prevailed on, after two or three similar failures, to
leave the work to others.

Meanwhile the mountains and valleys of Ungava
were traversed far and near by the agonised father
and his men. The neighbourhood of the lake was the
first place searched, and they had not sought long ere
they discovered the little sledge sticking fast among

the rocks of the sea-coast, and Chimo lying in the traces almost dead with cold and hunger. The dog had kept himself alive by gnawing the deerskin of which the traces were made. Around this spot the search was concentrated, and the Eskimos of the neighbouring camp were employed in traversing the country in all directions; but, although scarce a foot of ground escaped the eager scrutiny of one or other of the party, not a vestige of Edith was to be seen—not so much as a footprint in the snow.

Days and nights flew by, and still the search was continued. Frank quickly recovered under the affectionate care of the almost heartbroken mother, who found some relief from her crushing sorrow in ministering to his wants. But the instant he could walk without support, and long before it was prudent to do so, Frank joined in the search. At first he could do little, but as day after day passed by his strength returned so rapidly that the only symptoms that remained to tell of his late accident were his pale cheek and the haggard expression of his countenance. But the mysterious disappearance of Edith had more to do with the latter than illness.

Weeks passed away, but still the dark cloud of sorrow hung over Fort Chimo, for the merry young voice that was wont to awake the surrounding echoes was gone. The systematic search had now been given up, for every nook, every glen, and gorge, and corrie within fifteen miles of the spot where they had found the little sledge, had been searched again and again without success. But hope clung with singular tenacity to the parents' hearts long after it had fled from those of the men of the fort and of the Eskimos. Every alternate day Stanley and Frank sallied forth with heavy steps and furrowed brows to explore more carefully those places where the child was most likely to have strayed, expecting, yet fearing, to find her dead body. But they always returned to the bereaved mother with silent lips and downcast looks.

They frequently conversed together about her, and always in a hopeful tone, each endeavouring to conceal from the other the real state of his own mind. Indeed, except when necessity required it, they seldom spoke on any other subject.

One day Stanley and Frank were seated by the blazing stove in the hall conversing as usual about the plan of the search for that day. Mrs. Stanley was busied in preparing breakfast.

"'Tis going to blow hard from the north, Frank," said Stanley, rising and looking out of the window; "I see the icebergs coming into the river with the tide. You will have a cold march, I fear."

Frank made no reply, but rose and approached the window. The view from it was a strange one. During the night a more than usually severe frost had congealed the water of the lake in the centre, and the icebergs that sailed towards the Caniapuscaw River in stately grandeur went crashing through this young ice as if it had been paper, their slow but steady progress receiving no perceptible check from its opposition. Some of these bergs were of great size, and in proceeding onwards they passed so close to the fort that the inhabitants feared more than once that a falling pinnacle might descend on the stores, which were built near to the water's edge, and crush them. As the tide gradually rose it rushed with violence into the cavities beneath the solid ice on the opposite shore, and finding no escape save through a few rents and fissures, sent up columns or spouts of white spray in all directions, which roared and shrieked as they flew upwards, as if the great ocean were maddened with anger at finding a power strong enough to restrain and curb its might. At intervals the main ice rent with a crash like the firing of artillery; and as if nature had designed to carry on and deepen this simile, the shore was lined with heaps of little blocks of ice which the constantly recurring action of the tide had moulded into the shape and size of cannon balls.

But such sights were common to the inhabitants of Fort Chimo, and had long ago ceased to call forth more than a passing remark.

"May it not be possible," murmured Stanley, while he leant his brow on his hand, "that she may have gone up False River?"

"I think not," said Frank. "I know not how it is, but I have a strange conviction that she is yet alive. If she had perished in the snow, we should certainly have found her long ago. I cannot explain my feelings, or give a reason for them, but I feel convinced that darling Eda is alive."

"Oh, God grant it!" whispered Stanley in a deep voice, while his wife hastened from the room to conceal the tears which she could not restrain.

While Frank continued to gaze in silence on the bleak scene without, a faint sound of sleigh-bells broke upon his ear.

"Hark!" he cried, starting, and opening the door.

The regular and familiar sound of the bells came floating sweetly on the breeze. They grew louder and louder, and in a few seconds a team of dogs galloped into the fort, dragging a small sled behind them. They were followed by two stalwart Indians, whose costume and manner told that they were in the habit of associating more with the fur-traders than with their own kindred. The dogs ran the sled briskly into the centre of the fort, and lay down panting on the snow, while the two men approached the hall.

"'Tis a packet," cried Stanley, forgetting for the moment his sorrow in the excitement of this unexpected arrival.

In a moment all the men at the fort were assembled in the square.

"A packet! Where come you from?"

"From Moose Fort," replied the elder Indian, while his comrade unfastened from the sled a little bundle containing letters.

"Any news? Are all well?" chorused the men.

"Ay, all well. It is many day since we left. The way is very rough, and we did not find much deer. We saw one camp of Indian, but they 'fraid to come. I not know why. But I see with them one fair flower which grow in the fields of the Eskimos. I suppose the Indian pluck her, and dare not come back here."

Stanley started, and his cheek grew pale.

"A fair flower, say you? Speak literally, man: was it a little white girl that you saw?"

"No," replied the Indian, "it was no white girl we saw. It was one young Eskimo woman."

Stanley heaved a deep sigh and turned away, muttering, "Ah! I might have known that she could not have fallen into the hands of Indians so far to the south."

"Well, lads, take care of these fellows," he cried, crushing down the feelings that had been for a brief moment awakened in his heart by the Indian's words, "and give them plenty to eat and smoke." So saying he went off with the packet, followed by Frank.

"Niver fear ye; come along, honey," said Bryan, grasping the elder Indian by the arm, while the younger was carried off by Massan, and the dogs taken care of by Ma-istequan and Gaspard.

On perusing the letters, Stanley found that it would be absolutely necessary to send a packet of dispatches to headquarters. The difficulties of his position required to be more thoroughly explained, and erroneous notions corrected.

"What shall I do, Frank?" said he, with a perplexed look. "These Indians cannot return to Moose, having received orders, I find, to journey in a different direction. Our own men know the way, but I cannot spare the good ones among them, and the second-rate cannot be depended on without a leader."

Frank did not give an immediate reply. He seemed to be pondering the subject in his mind. At length he said, "Could not Dick Prince be spared?"

"No; he is too useful here. The fact is, Frank, I

think I must send you. It will do you good, my dear boy, and tend to distract your mind from a subject which is now hopeless."

Frank at first objected strongly to this plan, on the ground that it would prevent him from assisting in the forlorn search for Edith; but Stanley pointed out that he and the men could continue it, and that, on the other hand, his (Frank's) personal presence at headquarters would be of great importance to the interests of the Company. At length Frank was constrained to obey.

The route by which he purposed to travel was overland to Richmond Gulf on snow-shoes; and as the way was rough, he determined to take only a few days' provisions, and depend for subsistence on the hook and gun. Maximus, Oolibuck, and Ma-istequan were chosen to accompany him; and three better men he could not have had, for they were stalwart and brave, and accustomed from infancy to live by the chase, and traverse trackless wastes, guided solely by that power of observation or instinct with which savages are usually gifted.

With these men, a week's provisions, a large supply of ammunition, a small sledge, and three dogs, of whom Chimo was the leader, Frank one morning ascended the rocky platform behind the fort, and bidding adieu to Ungava, commenced his long journey over the interior of East Main.

Chapter XXX

AN OLD FRIEND AMID NEW FRIENDS AND NOVELTIES—A
DESPERATE BATTLE AND A GLORIOUS VICTORY.

The scene of our story is now changed, and we request our patient reader to fly away with us deeper into the north, beyond the regions of Ungava, and far out upon the frozen sea.

Here is an island which for many long years has formed a refuge to the roedeer during the winter, at which season these animals, having forsaken the mainland in autumn, dwell upon the islands of the sea. At the time of which we write the island in question was occupied by a tribe of Eskimos, who had built themselves as curious a village as one could wish to see. The island had little or no wood on it, and the few willow bushes that showed their heads above the deep snow were stunted and thin. Such as they were, however, they, along with a ledge of rock over which the snow had drifted in a huge mound, formed a sort of protection to the village of the Eskimos, and sheltered it from the cold blasts that swept over the frozen sea from the regions of the far north. There were about twenty igloos in the village, all of which were built in the form of a dome, exactly similar to the hut constructed by Maximus on the lake. They were of various sizes, and while some stood apart with only a small igloo attached, others were congregated in groups and connected by low tunnels or passages. The doorways leading into most of them were so low that the natives were obliged to creep out and in on their hands and knees; but the huts themselves were high enough to permit the tallest man of the tribe to stand erect, and some of them so capacious that a family of six or eight persons could dwell in them easily. We may remark, however, that Eskimo ideas of roominess and comfort in their dwellings differ very considerably from ours. Their chief aim is to create heat, and for this end they cheerfully submit to what we would consider the discomfort of crowding and close air.

The village at a little distance bore a curious resemblance to a cluster of white beehives; and the round, soft, hairy natives, creeping out and in continually, and moving about amongst them, were not unlike (with the aid of a little imagination) to a swarm of monstrous black bees—an idea which was further strengthened by the continuous hum that floated on the air over the busy settlement. Kayaks and oomiaks lay about in several places supported on blocks of ice, and seal-spears, paddles, dans, lances, coils of walrus-line, and other implements, were intermingled in rare confusion with sledges, sealskins, chunks of raw meat and bones, on which latter the numerous dogs of the tribe were earnestly engaged.

In the midst of this village stood a hut which differed considerably from those around. It was built of clear ice instead of snow. There were one or two other igloos made of the same material, but none so large, clean, or elegant as this one. The walls, which were perpendicular, were composed of about thirty large square blocks, cemented together with snow, and arranged in the form of an octagon. The roof was a dome of snow. A small porch or passage, also of ice, stood in front of the low doorway, which had been made high enough to permit the owner of the mansion to enter by stooping slightly. In front and all around this hut the snow was carefully scraped, and all offensive objects—such as seal and whale blubber—removed, giving to it an appearance of cleanliness and comfort which the neighbouring igloos did not possess. Inside of this icy residence, on a couch of deerskin was seated Edith Stanley!

On that terrible night when the child lost her way in the dreary plain, she had wandered she knew not whither, until she was suddenly arrested by coming to the edge of the solid ice on the shores of Ungava Bay. Here the high winds had broken up the ice, and the black waters of the sea now rolled at her feet and checked her progress. Terrified at this unexpected sight, Edith endeavoured to retrace her steps; but she found to her horror that the ice on which she stood was floating, and that the wind, having shifted a point to the eastward, was driving it across to the west side of the bay. Here, in the course of the next day, it grounded, and the poor child, benumbed with cold and faint with hunger, crept as far as she could on to the firm land, and then lay down, as she thought, to die.

But it was otherwise ordained. In less than half an hour afterwards she was found by a party of Eskimos. These wild creatures had come from the eastward in their dog-sledges, and having passed well out to the seaward in order to avoid the open water off the mouth of False River, had missed seeing their countrymen there, and therefore knew nothing of the establishment of Fort Chimo. In bending towards the land again after passing the bay they came upon Edith's tracks, and after a short search they found her lying on the snow.

Words cannot convey an adequate impression of the unutterable amazement of these poor creatures as they beheld the fair child, so unlike anything they had ever seen or imagined; but whatever may have been their thoughts regarding her, they had sense enough to see that she was composed of flesh and blood, and would infallibly freeze if allowed to lie there much longer. They therefore lifted her gently upon one of the large sleighs, and placed her on a pile of furs in the midst of a group of women and children, who covered her up and chafed her limbs vigorously. Meanwhile the drivers of the sledges, of which there were six, with twenty dogs attached to each, plied their long whips energetically; the dogs yelled in consternation, and, darting away with the sledges as if they had been feathers, the whole tribe went hooting, yelling, and howling away over the frozen sea.

The surprise of the savages when they found Edith was scarcely, if at all, superior to that of Edith when she opened her eyes and began to comprehend, somewhat confusedly, her peculiar position. The savages watched her movements, open-mouthed, with intense curiosity, and seemed overjoyed beyond expression when she at length recovered sufficiently to exclaim feebly,— "Where am I? Where are you taking me to?"

We need scarcely add that she received no reply to her questions, for the natives did not understand a word of her language, and with the exception of the names of one or two familiar objects, she did not understand a word of theirs. Of how far or how long they travelled Edith could form no idea, as she slept profoundly during the journey, and did not thoroughly recover her strength and faculties until after her arrival at the camp.

For many days after reaching the Eskimo village poor Edith did nothing but weep; for, besides the miserable circumstances in which she was now placed, she was much too considerate and unselfish in her nature to forget that her parents would experience all the misery of supposing her dead, and added to this was the terrible supposition that the natives into whose hands she had fallen might never hear of Fort Chimo. The distracted child did her utmost by means of signs to make them understand that such a place existed, but her efforts were of no avail. Either she was not eloquent in the language of signs, or the natives were obtuse. As time abated the first violence of her grief, she began to entertain a hope that ere long some wandering natives might convey intelligence of her to the fur-traders. As this hope strengthened she became more cheerful, and resolved to make a number of little ornaments with her name inscribed on them, which she meant to hang round the necks of the chief men of the tribe, so that should any of them ever chance to meet with the fur-traders, these ornaments might form a clue to her strange residence.

A small medal of whalebone seemed to her the most appropriate and tractable material, but it cost her many long and weary hours to cut a circular piece of this tough material with the help of an Eskimo knife. When she had done it, however, several active boys who had watched the operation with much curiosity and interest, no sooner understood what she wished to make than they set to work and cut several round pieces of ivory or walrus-tusk, which they presented to their little guest, who scratched the name EDITH on them and hung them round the necks of the chief men of the tribe. The Eskimos smiled and patted the child's fair head kindly as they received this piece of attention, which they flattered themselves, no doubt, was entirely disinterested and complimentary.

Winter wore gradually away, and the ice upon the sea began to show symptoms of decay opposite to the camp of the Eskimos. During the high winds of spring the drift had buried the village so completely that the beehives were scarcely visible, and the big black bees walked about on the top of their igloos, and had to cut deep down in order to get into them. For some time past the natives had been unsuccessful in their seal-hunting; and as seals and walruses constituted their chief means of support, they were reduced to short allowance. Edith's portion, however, had never yet been curtailed. It was cooked for her over the stone lamp belonging to an exceedingly fat young woman whose igloo was next to that of the little stranger, and whose heart had been touched by the child's sorrow; afterwards it was more deeply touched by her gratitude and affection. This woman's name was Kaga, and she, with the rest of her tribe, having been instructed carefully by Edith in the pronunciation of her own name, ended in calling their little guest Eeduck! Kaga had a stout, burly husband named Annatock, who was the best hunter in the tribe; she also had a nephew about twelve or fourteen years old, named Peetoot, who was very fond of Edith and extremely attentive to her. Kaga had also a baby—a mere bag of fat—to which Edith became so attached that she almost constituted herself its regular nurse; and when the weather was bad, so as to confine her to the house, she used to take it from its mother, carry it off to her own igloo, and play with it the whole day, much in the same way as little girls play with dolls—with this difference, however, that she considerately restrained herself from banging its nose against the floor or punching out its eyes!

It was a bright, clear, warm day. Four mock suns

encircled and emulated in brilliancy their great original. The balmy air was beginning to melt the surface of the snow, and the igloos that had stood firm for full half a year were gradually becoming dangerous to walk over and unsafe to sit under. Considerable bustle prevailed in the camp, for a general seal-hunting expedition was on foot, and the men of the tribe were preparing their dog-sledges and their spears.

Edith was in her igloo of ice, seated on the soft pile of deerskins which formed her bed at night and her sofa by day, and worrying Kaga's baby, which laughed vociferously. The inside of this house or apartment betokened the taste and neatness of its occupant. The snow roof, having begun to melt, had been removed, and was replaced by slabs of ice, which, with the transparent walls, admitted the sun's rays in a soft, bluish light, which cast a fairy-like charm over the interior. On a shelf of ice which had been neatly fitted into the wall by her friend Peetoot lay a rude knife, a few pieces of whalebone and ivory (the remains of the material of which her medals had been made), and an ivory cup. The floor was covered with willow matting, and on the raised half of it were spread several deerskins with the hair on. A canopy of willow boughs was erected over this. On another shelf of ice, near the head of the bed, stood a small stone lamp, which had been allowed to go out, the weather being warm. The only other articles of furniture in this simple apartment were a square table and a square stool, both made of ice blocks and covered with sealskins.

While Edith and her living doll were in the height of their uproarious intercourse, they were interrupted by Peetoot, who burst into the room, more like a hairy wild-man-o'-the-wood than a human being. He carried a short spear in one hand, and with the other pointed in the direction of the shore, at the same time uttering a volley of unintelligible sounds which terminated with an emphatic "Eeduck!"

Edith's love for conversation, whether she made herself understood or not, had increased rather than abated in her peculiar circumstances.

"What is it, Peetoot? Why do you look so excited? Oh dear, I wish I understood you—indeed I do! But it's of no use your speaking so fast.—(Be quiet, baby darling.)—I see you want me to do or say something; what can it be, I wonder?"

Edith looked into the boy's face with an air of perplexity.

Again Peetoot commenced to vociferate and gesticulate violently; but seeing, as he had often seen before, that his young friend did not appear to be much enlightened, he seized her by the arm, and, as a more summary and practical way of explaining himself, dragged her towards the door of the hut.

"Oh, the baby!" screamed Edith, breaking from him and placing her charge in the farthest and safest part of the couch. "Now I'll go with you, though I don't understand what you want. Well, I suppose I shall find out in time, as usual."

Having led Edith towards the beach, Peetoot pointed to his uncle's sledge, to which the dogs were already harnessed, and made signs that Edith should go with them.

"Oh, I understand you now. Well, it is a charming day; I think I will. Do you think Annatock will let me? Oh, you don't understand. Never mind; wait till I put on my hood and return the baby to its mother."

In two minutes Edith reappeared in her fur cloak and Indian hood, with the fat baby sprawling and laughing on her shoulder. That baby never cried. It seemed as though it had resolved to substitute laughing in its stead. Once only had Edith seen tears in its little black eyes, and that was when she had given it a spoonful of soup so hot that its mouth was scalded by it.

Several of the sledges had already left the island, and were flying at full speed over the frozen sea, deviating ever and anon from the straight line in order to avoid a hummock of ice or a gap of open water caused by the separation of masses at the falling of the tide, while the men shouted, and the dogs yelled as they observed the flourish of the cruelly long and heavy lash.

"Shall I get in?" said Edith to Annatock, with an inquiring look, as she approached the place where the sledge was standing.

The Eskimo nodded his shaggy head, and showed a row of remarkably white teeth environed by a thick black beard and moustache, by way of reply to the look of the child.

With a laughing nod to Kaga, who stood watching them, Edith stepped in and seated herself on a deerskin robe; Annatock and Peetoot sat down beside her; the enormous whip gave a crack like a pistol-shot, and the team of fifteen dogs, uttering a loud cry, bounded away over the sea.

The sledge on which Edith was seated was formed very much in the same manner as the little sled which had been made for her at Fort Chimo. It was very much larger, however, and could have easily held eight or ten persons. The runners, which were shod with frozen mud (a substance that was now becoming nearly unfit for use owing to the warm weather), were a perfect wonder of ingenuity—as, indeed, was the whole machine—being pieced and lashed together with lines of raw hide in the most complicated manner and very neatly. The dogs were each fastened by a separate line to the sledge, the best dog being placed in the centre and having the longest line, while the others were attached by lines proportionably shorter according to the distance of each from the leading dog, and the outsiders being close to the runners of the sledge. All the lines were attached to the front bar of the machine. There were many advantages attending this mode of harnessing, among which were the readiness with which any dog could be attached or detached without affecting the others, and the ease with which Annatock, when so inclined, could lay hold of the line of a refractory dog, haul him back without stopping the others, and give him a cuffing. This, however, was seldom done, as the driver could touch any member of the team with the point of his whip. The handle of this terrible instrument was not much more than eighteen or twenty inches long, but the lash was upwards of six yards! Near the handle it was about three inches broad, being thick cords of walrus-hide platted; it gradually tapered towards the point, where it terminated in a fine line of the same material. While driving, the long lash of this whip trails on the snow behind the sledge, and by a peculiar sleight of hand its serpentine coils can be brought up for instant use.

No backwoodsman of Kentucky was ever more perfect in the use of his pea-rifle or more certain of his aim than was Annatock with his murderous whip. He was a dead shot, so to speak. He could spread intense alarm among the dogs by causing the heavy coil to whiz over them within a hair's-breadth of their heads; or he could gently touch the extreme tip of the ear of a skulker, to remind him of his duty to his master and his comrades; or, in the event of the warning being neglected, he could bring the point down on his flank with a crack like a pistol-shot, that would cause skin and hair to fly, and spread yelping dismay among the entire pack. And how they did run! The sledge seemed a mere feather behind the powerful team. They sprang forth at full gallop, now bumping over a small hummock or diverging to avoid a large one, anon springing across a narrow gap in the ice, or sweeping like the snowdrift over the white plain, while the sledge sprang and swung and bounded madly on behind them; and Annatock shouted as he flourished his great whip in the excitement of their rapid flight, and Peetoot laughed with wild delight, and Edith sat clasping her hands tightly over her knees—her hood thrown back, her fair hair blown straight out by the breeze, her cheeks flushed, her lips parted, and her eyes sparkling with emotion as they whirled along in their mad and swift career.

In half an hour the low village was out of sight, and in half an hour more they arrived at the place where a number of the Eskimos were scattered in twos and threes over the ice, searching for seal-holes, and preparing to catch them.

"What is that man doing?" cried Edith, pointing to an Eskimo who, having found a hole, had built a semicircular wall of snow round it to protect him from the light breeze that was blowing, and was sitting, when Edith observed him, in the attitude of one who listened intently. The hood of his sealskin coat was over his head, so that his features were concealed. At his feet lay a stout, barbed seal-spear, the handle of which was made of wood, and the barb and lower part of ivory. A tough line was attached to this, and the other end of it was fastened round the man's waist; for when an Eskimo spears a seal, he prepares to conquer or to die. If he does not haul the animal out of the hole, there is every probability that it will haul him into it. But the Eskimo has laid it down as an axiom that a man is more than a match for a seal; therefore he ties the line round his waist, which is very much like nailing the colours to the mast. There seems to be no allowance made for the chance of an obstreperously large seal allowing himself to be harpooned by a preposterously small Eskimo; but we suppose that this is the exception to the rule.

As Edith gazed, the Eskimo put out his hand with the stealthy motion of a cat and lifted his spear. The next instant the young ice that covered the hole was smashed, and, in an instant after, the ivory barb was deep in the shoulder of an enraged seal, which had thus fallen a sacrifice to his desire for fresh air. The Eskimo immediately lay back almost at full length, with his heels firmly imbedded in two notches cut in the ice at the edge of the hole; the seal dived, and the man's waist seemed to be nearly cut in two. But the rope was tough and the man was stout, and although the seal was both, it was conquered in the course of a quarter of an hour, hauled out, and thrown exultingly upon the ice.

This man had only watched at the seal-hole a couple of hours, but the natives frequently sit behind their snow walls for the greater part of a day, almost without moving hand or foot.

Having witnessed this capture, Annatock drove on until the most of his countrymen were left behind. Suddenly he called to the dogs to halt, and spoke in a deep, earnest tone to his nephew, while both of them gazed intently towards a particular quarter of the sea. Edith looked in the same direction, and soon saw the object that attracted their attention, but the only thing it seemed like to her was an enormous cask or barrel.

"What is it?" said she to Peetoot, as Annatock selected his largest spear and hastened towards the object.

Of course Edith received no reply save a broad grin; but the little fellow followed up this remark, if we may so call it, by drawing his fingers through his lips, and licking them in a most significant manner. Meanwhile Annatock advanced rapidly towards the object of interest, keeping carefully behind hummocks of ice as he went, and soon drew near enough to make certain that it was a walrus, apparently sound asleep, with its blunt snout close to its hole, ready to plunge in should an enemy appear.

Annatock now advanced more cautiously, and when within a hundred yards of the huge monster, lay down at full length on his breast, and began to work his way towards it after the manner of a seal. He was so like a seal in his hairy garments that he might easily have been mistaken for one by a more intellectual animal than a walrus. But the walrus did not awake, and he approached to within ten yards. Then, rising suddenly to his feet, Annatock poised the heavy weapon, and threw it with full force against the animal's side. It struck, and, as if it had fallen on an adamantine rock, it bounded off and fell upon the ice, with its hard point shattered and its handle broken in two.

For one instant Annatock's face blazed with surprise; the next, it relapsed into fifty dimples, as he roared and tossed up his arms with delight at the discovery that the walrus had been frozen to death beside its hole!

This catastrophe is not of unfrequent occurrence to these elephants of the northern seas. They are in the habit of coming up occasionally through their holes in the ice to breathe, and sometimes they crawl out in order to sleep on the ice, secure, in the protection of their superabundant fat, from being frozen—at least easily. When they have had enough of sleep, or when the prickling sensation on their skin warns them that nothing is proof against the cold of the Polar Seas, and that they will infallibly freeze if they do not make a precipitate retreat to the comparatively warm waters below, they scramble to their holes, crush down the new ice with their tusks and thick heads, and plunge in. But sometimes the ice which forms on the holes when they are asleep is too strong to be thus broken, in which case the hapless monster lays him down and dies.

Such was the fate of the walrus which Annatock was now cutting up with his axe into portable blocks of beef. For several days previous to the thaw which had now set in, the weather had been intensely cold, and the walrus had perished in consequence of its ambitious desire to repose in the regions above.

Not far from the spot where this fortunate discovery had been made, there was a large sheet of recently-formed black ice, where the main ice had been broken away and the open water left. The sheet, although much melted by the thaw, was still about three inches thick, and quite capable of supporting a man. While Annatock was working with his back to this ice, he heard a tremendous crash take place behind him. Turning hastily round, he observed that the noise was caused by another enormous walrus, the glance of whose large round eyes and whose loud snort showed clearly enough that he was not frozen like his unfortunate companion. By this time the little boy had come up with Edith and the sledge. So Annatock ordered him to take the dogs behind a hummock to keep them out of sight, while he selected several strong harpoons and a lance from the sledge. Giving another lance to Peetoot, he signed to Edith to sit on the hummock while he attacked the grisly monster of the deep.

While these preparations were being made, the walrus dived; and while it was under water, the man and the boy ran quickly forward a short distance, and then lay down behind a lump of ice. Scarcely had they done so when the walrus came up again with a loud snort, splashing the water with its broad, heavy flippers—which seemed a sort of compromise between legs and fins—and dashing waves over the ice as it rolled about its large, unwieldy carcass. It was truly a savage-looking monster, as large as a small elephant, and having two tusks of a foot and a half long. The face bore a horrible resemblance to that of a man. Its crown was round and bulging, its face broad and massive, and a thick, bristling moustache—rough as the spines of a porcupine—covered its upper lip, and depended in a shaggy dripping mass over its mouth. After spluttering about a short time it dived again.

Now was Annatock's time. Seizing a harpoon and a coil of line, he muttered a few words to the boy, sprang up, and running out upon the smooth ice, stood by the edge of the open water. He had not waited here more than a few seconds when the black waters were cleft by the blacker head of the monster, as it once more ascended to renew its elephantine gambols in the pool. As it rose, the Eskimo threw up his arm and poised the harpoon. For one instant the surprised animal raised itself breast-high out of the water, and directed a stare of intense astonishment at the man. That moment was fatal. Annatock buried the harpoon deep under its left flipper. With a fierce bellow the brute dashed itself against the ice, endeavouring in its fury to reach its assailant; but the ice gave way under its enormous weight, while Annatock ran back as far as the line attached to the harpoon would permit him.

The walrus, seeing that it could not reach its enemy in this way, seemed now to be actually endued with reason. It took a long gaze at Annatock, and then dived. But the Eskimo was prepared for this. He changed his position hastily, and played his line the meanwhile, fixing the point of his lance into the ice, in order to give him a more effective hold. Scarcely had he done so than the spot he had just left was smashed up, and the head of the walrus appeared, grinning and bellowing as if in disappointment. At this moment Peetoot handed his uncle a harpoon, and, ere the animal dived, the weapon was fixed in his side. Once more Annatock changed his position; and once again the spot on which he had been standing was burst upwards. It was a terrible sight to see that unearthly-looking monster smashing the ice around it, and lashing the blood-stained sea into foam, while it waged such mortal war with the self-possessed and wary man. How mighty and strong the one! How comparatively weak and seemingly helpless the other! It was the triumph of mind over matter—of reason over blind brute force. But Annatock fought a hard battle that day ere he came off conqueror. Harpoon after harpoon was driven into the walrus; again and again the lance pierced deep into its side and drank its life-blood; but three hours had passed away before the dead carcass was dragged from the deep by the united force of dogs and man. During this terrible combat Edith had looked on with such intense interest that she could scarcely believe her eyes when she found, from the position of the sun, that the day was far advanced. It was too late now to think of cutting up the carcasses without assistance, so Annatock determined to return home and tell his countrymen of his good fortune.

It is a custom among the Eskimos to consider every animal that is killed as the common property of all—the successful hunter being entitled to all the titbits, besides his portion of the equal dividend; so that Annatock knew he had only to give the signal, and every able-bodied man in the village, and not a few of the women and children, would descend like vultures on the spoil. Jumping into his sledge, he stretched out his exhausted frame at full length beside Edith, and committed the whip to Peetoot.

"I'm so glad," cried Edith, with a beaming face, "that we have killed this beast. The poor people will have plenty to eat now."

"Ha! ha! ha!" roared Peetoot, giving increased emphasis to each successive shout, and prolonging the last into a yell of delight, as he cracked the ponderous whip from side to side like a volley of pistolry.

"O Peetoot!" exclaimed Edith, in a remonstrative tone, as the sledge swayed to and fro with the rate at which they were sweeping over the plain, "don't drive so fast; you will kill the poor dogs!"

"Ho! ho! ho-o-o! Eeduck!" roared the boy, aiming a shot at the leader's left ear, and bringing the thick end of the whip down on the flanks of the six hindmost dogs.

Thus, amid a volley of roars, remonstrances, yells, yelps, and pistolry, Edith and her friends scoured over the frozen sea, and swept into the Eskimo camp like a whirlwind.

Chapter XXXI

ANOTHER DESPERATE BATTLE, AND A DECIDED
VICTORY—THE ESKIMOS SUFFER A SEVERE LOSS.

The night that followed the day of which we have given an account in the last Chapter was a night of rest to Edith, but not to the Eskimos.

Scarcely allowing themselves time to harness their dogs, after the news reached them, they set off for the scene of action in a body. Every sledge was engaged, every able-bodied male and female started. None were left in camp except the sick, of whom there were few; and the aged, of whom there were fewer. While engaged in the hurried preparations for departure the women sang with delight, for they had been living on very short allowance for some weeks past, and starvation had been threatening them; so that the present success diffused among these poor creatures a universal feeling of joy. But their preparations were not numerous. A short scene of excited bustle followed Annatock's arrival, a few yells from the dogs at starting, and the deserted camp was so silent and desolate that it seemed as if human beings had not been there for centuries.

It did not continue long, however, in this state. Two or three hours later, and the first of the return parties arrived, groaning under the burdens they carried and dragged behind them. The walrus-flesh was packed on the dog-sledges; but as for the few seals that had been caught, they were sledges to themselves—cords being tied to their tails, to which a dozen natives attached themselves, and dragged the carcasses over the snow.

Peetoot, whose spirit that night seemed to be intoxicated with success, and who felt that he was the lion of the night (after Annatock!), seated himself astride of one of the dead seals, and was dragged into camp on this novel sledge, shouting a volley of unintelligible jargon at the top of his voice, in the midst of which "Eeduck" frequently resounded. At length the last lingerer arrived, and then began a feast of the most extraordinary kind. The walrus-flesh was first conveyed to the igloo of Annatock, where it was cut up and distributed among the natives. The women seemed quite frantic with joy, and went about from hut to hut embracing one another, by way of congratulation. Soon the lamps of the village were swimming with oil, the steaks stewing and roasting, the children provided with pieces of raw blubber to keep them quiet while the larger portions were being cooked, and the entire community gormandising and rejoicing as savages are wont to do when suddenly visited with plenty in the midst of starvation.

During all this scene, Edith went about from hut to hut enjoying herself. Nay, reader, be not horrified; thou knowest not the pliable and accommodating nature of humanity. Edith did not enjoy the filth by which she was surrounded—far from it; neither did she enjoy the sight of raw blubber being sucked by little babies, especially by her own favourite; but she did enjoy the sight of so much plenty where, but a few hours ago, starvation had begun to threaten a visit; and she did enjoy and heartily sympathise with the undoubted and great happiness of her hospitable friends. A very savoury dish, with a due proportion of lean to the fat, cut specially to suit her taste, smoked on Eeduck's table that night, and Peetoot and the baby helped her to eat it. Really it would be a matter of nice calculation to ascertain whether Peetoot or the baby laughed most on this jovial occasion. Undoubtedly the former had the best of it in regard to mere noise; nevertheless the pipe of the latter was uncommonly shrill, and at times remarkably racy and obstreperous. But as the hours flew by, the children throughout the camp generally fell asleep, while their seniors sat quietly and contentedly round their kettles and lamps, eating and slumbering by turns. The amount of food consumed was enormous, and quite beyond the belief of men accustomed to the appetites of temperate zones; but we beg them to remember that arctic frosts require to be met with arctic stimulants, and of these an immense quantity of unctuous food is the best.

Next morning the Eskimos were up and away by

daybreak, with their dogs and sledges, to bring home
the remainder of the walrus-meat; for these poor
people are not naturally improvident, and do not idle
their time in luxurious indolence until necessity urges
them forth again in search of food. In this respect
they are superior to Indians, who are notoriously
improvident and regardless of the morrow.

This day was signalised by another piece of success
on the part of Annatock and his nephew, who went to
the scene of yesterday's battle on foot. Edith remained
behind, having resolved to devote herself entirely to
the baby, to make up for her neglect of the previous
day. On reaching the place where the walrus had been
slain, Annatock cut off and bound up a portion with
which he intended to return to the camp. While he
was thus employed, along with a dozen or more of
his countrymen, Peetoot came running towards him,
saying that he thought he saw a seal lying on the ice far
ahead. Having a harpoon and two spears with them,
Annatock left his work and followed his nephew to the
spot where it was supposed to be lying. But on reaching
the place they found that it was gone, and a few bells
floating at the surface of the hole showed where it
had made its descent to the element below. With the
characteristic indifference of a man accustomed to the
vicissitudes and the disappointments of a hunter's life,
the elder Eskimo uttered a grunt and turned away. But
he had not proceeded more than a few paces when
his eye became riveted on the track of some animal
on the ice, which appeared to his practised eye to be
quite fresh. Upon examination this proved to be the

case, and Annatock spoke earnestly for a few minutes with his nephew. The boy appeared from his gestures to be making some determined remarks, and seemed not a little hurt at the doubting way in which his uncle shook his head. At length Peetoot seized a spear, and, turning away, followed the track of the animal with a rapid and determined air; while Annatock, grasping the other spear, followed in the boy's track.

A brisk walk of half an hour over the ice and hummocks of the sea carried them out of sight of their companions, but did not bring them up with the animal of which they were in chase. At length Peetoot halted, and stooped to scrutinise the track more attentively. As he did so an enormous white bear stalked out from behind a neighbouring hummock of ice, and after gazing at him for a second or two, turned round and walked slowly away.

The elder Eskimo cast a doubtful glance at his nephew, while he lowered the point of his spear and seemed to hesitate; but the boy did not wait. Levelling his spear, he uttered a wild shout and ran towards the animal, which instantly turned towards the approaching enemy with a look of defiance. If Annatock had entertained any doubts of his nephew's courage before, he had none now; so, casting aside all further thought on the subject, he ran forward along with him to attack the bear. This was a matter attended with much danger, however, and there was some reason in the man feeling a little uncertainty as to the courage of a youth who, he was aware, now faced a bear for the first time in his life!

At first the two hunters advanced side by side towards the fierce-looking monster, but as they drew near they separated, and approached one on the right, the other on the left of the bear. As it was determined that Annatock should give the death-wound, he went towards the left side and hung back a moment, while Peetoot advanced to the right. When about three yards distant the bear rose. The action had a powerful and visible effect upon the boy; for as polar bears are comparatively long-bodied and short-legged, their true proportions are not fully displayed until they rear on their hind legs. It seemed as if the animal actually grew taller and more enormous in the act of rising, and the boy's cheek blanched while he shrank backwards for a moment. It was only for a moment, however. A quick word of encouragement from Annatock recalled him. He stepped boldly forward as the bear was glancing savagely from side to side, uncertain which enemy to attack first, and, thrusting his lance forward, pricked it sharply on the side. This decided the point. With a ferocious growl the animal turned to fall upon its insignificant enemy. In doing so its left shoulder was fully exposed to Annatock, who, with a dart like lightning, plunged his spear deep into its heart. A powerful shudder shook the monster's frame as it fell dead upon the ice.

Annatock stood for a few minutes leaning on his spear, and regarding the bear with a grim look of satisfaction; while Peetoot laughed, and shouted, and danced around it like a maniac. How long he would have continued these wild demonstrations it is difficult to say—probably until he was exhausted—but his uncle brought them to a speedy termination by bringing the butt-end of his spear into smart contact with Peetoot's flank. With a howl, in which consternation mingled with his glee, the boy darted away over the ice like a reindeer to convey the glad news to his friends, and to fetch a sledge for the bear's carcass.

On returning to the village there was immediately instituted another royal feast, which continued from day to day, gradually decreasing in joyous intensity as the provender decreased in bulk, until the walruses, the bear, and the seals were entirely consumed.

Soon after this the weather became decidedly mild, and the power of the sun's rays was so great that the snow on the island and the ice on the sea began to be resolved into water. During this period several important changes took place in the manners and customs of the Eskimos. The women, who had worn deerskin shoes during the winter, put on their enormous waterproof summer boots. The men, when out on the ice in search of seals, used a pair of wooden spectacles, with two narrow slits to peep through, in order to protect their eyes from the snow-blindness caused by the glare of the sun on the ice and snow—a complaint which is apt to attack all arctic travellers in spring if not guarded against by some such appliance as the clumsy wooden spectacles of the Eskimos. Active preparations were also made for the erection of skin summer tents, and the launching of kayaks and oomiaks. Moreover, little boys were forbidden to walk, as they had been wont to do, on the tops of the snow-houses, lest they should damage the rapidly-decaying roofs; but little boys in the far north inherit that tendency to disobedience which is natural to the children of Adam the world over, and on more than one occasion, having ventured to run over the igloos, were caught in the act by the thrusting of a leg now and then through the roofs thereof, to the indignation of the inmates below.

A catastrophe of this sort happened to poor Peetoot not long after the slaying of the polar bear, and brought the winter camp to an abrupt termination.

Edith had been amusing herself in her house of ice all the morning with her adopted baby, and was in the act of feeding it with a choice morsel of seal-fat, partially cooked, to avoid doing violence to her own prejudices, and very much under-done in order to suit the Eskimo baby's taste—when Peetoot rushed violently into the hut, shouted Eeduck with a boisterous smile, seized the baby in his arms, and carried it off to its mother. Edith was accustomed to have it thus torn from her by the boy, who was usually sent as a messenger when Kaga happened to desire the loan of her offspring.

The igloo in which Kaga and her relations dwelt was the largest in the village. It was fully thirty feet in diameter. The passage leading to it was a hundred yards long, by five feet wide and six feet high, and from this passage branched several others of various lengths, leading to different storehouses and to other dwellings. The whiteness of the snow of which this princely mansion and its offices were composed was not much altered on the exterior; but in the interior a long winter of cooking and stewing and general filthiness had turned the walls and roofs quite black. Being somewhat lazy, Peetoot preferred the old plan of walking over this palace to going round by the entrance, which faced the south. Accordingly, he hoisted the fat and smiling infant on his shoulder, and bounded over the dome-shaped roof of Kaga's igloo. Alas for the result of disobedience! No sooner had his foot touched the key-stone of the arch than down it went. Dinner was being cooked and consumed by twenty people below at the time. The key-stone buried a joint of walrus-beef, and instantly Peetoot and the baby lay sprawling on the top of it. But this was not all. The roof, unable to support its own weight, cracked and fell in with a dire crash. The men, women, and children struggled to disentomb themselves, and in doing so mixed up the oil of the lamps, the soup of their kettles, the black soot of the walls and roof, the dogs that had sneaked in, the junks of cooked, half-cooked, and raw blubber, and their own hairy-coated persons, into a conglomerate so atrocious to behold, or even think upon, that we are constrained to draw a curtain over the scene and spare the reader's feelings. This event caused the Eskimos to forsake the igloos, and pitch their skin tents on a spot a little to the southward of their wintering ground, which, being more exposed to the sun's rays, was now free from snow.

They had not been encamped here more than three days when an event occurred which threw the camp into deep grief for a time. This was the loss of their great hunter, Annatock, the husband of Kaga.

One of those tremendous north-west gales, which now and then visit the arctic seas and lands with such devastating fury, had set in while Annatock was out on the ice-floe in search of seals. Many of his comrades had started with him that day, but being a bold man, he had pushed beyond them all. When the gale came on the Eskimo hunters prepared to return home as fast as possible, fearing that the decaying ice might break up and drift away with them out to sea. Before starting they were alarmed to find that the seaward ice was actually in motion. It was on this ice that Annatock was employed; and his countrymen would fain have gone to warn him of his danger, but a gap of thirty feet already separated the floe from the main ice, and although they could perceive their friend in the far distance, busily employed on the ice, they could not make their voices heard. As the gale increased the floe drifted faster out to sea, and Annatock was observed running anxiously towards the land; but before he reached the edge of the ice-raft on which he stood, the increasing distance and the drifting clouds of snow hid him from view. Then his companions, fearful for their own safety, hastened back to the camp with the sad news.

At first Kaga seemed quite inconsolable, and Edith exerted herself as a comforter without success; but as time wore on the poor woman's grief abated, and hope began to revive within her bosom. She recollected that the event which had befallen her husband had befallen some of her friends before in exactly similar circumstances, and that, although on many occasions the result had been fatal, there were not a few instances in which the lost ones had been driven on their ice-raft to distant parts of the shore, and after months, sometimes years, of hardship and suffering, had returned to their families and homes.

Still this hope was at best a poor one. For the few instances there were of return from such dangers, there were dozens in which the poor Eskimos were never heard of more; and the heart of the woman sank within her as she thought of the terrible night on which her husband was lost, and the great, stormy, ice-laden sea, over whose surging bosom he was drifted. But the complex machinery of this world is set in motion and guided by One whose power and wisdom infinitely transcend those of the most exalted of His creatures; and it is a truth well worthy of being reiterated and re-impressed upon our memories, that in His hands those events that seem most adverse to man often turn out to be for his good.

Chapter XXXII

EDITH WAXES MELANCHOLY, BUT HER SADNESS IS
SUDDENLY TURNED INTO JOY; AND THE ESKIMOS RECEIVE
A SURPRISE, AND FIND A FRIEND, AND LOSE ONE.

The sea! How many stout hearts thrill and manly
bosoms swell at the sound of that little word, or
rather at the thought of all that it conveys! How many
there are that reverence and love thy power and beauty,
thy freedom and majesty, O sea! Wherein consists the
potent charm that draws mankind towards thee with
such irresistible affection? Is it in the calm tranquillity
of thy waters, when thou liest like a sheet of crystal,
with a bright refulgent sky reflected in thy soft bosom,
and the white ships resting there as if in empty space,
and the glad sea-mews rippling thy surface for a brief
moment and then sailing from the blue below to the
deeper blue above, and the soft song of thy wavelets
as they slide upon the shingly shore or lip among the

caves and hollows of the rocks! Or is it in the loud roar of thy billows, as they dash and fume and lash in fury on the coasts that dare to curb thy might? That might which, commencing, mayhap, in the torrid zone of the south, has rolled and leaped in majesty across the waste of waters, tossed leviathans as playthings in its strength, rushed impetuously over half the globe, and burst at last in helplessness upon a bed of sand! Or does the charm lie in the yet fiercer strife of the tempest and the hurricane, when the elements, let loose, sweep round the shrinking world in fury; or in the ever-changing aspect of thy countenance, now bright and fair, now ruffled with the rising breeze, or darkened by the thunder-cloud that bodes the coming storm!

Ah yes! methinks not one but all of these combined do constitute the charm which draws mankind to thee, bright ocean, and fills his soul with sympathy and love. For in the changeful aspects of thy visage there are talismans which touch the varied chords that vibrate in the hearts of men. Perchance, in the bold whistle of thy winds, and the mad rolling of thy waves, an emblem of freedom is recognised by crushed and chafing spirits longing to be free. They cannot wall thee round. They cannot map thee into acres and hedge thee in, and leave us naught but narrow roads between. No ploughshare cleaves thee save the passing keel; no prince or monarch owns thy haughty waves. In thy hidden caverns are treasures surpassing those of earth; and those who dwell on thee in ships behold the wonders of the mighty deep. We bow in adoration to thy great Creator; and we bow to thee in love and reverence and sympathy, O sea!

Edith sat on the sea-shore. The glassy waves were no longer encumbered with ice, but shone like burnished gold in the light of the summer sun. Here and there, however, a large iceberg floated on the deep—a souvenir of winter past, a guarantee of winter yet to come. At the base of these blue islands the sea, calm though it was, broke in a continual roar of surf, and round their pinnacles the circling sea-birds sailed. The yellow sands on which the child sat, the green willows that fringed the background of brown rocks, and the warm sun, contrasted powerfully with the vestiges of winter on the sea, while a bright parhelia in the sky enriched and strengthened these characteristics of an arctic summer.

There was busy life and commotion in the Eskimo camp, from which Edith had retired to some distance to indulge in solitude the sad reveries of home, which weighed more heavily on her mind as the time flew by and the hope of speedy delivery began to fade.

"O my own dear mother," sighed the child aloud, while a tear trickled down each cheek, "shall I never see you more? My heart is heavy with wishing, always wishing. But no one comes. I never see a boat or a ship on that wide, wide sea. Oh, when, when will it come?"

She paused, and, as she had often done before, laid her face on her hands and wept. But Edith soon recovered. These bursts of grief never lasted long, for the child was strong in hope. She never doubted that deliverance would come at last; and she never failed to supplicate at the throne of mercy, to which her mother had early taught her to fly in every time of trouble and distress.

Soon her attention was attracted from the sea, over whose wide expanse she had been gazing wistfully, by the loud voices of the Eskimos, as a number of them prepared to embark in their kayaks. Several small whales had been descried, and the natives, ever on the alert, were about to attack them. Presently Edith observed Peetoot running along the beach towards her with a seal-spear or harpoon in his hand. This youth was a remarkably intelligent fellow, and had picked up a few words and sentences of English, of which he made the most.

"Eeduck! Eeduck!" he cried, pointing to one of the oomiaks which the women were launching, "you go kill whale—funny; yes, Eeduck."

"I don't think it will be very funny," said Edith, laughing; "but I'll go to please you, Peetoot."

"Goot, Eeduck; you is goot," shouted the boy, while he flourished his harpoon, and seizing his companion by the hand, dragged her in the direction of the kayaks.

In a few minutes Edith was ensconced in the centre of the oomiak amid a pack of noisy Eskimo women, whose tongues were loosed and spirits raised by the hope of a successful hunt. They went merely for the purpose of witnessing the sport, which was to be prosecuted by twelve or thirteen men, each in his arrow-like kayak. The women sat round their clumsy boat with their faces to the bow, each wielding a short, broad paddle, with which they propelled their craft at good speed over the glassy wave; but a few alternate dips of the long double-bladed paddles of the kayaks

quickly sent the men far ahead of them. In the stern
of the oomiak sat an old grey-headed man, who filled
the office of steersman; a duty which usually devolves
upon old men after they become unfit to manage
the kayak. Indeed, it requires much vigour as well as
practice to paddle the kayak, for it is so easily upset
that a man could not sit in it for a minute without the
long paddle, in the clever use of which lies the security
of the Eskimo.

When the flotilla had paddled out a short distance
a whale rose, and lay as if basking on the surface of
the water. Instantly the men in the kayaks shot towards
it, while the oomiak followed as fast as possible. On
drawing near, the first Eskimo prepared his harpoon.
To the barb of this weapon a stout line, from eight to
twelve fathoms long, was attached, having a dan, or
float, made of a sealskin at the other end of it. The dan
was large enough to hold fifteen gallons or more.

Having paddled close to the whale, the Eskimo
fixed the harpoon deep in its side, and threw the dan
overboard. The whale dived in an agony, carrying the
dan down along with it, and the Eskimo, picking up
the liberated handle of the harpoon as he passed,
paddled in the direction he supposed the whale
must have taken. In a short time the dan re-appeared
at no great distance. The kayaks, as if shot from a
bow, darted towards the spot, and before the huge
fish could dive a second time, it received two more
harpoons and several deep stabs from the lances of
the Eskimos. Again it dived, carrying two additional
dans down with it. But the dragging tendency of these

three large floats, combined with the deep wounds it had received, brought the fish sooner than before to the surface, where it was instantly met and assailed by its relentless pursuers, who, in the course of little more than an hour, killed it, and dragged it in triumph to the shore.

The natives were still occupied in towing the captured fish, when one of the men uttered a wild shout, and pointed eagerly out to sea. At first Edith imagined that they must have seen another whale in the distance; but this opinion was quickly altered when she observed the eager haste with which they paddled towards the land, and the looks of surprise with which, ever and anon, they regarded the object on the horizon. This object seemed a mere speck to Edith's unaccustomed eyes; but as she gazed long and earnestly at it, a thought flashed across her mind. She sprang up; her sparkling eyes seemed as though they would burst from their sockets in her eager desire to make out this object of so great interest. At this moment the oomiak touched the land. With a bound like a gazelle Edith sprang on shore and ran panting with excitement to the top of a rocky eminence. Here she again directed her earnest gaze out to sea, while her colour went and came as she pressed her hands upon her breast in an agony of hope. Slowly but surely the speck came on; the wind shifted a point, which caused a gleam of sunlight to fall upon a sail. It was a boat! there could be no doubt of it—and making directly for the island! Unable to contain herself, Edith, uttering a piercing cry, sank upon the ground and burst into a passionate flood of tears. It was the irresistible impulse of hope long deferred at length realised; for the child did not entertain a doubt that this was at length the answer to her prayers.

Meanwhile the Eskimos ran about in a state of extraordinary excitement. These people had very probably heard of the ships which once a year pass through Hudson's Straits on their way to the depots on the shores of Hudson's Bay; but they had never met with them, or seen a Kublunat (white face) before that great day in their annals of discovery when they found little Edith fainting in the snow. Their sharp eyes had at once detected that the approaching boat was utterly different from their own kayaks or oomiaks. And truly it was; for as she drew near with her white sails bending before the evening breeze that had recently sprung up, and the Union Jack flying from her peak, and the foam curling before her sharp prow, she seemed a very model of grace and symmetry.

There were only three figures in the boat, one of whom, by the violent gesticulations that he made as they approached, bespoke himself an Eskimo; the other two stood erect and motionless, the one by the tiller, the other by the sheet.

"Let go," said a deep soft voice, when the boat was within a stone's-cast of the shore.

The sheet flapped in the wind as the peak fell, and in another instant the keel grated on the sand.

For one moment a feeling of intense disappointment filled Edith's heart as she sought in vain for the face of her father or Frank; then with a cry of joy she sprang forward and flung herself into the arms of her old enemy, Gaspard!

"Thank God!" said Dick Prince, with a tremulous voice, as he leaped lightly from the boat and clasped the child in his arms; "thank God we have found you, Miss Edith! This will put new life into your poor mother's heart."

"Oh! how is she? Why did she not come with you?" sobbed Edith; while Dick Prince, seating himself on a rock, drew her on his knee and stroked her fair head as she wept upon his shoulder.

Meanwhile Annatock was being nearly devoured by his wife and child and countrymen, as they crowded round him to obtain information, and to heap upon him congratulations; and Gaspard, in order to restrain, and at the same time relieve his feelings, essayed to drag the boat out of the water, in which attempt, giant though he was, being single-handed, he utterly failed.

After the first eager questions were answered on both sides, the natives were informed by their comrade of the nature and objects of the establishment at Ungava, and they exhibited the most extravagant signs of joy on hearing the news. When their excitement was calmed down a little, they conducted the party to their principal tent, and set before them the choicest viands they possessed, talking vehemently all the while, and indulging in a few antics occasionally, expressive of uncontrollable delight.

"Ye see, Miss Edith," began Prince, when he and Gaspard were seated before a round of walrus-beef, "the way we came to know your whereabouts was this:

Gaspard and me was sent down to the coast to hunt seals, for we were getting short o' blubber, and did not like to be obleeged to give deer's-meat to the dogs. Your father gave us the boat; 'for,' says he, 'Prince, it'll take ye down faster than the canoe with this wind; and if ye see any o' the natives, be sure ye don't forget to ask about her, Prince.' Ye see, Miss Edith, ever since ye was lost we never liked to mention your name, although we often spoke of you, for we felt that we might be speakin' o' the dead. Hows'ever, away we went for the shores o' the bay, and coasted along to the westward a bit. Then we landed at a place where there was a good lot o' field-ice floatin', with seals lyin' on it, and we began to catch them. One day, when we was goin' down to the ice as usual, we saw a black object sittin' on a floe that had drifted in the night before with a stiff breeze.

"'That's a queer-lookin' seal,' says Gaspard.

"'So 'tis,' said I. 'If there was ever black bears up hereabouts, I would say it was one o' them.'

"'Put a ball in yer gun,' says Gaspard; for ye see, as we had been blazin' at small birds the day before, there was nothing but shot in it. So I put in a ball, and took aim at the beast, intendin' to give it a long shot. But I was mercifully prevented from firin'. Jist as I squinted along the barrel, the beast rose straight up, and held up both its fore paws. 'Stop!' roars Gaspard, in an awful fright; and sure enough I lowered my gun, and the beast hailed us in the voice of a man, and began to walk to the shore. He seemed quite worn out when he landed, and I could understand enough of his jargon to make out that he had been blown out to sea on the floe, and that his name was Annatock.

"While we were talkin' to the Eskimo, Gaspard cries out, 'I say, Prince, look here! There's a sort o' medal on this chap's neck with somethin' written on it. You're a larned fellow, Prince; see if ye can make it out.' So I looked at it, and rubbed my eyes once or twice, I can tell you, for, sure enough, there was EDITH as plain as the nose on my face."

"Oh," exclaimed Edith, smiling through her tears, "that was the medal I hung round his neck long, long ago! I hoped that it might be seen some day by people who knew me."

"I thought so, miss," returned Prince—"I thought as much, for I knew that the Eskimo could never have invented and writ that out of his own head, ye see. But Gaspard and me had most awful trouble to get him to explain how he came by it, and where he came from. Howsoever, we made out at last that he came from an island in this direction; so we just made up our minds to take the boat and come straight away for the island, which we did, takin' Annatock to pilot us."

"Then does my father not know where you are, or anything about your having heard of me?" inquired Edith, in surprise.

"Why, no, Miss Edith," replied Prince. "You see, it would have lost us two or three days to have gone back to Fort Chimo; and, after all, we thought it might turn out a false scent, and only raise your poor mother's hopes for nothin'. Besides, we were sent away for a week or two, so we knew they wouldn't wonder at our absence; so we thought, upon the whole, it would be best to come at once, specially since it was sich a short distance."

"A short distance!" repeated Edith, starting up. "I thought we must be miles and miles, oh, ever so far away! Is the distance really short?"

"Ay, that it is, little one," said Prince, patting the child on the head. "It is not more than three days' rowing from this island, and a stiff breeze on the quarter would carry us there in less than two."

"And Frank, where is Frank?" said Edith, with a look of eager inquiry.

"Ah, miss," replied Prince, "he has been away almost as long as yourself. Soon after you were lost a packet came from the south, and he was obleeged to give up the sarch after you—though he was loath to do it—and set out with three o' the men for Moose. From that day to this we've heerd nothin' of him. But the journey he had to make was a long one—havin' to go round all the way to York Fort—so we didn't expect to hear o' him afore now. But I'll tell ye more about all your old friends when we git things ready for a start to-morrow."

The remainder of that day was spent in making preparation for setting sail on the following morning. The first intimation of the existence of the new trading-fort had thrown the child-like natives into rapturous delight; but when Prince told them he intended to go off the next day with the child who had been as a bright spirit in their camp so long, they fell into the depths of grief. Indeed, there was manifested a slight desire to offer forcible opposition to this; but when Edith told them, through the medium of Peetoot, who acted as her interpreter, that the distance to her father's fort was not great, and that she would expect them to come often there, and stay long, they became reconciled to her departure; and when she sought to turn their minds (a work of no great difficulty at any time) away from that subject by describing to them the treasures of the trading-store, they danced and laughed and sang like very children. Even Kaga's baby crowed with a racy richness of feeling, and smiled with an oily brilliancy of expression, compared with which all its former exhibitions were mere child's play.

But when the hour of departure really came, and Edith bade farewell to her kind friends, whose rude but warm hospitality she had enjoyed so long, they were again plunged into the deepest distress; and when the little boat finally put to sea, there was not a tearless eye among the tribe, while Edith was swiftly borne from their island shore before a strong and favouring breeze.

Chapter XXXIII

THE CLOUDS ARE BROKEN, THE SUN BURSTS
THROUGH AND ONCE MORE IRRADIATE FORT
CHIMO—HOPES AND FEARS FOR MAXIMUS.

The wings of time moved slowly and heavily along at Fort Chimo. Hope long deferred, expectation frequently reviving and as often disappointed, crushed the spirits of the little party. The song, and jest, and laugh seldom sounded from the houses of the men, who went through their daily avocations almost in silence. Not only had the loss of Edith—the bright spirit of the place, the tender rosebud in that savage wilderness—cast an overwhelming gloom upon the fort, but the failure of the trade, to a great extent, had added to the general depression, and now fresh anxiety was beginning to be felt at the non-appearance of Frank Morton.

"Jessie," said Stanley one day, as he rose from the

desk at which he had been writing, and put on his cap with the intention of taking a stroll along the beach, "will you come with me today? I know not how it is, but every time I go out now I expect to hear the ship's gun as it comes through the narrows."

Mrs. Stanley rose, and throwing on a shawl and hood, accompanied her husband in silence.

"Perhaps," she said at length, "you expect to hear the gun because the vessel ought to be here by this time."

As she spoke, La Roche came up and touched his cap. "Please, madame, vat you vill have pour dinner?"

"Whatever you please, La Roche. Repeat yesterday's," answered Mrs. Stanley, with the air of one who did not wish to be troubled further on the subject. But La Roche was not to be so easily put down.

"Ah, madame! pardonnez moi. Dat is impossible. Ve have fresh fish yesterday, dere be no fresh fish to-day. More de pity. C'est dommage— dat Gaspard him gone away—"

La Roche was interrupted by a sudden exclamation from his master, who pointed, while he gazed earnestly, towards the narrows of the river. It seemed as if the scene of last year were repeated in a vision. Against the dark rock appeared the white, triangular sail of a vessel. Slowly, like a phantom, it came into view, for the wind was very light; while the three spectators on the beach gazed with beating hearts, scarcely daring to credit their eyes. In a few seconds another sail appeared—a schooner floated into view; a white cloud burst from her bows, and once again the long, silent echoes of Ungava were awakened by the roaring of artillery.

The men of the fort left their several employments and rushed to the beach to welcome the vessel with a cheer; but although it was heartfelt and vigorous, it was neither so prolonged nor so enthusiastic as it was on the first occasion of the ship's arrival.

As the vessel dropped anchor opposite the fort, Frank Morton leaped on her bow, and along with the crew returned the cheer with a degree of energy that awakened memories of other days.

"There's Frank!" cried Stanley, turning on his wife a glance of joy. "Bless the boy! It warms my heart to see him. He must have picked up some Indian woman by the way. I see the flutter of a petticoat."

As he spoke, the boat pushed off from the vessel's side, and a few rapid strokes sent it bounding towards the shore.

"Eh! what's this?" exclaimed Stanley, as his wife broke from him, and with a wild shriek rushed into the lake.

The figure of a child stood on the boat's bow, with her arms extended to the shore.

"Hurrah, lads! give way!" shouted Frank's deep voice.

"Mother! Mother!" cried the child.

In another moment Frank bounded over the boat's side and placed Edith in her mother's arms!

Reader, there are incidents in the histories of men which cannot be minutely described without being marred. Such an one was the meeting between the father and mother and their long-lost child. We refrain from attempting to draw aside the curtain further than to say that the joy and gratitude in more than one heart at Ungava found vent that night in thanksgiving to Him who can bring light out of darkness and turn sorrow into joy.

The greater part of the day was spent at the fort in that feverish excitement which cannot calm down to steady conversation, but vents itself in eager, rambling questions and abrupt replies. Meanwhile, the necessity of discharging the cargo of the vessel, and preparing the furs for shipment, served to distract the attention and occupy the hands of the whole party.

As evening advanced, La Roche, true to his duty, placed supper on the table, and Stanley and his wife, along with Edith and Frank, while they partook of the meal, continued their inquiries.

"Whereabouts was it, Frank, that you fell in with the boat?" said Stanley.

"Not more than five miles from the mouth of the river, at about six this morning. We observed the boat beset by a pretty solid pack of ice, and you may be sure we were not a little surprised when we saw the Union Jack run up to her peak; so I ordered our boat to be lowered, intending to go to her assistance. While the men were doing this, I examined her with the glass, and then it was that I found, to my amazement and inexpressible joy, that the boat contained Prince, Gaspard, and Edith."

"Ah! Frank," said Mrs. Stanley, "was it not a strange providence that you, who were so sad at being compelled to give up the search, should be the one appointed to find our beloved child, and bring her back to us?"

"Nay," replied Frank, "it was not I who found her.

Let me not rob Dick Prince and Gaspard of the honour and gratitude which they have nobly won."

"And what do you think of the non-arrival of Maximus?" said Stanley, whose feelings were still too much perturbed to allow him to dwell for more than a few minutes at a time on any subject. Frank shook his head.

"I know not what to think," said he. "As I have told you already, we left him at Moose Fort with his recovered bride, and we got the missionary to marry them there in due form. Next day they started in a small canoe on their return voyage to Ungava, and the day following I left for Lake Superior. I fully expected to find them here on my return."

Stanley looked grave. "I fear much," said he, "that some mischance has befallen the good-hearted Eskimo. He was well armed, you say, and amply supplied with provisions?"

"Ay, most certainly. He took two guns with him, saying that his wife was as good a shot as himself."

"The men wish to know where the heavy goods are to be put," said Massan, as he opened the door, and stood, cap in hand, awaiting orders.

Stanley rose to leave the room.

"I'll be with you in a minute, Massan. Then, Frank, we'll expect an account of your journey to-night. Eda is very anxious that we should be told all about your wonderful adventures in the mountains. Meanwhile I shall be off to look after the men."

When the sun had set that night, and the song of the sailors had ceased, and most of the wearied inhabitants of Fort Chimo were enjoying a fragrant pipe after the labours of the day, Frank and Stanley seated themselves, one on either side of the fire-place, with Mrs. Stanley and Edith in front of the hearth between them. An extra pine-knot was thrown on the fire, which, in a few minutes, rendered the candle on the table unnecessary. Stanley lit his pipe, and after drawing one or two whiffs to make sure that it would keep alight, said,—"Now, Frank, my boy, we're ready for you; fire away."

Frank fired away, literally, for he applied a piece of glowing charcoal to his pipe, and fired off half a dozen rapid puffs in reply, as it were, to his friend opposite. Then he began.

Chapter XXXIV

ROUGH AND TUMBLE—A POLAR BEAR MADE
USEFUL—FISHING AND FLOUNDERING, AND
NARROW ESCAPES—AN UNEXPECTED DISCOVERY,
PRODUCTIVE OF MINGLED PERPLEXITY AND JOY.

"You remember, I daresay, that the day on which
I left Ungava, last spring, was an unusually fine
one—just such a day, Eda, as those on which you and
I and Chimo were wont to clamber up the berry-glen.
But the clambering that we went through there was
nothing to the work we went through on our third
day from the fort. Maximus and Oolibuck were first-
rate climbers, and we would have got over the ground
much faster than we did but for the dogs, which could
not travel easily over the rough ground with their
loaded sled. Chimo, indeed, hauled like a hero, and
if the other dogs had been equal to him we would
have been here before to-day. Well, as I said, our third

day was one of considerable toil. Leaving the river we struck into the mountains, but after nearly breaking our sled to pieces, and endangering our necks more than once, we found it necessary to return to the river and follow its windings into the interior.

"After many days of as rough travelling as I ever experienced, we came to the lake district on the height of land, and travelled for some time more rapidly and with much greater ease. There were plenty of ptarmigan here, so that we saved our provisions—a matter of importance, as you know, in a country where we might have found nothing fit for food. One evening, towards sunset, as we were crossing a large lake, it came on to snow heavily, and ere long we could not see the land.

"'What shall we do, Maximus?' said I; 'it seems to me that if we go on we may wander out of our course and lose much time ere we find it again. Shall we turn back?'

"'Better go on,' replied Maximus.

"Oolibuck seemed to be of the same opinion, so I gave my whip a flourish to urge on the dogs, which were beginning to flag, owing to the difficulty of drawing the sled through the deepening snow. But the two rear dogs could hardly be prevailed on to move. Even Chimo was knocked up. In this dilemma Maximus came to my aid. He hung one of the ptarmigan at his belt, and letting the dogs smell it, walked on before. The hungry animals brightened up instantly, and went forward for a considerable distance with alacrity.

"But after trudging on for two or three miles, the snow fell so thickly that we thought proper to call a halt and hold another council of war.

"'Now,' said I, 'it is my opinion that we should encamp on the ice; there is no use in wearying the dogs, and ourselves in uncertainty; what think you, lads?'

"'Me t'ink so too,' said Oolibuck.

"Maximus nodded his head by way of assent, so we immediately set to work to make our encampment. You recollect the hut we built on the lake when I was so badly hurt, and when you were lost, Eda? Well, we made a snow-house just like that one; and as we worked very hard, we had it up and were all snug under its shelter in little more than two hours. Meanwhile, the dogs were fed; and a small piece of wood, that we fortunately brought with us on the sled, was cut up, and a fire kindled. But this only served long enough to boil the kettle; and then it went out, leaving us to eat our supper in the dark, for by this time the sun had set. However, we did not mind that much; and when we had finished, and were stretched out side by side on the snow, smoking our pipes, while the dogs lay at our feet and kept us warm, I thought that a palace could not have been more comfortable than our snow-house.

"As we had no wood wherewith to make another fire, and so could not procure water except by the tedious process of digging through the ice, I resolved to try an experiment which I had once heard had been attempted with success. This was, to fill a bottle with snow and take it to bed with me. During the night the heat of my body melted the snow, and in the morning we had sufficient water to give us each a draught at breakfast.

"When morning came we found that it was blowing

and drifting so hard that we could not venture to move; so we made up our minds to remain where we were until the weather should moderate.

"'Maximus,' said I, after our breakfast of cold boiled ptarmigan was over, 'set to work outside and dig a hole through the ice. I have no doubt we shall find fish in this lake. If we do, they will form an excellent addition to our fare. I will prepare the lines and hooks.'

"Maximus, whose huge body was stretched out at full length, while he enjoyed his pipe, rose to obey; but as he was about to leave the hut Oolibuck said a few words to him.

"'Please, sir,' said Oolibuck, with his usual oily smile, 'my countrymen fish in igloo when blow hard. Pr'aps ve make hole here, if you like.'

"'Very good,' said I; 'make the hole where you please, and look sharp about it, else I shall have my lines prepared before you reach the water.'

"The two Eskimos immediately set to work, and in less than an hour a hole about six feet deep was yawning in the middle of our floor. Through this we set two lines, and our usual luck attended us immediately. We caught five or six excellent white-fish, and one or two trout, in the first half-hour, so that we were enabled to give the dogs a capital feed. Moreover, we froze as many as we could carry along with us for future use; but we had not the satisfaction of having a good dinner of them that day, as we had no wood wherewith to make fire. You would have been greatly amused had you peeped in at the ice-window of our igloo that day, as we sat round the hole in the floor with eager, excited looks. I confess, however, that I left the work principally to the two men, who seemed to relish it amazingly. Maximus was earnest and energetic, as he always is; but the expression of Oolibuck's face underwent the most extraordinary transformations—now beaming with intense hope, as he felt, or thought he felt, a tug; anon blazing with excitement, while his body jerked as if a galvanic shock had assailed it, under the influence of a decided pull. Then his visage was elongated as the fish escaped, and was again convulsed by another pull, or shone in triumph as he hauled the wriggling captive into the light of day.

"Towards evening the wind fell, and we resumed our journey. We were not again interrupted by weather for more than a week after this, but were much perplexed by the chains of small lakes into which we came. At last we reached Clearwater Lake, and had a long consultation as to the best course to pursue, because it was now a question whether we should follow the chain of lakes by which we came up to Ungava in our canoes, or make a straight cut for the coast and take our chance of finding it. While we were yet uncertain what to do, our course was decided by a polar bear!"

"A polar bear!" cried Edith, in surprise.

"Ay; a polar bear and her cub settled the question for us, as you shall hear presently," replied Frank. "But first hand me Papa's tobacco-pouch, please, as my pipe is exhausted.

"There, now," continued Frank, re-lighting his pipe, and throwing a fresh log on the fire, "that's comfortable. Well, as I said, we were somewhat perplexed as to what we should do, when, in wandering about the lake endeavouring to find the outlet, I came upon the track of a polar bear; and by the side of it were little foot-prints, which showed me that it was a she-bear with her cub. I observed that the tracks were quite fresh.

"'Now, then, Maximus,' said I, pointing to the tracks, which went to the westward, 'there is a sure guide who will conduct us by the quickest route to the coast.' I could tell this, Eda, because I knew that the bear had found food rather scarce in those high regions, and would descend Clearwater River in order to fish in the open water at the falls, which are very numerous in that river. On reaching the coast it would find plenty seals in the sea. In the meantime I had nothing to do but follow its track to be conducted by the shortest route to Clearwater River, the commencement of which was difficult to find owing to the flatness of the margin of the lake at this end. Away we went then, and, as I had expected, were soon led to the river, down the banks of which we scrambled, over rocks and crags, through bushes and snow, until we came to the coast at Richmond Gulf.

"But it took us many weeks to accomplish the journey which I have briefly sketched thus far, and when we reached the coast, worn with hard travel, and our clothing uncomfortably ragged, the spring was well advanced—rivers were breaking up, ducks and geese were passing to the north, and there were thousands of deer, so that we found ourselves suddenly in the midst of abundance. Just before reaching the gulf I witnessed the breaking up of a river, which was one of the grandest sights I ever saw.

"The river was not a very large one. On reaching it we were much struck with a curious barrier of ice that was jammed across it. On examination I saw that the ice had given way some time before we arrived there, and an enormous cake, of many yards surface and fully six feet thick, had, while being hurled along by the swelling water, caught upon the rugged rocks and been tilted upon end. Thus it formed a temporary barrier, against which other masses were forced until the outlet was completely checked, and the water began to rise with great rapidity. As we stood on the high cliff, looking down on the wild ravine in which this was going on, I heard a loud crack. In another instant the obstructing barrier burst like a thunderclap, and the pent-up waters leaped with one mighty roar into their accustomed channel! The devastation created was inconceivably grand. Rocks of many tons weight were torn up, cast like playthings on the rushing ice, and hurled on the cliffs below, while trees, and ice, and water swept down the gorge in a mad whirl, that made my brain reel as I gazed at it. In an hour the worst of this awful scene was over, but the unutterable desolation that was left will remain for centuries, I believe, to tell of the mighty rush that happened there.

"Our first experience of Richmond Gulf was not by any means pleasant. When we arrived it was covered with ice; but we did not know that, although it appeared to be solid enough, it was in reality little better than frozen sludge or foam. Oolibuck happened to be walking first, with the line of his little sled over his shoulder. For a short distance we plodded on, intending to cross the gulf; but I was suddenly aroused from a reverie by a shout from Maximus. Looking hastily up, I beheld nothing of Oolibuck except his head above the ice, while Maximus was trying to pull him out by hauling at the tail-line of the sled. Luckily Oolibuck had kept fast hold of the line which was over his shoulder, and after much trouble we succeeded in dragging him out of the water. A sharp frost happened to have set in, and before we got back to the shore the poor fellow's garments were frozen so stiff that he could not run.

"'This is a bad job, Maximus,' said I; 'we must carry him. Do you lift his head, and I'll take the feet.'

"'Oh be queek! I is frizzen up,' cried Oolibuck, casting a rueful look through his tangled locks, which were a mere mass of icicles!

"Maximus gave a loud chuckle, and before I could assist him he seized his comrade in his powerful arms, heaved him over his shoulder like a sack, and ran towards the shore as lightly as if his burden were a child instead of a big over-fed Eskimo!

"Arrived at the woods, we wrapped Oolibuck in our blankets; then we kindled a fire, and in two hours after his clothes were dried and himself ready to proceed. This might have turned out a more serious accident, however, and we felt very thankful when we had our damp companion steaming beside a good fire. The lesson was not thrown away, for we coasted round Richmond Gulf instead of attempting to cross it.

"And now," continued Frank, stirring the fire and re-lighting his pipe, which invariably went out at the interesting parts of his narrative—"now I come to that part of my story which bears on the fate of Maximus.

"As I have said, we had arrived at the coast, and began to look forward to Moose Fort as the first resting-place on our journey. By far the greater part of the journey lay before us, Eda; for, according to my calculation, I have travelled since last spring a distance of three thousand miles, nearly a thousand of which have been performed on foot, upwards of a thousand in boats and canoes, and a thousand by sea; and in the whole distance I did not see a civilised spot of ground or a single road—not so much as a bridle-path. As Bryan's favourite song has it—

"'Over mountains and rivers I was pelted to shivers.'

"But I'm happy to say I have not, as the same song continues, 'met on this land with a wathery grave.' I was very near it once, however, as you shall hear.

"Well, away we went along the coast of James's Bay, much relieved to think that the mountains were now past, and that our road henceforth, whatever else it might be, was level. One evening, as we were plodding wearily along, after a hard day's march over soft snow alternated with sandy beach—for the spring was fast advancing—we came suddenly on a camp of Indians. At first I thought they must be some of the Moose Indians, but on inquiry I found that they were a party of Muskigons, who had wandered all over East Main, and seemed to be of a roving, unsettled disposition. However, we determined to encamp along with them for that night, and get all the information we could out of them in regard to their hunting-grounds.

"We spent a great part of the night in the leathern wigwam of the principal chief, who was a sinister-looking old rascal, though I must say he received us hospitably enough, and entertained us with a good deal of small-talk, after time and the pipe had worn away his reserve. But I determined to spend part of the night in the tent of a solitary old woman who had recently been at Moose Fort, and from whom I hoped to hear some news of our friends there. You know I have had always a partiality for miserable old wives, Eda; which accounts, perhaps, for my liking for you! This dame had been named Old Moggy by the people at Moose; and she was the most shrivelled, dried-up, wrinkled old body you ever saw. She was testy too; but this was owing to the neglect she experienced at the hands of her tribe. She was good-tempered by nature, however; a fact which became apparent the longer I conversed with her.

"'Well, Old Moggy,' said I, on entering her tent, 'what cheer, what cheer?'

"'There's no cheer here,' she replied peevishly, in the Indian tongue.

"'Nay, then,' said I, 'don't be angry, mother; here's a bit o' baccy to warm your old heart. But who is this you have got beside you?' I asked, on observing a good-looking young girl, with a melancholy cast of countenance, seated in a dark corner of the wigwam, as if she sought concealment. I observed that she was whiter than Indians usually are, and supposed at first that she was a half-breed girl; but a second glance convinced me that she had little if any of the Indian blood in her veins.

"'She is my only friend,' said Old Moggy, her dark eye brightening as she glanced towards the girl. 'She was to have been my son's wife, but the Great Spirit took my son away. She is all that is left to me now.'

"The old woman's voice trembled as she spoke the last few words, and she spread her skinny hands over the small fire that smouldered in the centre of the floor.

"I was proceeding to make further inquiries into this girl's history, when the curtain-door of the tent was raised and Oolibuck thrust in his shaggy head.

"'Please, sir, de ole chief him wants baccy. I have smoke all mine. Vill you give some?'

"'Here you are,' said I, throwing a lump to the Eskimo. 'Send Maximus to me; I want to speak with him.'

"'I is here,' said Maximus, outside the tent.

"'Ah! that's right. Now, Old Moggy, I'll be back in a few minutes, so don't go to sleep till I return.'

"As I was about to issue from the tent, the young girl passed me hastily, and, drawing the hood over her head and face, darted through the opening. I found Maximus gazing after her in surprise.

"'Hallo, Maximus! what's wrong? Do you think the girl's a witch?'

"'No; but I t'ink she be funny. She look close into my face, and fly 'way when you come hout o' tent.'

"'That's odd. Did you ever see her before?'

"'I not see her yet. She keep face covered up.'

"'Well, come along, it doesn't signify. I want you to

go with me to the chief's wigwam, to ask where we are to put the dogs for the night, and to see about our own quarters.'

"Old Moggy's wigwam stood at the distance of several hundred yards from the other tents of the village, from which it was separated by a belt of stunted trees and willows. Through this copsewood Maximus and I took our way, following one of the many beaten tracks made by the Indians. The night was clear, and we found no difficulty in picking our steps among the low shrubs. When we were about half-way through this wood, I observed a female form gliding among the bushes. She ran towards Maximus, who walked in advance and concealed me with his bulky form. But a slight bend in the road revealed my figure, and the woman paused, as if uncertain what to do.

"'Surely that is your unknown friend again,' said I, as we both halted. Then I beckoned her to approach. At first she appeared unwilling to do so; but suddenly she seemed to change her mind, and walking boldly up to Maximus, she threw back her hood and stood before him. I observed that she was Moggy's young friend, but a wondrous change had come over her. The pale cheeks were now covered with a bright blush, and the sad eyes were sparkling with animation, as she gazed intently into the face of the Eskimo. For a few seconds Maximus looked like one thunder-struck. 'Aneetka!' he exclaimed vehemently, and, striding forward with a suppressed cry, clasped the girl in his arms.

"You may easily conceive my surprise at this scene. Immediately the recollection of the attack by the

Indians on the Eskimo camp, and of Maximus's young bride having been carried off, flashed upon me, and I had no doubt that the Eskimo girl now stood before me. Indeed, the fact of the broken exclamations uttered by the pair being in the Eskimo tongue put this beyond a doubt. A feeling of great delight filled my heart as I looked upon the couple thus unexpectedly reunited; while they, quite oblivious of my presence, poured out a flood of question and reply, in the midst of which they ever and anon embraced, to make sure, no doubt, of their physical identity. Then it suddenly occurred to me that I was behaving very ill, so I wheeled about and sauntered away to a little distance in the direction of the shore, in order to take some astronomical observations of the sky, and gaze inquiringly up at the moon, which at that moment broke through a bank of clouds, tipping the icebergs on the sea and the branches of the overhanging trees with silver light.

"In quarter of an hour Maximus came to me and presented his long-lost bride, Aneetka, whose pretty face beamed with joy, while her lover's frame appeared to expand with felicity until he looked like an exaggerated Hercules. But we had no time to waste in talking of the past. The present required our instant and earnest attention; so we sat down on the stem of a fallen tree to consult as to how we were to get Aneetka out of the hands of her Indian captors. Her brief history, after she was captured at Ungava, was as follows—

"The Indian who had intended to make her his bride found her resolved rather to die than to marry him;

but hoping that time would overcome her objection, he placed her under the care of his widowed mother, Old Moggy, on returning to his village in the interior. Soon afterwards this Indian was killed by a brown bear, and the poor mother became a sort of outcast from the tribe, having no relations to look after her. She was occasionally assisted, however, by two youths, who came to sue for the hand of the Eskimo girl. But Aneetka, true to her first love, would not listen to their proposals. One of these lovers was absent on a hunting expedition at the time we discovered Aneetka; the other, a surly fellow, and disliked by the most of his comrades, was in the camp. From the day of her son's death, a feeling of sympathy had sprung up between Old Moggy and the Eskimo girl, and this had gradually strengthened into affection.

"Thus matters stood when we fell in with her. After much deliberation, it was resolved that I should go to the old chief and tell him that Old Moggy and her adopted child wished to quit the tribe and go to Moose with us, to live there; while Aneetka should go and acquaint her old protectress with our plans and her own altered circumstances.

"'Adieu, then, Aneetka,' said I, as the girl pushed her lover away and bounded into the woods. 'Now, Maximus, nothing will do for it but stout hearts and strong arms. Come along, lad.'

"I found, to my surprise, that the old chief had no objection to the arrangement I proposed. A few of the others did not seem inclined to part with their captive; but I explained to them the advantage it would be to them to have friends at court, as it were, and said that the fur-traders would be glad to support Moggy in her old age—which was true enough, for you all know as well as I do that there is not a post in the country where there are not one or more old or otherwise helpless Indians supported gratuitously by the Hudson's Bay Company. The only man who resolutely opposed the proposal was Meestagoosh, the rejected lover; but I silenced him in a novel manner. He was a tall, powerful fellow, of about my own size.

"'Come,' said I to his assembled comrades, in the Indian language, for I found they understood my bad mixture of Cree and Sauteaux very well—'come, friends, let us deal fairly in this matter. My man there has taken a fancy to the girl—let Meestagoosh and Maximus wrestle for her.'

"A loud laugh greeted this proposal, as the Indians surveyed the huge proportions of my Eskimo.

"'Well, then,' I continued, 'if Meestagoosh is afraid of the Eskimo, I have no objections to try him myself.' The Indian looked at me with an angry glance, and seemed, I thought, half inclined to accept the challenge; so, to cut the matter short, I took him by the throat and hurled him to the ground—a feat which was evidently enjoyed by his countrymen.

"Meestagoosh rose and retired with a savage scowl on his face, and I saw no more of him. Indeed, I believe he left the camp immediately.

"After this no opposition was offered, and I made the matter sure by distributing a large quantity of powder, shot, and tobacco to the chiefs. Old Moggy made no objection to our plan, so we set out the next day with an additional dog purchased from the Indians in order to make our team strong enough to haul the old woman when she got knocked up with walking. Six days brought us to Moose Fort, just as the ice on the river was breaking up. Here, as I have already told you, Maximus and Aneetka were married in due form by the Wesleyan missionary, after they had received some instruction and expressed their desire to become Christians. Then they were supplied with a canoe and all necessary provisions, and sent off to go round the coast to Ungava, accompanied by our good dog Chimo, for whom we had now no further use, and by Old Moggy, who would not consent to be separated from her friend Aneetka. They started along the coast on a fine spring day, and the back of his sealskin coat, shining in the sun's rays like velvet, as the canoe swept out to sea, and disappeared behind a low point, was the last that I saw of Maximus.

"I will not weary you just now," continued Frank, "with the details of my subsequent journeying, as, although full of incidents, nothing of a very thrilling character occurred except once. At Moose I remained till the rivers were clear of ice, and then set off into the interior of the country with a small canoe and five men, Oolibuck being bowsman. For many days we voyaged by rivers and lakes, until we arrived at the Michipicoten River, which is a very rough one, and full of tremendous falls and rapids. One day, while we were descending a rapid that rushed through a dark gorge of frowning rocks, and terminated in a fall, our canoe was broken in two, and the most of us thrown into the water. We all swam ashore in safety, with the exception of one man, who clung to the canoe, poor fellow, and was carried along with it over the fall. We never saw him more, although we searched long and carefully for his body.

"We now found ourselves in a very forlorn condition. We were dripping wet, without the means of making a fire, and without provisions or blankets, in the midst of a wild, uninhabited country. However, we did not lose heart, but set off on foot to follow the river to its mouth, where we knew we should find relief at Michipicoten Fort. The few days that followed were the most miserable I ever passed. We allayed the cravings of hunger by scraping off the inner bark of the trees, and by a few of last year's berries which had been frozen and so preserved. Once or twice we crossed the river on rafts of drift-wood, and at night lay down close to each other under the shelter of a tree or cliff. At length we arrived at the fort on Lake Superior, quite worn out with fatigue and starvation. Here we waited until the canoes from Canada passed; and after a somewhat similar voyage, through woods, rivers, and lakes, arrived at length, about the beginning of autumn, at York Fort, on Hudson's Bay.

"Here I spent some weeks in recalling to memory and recording on paper the contents of my dispatches, which had been lost, along with our canoe and baggage, in Michipicoten River; and when these were finished and delivered, I embarked, along with our outfit of goods, in the Beaver, and sailed for Ungava. I need scarcely add that the voyage was a prosperous one, and that the brightest day in it all was that on which we found the boat, with our dear little Edith, beset among the ice near the entrance to Ungava Bay."

While Frank was thus occupied in narrating the events of his long journey in the hall of Fort Chimo, Oolibuck was similarly employed in entertaining the men. After the day's toil of unloading the ship was over, he was placed in the middle of the circle, directly in front of the blazing fire, by Dick Prince and Massan; while Moses, Oostesimow, Gaspard, and Ma-istequan sat on his right; and Bryan, La Roche, Francois, and Augustus supported him on the left—all having pipes in their mouths, which were more or less blackened by constant use. A pipe was then handed to Oolibuck, and the order given, generally by Bryan, "to blaze away."

This the oily-visaged Eskimo did with right good-will; and the shouts of laughter which issued from the house occasionally, as he proceeded with his interminable narration, proved that the spirit and humour of the stout voyageur had not been crushed by the trials and dangers of his long, eventful journey.

Chapter XXXV

A STIRRING PERIOD IN THE LIFE OF MAXIMUS.

Intermingled joy and sorrow is the lot of man. Thus it has ever been; thus, no doubt, it shall continue to be until the present economy shall have reached its termination. "Shall not the Judge of all the earth do right?" is a sufficient reply to those who would fain have it otherwise. But, independently of this view of the subject, may we not, with the painter's eye, regard joy as the light, sorrow as the shade, in the picture of life? And who would have a painting all light or all shadow?

Maximus found it so in his experience. The shadows in the picture of his life had of late been broad and dark, but a flash of vivid brilliancy had crossed it when he found his bride. Afterwards the light and shade were chequered, as we shall see.

On leaving Moose, Maximus proceeded a day's journey along the coast, and at night, as the weather was fine, he encamped with his wife and Old Moggy and Chimo on the open seashore. Here he held a consultation as to their future proceedings. As long as they were on the shore of James's Bay they were in danger of being found by Indians; but once beyond Richmond Gulf they would be comparatively safe, and in the land of the Eskimos. After mature deliberation it was resolved that they should travel during the night, and rest and cook their food during the daytime, when a fire would not be so likely to attract attention if kindled in sequestered places.

This plan answered very well, and they passed stealthily along the coast when the Indians, if there were any there, were buried in repose. On approaching the camp of the tribe, however, from whom Aneetka had been taken, Maximus deemed it advisable to paddle far out to sea—the weather being fortunately calm—and to rest for a day and a night as well as they could in their frail bark. Maximus sat in the stern of the canoe and steered; his wife sat in the bow and paddled day after day as vigorously as if she had been a man. As for poor Old Moggy, she sat in the middle and paddled a little when she felt cold; but she slept during the greater part of the journey. Chimo conceived it to be his duty to enjoy himself, and did so accordingly, at all times and in every possible way.

During that livelong day and night, and all the following day, the giant's arm never flagged; Aneetka, too, rested only once or twice at the earnest request of her husband; but the little bark never once slackened its speed until the second night. Then Old Moggy was awakened.

"Mother," said Aneetka, who acted as interpreter between her husband and the old woman, "we want to sleep for an hour or two. You seem to have rested well. Will you wake and watch?"

The old woman yawned, rubbed her eyes, and assented, after the question had been twice repeated. Then laying their heads on opposite sides of the canoe, without otherwise changing their positions, the husband and wife sank into repose.

Two hours afterwards the old Indian woman, who had remained motionless as a dark statue all the time, uttered a slight sound. Instantly the sleepers awoke, for those who are in the midst of danger sleep lightly.

"It is time to go on," said the old woman, as she lay back again in her lair, rolled herself up into a bundle, and went to sleep.

Maximus and his wife resumed their paddles, and the light craft glided swiftly on its way to the far north.

As the sun rose they neared the land, and soon after they were seated not far from a high cliff, eating their breakfast beside a small fire, which sent so thin a column of smoke into the air that it was almost dissipated ere it reached the tree-tops. It was hoped that the Indians had been now so far overshot that there was no danger of even a straggler being near them. But they took the precaution to load their two guns with ball, and lean them against a tree within reach of their hands. When the meal was over, Maximus retired from the fire a few paces, and throwing himself at full length on the green moss beneath a tree, he fell into a sound sleep.

He had not lain thus more than quarter of an hour

when he was startled by the report of a gun, which was followed by a wild scream and a chorus of unearthly yells. At the same instant, and ere he could attempt to rise, his legs and arms were pinioned to the ground by four powerful Indians. For an instant Maximus was paralysed. Then the terrible reality of his position, the scream of Aneetka, and the sight of the thong with which his captors were about to bind him, caused his spirit to rebound with a degree of violence that lent him for the moment the strength of a giant. With a shout, in which even a tone of contempt seemed to mingle the Eskimo hurled his captors right and left, and sprang to his feet. The Indians fled; but one, who was a moment later in rising than the others, received a blow that felled him instantly. Maximus glanced quickly round in search of his wife, and observed her being hurried away by two Indians. As the arrow leaps from the bow the Eskimo sprang forward in pursuit. The Indians saw him coming. In bitter anger they prepared to let her go and fly, for having dropped their guns in the scuffle they were unable to fire upon their approaching foe. But there were other Indians in the bush whose weapons were levelled at the breast of Maximus, and the next moment would have been his last, but for a stone thrown from the cliffs above, which struck him on the forehead and stretched him bleeding and insensible upon the ground.

When Maximus recovered from the effects of the blow, he found himself lying on the cold earth in total darkness, and firmly bound hand and foot. It is impossible to describe the agony of that bold spirit as he lay writhing on the ground, in the vain effort to burst the cords that bound him. He thought of Aneetka and his own utter helplessness, while she was, no doubt, in urgent need of his strong arm to deliver her. The thought maddened him, and again he strove in vain to burst his fetters, and yelled aloud in despair. The echoing rocks gave back his cry, and then all was silence. The dreadful thought now flashed across him that the Indians had buried him alive in some dark cavern, and brave though he was, he trembled in every limb with agony.

Thus Maximus lay until the grey dawn shone in upon him, and showed that he was in a cave. Scarcely had he noted this fact when the figure of a man darkened the cave's mouth and approached him. As the Indian bent over his helpless foe he revealed the savage features of Meestagoosh. For an instant he cast a look of mingled hatred and triumph on his enemy; then drawing a scalping-knife from his girdle, he stooped and cut the thong that bound his feet, at the same time signing to him to rise, for he knew that Maximus did not understand Indian. The Eskimo obeyed, and was led by the Indian through the woods towards the cliff where the struggle of the previous night had taken place. Here they came suddenly into view of the Indian camp.

There were no tents: several green blankets that lay on the moss under the trees indicated where the party had lain during the night; and at a considerable distance apart from these sat Old Moggy, with her face buried in her skinny hands. Beside her stood Aneetka, with a calm but slightly anxious expression on her pale countenance. Chimo was held in a leash by an Indian. From the fact of the Indians being without tents or women, and having their faces daubed with red paint, besides being armed with knives, guns, and tomahawks, Maximus concluded that they composed a war party.

On seeing her husband, Aneetka uttered a suppressed cry and bounded towards him; but ere she had proceeded two paces an Indian laid his hand on her arm, and led her back to where the old woman sat. Meestagoosh led Maximus to the same spot, and having confronted him with his wife, he said to the latter, "Now, she-bear of the north, translate between us. If I think you tell lies, the dogs shall have your bones to pick."

Aneetka replied meekly, "You cannot hurt one hair of our heads unless the Great Spirit permit you."

"We shall see," retorted the Indian with a scornful laugh. "Tell the polar bear," continued Meestagoosh, in a contemptuous tone, "that I did not expect to catch him so soon. I have been fortunate. It was kind of him to come in my way, and to bring his she-bear with him. Tell him that I and my braves are going to pay a visit to his nation, to take a few scalps. I let him know this piece of good news because he will never know it from his friends, as he shall be food for dog very soon."

On this being translated, the face of Maximus assumed an expression of deep gravity mingled with sadness. His mind flew to the far north, and he thought of the midnight assault and the death-cry of women and children. The nature of the Eskimo was too noble and generous to be easily ruffled by the contemptuous tone of such a man as Meestagoosh; but his heart sank within him when he thought of the power as well as the will that the Indian had to put his threat into execution.

"Tell him," said Maximus quietly, "that I have no wish to talk with him, but remind him that Indians are not gods; they are men."

"Yes, he says truly," retorted Meestagoosh, "the Indians are men, but Eskimos are dogs."

While this conversation was going on, and the Indians were intent upon the scene, Old Moggy, who was not deemed worthy of being noticed, contrived unobserved to possess herself of a knife, and springing suddenly towards Maximus with an agility of which she seemed utterly incapable, she endeavoured to cut the thongs that bound his arms. Her hand was caught, however, by Meestagoosh, in time to frustrate her intention. Without deigning a word of remark, the Indian struck her a heavy blow on the cheek with the back of his open hand, which nearly stunned her. Staggering backward, she fell upon the ground with a low wail.

The bosom of Maximus felt as if it would burst with rage. Before any one could prevent him, he raised his foot and struck Meestagoosh so violently on the chest that he fell as if he had been shot. In a moment he recovered, drew his knife, and springing like an infuriated tiger at his enemy, drove it with deadly force at his throat. Fortunately the arms of Maximus were tied in front of him, so that by raising them he was enabled to guard his chest and receive the stab on his wrist. The knife passed quite through the fleshy part of his left arm, but in doing so it severed one of the cords that bound him. Thought is not quicker than the mighty wrench with which the Eskimo burst the remaining cord and dashed his opponent to the ground. Before the astonished Indians could level their guns, Maximus had seized Aneetka in his arms and was bounding madly towards the cliff, which was not more than fifty yards distant. Every gun poured forth its deadly contents before he gained it; but his very nearness to the Indians seemed to contribute to his safety, and the suddenness of his flight rendered their hasty aim uncertain. In another moment he was round the point and behind the sheltering cliff, while the Indians uttered a terrific yell and darted forward in pursuit. Just about thirty paces beyond the point of the cliff that hid him for a few moments from view was the cave in which Maximus had spent the night. Quick as thought he sprang up the steep short ascent that led to its narrow entrance and darted in.

Scarcely had he placed Aneetka behind a projection that formed an ample shelter at the mouth of the cave, when Chimo, who had broken from his captors, also darted in and crouched at his master's feet. Meanwhile the Indians came sweeping round the point, and seeing by the entrance of the dog where the fugitives had taken shelter, they bounded up the ascent. The first who reached the cave's mouth rashly passed the entrance. Ere he could fire his piece he received a blow from the fist of the Eskimo that fractured his skull, hurled him down the steep ascent, and dashed him against his comrades in the rear. This sudden repulse effectually checked the Indians, who are notoriously bad at storming. Indeed they would never have ventured to enter the cave in this manner had they not known that Maximus was totally unarmed.

Withdrawing to a distance of about forty yards, the Indians now formed in a line, and loading their guns, fired volley after volley into the cave's mouth. But Maximus and his wife crouched with the dog behind the ledge of rock at the entrance, and remained there in perfect safety. In a few minutes the Indians ceased firing, and one of their number cautiously approached the cave, supposing, no doubt, that the fusillade must have wounded if it had not killed those within; but the instant he passed the entrance, knife in hand, he was caught in the powerful arms of Maximus and hurled down the slope.

A yell of indignation from the Indians followed this feat, and another volley was fired into the cave, but without effect; and the savages, seeing that it was impossible in this way to dislodge their foe, assembled in a group to consult.

Meanwhile Old Moggy had made good use of the opportunity thus afforded her to effect her escape. She darted into the bushes and made for the rocky ground in the rear of the camp. In doing so she happened to pass the tree against which leaned the two guns belonging to her friends. They had escaped notice during the melee of the previous day, and, with the shot-belts and powder-horns, remained where they had been placed when she and her companions landed. The old woman eagerly seized these, and clambered with them over the rocks at a rate that would have done credit to more youthful limbs. On reaching a ridge of rock that overlooked the cave where Maximus was sheltered, Old Moggy became aware of how matters stood. She could also see, from her elevated position, that a track, or the bed of a dried-up watercourse, led through the bushes towards the cave. Without a moment's delay she descended it; but, on drawing near to the cave, she found that there was a barren spot of about thirty yards in extent between the place of refuge and the edge of the bushes. This open space was completely exposed to the view of the natives, who at that time were firing across it into the cavern; for, after their consultation, they had changed their position and renewed the fusillade. Moggy was now in despair. She knew that it would be impossible to pass the open ground without being shot, and she also felt certain that, when the Indians found their present attempts were fruitless, they would resort to others, in prosecuting which they would in all probability discover her. While she meditated thus, she looked earnestly towards the cave, and observed the astonished gaze of Maximus fixed upon her; for, from his position behind the ledge of rock, he could see the old woman without exposing himself to the Indians. While they gazed at each other a thought occurred to Old Moggy. She made a series of complicated signs, which, after frequent repetition, were understood by Maximus to mean that he was to expose himself to the view of the Indians. Instantly comprehending her meaning, the Eskimo stepped boldly from his place of concealment and shook his fist contemptuously in the face of his enemies. A shower of bullets and a yell of rage followed the act. This was just what Old Moggy had expected and desired. Not a gun remained undischarged, and before they could reload, she passed quickly over the open ground and bounded into the cave, where she turned and shook aloft the two guns with a hoarse laugh of triumph ere she sought the shelter of the ledge of rock.

The Indians were so filled with fury at being thus outwitted by an old woman, that they forgot for a moment their usual caution, and rushed in a body up the slope; but ere they had accomplished half the distance two of their number fell, to rise no more. This was sufficient to check their career. Howling with baffled rage, and without waiting to pick up their fallen comrades, they darted right and left to seek the shelter of the bushes, for they could no longer remain in the open ground, now that their enemies were armed.

For nearly an hour after this all was silence. Maximus and his companions could only form conjectures as to the movements of the Indians, for none of them were to be seen. However, as they had no resource but to remain in their retreat until night-fall, they endeavoured to make the place as comfortable as possible, and busied themselves in cleaning their arms.

It happened that from the cave's mouth they could see their canoe, which still lay on the beach where they had originally left it; and, while they were looking at it, they perceived one of the Indians stealing down towards it. Fortunately Maximus had a gun in his hand ready loaded, and the instant the Indian appeared he fired and shot him. No second Indian dared to venture towards the little craft, although it lay only a few yards distant from the edge of the forest; for they knew that the watchful eye of the Eskimo was upon them, and that instant death would be the fate of him who should make the attempt. The little canoe now became an object of intense interest to both parties. The Indians knew that if their foe should succeed in reaching it he could easily escape. This, of course, he could not hope to do as long as daylight lasted; nor even when night should arrive, unless it were a very dark one. But, on the other hand, they knew that they did not dare to venture near it so long as there was sufficient light to enable Maximus to take aim at them with his deadly gun. Both parties, therefore, remained silent and apparently inactive during the remainder of the day.

But the busy brains both of Indians and Eskimos were, during this weary interval, employed in planning how to circumvent each other. As the shades of night deepened, each became more watchful. Once only did Maximus move from his post, in order to go to the farther end of the cave, where the large powder-horn had been placed for safety. As he did so, Chimo, who was tied to a rock, tried to follow him, and on finding that he was restrained, uttered a loud, mournful howl. This cry sent a thrill to the heart of Maximus, for it immediately occurred to him that any attempt to leave the cave stealthily would instantly be intimated to the watchful foe by the dog, and to take Chimo with them was impossible.

"The dog must die," said Old Moggy, who divined at once what was passing in the man's mind.

Maximus shook his head sadly.

"I cannot kill Chimo," he said to Aneetka; "he is Edith's dog."

Aneetka made no reply, for she felt the power of her husband's objection to injure the dog of his little favourite; yet she could not but perceive that the cry—which was invariably repeated when any of the party moved away from the animal—would betray them in the moment of danger. Nothing further was said for some time, but Old Moggy, who had no tender reminiscences or feelings in regard to the dog, proceeded quietly and significantly to construct a running-noose on the stout thong of leather that encircled her waist and served as a sash.

While she was thus engaged the sun's last rays faded away and the night began to deepen around them. To the satisfaction of both parties the sky was draped with heavy clouds, which gave promise of a night of intense darkness. This was absolutely essential not only to the Indians but to Maximus, who had at length formed a plan by which he hoped to turn the dreaded cry of the dog to good account, although he had little hope of saving it from the Indians, should he succeed in escaping with the women. As the night grew darker he began to put this plan in execution.

Taking his station at the entrance of the cave, he

took a long and steady aim at the bow of the canoe, which could now be only seen dimly. Having adjusted the gun to his satisfaction he marked its position exactly on the rock, so that, when the canoe should be entirely hid from sight, he could make certain of hitting any object directly in front of it. Then he ordered Moggy and his wife to keep moving about the cave, so that the howling of Chimo should be kept up continually, and thus not appear unusual when they should really forsake the cave and attempt their escape. In order to show that he was still on the alert, he shortly after aimed at the canoe, which was now quite invisible, and fired. The effect was more startling than had been expected. A death-cry rent the air and mingled with the reverberations of the shot, proving that it had taken deadly effect on one of the Indians, who, under cover of the darkness, had ventured to approach the coveted canoe. A volley was instantly fired in the direction of the cave from various parts of the bushes, but without effect.

Maximus now kept up a continued fire, sometimes discharging a succession of rapid shots, at other times firing at irregular intervals of from three to ten minutes. This he did purposely, with a view to his future plans. In the meantime the dog was made to keep up a continuous howling.

"Now, Aneetka," said Maximus, as the ring of his last shot died away, "go, and may the Great Spirit guide thee!"

Without a word of reply, the two women glided noiselessly like shadows into the thick darkness. About two minutes after they had disappeared, Maximus again fired several shots, taking care, however, to point considerably to the right of the canoe. Then he ceased for three minutes, and again fired several shots irregularly. At the last shot he passed from the cave so silently and quickly that even Chimo was deceived, and snuffed the air for a moment ere it renewed its sad wailing. In less than two minutes the Eskimo had glided, with the noiseless tread of a panther, to the spot where the canoe lay. Here he found his wife and the old woman crouching beside it. The water's edge was about ten yards distant. A few seconds would suffice to lift the light bark in his powerful arms and launch it. Aneetka and the old woman, who had already received minute instructions what to do, had glided quietly into the sea the instant Maximus touched them; for, as we have said, it was intensely dark and they could not see a yard before them. The women now stood up to the knees in water, with their paddles in their hands ready to embark.

Stooping down, the Eskimo seized the canoe; but, just as he was about to lift it, he observed a tall dark object close to his side.

"Wah!" whispered the Indian, "you are before me. Quick! The Eskimo dog will fire again."

The words of the Indian were cut short by the iron gripe of Maximus on his throat, and the next instant he was felled by a blow that would have stunned an ox. So decided and quick was the action that it was not accompanied by more noise than might have been caused by the Indian endeavouring to lift the canoe,

so that his comrades were not alarmed. Next moment
the canoe was in the water. But the long silence, which
had now been unbroken for eight or ten minutes,
except by the howling of Chimo in the cave, began to
arouse the suspicion of the red men; and no sooner
was this the case than they glided from the bushes
in all directions with noiseless tread. In a second or
two the body of their fallen comrade was discovered,
and a yell of fury rent the air (for concealment was
now unnecessary), while they dashed into the water
in pursuit. The darkness favoured the fugitives for
a few seconds, and enabled the women to embark;
but just as Maximus was about to step into his place,
Meestagoosh seized him by the throat!

Maximus was possessed of that ready presence of
mind and prompt energy of character which are so
necessary to a warrior, especially to him who wars with
the prowling and stealthy savage. Almost in the same
instant he gave the canoe a shove that sent it bounding
out to sea, and raised his hand to catch the invisible
arm which he knew must be descending with the
deadly knife towards his heart. He succeeded so far
that, although he did not arrest it, he turned the blow
aside, receiving only a slight wound on the shoulder.
Ere it could be repeated, he dealt his adversary a blow
on the forehead, and hurled him back insensible into
the water.

The Eskimo immediately glided out into deep
water; and now, for the first time in his life, he felt
keenly the disadvantage of not being able to swim.
This is an art which the inhabitants of the icy seas have

never acquired, owing probably to the shortness of the season of open water, and the intense cold of the ice-laden seas, even in summer. The Indians, on the contrary, who live beside the warm lakes and rivers of the interior, are many of them pretty expert swimmers. Thus it happened that Maximus was obliged to stand up to his neck in the water, not daring to move or utter a sound, while his friends and foes alike sought in vain for him in the darkness.

While he stood thus, uncertain how to act, he heard the water rippling near to him, and distinguished the hard breathing of a swimmer. Soon he observed a dark head making straight towards him. A sarcastic smile played for a moment on the face of the gigantic Eskimo, as he thought of the ease with which he should crush his approaching foe; and his hand was already raised to strike when it was arrested by a low whine, and the next moment Chimo was endeavouring to clamber upon his shoulder!

It instantly occurred to Maximus that he might turn the dog's swimming powers to good account. Seizing Chimo by the flanks with both hands, he turned its head out to sea, and keeping it in that position, was dragged into deep water. When he had been thus conveyed what appeared to be about fifty yards, he uttered a low cry. He was heard by the Indians as well as by those in the canoe; but the latter happened to be nearer to the spot, and a few strokes of the paddles sent them alongside of their comrade, who quickly caught the stern of the bark. The women plied their paddles, the Eskimo gave a shout of triumph, and half immersed in the water, was dragged away from shore. A yell of anger, and, soon after, a desultory discharge of firearms, told that the Indians had given up the chase.

But it was now a question how Maximus was to be got into the canoe. The frail bark was so crank that a much lighter weight than that of the burly Eskimo would have upset it easily; and as the stern was sharp, there was no possibility of climbing over it. This was a matter of considerable anxiety, for the water was excessively cold, being laden with ice out at sea. While in this dilemma, the canoe grated on a rock, and it was discovered that in the dark they had well-nigh run against a low cape that jutted far out from the land at this part of the coast. Here Maximus and the dog landed, and while the one shook its wet sides, the other wrung the moisture from his garments; after which necessary operation he leaped, with his canine friend, into the canoe, and they pushed well out to sea.

When daylight returned, they were far beyond the reach of their Indian enemies.

Chapter XXXVI

HAPPY MEETINGS AND JOYOUS FEASTINGS—LOVE,
MARRIAGE, DESERTION, DESOLATION, AND CONCLUSION.

After the escape narrated in the last Chapter, the stout Eskimo and his companions travelled in safety; for they had passed the country of the Indians, and were now near the lands of their own people.

But if Maximus had not now to fight with men, he was not exempted from doing fierce battle with the elements of these inhospitable climes. For hundreds of miles he travelled along the east coast of Hudson's Bay and the southern shores of the Straits, now driven ashore by the storm, anon interrupted by drift-ice, and obliged to carry his canoe for miles and miles on his shoulders, while the faithful Aneetka trudged by his side, happy as the day was long; for, although her load was necessarily a heavy one, her love for Maximus made it rest lighter than the eider-down that floated from her fingers when she plucked the wild birds for their evening meal. Moggy, too, waddled along after her own fashion, with a resolution and energy that said much for her strength and constitution. She only carried the light paddles and a few trifling articles that did not incommode her much.

During the spring and summer and autumn they pursued their arduous journey, living from hand to mouth on the produce of their guns, nets, seal-spears, and fishing-lines, which generally supplied them with enough for their daily wants, sometimes with abundance, but not unfrequently with just sufficient to keep them alive. Three or four times they met with Eskimos, and rendered essential service to them, and to the fur-traders, by telling them of the new fort at Ungava, recounting the wonders of the store there, and assuring them that the chief desire of the traders, after getting their furs, was to do them good, and bring about friendly intercourse between them and the Indians.

Late in the autumn the three voyageurs drew near to Ungava Bay, and in passing along the coast opposite to the island on which Edith had spent the winter, they overtook Annatock and his whole tribe, with a flotilla of oomiaks and kayaks, on their way to the same place. At the mouth of the bay they were joined by the Eskimos of False River, who were carrying supplies of seal-blubber to the fort for the use of the dogs in winter, and a few deerskins to trade.

It was a bright and beautiful autumn afternoon (a rare blessing in that dreary clime) when they passed the narrows of the river, and came in sight of Fort Chimo.

On that day an unusually successful deer-hunt had taken place, and the fiddle had, as Bryan expressed it, been "sarved out" to the men, for the purpose of rejoicing their hearts with sweet sounds. On that day a small band of Indians had arrived with a rich and unusually large stock of furs, among which there were one or two silver foxes and a choice lot of superb martens. This tended to gladden the heart of Stanley; and truly he needed such encouragement. At one of the Company's inland trading-posts such a bundle of furs would have been received as a matter of common occurrence; but it was otherwise with the poverty-stricken Ungava, from which so much had been expected before its dreary, barren character was known.

On that day, too, a picturesque iceberg had grounded near the fort at high water, and Frank took Edith in the small canoe to paddle her among its peaked and fantastic fragments.

"You will be steersman and sit in the stern, Eda," said Frank, as they embarked. "I will stand in the bow and keep you clear of ice-tongues."

"How beautiful!" exclaimed the delighted child, as their light craft glided in and out among the icy pinnacles which overhung them in some places as they passed. "Don't you hear a strange noise, Frank?"

Truly Frank did hear a strange noise, and beheld a strange sight, for at that moment the Eskimo flotilla passed the narrows and swept round the bay; while the natives, excited by their unusual numbers and the unexpected return of Maximus, yelled and screamed and threw about their arms in a manner that defies description.

"There must be strangers among them," said Frank, as he paddled towards the shore; "they are too numerous for our friends of False River."

"That seems to be an Indian canoe coming on ahead," remarked Stanley, who, along with his wife and most of the men, had hurried to the beach on hearing the shouts of the approaching multitude.

"Can it be possible?" exclaimed Frank, as the canoe drew near; "does it not look like Maximus—eh?"

"Oh! o-o-o-oh! there's Chimo!" screamed Edith, her eyes dancing with mingled amazement and delight.

The dog in his anxiety to reach the shore had leaped into the water; but he had miscalculated his powers of swimming, for the canoe instantly darted ahead. However, he was close on the heels of Maximus.

"Give him a chare, bays," cried Bryan, as he ran down to the beach waving a large hammer round his head. "Now thin, hooray!"

The appeal was responded to with heartfelt energy by the whole party, as their old comrade sprang from the canoe, and leaving his wife to look after herself, ran toward Stanley and Frank and grasped them warmly by the hands, while his huge face beamed with emotion.

"I hope that's your wife you've brought with you, Maximus," said Stanley.

"I can answer for that," said Frank; "I know her pretty face well."

"Ah! le poor chien," cried La Roche; "it vill eat Miss Edith, I ver' much b'lieve, voila!"

This seemed not unlikely, for the joy manifested by

poor Chimo at the sight of his young mistress was of a most outrageous character, insomuch that the child was nearly overturned by the dog's caresses.

"Musha! What have ye got there, Maximus?" said Bryan, who had been gazing for some time past in solemn wonder at the figure of Old Moggy, who, regardless of the noise and excitement around her, was quietly carrying the goods and chattels from the canoe to the beach. "Shure ye've found yer ould grandmother. She's the mortial parsonification of my own mother. Faix if it wasn't that her proboscis is a taste longer, I'd swear it was herself."

At this point Massan stepped forward and took Maximus by the arm.

"Come along, lad; there's too much row here for a comfortable palaver; bring your wife wi' you. Ye've run out o' baccy, now? Of coorse ye have. Come, then, to the house; I'll fill yer pipe and pouch, too, boy. See after his canoe, La Roche; and bring the old ooman, Bryan."

"Mind yer own consarns an' let yer shupariors proceed ye," said Bryan, as he shoved past, and tucking Old Moggy's arm within his own, marched off in triumph to the fort.

Meanwhile, the main body of Eskimos had landed, and the noise and confusion on the shore were so great that scarcely an intelligible sound could be heard. In the midst of all this, and while yet engaged in caressing Chimo, Edith felt some one pluck her by the sleeve, and on looking round she beheld the smiling faces of her old friends Arnalooa and Okatook. Scarcely had she bestowed a hearty welcome on them, when she was startled by an ecstatic yell of treble laughter close to her ear; and turning quickly round, she beheld the oily visage of Kaga with the baby—the baby—in her hood, stark naked, and revelling in mirth as if that emotion of the mind were its native element—as indeed it was, if taken in connection with seal-fat.

Scarcely had she recovered from her delight at this meeting, when she was again startled by a terrific shout, and immediately after Peetoot performed a violent dance around her, expressive of unutterable joy, and finished off by suddenly seizing her in his arms, after which he fled, horrified at his own presumption.

To escape from this scene of confusion the traders returned to the fort, having directed the Eskimos to pitch their camp on the point below; after which they were to assemble in the yard, for the double purpose of palavering and receiving a present of tobacco.

That night was spent by the inhabitants of Fort Chimo in rejoicing. In her own little room Edith entertained a select tea-party, composed of Arnalooa, Okatook, Peetoot, Chimo, and the baby; and really it would be difficult to say which of them made most noise or which behaved most obstreperously. Upon mature consideration we think that Chimo behaved best; but that, all things considered, is not saying much for him. We rather think the baby behaved worst. Its oily visage shone again like a lustrous blob of fat, and its dimples glided about the surface in an endless game of hide-and-seek! As for Peetoot, he laughed and yelled until the tears ran over his cheeks, and more than once, in the excess of his glee, he rubbed noses with Chimo—a piece of familiarity which that sagacious animal was at length induced to resent and put a stop to by a gentle and partial display of two tremendous rows of white ivory.

In the hall Stanley held a levee that lasted the greater part of the evening; and in the men's house a ball was got up in honour of the giant's return with his long-lost Aneetka.

Ah, reader! Although the countenances of the men assembled there were sunburnt and rough, and their garments weather-worn and coarse, and their language and tones unpolished, think not that their hearts were less tender or sympathetic than the hearts of those who are nurtured in softer scenes than the wilds of Ungava. Their laugh was loud and uproarious, it is true, but there was genuine, heartfelt reality in it. Their sympathy was boisterously expressed, mayhap, if expressed at all, but it was truly and deeply felt, and many an unbidden tear glanced from the bronzed cheeks of these stalwart men of the north, as they shook their gigantic comrade by the hand and wished him joy, and kissed his blooming bride.

Aneetka had long since laid aside her native garb, and wore the more graceful and womanly costume of the Indian women, and Maximus wore the capote and leggings of the voyageur. But there were not wanting gentlemen from the camp at the point whose hairy garments and hoods, long hair and beards, did honour to the race of the Eskimos; and there were present ladies from the same place, each of whom could a tail unfold that would have been the admiration and envy of tadpoles, had any such creatures been there to see them. They wore boots too, to which, in width at least, those worn by fishermen are nothing. Some of them carried babies in their hoods—little naked imps, whose bodies and heads were dumplings (suet dumplings, we may add, for the information of the curious), and whose arms and legs were sausages.

Bryan was great that night—he was majestic! The fiddle all but spoke, and produced a sensation of dancing in the toes of even those who happened to be seated. Bryan was great as a linguist, too, and exhibited his powers in this respect with singular felicity in the vocal entertainment that followed the dancing. The Eskimo language seemed a mere trifle to him, and he conversed, while playing the violin, with several "purty craytures" in their native tongue, with an amount of volubility quite surprising. Certainly it cannot be said that those whom he addressed expressed much intelligence; but Eskimos are not usually found to be quick in their perceptions. Perchance Bryan was metaphysical!

Mirth, hearty, real mirth reigned at the fort, not only that day, but for many a day afterwards; for the dangers, and troubles, and anxieties of the first year were past. Hope in the future was strong, despite the partial failures that had been experienced; and through the goodness of God, all those who composed the original band of the "forlorn hope" were reunited, after many weary months of travel, danger, and anxiety, during part of which a dark and dreary cloud (now happily dispelled) had settled down on Fort Chimo.

Years have rolled away since the song and shout of the fur-trader first awakened the echoes of Ungava. Its general aspect is still the same, for there is no change in the everlasting hills. In summer the deer still wander down the dark ravines and lave their flanks in the river's swelling tide, and in winter the frost-smoke still darkens the air and broods above the open water of the sea; but Fort Chimo, the joy and wonder of the Eskimos and the hope of the fur-trader, is gone, and a green patch of herbage near the flat rock beside the spring alone remains to mark the spot where once it stood.

In the course of time the changes that took place in the arrangements of the Fur Company required the presence of Stanley at another station, and he left Ungava with his wife and child. The gentleman who succeeded him was a bold, enterprising Scottish Highlander, whose experience in the fur trade and energy of character were a sufficient guarantee that the best and the utmost would be done for the interests of the Company in that quarter. But however resolute a man may be, he cannot make furs of hard rocks, nor convert a scene of desolation into a source of wealth. Vigorously he wrought and long he suffered, but at length he was compelled to advise the abandonment of the station. The Governor of the Company—a man of extraordinary energy and success in developing the resources of the sterile domains over which he ruled—was fain to admit at last that the trade of Ungava would not pay. The order to retreat was as prompt and decisive as the command to advance. A vessel was sent out to remove the goods, and in a brief space of time Fort Chimo was dismantled and deserted.

The Eskimos and Indians soon tore down and

appropriated to their own use the frames of the buildings, and such of the materials of the fort as had been left standing; and the few remnants that were deemed worthless were finally swept away and every trace of them obliterated by the howling storms that rage almost continually around these desolate mountains.

And now, reader, it remains for me to dismiss the characters who have played their part in this brief tale. Of most of them, however, I have but little to say, for they are still alive, scattered far and wide throughout the vast wilderness of Rupert's Land, each acting his busy part in a new scene; for it is frequently the fate of those who enter this wild and stirring service to be associated for a brief season under one roof, and then broken up and scattered over the land, never again to be reunited.

George Stanley, after a long sojourn in the backwoods, retired from the service, and, with his family, proceeded to Canada, where he purchased a small farm. Here Edith waxed strong and beautiful, and committed appalling havoc among the hearts of the young men for thirty miles around her father's farm. But she favoured no one, and at the age of seventeen acquired the name of being the coldest as well as the most beautiful and modest girl in the far west.

There was a thin young man, with weak limbs and a tendency to fall into a desponding state of mind, who lived about three miles from Mr. Stanley's farm. This young man's feelings had been so often lacerated by hopes and fears in reference to the fair Edith, that he mounted his pony one evening in desperation, and galloped away in hot haste to declare his passion, and realise or blast his hopes for ever. As he approached the villa, however, he experienced a sensation of emptiness about the region of the stomach, and regretted that he had not taken more food at dinner. Having passed the garden gate, he dismounted, fastened his pony to a tree, and struck across the shrubbery towards the house with trembling steps. As he proceeded, he received a terrific shock by observing the flutter of a scarf, which he knew intuitively belonged to Edith. The scarf disappeared within a bower which stood not more than twenty yards distant from him, close beside the avenue that led to the house. By taking two steps forward he could have seen Edith, as she sat in the bower gazing with a pensive look at the distant prospect of hill and dale, river and lake, in the midst of which she dwelt; but the young man could as easily have leaped over Stanley's villa, farm and all, as have taken these two steps. He essayed to do so; but he was rooted to the ground as firmly as the noble trees under which he stood. At length, by a great effort, he managed to crawl—if we may so express it—to within a few yards of the bower, from which he was now concealed only by a few bushes; but just as he had screwed up his soul to the sticking point, and had shut his eyes preparatory to making a rush and flinging himself on his knees at Edith's feet, he was struck powerless by the sound of a deep sigh, and, a moment after, was all but annihilated by a cough!

Suddenly the sound of horse-hoofs was heard clattering up the avenue. On came the rider, as if in urgent haste. In a few seconds a curve in the avenue brought him into view. He was a man of handsome and massive proportions, and bestrode a black charger that might have carried a heavy dragoon like a feather. A wheel-barrow had been left across the track, over which the steed went with an easy yet heavy bound, betokening well-balanced strength and weight; and a bright smile lighted up the rider's bronzed face for an instant, as his straw-hat blew off in the leap and permitted his curling hair to stream out in the wind. As he passed the bower at a swinging gallop, an exclamation of surprise from Edith attracted his attention. The charger's hoofs spurned the gravel while he was reined up so violently that he was thrown on his haunches, and almost before the thin young man could wink in order to clear his vision, this slashing cavalier sprang to the ground and entered the bower.

There was a faint scream, which was instantly followed by a sound so peculiar that it sent a thrill of dismay to the cavity in which the heart of the weak young man had once lodged. Stretching out his hand he turned aside the branches, and was brought to the climax of consternation by beholding Edith in the arms of the tall stranger! Bewildered in the intellect, and effectually crippled about the knees and ankles, he could only gaze and listen.

"So you have come—at last!" whispered Edith, while a brilliant blush overspread her fair cheek.

"O Edith!" murmured the stalwart cavalier, in a deep musical voice, "how my heart has yearned for this day! How I have longed to hear your sweet and well-remembered voice! In the desolate solitudes of the far north I have thought of you. Amid the silent glades of the forest, when alone and asleep on my mossy couch or upon my bed of snow, I have dreamed of you— dreamed of you as you were, a fair, sweet, happy child, when we wandered together among the mountains of Ungava—and dreamed of you as I fancied you must have become, and as I now find you to be. Yes, beloved girl, my heart has owned but one image since we parted, years ago, on the banks of the Caniapuscaw River. Your letters have been my bosom friends in all my long, long wanderings through the wilderness; and the hope of seeing you has gladdened my heart and nerved my arm. I have heard your sighs in every gentle air that stirred the trees, and your merry laugh in the rippling waters. Even in the tempest's roar and the thundering cataract I have fancied that I heard you calling for assistance; and many a time and oft I have leaped from my couch to find that I did but dream. But they were pleasant and very precious dreams to me. O Edith! I have remembered you, and thought of you, and loved you, through months and years of banishment! And now—"

Again was heard the peculiar sound that had thrilled with dismay the bosom of the weak young man.

"Halo! Whence came this charger?" shouted a hale, hearty voice, as Stanley walked towards the bower. "Eh! what have we here?" he exclaimed, rushing forward and seizing the stranger in his arms,—"Frank—Frank Morton!"

This was too much. The weak young man suddenly became strong as Hercules. He turned and fled down the avenue like a deer. The pony, having managed to unfasten its bridle, stood in the centre of the way gazing down the avenue with its back towards its master. Unwonted fire nerved the youth's limbs; with one bound he vaulted leap frog over the animal's back into the saddle, dashed his spurs into its sides, and fled like a whirlwind from the scene of his despair.

Frank Morton and George Stanley, being both men of promptitude and decision, resolved that one month was long enough to make preparations for the marriage; and Edith, being the most dutiful daughter that ever lived, did what she was bid.

That beautiful cottage which stands in the midst of most exquisite scenery, about two miles from Stanley's villa, is inhabited by Frank Morton and his family. That crow which you have just heard proceed from the nursery was uttered by the youngest of five; and yonder little boy with broad shoulders, who thrusts his hands into his pockets in a decided manner, and whistles vociferously as he swaggers down the avenue, is Master George F. Morton, on his way to school.

La Roche and Bryan were so fortunate as to be appointed to the same establishment after leaving Ungava—somewhere near the mouth of the Mackenzie River, and within the region of all but perpetual frost and snow. They are sometimes visited by Eskimos, which is fortunate; for, as Bryan says, "it guves him an opportunity o' studyin' the peecoolier dialects o' their lingo."

Dick Prince was the only one who lost his life in the "forlorn-hope." He was drowned while out shooting in the bay alone in his canoe. A sudden storm upset his frail bark and left him struggling in the water. Prince was a strong swimmer, and he battled long for his life; but the ice-laden sea benumbed his hardy limbs, and he sank at last, without a cry, to rise no more. He was a noble specimen of his class—a brave, modest, unobtrusive son of the forest, beloved and respected by his companions; and when his warm heart ceased to beat, it was felt by all that a bright star of the wilderness had been quenched for ever. His body was found next day on the beach, and was interred by his mourning comrades in a little spot of ground behind the fort. It was many a long day after this melancholy event ere Massan could smile; and when the fort was finally deserted, he put in practice his long-meditated intention of becoming a hunter and taking to the Rocky Mountains, where he wanders now, if he has escaped the claws of the dreaded grizzly bear and the scalping-knife of the Red Indian.

Moses, finding the life of a fur-trader not quite to his taste, rejoined his countrymen, and reverted to killing seals and eating raw blubber. The two Indians also returned to a purely savage life, which, indeed, they had only forsaken for a time. Augustus and Oolibuck died; and the latter left a son, who has already rendered good service as interpreter to the arctic expeditions, as his worthy father did before him. Francois and Gaspard are still together at one of the posts of the interior. They are now fast friends, and have many a talk over the days when they quarrelled and messed together at Fort Chimo.

As for the poor Eskimos, they were for a time quite

inconsolable at the departure of the fur-traders, and with a species of childlike simplicity, hung about the bay, in the hope that they might, after all, return. Then they went off in a body to the westward, and the region of Ungava, to which they had never been partial, was left in its original dreary solitude. It may be that some good had been done to the souls of these poor natives during their brief intercourse with the traders. We cannot tell, and we refrain from guessing or speculating on a subject so serious. But of this we are assured—if one grain of the good seed has been sown, it may long lie dormant, but it cannot die.

Maximus accompanied his countrymen, along with Aneetka and Old Moggy, who soon assumed the native costume, and completely identified herself with the Eskimos. Maximus was now a great man among his people, who regarded with deep respect the man who had travelled through the lands of the Indians, had fought with the red men, single-handed, and had visited the fur-traders of the south. But the travelled Eskimos was in reality a greater man than his fellows supposed him to be. He fully appreciated the advantages to be derived from a trading-post near their ice-girt lands, and resolved, when opportunity should offer, to do all in his power to strengthen the friendship now subsisting between the Indians and the Eskimos of Ungava, and to induce his countrymen, if possible, to travel south towards the establishment on James's Bay.

He still retains, however, a lingering affection for the spot where he had spent so many happy days, and at least once a year he undertakes a solitary journey to the rugged mountains that encircled Fort Chimo. As in days of yore, with wallet on shoulder and seal-spear in hand, the giant strides from rock to rock along the now silent banks of the Caniapuscaw River. Once again he seats himself on the flat rock beside the spring, and gazes round in sadness on those wild, majestic hills, or bends his eye upon the bright green spot that indicates the ancient site of the trading-post, not a vestige of which is now visible, save the little wooden cross that marks the lonely grave of Dick Prince; and the broad chest of the giant heaves with emotion as he views these records of the past, and calls to mind the merry shouts and joyous songs that used to gladden that dreary spot, the warm hearth at which he was wont to find a hearty welcome, and the kind comrades who are now gone for ever. Ungava spreads, in all its dark sterility, around him, as it did in the days before the traders landed there; and that bright interval of busy life, in which he had acted so prominent a part, seems now but the fleeting fancy of a bright and pleasant dream.

THE END.